J

This book should be returned to any branch of the
Lancashire County Library on or before the date

JS R10

20 JUN 2017

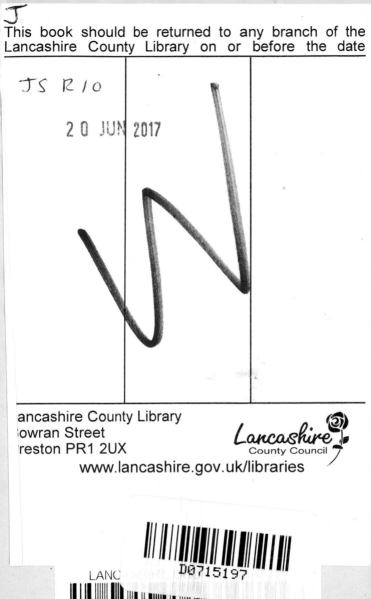

ancashire County Library
owran Street
reston PR1 2UX

www.lancashire.gov.uk/libraries

Lancashire
County Council

Midwives On-Call at Christmas

*Mothers, midwives and mistletoe—
lives changing for ever at Christmas!*

Welcome to Cambridge Royal Hospital—
and to the exceptional midwives
who make up its special Maternity Unit!

They deliver tiny bundles of joy on a daily
basis, but Christmas really is a time for
miracles—as midwives Bonnie, Hope,
Jessica and Isabel are about to find out.

Amidst the drama and emotion of babies
arriving at all hours of the day and night,
these midwives still find time for some
sizzling romance under the mistletoe!

This holiday season, don't miss the festive,
heartwarming spin-off to the dazzling
Midwives On-Call continuity
from Mills & Boon Medical Romance:

A Touch of Christmas Magic
by Scarlet Wilson

Her Christmas Baby Bump
by Robin Gianna

Playboy Doc's Mistletoe Kiss
by Tina Beckett

Her Doctor's Christmas Proposal
by Louisa George

A TOUCH OF CHRISTMAS MAGIC

BY
SCARLET WILSON

Published in Great Britain 2015
by Mills & Boon, an imprint of Harlequin (UK) Limited,
Eton House, 18-24 Paradise Road, Richmond, Surrey, TW9 1SR

© 2015 Harlequin Books S.A.

ISBN: 978-0-263-24741-1

Special thanks and acknowledgement are given to Scarlet Wilson
for her contribution to the Midwives On-Call at Christmas series.

Harlequin (UK) Limited's policy is to use papers that are natural,
renewable and recyclable products and made from wood grown in
sustainable forests. The logging and manufacturing processes conform
to the legal environmental regulations of the country of origin.

Printed and bound in Spain
by CPI, Barcelona

Dear Reader,

I was really delighted to be asked to take part in the Midwives On-Call at Christmas series—as you might have guessed by now, I like nothing better than writing Christmas books!

It seemed fitting that my heroine was from Scotland, and I loved the thought of her putting her past behind her and trying to build a new and exciting future for her and her daughter.

Jacob was a whole different matter... The first thing I did was visualise his house and how empty it looked without any love or significant others in it. It was so easy to imagine how gorgeous it might look for Christmas, and a whole part of the story is built around this idea.

Wishing you all a wonderful time—whatever your celebrations at this time of year. I will be frantically wrapping presents, trying to buy Christmas food and hoping I haven't forgotten anything!

Please feel free to contact me at my website: scarlet-wilson.com.

Best wishes,

Scarlet

This book is dedicated to my fabulous fellow authors
Louisa George, Tina Beckett and Robin Gianna.

It's been a pleasure working with you, ladies!

Scarlet Wilson wrote her first story aged eight and
has never stopped. Her family have fond memories of
Shirley and the Magic Purse, with its army of mice all
with names beginning with the letter 'M'. An avid reader,
Scarlet started with every Enid Blyton book, moved on
to the Chalet School series and many years later found
Mills & Boon. She trained and worked as a nurse and
health visitor, and currently works in public health. For
her, finding Mills & Boon Medical Romances was a
match made in heaven. She is delighted to find herself
among the authors she has read for many years. Scarlet
lives on the West Coast of Scotland with her fiancé and
their two sons.

Books by Scarlet Wilson

Mills & Boon Medical Romance

Rebels with a Cause
The Maverick Doctor and Miss Prim
About That Night...

The Boy Who Made Them Love Again
West Wing to Maternity Wing
A Bond Between Strangers
Her Christmas Eve Diamond
An Inescapable Temptation
Her Firefighter Under the Mistletoe
200 Harley Street: Girl from the Red Carpet
A Mother's Secret
Tempted by Her Boss
Christmas with the Maverick Millionaire
The Doctor She Left Behind

Visit the Author Profile page at
millsandboon.co.uk for more titles.

CHAPTER ONE

THE LITTLE FACE stared back out of the window as Freya gave her a nervous wave from the new school. Bonnie sucked in a breath and kept the smile plastered to her face, waving back as merrily as she could. *Please be okay.*

Her thick winter coat was stifling her already. Even at this time of year, Cambridge was unexpectedly warmer than Scotland. She could feel an uncomfortable trickle of sweat run down her spine. The teacher came to the window and, glancing at Bonnie, ushered Freya away. Freya's red curls had already started to escape from the carefully styled pleat. By the time she came home later her hair would be back to its usual fluffy head style. She could almost hear the teacher's thoughts in her head: *over-anxious parent.*

She wasn't. Not really. But travelling down from Scotland yesterday with their worldly goods stuffed into four suitcases was hardly ideal. The motel they'd ended up staying in was even less pleasant. The smell of damp and mildew in the room had set off alarm bells that it might cause a flare-up of Freya's asthma. With Christmas not too far away, she desperately needed to sort out somewhere more suitable to stay. And the combination of everything, plus dropping Freya at a brand-new school this morning, had left her feeling rattled.

The director of midwifery at Cambridge Royal Maternity Unit had been quite insistent on her start date. No compromise. The ward sister had just taken early maternity leave due to some unexpected problems. They needed an experienced member of staff as soon as possible. And she hadn't felt in a position to argue—despite the fact they'd had nowhere to stay. The job in Cambridge was her way out of Scotland. And, boy, did she need out.

Working at such a prestigious hospital was appealing. Everyone knew about the two-hundred-year-old hospital and one night, midway between tears and frustration, she'd applied. When they'd emailed back the next day to arrange a telephone interview she'd been surprised. And when they'd told her the next day she had the job she'd been stunned. Things had moved at a rapid pace ever since. References, occupational health forms and a formal offer telling her they wanted her to start straight away.

Thankfully, she'd had a sympathetic community manager in Scotland who knew about her circumstances and had done a little jigging to allow her to take annual leave and special leave to let her only work two weeks' notice. The last two weeks had passed in a complete blur.

This morning had been hard. There had been tears and sniffles from Freya, a normally placid child. Bonnie held her breath. The school window remained empty; it was clear the teacher had successfully distracted her.

With a sigh of relief she glanced at her watch. Yikes. First day and she was going to be late. She hurried back to the bus stop. Getting a car was next on the 'to do' list. She phoned and left a message on the director of midwifery's answerphone—hardly a good start for her first day on the job. But it couldn't be helped. The woman knew she wasn't arriving until last night and that her daughter was starting a new school today. She still had to hand some paperwork into HR and pick up her uniforms before she could start on the labour ward.

For once, she was in luck. The bus appeared almost immediately. Now it was daylight and she could actually see a bit of the beautiful city she'd decided to live in on almost a whim.

Well, a whim that was a result of catching her husband in bed with her best friend. She should still feel angry and hurt. But all she really felt was relief. As soon as the ink was dry on the divorce papers she'd started job hunting. She needed a fresh start and there was something so exciting about coming to a historic city like Cambridge. She watched as the Victorian-style shops and Grade II listed buildings whizzed past and allowed herself to smile a little. Cambridge was truly an atmospheric city; seeing it in daylight made her all the more excited to get a chance to see round about.

The hospital came into a view. A large, imposing building based in the heart of the bustling city. A little tremor of anticipation went down her spine. This was it. This was where she worked. As the bus drew to a halt, climbing down, she took a final glance around the city of Cambridge. *Her city.* Full of possibilities.

This was now home.

Jacob Layton was more than mildly irritated. He was mad—but, these days, that was nothing unusual for him.

He hated disorganisation. Hated chaos. He prided himself on the fact that his unit ran like clockwork. Any midwife or medic not up to the job at this hospital was quickly rooted out and dealt with.

It might sound harsh. But in Cambridge Royal Maternity Unit the lives of women and babies were on the line every day. He was a firm believer that all expectant mothers deserved the best possible care and it was his job to ensure they got it.

This morning, he stood at the nurses' station with his hands on his hips as his temper bubbled just beneath the surface. There was no sign of any member of staff. None of the whiteboards were up to date—he didn't even know which patient was in which room. Case notes were spread all over the desk with a whole variety of scribbled multicoloured sticky notes littering the normally immaculate desk.

'Where is everyone?' he yelled.

The frightened faces of a midwife and junior doctor appeared simultaneously from separate rooms. The midwife hurried towards him, her eyes fixed on her shoes. The junior doctor walked slowly, obviously hoping the midwife would get the brunt of Jacob's rage this morning. He should be so lucky.

The midwife handed over a set of notes with slightly shaking hands. 'I think this is the set of notes you wanted. I was just doing Mrs Clark's observations. Everything seems fine.'

He snatched them from her hands and reviewed them quickly. Relief. Things were looking better for Mrs Clark. He raised his head, keeping his voice in check. 'Good. Tell Mrs Clark I'll be in to see her shortly.'

The midwife disappeared in a flash. The junior doctor's legs practically did a U-turn in the corridor. He didn't want to be left with Jacob.

'Dr Jenkins.'

The young guy's legs froze midstride. Jacob flung case notes onto the desk one after another. 'Ms Bates needs her bloods done, Mrs Kelly needs her bloods repeated, where is the cardiac consult for Lucy Evans—she's been here more than six hours—and how long ago did I ask you to arrange another ultrasound for Ms Shaw? Get it done, now!' His voice rose as the anger he was trying to contain started to erupt. He hated incompetence. These patients were in the best maternity unit for miles. They should be receiving top-quality care.

The doctor's face paled and he gathered up the notes in his arms. 'Right away, Dr Layton,' he said, practically scampering down the corridor to the nearest office.

He sighed. This place—normally his pride and joy—was becoming a disaster zone.

Ever since he'd diagnosed the ward manager with pre-eclampsia and sent her home with the instructions not to come back until she had her baby, this place had gone to pot. There were four other senior midwives. All of them excellent at clinical care—and none with an organisational bone in their body.

The director of midwifery had promised him that their new employee would be able to help with all this. But he'd just read her CV, and was struggling to see why a Scottish community midwife would be able to do anything to help a busy city labour ward.

But the thing that was really making him mad was the fact that she wasn't here. He glanced at his watch again. First day on a new job—after nine-thirty—and the new start wasn't here.

The doors at the bottom of the corridor swung open right on cue. Bonnie Reid. It had to be. Jacob knew everyone who worked here and he didn't recognise her at all. Dressed in the blue scrubs that the labour ward midwives wore and bright pink trainers, she had her red hair coiled up on top of her head in a strange kind of knot. How on earth did she do that? That, coupled with the curves not hidden by the shapeless scrubs, reminded him of a poster he'd had on his wall as a teenager. He felt a smile form on his lips.

Was she nervous? Her hands fidgeted with her security pass and she seemed to make a conscious effort to slow her steps. What irritated him most of all was the fact she didn't seem to notice him standing, waiting for her. Instead, she stopped at every room on the way along the corridor, nodding and introducing herself to the members of staff. She even disappeared for a second to obviously help with a patient.

Then, she appeared with a load of laundry, which she put into the laundry bags, reorganised two of the hand scrubs outside the doors and tidied the top of the cardiac-arrest trolley on her way past.

He waited until she'd almost reached him. 'Bonnie Reid?' His voice dripped with sarcasm. 'Nice of you to finally join us.'

Something flickered across her face. Her skin was pale under the bright hospital lights and he could see a few tiny freckles under her make-up. She'd looked good from a distance. Up close, she was much more interesting.

She had real knockout eyes. Dark, dark blue. Not the pale blue normally associated with a redhead. But then her hair wasn't the average red either. It was a dark deep auburn. The kind of colour normally associated with Hollywood actresses who probably had a whole team of people to get it that colour. Almost instantly he knew that

Bonnie Reid's was entirely natural. She gave him the slightest glance from those eyes. And for the first time, in a long time, he took a deep breath.

It had been a long time since a woman had ignited something in his system. Maybe it was her dark blue eyes against her pale skin? Or the look of disdain she gave him as she walked past into the treatment room and started washing her hands.

Had he just imagined it? No. Something in her eyes told him this was a woman who had lived—had experienced life. She must be in her early thirties. As she finished washing her hands he glanced at her finger—no ring. It had been a long time since he'd done that too.

She turned to face him. 'Bonnie Reid, new midwife at Cambridge Royal Maternity Unit.' Her eyebrows rose. 'And you are?'

It was her tone. It rankled him right away. He'd never been a person to pull rank. 'Jacob Layton, Head Obstetrician, CRMU.'

It was almost as if a box of chocolates or tray of cakes had appeared out of thin air at the nurses' station. Just about every door in the corridor opened and a whole host of previously hidden staff appeared. Did they avoid him every morning?

Bonnie didn't appear to notice. She blinked and pointed towards his scrubs. 'You should wear an ID badge, Dr Layton. You could be absolutely anyone. I expect all staff members I work with to be clearly identified.'

She was just here. His skin prickled. Patience was not his friend. In any other set of circumstances he might have said their new staff member had an attitude problem. But he got the distinct impression that Bonnie Reid was only reacting to his initial barb.

He didn't know whether to give her a dressing-down or to smile. 'It's Jacob,' he said quietly. 'Everyone calls me Jacob.' Not true. Only the few people not terrified by him called him Jacob. For a second their gazes meshed. It startled him, sending a little jolt around his system.

More than a year. That was how long it had been since he'd felt a spark with someone.

She gave the slightest nod of her head and extended her hand towards his. 'Bonnie. Everyone calls me Bonnie.'

As soon as he connected with her skin he knew he'd made a mistake. The warm feeling of her palm against his. Touch. That was what he'd missed most of all in the last year. The warmness of someone's touch. He pulled his hand back sharply as her eyes widened at his reaction.

'You're late.' It came out much snappier than he intended. Her hand was still in mid-air, suspended from their shake. She drew it back slowly and her gaze narrowed as she took a deep breath and her shoulders went back.

She met his gaze full on. 'Yes, I'm late.' It was clear she had no intention of giving anything else away. He couldn't believe how much one meeting with one woman could irk him.

She was new. She was working in his unit. And, after talks with the director of midwifery, this was the person he was supposed to offer a promoted post to. *If* he deemed her suitable. Tardiness was not an option.

He felt his normal persona resume. The one that had held most of the staff at arm's length for the last year. 'Staff and patients rely on us. Lateness is not acceptable at CRMU. I expected you here at nine a.m.'

It was the first time she looked a little worried. 'I had to take my daughter to school. We arrived late last night from Scotland. She was upset. I had to make sure she was okay.' She glanced over her shoulder as if she expected someone else to be there. 'I left a message for the director of midwifery—she knew my circumstances.'

Those words annoyed him. He'd seen her CV, but the director hadn't told him anything about their new employee's 'circumstances'. He hated it when staff used excuses for not being able to do a shift, or being late for work.

'We all have circumstances. We all still have to be at work for nine. Work is our priority. Patients are our priority.'

Her face flamed and her eyes sparked. 'Patients are always my priority and I've already dealt with two on my way along the ward. Exactly how many have you dealt with while you've been standing there waiting for me to arrive? Hardly a good use of consultant time.'

She was questioning him. She was challenging him and she'd only been here five minutes. He'd love to sack her on the spot. But they desperately needed the staff right now, and if she was as competent as she was mouthy he'd be in serious trouble with the director of midwives. She was almost questioning his competence. Let them see how she was when someone questioned hers.

'I saw from your CV that you were a community midwife in Scotland. It's a bit of a leap coming to work in an inner city labour ward. Don't you think that might stretch your current capabilities? Are you going to have to refresh your skills?'

It was a reasonable question. At least he felt it was. He still wasn't entirely sure why the director thought a community midwife was a suitable replacement for their ward sister.

It took about a millisecond to realise he'd said exactly the wrong thing.

Bonnie glared at him and put her hands on her hips. 'Please do not question my capabilities or qualifications. In the last year, I've dealt with a shoulder dystocia, umbilical cord prolapse, two women who failed to progress, a footling breech, a cervical lip and an intrapartum haemorrhage. Is that enough for you?' She turned to walk away, then obviously decided she wasn't finished. 'And just so we're clear—' she held out her hands '—I didn't have a fancy unit, staffed with lots of other people to help me. These were home deliveries. I was on my own, with no assistance. Still think I need to *refresh my skills*?'

Her pretty brow was marred by a frown and he could practically feel the heat sparking from her eyes. It was an impressive list—even for a midwife based in a busy labour ward. For a community midwife, some of those situations must have been terrifying. He had a whole new respect for his new midwife.

But Bonnie wasn't finished. It was obvious he'd lit a fire within her and probably touched a nerve. Maybe she was nervous about starting work in a new hospital? Worse, he'd just called her qualifications into question in front of the rest of the staff. He hadn't even considered that might not be entirely appropriate—especially when these could be the people she would be in charge of. Mentally, he was kicking himself.

'My experience with women isn't just in the labour suite, *Dr* Layton.' Oh, boy, she was mad. It was clear, if he was patronising her, they weren't on first-name terms. 'I've spent the last ten years looking after women from the moment they're pregnant until long after the baby is delivered. I've picked up on lots of factors that affect their pregnancy, both clinical and social. And as a community midwife I've dealt with lots of post-delivery problems for both mother and child. Looking after patients at home is a whole lot different from looking after them in a clinical setting. Isolation, post-op complications, neonatal problems, postpartum psychosis, depression, domestic abuse...' She fixed him with her gaze. 'The list goes on and on.'

He didn't want to smile. He should be annoyed. This woman was practically putting him in his place. But he couldn't help but feel he might have deserved it.

He wondered how on earth she'd ended up here. She'd already mentioned a daughter. And she clearly wasn't wearing a wedding ring. It was absolutely none of his business. But Jacob Layton's curiosity was definitely sparked. He liked this feisty midwife.

He spoke steadily. 'That certainly seems like enough experience. So what made you come down to Cambridge? It's a long way from Scotland.'

She didn't even stop to think. Her eyes were still flashing. Bonnie Reid was on a roll. 'That's the thing about finding your husband in bed with your best friend—it makes you want to get as far away as possible.'

Silence.

You could have heard a proverbial pin drop. Bonnie felt the colour rush to her cheeks and she lifted her hand to her mouth. Oh, no. Why on earth would she say something like that out loud?

It was that darn man. Jacob Layton. It wasn't bad enough that the handsomest man on the planet had watched her walking down the corridor as if he were undressing her with his eyes. Then he'd started talk-

ing to her and everything he'd said had put her back up.
Now she'd lost her rag with him. Hardly the best start
in a new job.

But Bonnie Reid didn't take any prisoners. In this life,
she meant to start the way she was going to continue. The
part of her life where she put up with bad behaviour, in-
difference and rudeness was over.

Maybe it was the fact he was so good-looking that was
unnerving her. If she got any closer she was sure she'd
see gold flecks in those intense green eyes. Or maybe it
was the fact that no man had even flickered on her radar
since she'd walked away from her ex. Certainly not a
brown-haired, green-eyed Hollywood-style hunk.

Her insides were cringing. She couldn't believe what
she'd just said. And it was clear from the faces around
her that no one else could either.

But what made it all the more excruciating was the
fact that the edges of Jacob Layton's mouth seemed to
be turning upwards.

He was laughing at her.

'Please come with me,' he said sharply and walked
over, ushering her towards an office door with Head Obstetrician emblazoned across it, and away from the gap-
ing mouths.

He closed the door firmly behind them and walked
around his desk. 'Take a seat.' His voice was firm and
she felt a wave of panic sweep over her.

She hadn't even officially started—was she about to
be fired? 'I'm sorry. I've no idea where that came from.'

Her stomach did a little flip-flop. It didn't matter. It
really didn't matter but she'd just made a fool of herself
in front of the resident hunk and her new boss. She'd
just told him that her husband had cheated on her. It was

hardly a placard that she wanted to wave above her head. She might as well be holding a sign saying 'I'm plain and boring in bed'.

The humiliation burned her cheeks. Right now she wanted to crawl into a hole.

He fixed on her with those green eyes and she felt her skin prickle under her thin scrubs. At times like this she longed for her thicker white tunic and navy trousers. But scrubs were the order of the day in most labour wards.

He pointed to the chair again. 'Sit down.'

Her feet were shuffling nervously on the carpet and she couldn't stop wringing her hands together. Sitting down seemed quite claustrophobic. Particularly with Jacob sitting at the other side of the desk and the door closed behind them.

'Don't ever speak to me like that again in front of my colleagues.' The words were out before she could stop them. And she wasn't finished. 'It was unprofessional. If you want to question my clinical capabilities take it up with me privately, or take it up with the director of midwives who employed me.' She waved her hand. 'On second thoughts, why don't you actually wait until you've worked with me, *before* you question my clinical capabilities?' She stuck her hands on her hips. 'And maybe I'll wait until then to question yours.'

Too much. It was too much. Even she knew that. The shocked expression on his face almost made her want to open the door and run back down the corridor.

Definitely not her best start.

She took a deep breath and sat down. 'Look—' she started but Jacob lifted his hand.

She froze mid-sentence. This was the way she always got when she was nervous. Her mouth started running away with her, a prime example being what had happened outside.

Jacob ran his hand through his hair. It struck her as an odd act. Usually a sign of someone being tired or frustrated. Jacob Layton didn't strike her as any of those things.

He lifted his eyes to meet hers. 'You're right. I shouldn't have questioned your capabilities. But let's start with the basics. Bonnie, I would have preferred it if you could have been here at nine this morning. It would have made our meeting a little easier. Is timing going to be an issue for you?'

She shook her head quickly, wondering if she should be offended by the question. 'No. Not at all. This morning was a one-off.'

He gave the tiniest nod. 'I appreciate you just arrived last night, and that you were asked to start at short notice.' His brow furrowed a little. 'Do you have adequate arrangements in place for your daughter?'

She straightened her shoulders. He was putting her on edge again. Dr Handsome just seemed to rub her up the wrong way. 'I hope so. I have a friend who is a registered childminder. She's agreed to take Freya in the mornings and after school.'

'What about weekends and night shifts?'

Bonnie felt herself pull back a little. 'I was told there was no requirement for night shifts—that you had permanent night shift staff here?' The statement had turned into a question. She had the mildest feeling of panic.

A wave of recognition flickered across his face. 'What about shift work? Will that cause you a problem?

Now he was really getting her back up. She couldn't fathom this guy out at all. One minute he was fiercely professional, the next he looked amused by her. As for the sparks that had shot up her arm when they'd touched…

She'd already snapped at this guy once. She didn't want to do it again. It wasn't his fault she was tired. It wasn't his fault that the journey from Scotland had taken much more out of her and Freya than she'd really expected. It wasn't his fault Freya had been upset this morning, or that the motel room was totally inappropriate for them both. None of this was his fault.

She wanted to respect her boss and get on well with him. He was a bit grumpy, but she'd met worse, and she was sure she could knock it out of him. She'd already embarrassed herself once in front of her boss. It was time for a new tack.

She met his gaze straight on. 'Jacob, I don't think you're actually allowed to ask me questions like that.'

'Aren't I?' He sat back quickly and frowned.

She held up her hands. 'Would you ask a guy these questions?' She was so aware it was all about the tone here. It was a serious subject, but she was quite sure he wasn't even aware of what he was doing. 'What if I asked you, right now, about childcare arrangements for any kids you might have? Would that seem appropriate to you?'

The recognition dawned quickly on his face. 'Well… no.' He put his head in his hands for a second and shook it. When he pulled his head back up he had a sorry smile on his face and shrugged his shoulders. 'Sorry.'

She gave a little nod of her head. 'No problem.'

She heard him suck in a breath and his shoulders relaxed a little. 'I do have a good reason for asking you.'

She raised her eyebrows. 'You do?'

He nodded slowly. 'I do.' He was being serious now.

'Valerie Glencross, the director of midwifery, suggested we should offer you a promoted post.'

Bonnie sat bolt upright in her chair. It was the last thing she'd expected to hear. 'She did?'

His gaze connected with hers. 'She did.' For a second it felt as if time had frozen. She was looking into the brightest pair of green eyes she'd ever seen. She'd been right. He had little gold flecks in his irises. It made them sparkle. It was making her hold her breath as she realised exactly what kind of an effect they were having on her.

'She did,' he reiterated. 'It seems your CV had already impressed her. I'm guessing that your telephone interview with her went well. She wanted me to meet you and ask if you'd consider being Ward Sister on a temporary basis.'

'Me?' Bonnie was more than a little surprised. 'But you must have senior staff working here already. Wouldn't it make more sense to have someone take charge who is familiar with the set-up?'

He gave a little laugh. 'You would think so. Our senior staff are excellent. But none of them have the talent of organisation. Valerie said that before you were a community midwife you were a ward sister. I think she thought it would be good to have a new broom, so to speak. Someone who didn't have any preconceived ideas about CRMU and could bring some fresh ideas about how things should run.' He gave a little sigh. 'Our ward sister Abby has been gone less than two weeks and it's chaos out there. She left sooner than expected and we obviously didn't appreciate just how much she kept on top of things.' He gave his head a little shake. 'I'm feeling bad. I'm wondering if the stress of the ward was a factor in her pre-eclampsia.'

'Is she okay?' It was the first thing that sprang to mind.

He gave a quick nod and Bonnie shot him a smile. 'In that case, you're not making it sound like my dream job. Shouldn't you be giving me the hard sell? And after our first meeting—do you really want to offer it to me at all?' Jacob Layton wasn't good at this. He was being too honest.

He groaned again and sat straighter, giving her a grin that sent tingles to her toes. 'Let me start again. Bonnie Reid—from your extensive experience on your CV we've decided you would be a great addition to our team. You'll know the reputation of Cambridge Royal Maternity Unit. We employ the best obstetricians and midwives and are known as a centre of medical excellence. We have links with Cambridge University and are pioneers in the development and research of many groundbreaking medical techniques. We have a great bunch of staff working in the labour delivery suite. We just need someone who can bring some new organisational skills to the ward.' He leaned across the table towards her. 'How's that for the hard sell?'

She couldn't pull her eyes away from his. He was closer to her than ever before. She could see every strand of his dark brown hair. See the tiny lines around his eyes. And exactly just how straight and white his teeth were.

He nodded towards her. 'And yes, I do want to offer it to you. You're the first person to answer back in about five years.'

Boy, he was handsome. But there was something else. Something so much more than just good looks. Beneath the flecks of gold in his eyes she could see another part of Jacob Layton. There was so much more there than a handsome but grumpy obstetrician. He seemed the single-minded, career-driven type. But what lay beneath the driven exterior?

She returned his smile. 'That was much better.'

He relaxed back in his chair and she was almost sorry she'd replied. 'Thank goodness.' He was so much nicer like this. Why did he act so grumpy around the staff?

She took a deep breath. 'I want this to work. I want this to work for me and for Freya—my little girl. This is a fresh start. I want to leave everything else behind us.' She rolled her eyes and gave her head a little shake. 'And I definitely want to leave men behind. I just want to focus on my new job and getting me and my daughter settled.'

Jacob gave a little nod of acknowledgement as he tapped his fingers on the desk. 'The reason I asked about your childcare arrangements—if you're working as ward sister we'd generally expect you to work nine to five. You'd only occasionally be expected to work late shifts if there were staffing issues, and join part of the hospital on-call rota to do weekends.'

Bonnie frowned. 'How does that work?'

'All of our ward sisters take turns in covering weekends. You're not actually there as a member of the team that weekend. You're covering the management for the whole hospital. Sorting out staffing problems, dealing with any difficult cases or issues across the whole of maternity. It usually works out once every nine weeks.'

Bonnie nodded. 'That's understandable. This would make things much easier with my childcare arrangements. Freya will be much happier if I'm working more or less regular hours. I'll get to put her to bed most nights. And, as I've mentioned, Lynn will happily take Freya every weekday before and after school, and for the occasional late night or weekend.' She gave a visible sigh of relief. 'I'm happy to do the job—in fact, I'm really excited to be asked.'

He seemed relieved. 'So you'll take the job?' His voice went up a little, as if he was still a bit anxious she might turn down this fabulous opportunity.

She stood up and held out her hand towards him. 'Of course I will. I'm a little nervous but am sure in a few days it will feel like I've been here for weeks. That's always the way of it, isn't it?'

He smiled again; this time the relief was definitely reaching right up into his eyes. His hand grasped hers. There it was again.

She hadn't been mistaken first time around. Coming into contact with Jacob Layton's hand was doing strange things to her skin receptors—currently it was the dance of a thousand butterflies. Just as well she'd made it clear she was a man-free zone.

'Perfect. I'll let Valerie know you've accepted. She'll arrange for a new contract.' He held open the door for her. 'Now, let's go and tell the staff.'

Her stomach did another little flip-flop as she walked through, but she couldn't work out if that was the thought of telling her new peers about her role, or from the burn coming from Jacob's hand at the small of her back.

One thing was for sure—CRMU was going to be interesting.

CHAPTER TWO

JACOB HADN'T BEEN WRONG. The labour suite was in chaos. And it was all basics.

Bonnie grabbed a ward clerk and made some immediate requests about sorting out case notes, filing things appropriately and keeping the boards up to date. Then she asked for new lists of contact numbers. The one she found on the wall was obviously out of date and, with doctors changing every six months, she didn't want any problems with pagers in case of emergency.

She spent the next two hours working with various members of staff and patients. After a few hours she was confident in the clinical capabilities of the staff that were on duty. They all wanted to do their jobs and work with patients. They just didn't want to bother with 'ward' stuff. Ordering, stocking, rotas, outpatient appointments, pharmacy prescriptions. It quickly became apparent that her predecessor had dealt with all these things and her quick departure meant there had been no handover.

Bonnie gave a sigh. She'd like to spend all day working with patients too—but that wasn't the way a ward was run. She started making a 'to do' list that she'd have to work her way through.

The other issue was the phones. They rang constantly—

often with no one answering. First thing tomorrow she was going to ask about a regular ward clerk for the unit. Just as she finished making a few notes about the off-duty rota the phone rang again.

'CRMU, Bonnie Reid, can I help you?'

'Ambulance Control. We need a team on-site at a crash on one of the motorway slip roads. We have a trapped, unconscious pregnant woman. She's reported to be thirty-four weeks. Ambulance is on its way to pick you up.'

Bonnie put down the phone. First day on the job. You had to be joking. She automatically dialled the page for the on-call obstetrician. Most big maternity units had supplies for emergencies like these. It was just a pity she hadn't had a chance to find out where they were.

A few seconds later Jacob appeared from his office just as Bonnie was relaying the message to one of the senior midwives. He was holding his page. 'What have we got?'

She handed over the piece of paper she'd scribbled on. Jacob gestured towards her. 'Follow me. Equipment is in here. Grab a jacket and a bag.' He turned to face her. 'You are coming, aren't you?'

She hesitated for only the briefest of seconds. 'If you want me to.'

No. I'm terrified. This sounds like an initiation of fire. It's my first day, I've just agreed to act as temporary sister in one of the most prestigious maternity units in the country and now you want me to be part of the emergency response team.

He acted as if he did this every day, grabbing a jacket with 'Doctor' emblazoned across the back and handing her the one with 'Midwife'. He shot her a smile as he helped her lift the emergency pack onto her shoulders.

'Let's go. Leave instructions with Miriam, the senior midwife. She'll deal with the calls until we get back.' He walked away, his long strides crossing the corridor quickly, only stopping to wheel a portable incubator to the door.

She could feel the wave of panic lapping around her ankles. There was no way she could let it go any further. She started repeating in her head the list of emergencies that she'd dealt with on her own as a community midwife. She could do this. She could.

Miriam gave her a sympathetic nod as she handed over a few instructions. 'I'm so glad it's you and not me,' she murmured under her breath.

'What do you mean?'

Miriam rolled her eyes. 'If you think Dan Daring is harsh on the ward, you should see him at a roadside emergency. The patients love him. The rest of the staff need counselling by the time he's done.'

'Let's go, Bonnie!' The shout made her jump and she hurried to the exit and into the back of the waiting ambulance. As soon as the doors closed and the sirens switched on they were on their way.

Sitting in the back of the ambulance was more than a little bumpy. She only just managed to avoid practically bouncing onto Jacob's lap. But he barely noticed. He was holding on to the strap in the back with his eyes fixed on the road ahead.

'Any more news?'

One of the paramedics turned around. 'All bad. We've just had a report that they think her membranes might have ruptured. She's still unconscious and trapped. They're panicking. They think she's gone into labour.' He glanced at the clock. 'We'll be there in five minutes.'

Bonnie sucked in a breath. A thousand different potential diagnoses were flying through her head. From Jacob's serious expression he was thinking the same.

When they screeched to a halt Jacob didn't wait, he just flung open the doors, grabbed the bag and started running.

The first thing that struck her was the smell. Fire, burning metal, petrol and a whole lot more. There were four ambulances already on-site. A few casualties were sitting on the edge of the road. Two children with blood on their faces, a man cradling his arm and an older woman who looked completely shell-shocked. Police had cordoned off part of the motorway but the speed and noise of the cars still passing by was unnerving. Rubbernecking. That was what most of the passing cars were doing. Any minute now there would be another accident on the other side of the motorway. She shuddered and jumped out of the back of the ambulance, trying to spot Jacob's bright green jacket in amongst the melee of emergency people.

'Over here.' A policeman gestured her towards an upended car. She stepped around the pieces of car debris that littered the road. Somewhere, she could hear someone crying. The wails cutting through the rest of the sounds. It was horrible. It was unnerving.

She landed on her knees next to the upturned car. The only thing she could currently see of Jacob was the soles of his feet. His whole body was inside the car, his feet sticking out through the broken passenger-side window. 'Do you need anything?' she shouted through the gap.

She adjusted her position to get a better view. Inside the car a pregnant woman was trapped upside down, held precariously in position by her seat belt. It was obvious she was still unconscious, an oxygen mask to her face and a collar around her neck. Jacob was pushing back her coat and gently easing her stretched top over her abdomen. Bonnie didn't wait for instructions. She fished out a stethoscope and a foetal monitor and stuck her hand through a gap in the broken window where Jacob could grab them.

Even from here she could see the damp patch between the woman's trousers. It could be two things. It could be urine or it could be amniotic fluid. She was just praying it wasn't blood. She didn't even want to consider that— not under these conditions.

After a few minutes of wrestling around Jacob finally spoke. 'I've got a heartbeat—albeit a little quick. But I've just felt her contracting and there's absolutely no way to do any kind of examination.'

He shook his head as Bonnie tried to hand him the nitrazine strips. The best they could do in this situation was rub one against her damp clothes. 'There's no point checking. I'm fairly sure her membranes have ruptured. We need to get her out of here now. She's at risk of uterine or placental rupture. There's no way I'm delivering this baby upside down.'

Bonnie stood up and shouted over to the fire and rescue colleagues. 'We need to get this woman out. She's about to deliver. Can we have some assistance?'

One of them ran over. 'Sorry, got tied up trying to lift a car off someone's chest.'

Bonnie gulped. It was chaos all around them and even though the road seemed full of emergency staff, there probably still wasn't enough.

The fire-and-rescue guy pointed at the collar. 'She was conscious for only a few seconds after we arrived and had no feeling in her legs. That's why the collar's in place. The trauma doc said not to move her. He was waiting for you to arrive.'

She nodded. 'Well, tell the trauma doc we're here and she's in labour. We need assistance to move her as safely as possible now. Can you get us a backboard?'

She pushed her way around the other side of the car. The driver's door was wedged up against a van that was on its side. It was a struggle to push her arms through and try and wind a blood-pressure cuff around the lady's arm. 'Do we have a name?' she shouted to Jacob.

'Holly Burns.'

She pressed the button on the machine. Now she'd squeezed around the other side she could see him a little easier. There were deep furrows along his brow; he was clearly worried about this patient and so was she.

'BP's low,' she said quickly as the result displayed.

A number of the fire-and-rescue crew had collected around them, all talking in low voices. 'Doc, we're going to have to move the car. We need to cut the patient free and we can't do it while the van's in place. You'll need to come out.'

Jacob didn't hesitate. 'I'm going nowhere. This mother and her baby need monitoring every second. Move the car with me in it.'

One of them stepped forwards as Bonnie wriggled out from the other side. She could see clearly why they would need to separate the vehicles. There was no way they could get Holly out on a backboard otherwise. If she had spinal damage they had to do everything possible to try to minimise the movement.

She shook her head and touched the fire-and-rescue chief's arm. 'Don't waste your time arguing with him.

He won't change his mind and it'll just get ugly. This woman could deliver very soon and her position makes it dangerous for her life and her baby's.'

She was quite sure this went against every health and safety check imaginable. But she'd seen fire and rescue, paramedic and police services do similar things before. They all made the patient their priority.

She stood back as equipment was positioned and blankets shoved inside the car as Jacob was told to brace himself and his patient.

The car and van were wedged tightly together. The sound of metal ripping apart made her wince. Nothing about this was delicate. Both the car and van were juddering, wheels spinning in the air. It seemed to take for ever before they were finally yanked apart and the fire-and-rescue crew moved in with their cutting equipment.

It only took seconds for them to cut the side from the car. One of the other trauma doctors appeared with the backboard and had a quick confab with Jacob inside about the best way to cut Holly free from her seat belt and support her spine. It was a delicate operation. Twelve pairs of hands ended up all around her, ready to ease her gently onto the spinal board as the seat belt was cut. 'Hold it,' said Jacob abruptly. 'She's having another contraction. We'll have to wait a few seconds for it to pass.'

Bonnie swallowed anxiously. Jacob still had the foetal monitor on Holly's swollen abdomen. She could see the contraction clearly. As an experienced midwife she knew Holly wasn't in the early stages of labour, even though she was upside down. A thought flicked through her mind— had Holly already been in labour and on her way to the hospital before the crash? Or was this a trauma-induced labour brought on by the crash? One thing was for sure:

as soon as they got Holly into the ambulance, they'd better be prepared for a delivery.

As the seat belt was cut and Holly slid onto the back-board Bonnie glanced around. 'Does anyone know about next of kin?' she shouted. They were just about to take Holly away from the accident site. There hadn't been a chance to get all the information they needed.

One of the policemen appeared at her elbow. 'We've sent someone to contact her husband. Are you taking her to CRMU?'

Bonnie nodded. 'Can you give me her husband's name and contact details?'

He nodded and scribbled in his notebook, ripping out the page and handing it to her. By the time she turned around Holly was already being loaded onto the ambulance.

Jacob was ruthlessly efficient. The other trauma doctor secured Holly's head and neck, checking her airway before he left. He was part of the general team from Cambridge Royal. 'I have to accompany another patient back with a flail chest. I'll send an orthopod around to the maternity unit.' Jacob gave him the briefest nod as he attached the monitoring equipment. Bonnie barely got inside as the doors slammed shut and the ambulance started off at breakneck speed.

'There's another contraction coming,' she said as she finished attaching the BP cuff and heart monitor. She helped him slide off Holly's underwear and covered her abdomen with a blanket.

Jacob's frown deepened. 'She's crowning. This baby is coming out any minute.'

Bonnie turned towards the portable incubator, struggling to stay on her feet as the ambulance rocked from side to side. There had to be rules about this. She was sure they were supposed to be strapped in. But this baby wasn't waiting for anyone, and what use would two health professionals be at her head or at her side, while a baby slipped out?

She was doing rapid calculations in her head. 'She's thirty-four weeks. That's not too early. Hopefully the baby won't have any breathing difficulties.' She switched on the monitoring equipment in the incubator, ensuring it was warm and the oxygen was ready.

It was difficult to take up position in the swaying ambulance. She could only try and lift Holly's nearest leg, holding it in position to allow Jacob easier access to the presenting head.

She gulped. 'She's missing out on the birth of her baby.' She blinked back tears. 'I hope she doesn't miss out on anything else.'

This was awful. Her first delivery for CRMU with a mother that she didn't even know would wake up. Why was she still unconscious? The trauma doctor had only given her a quick once-over. There hadn't been time for anything else. A Glasgow Coma Scale chart dangled from a clipboard. As each contraction gripped there were facial twinges—as if she were reacting to some element of the labour pain. Reaction to pain was a crucial part of the head injury assessment. And she was breathing spontaneously. Bonnie tried to focus on the positives. She would hate to think this mother would never get to hold her new baby.

As another contraction gripped Holly's stomach the head delivered. Jacob had a quick check around the baby's neck for any sign of a cord. He glanced quickly in Bon-

nie's direction. 'No cord. Presentation is good.' He gave
an audible sigh of relief. 'Thank goodness.'

One minute later the baby slid into his hands and he
quickly handed it over to Bonnie.

A little girl. Just like Freya. A fist squeezed around her
heart. She'd heard Freya's first cries, felt her first little
breaths against her chest. Holly was missing all of this.

She quickly gave the pale little baby a rub, stimulating her first noisy breath, followed by some sharp cries.
She gave Jacob a quick smile before wrapping the baby
in the warming blanket and doing a quick assessment.
'APGAR six,' she said as she finished.

It was a little low, but would likely come up before
the second check in five minutes. It was certainly better
than she'd initially hoped for.

She looked up; they were pulling up in front of the
emergency entrance at the maternity unit. Three other
staff were waiting for them.

Jacob moved into position as the doors opened and
helped lift the incubator down. 'Take her to the nursery
and get a paed doc to check her over.'

Bonnie gave a brief nod and headed down the corridor with one of the nursery midwives by her side. The
handover was quick. The little girl was pinking up now
and was letting everyone know she wasn't entirely happy
with her entrance to the world.

By the time Bonnie got back to the labour suite, Jacob
was consulting with the orthopaedic doctor who'd come
over from the main hospital. Holly's notes had appeared
at the desk. Thankfully, she had no significant medical
history and her pregnancy seemed to have gone well.
Bonnie could see from the whiteboard that Miriam, the
senior midwife, was with her.

'Has she woken up yet?' She was having trouble getting her head around the fact that Holly had delivered a baby without being conscious. 'In ten years of midwifery I've never seen a woman labour while unconscious.' She blinked back the tears that threatened to spill over. 'Does she have some kind of head injury?'

The orthopaedic doctor glanced at Jacob, then leaned over and touched Bonnie's arm. 'It actually might not be as bad as first thought. She almost certainly has a head injury but her Glasgow Coma Scale responses are improving. I suspect Holly's in spinal shock from injuries sustained in the crash. She wouldn't have felt the intensity of the labour pains even though her body naturally delivered. Jacob and I were just discussing the fact that we think she might actually have been in labour prior to the accident. We've checked the ward call log. She hadn't called into the labour suite and she didn't have any bags in her car. We're wondering if she was going home to collect her things.'

Bonnie nodded. She could only remember a few things about spinal shock from her general nurse training. It was usually temporary but could cause loss of sensation and feeling. It certainly sounded better than some of the things she'd been imagining.

Jacob's voice cut across her thoughts. 'I take it the little girl is okay?' He was glaring and it took her a couple of seconds to realise it wasn't at her—well, not entirely. His eyes were fixed on the orthopaedic doctor's hand, which was still on Bonnie's arm.

Was Jacob this territorial around all his staff?

She gave a nod to the orthopod and walked behind the desk to pick up some paper notes. 'Baby Burns is doing fine. APGAR was eight at five minutes. The paediatrician was checking her as I left.' She waved the notes at Jacob. 'I'm just going to write up some midwifery notes for what happened out there. I'll get the clerk to put Holly and baby Burns into the hospital admission system.'

There was a bang at the bottom of the corridor as the doors were flung open. Both Bonnie and Jacob jumped to their feet. It wasn't entirely unusual for people to enter the labour suite in a rush. This time, though, there was no pregnant woman—just an extremely anxious man.

'My wife, Holly, is she here? They said there was a car accident. What happened? Is she okay? Is the baby okay?'

Jacob and the orthopaedic doctor exchanged glances. Jacob gestured towards his office. 'Mr Burns, why don't you come into my office and I'll let you know what has happened?'

The man's face paled even more and he wobbled. 'Are they dead?'

Jacob quickly reassured him. 'No, no, they're not dead. And you can see them both. Let's just have a chat first.' He turned to the orthopaedic doctor. 'Dr Connelly, will you join us, please?'

But the man's feet were welded to the floor. His eyes widened. 'Both? The baby is here?'

Bonnie walked over, putting her hand on his arm. 'You have a lovely daughter. I'll take you to see her once you've spoken to the doctors.' She helped usher him into the office and, once he was inside, closed the door behind him and left them to it.

'Debbie' The labour suite domestic was working in the kitchen. 'Would you mind taking a pot of tea into Dr Layton's office? I think the man he's talking to will need some.'

Debbie gave a little laugh. 'Tea, for Jacob? You've got to be joking. The guy drinks his coffee with three spoonfuls.' She shook her head. 'You'll soon learn he usually has a cup from the café across the street welded to his hand. Don't worry. I'll sort it out.'

For the rest of the day Bonnie's feet barely touched the ground. She finished her notes, took over from Miriam for a while, then took Mr Burns along to see his new daughter.

Holly had gradually started to come round. Things were complicated. Midwives really shouldn't be dealing with a patient with a head injury. But Holly had a few other complications with the delivery of her placenta. She really wasn't suitable to be on a general ward either. After some careful calls and juggling, Bonnie finally managed to make sure that either a midwife who was also trained as a general nurse was looking after her, or that an extra nurse be called over from the brief intervention unit. After the first twenty-four hours she'd need to be reassessed and other arrangements made.

By the time Jacob came to find her she'd no idea where the time had gone. Opening one store cupboard to have most of its contents fall on her head, followed by finding some out-of-date drugs in one of the cupboards was making her organisational skills go into overload. She wouldn't be able to sleep tonight with the 'to do' lists she currently had stored in her head.

'Just thought I should check how you are.'

She picked her way back through the untidy contents of the store cupboard. 'I'm fine, thanks.' She glanced at her watch. 'Is that the time already? The childminder will wonder where I am.'

She let out a groan. 'Darn it. I haven't found us somewhere else to stay.'

'What do you mean? You don't know where you are staying?'

Bonnie sucked in a deep breath. 'That's the thing about agreeing to start at short notice. I haven't managed to find somewhere to rent. I haven't even had a chance to view anywhere. The motel I booked is awful. We got in last night and it's damp and I'm pretty sure there are signs of mildew. It's going to play havoc with Freya's asthma. I need to find somewhere else as soon as I can. I had a quick look online last night and most places aren't available for rent until after Christmas. I've obviously come at the wrong time of year.' She kept shaking her head. She sighed and leaned against the doorjamb. 'I need to find somewhere quick. I just assumed that I'd be able to find somewhere without any problem. It is a city, after all.'

Accommodation wasn't something Jacob had even considered for their new start. As a mother she wouldn't have the option of staying in the hospital flats. They were only designed for singles.

He shook his head. 'Cambridge isn't like most cities. We don't have a huge turnover except when the university year starts. Most students find accommodation and stay in it for four full years.'

She shrugged. 'I'll just need to try a bit harder, I guess. More importantly I'll need to get a car. Relying on public transport is a bit of a nightmare. The sooner I get home to Freya, the better.'

He spoke before he thought. 'I'll give you a lift home.'

She blinked. The shock on her face was apparent. Had he really been that unfriendly to her earlier?

'You don't have to do that.'

'I know. But I will. You've had a bit of a baptism of fire today. I know you want to get home to Freya and the buses will be busy this time of day.' He shrugged. 'It's only five minutes out of my way. We'll go in ten minutes.'

The phone rang further along the ward and Hope Sanders, one of the other midwives, stuck her head out of one of the rooms. 'Jacob? Can you come and take this call?'

He didn't even give her a chance to respond before he walked swiftly along the corridor. He was impressed. Bonnie was doing a good job. He hadn't even given a thought to where she might be staying. If she was worried about that—would she be able to focus on her work?

Hope handed him the phone. 'It's Sean Anderson. He wants to know if you can help in Theatre tomorrow.'

The call only took a few minutes. Jacob liked Sean, the new Australian obstetrician, and he was happy to scrub in on a complicated case. Hope waited for him to finish the call, her arms folded across her chest, leaning on the door.

'What?' he asked as he replaced the receiver.

'How are you?' she asked steadily.

He felt himself flinch. Hope was one of the few people he classed as a friend. She knew exactly what kind of year he'd had. 'I'm fine.'

She nodded slowly. There was no way he'd get away with that kind of answer with Hope. 'When do you get your test results?'

He shifted uncomfortably on his feet. He hated being put on the spot. 'A few weeks.'

'And you're feeling well? Anything I can do?'

He shook his head and picked up some paperwork from his desk. 'I'm fine, Hope. There's no need to fuss.'

She gave him a tight smile. Hope was never bothered by his short answers or occasionally sharp tongue. She just ignored it and asked the questions she wanted to ask.

'Did you reconsider my suggestion?'

'What one?' Hope made lots of suggestions. He should socialise more. He should do less hours at work. He should eat better. He should be more pleasant at work.

She raised her eyebrows. 'About renting out one of your rooms?' Oh. That one. Her latest suggestion was a bid to encapsulate all her suggestions: it would force him to socialise, he might work less if he had someone to go home to, someone who could cook, maybe.

'Haven't had a chance.' He walked from behind the desk and gave her a cheeky wink. 'Been too busy at work.'

'Jacob…' Her voice tailed after him but he was already halfway down the corridor. Hope was about to go into interrogator mode. He could sense it. It was time to make a sharp exit.

Bonnie was just finishing at the desk and he welcomed the distraction. If Hope saw him talking to another woman she was bound to leave him alone.

'Good first day?' he asked.

Bonnie blinked. 'It's not over yet. Come with me a second.'

She took another quick glance over her shoulder at the bustling labour suite. *Her* bustling labour suite. She hadn't even started to make her mark here. They walked down the corridor together.

So many things needed organising to make the place

run more efficiently. Once she had things running the way she liked and she knew the staff a little better she'd start to delegate some tasks. All of the staff she'd met today seemed fine. No one had even mentioned what they'd overheard this morning, but she was sure—by the time she came on shift tomorrow—all members of staff would know about it. That was the thing about hospitals. Nothing was kept secret for long.

She'd met seven midwives, two doctors and one other consultant who all seemed good at their jobs. The ancillary staff seemed great too. CRMU's reputation appeared to be well founded. All the labour suite needed was its wheels oiled a little to help it run more smoothly.

She smiled. First day. After a bumpy start with Freya, and with Jacob, things appeared to be looking up. Good staff. A temporary promotion. Three healthy babies delivered while she was on shift. And another delivered in the back of an ambulance with a mother who appeared to be on the road to recovery.

Jacob had surprised her most with his offer of a ride home. At their first meeting he'd appeared a little detached. But at times today his mouth had betrayed him by turning up at the edges. There was a sense of humour in there somewhere. She'd just have to find a big spade to dig it out.

She pushed open the doors at the end of the ward and walked along to one of the side rooms between her ward and the special-care nursery. Both of them looked through the window. Holly had opened her eyes and was talking to one of the specialist midwives assigned to her. Her husband sat by her side holding the baby in his arms. Another midwife from the special-care nursery was there with the incubator. It was obvious this was the first time she'd got to see her baby.

The whole scene sent a warm glow around Bonnie's body. Coming here was the best decision she'd ever made.

She met Jacob's emerald gaze. There was a gleam in his eye. He knew exactly what kind of day she'd had. She kept her face straight. 'No. It's not been a good day.'

He raised his eyebrows and she broke into a beaming smile. 'It was a *great* day. I think I'm going to like Cambridge Maternity.'

CHAPTER THREE

JACOB TAPPED HIS fingers on the wheel of the car while he waited for Bonnie. He'd already had a few curious stares from members of staff who obviously wondered who he was waiting on. Bonnie appeared two minutes later and jumped in the car next to him. 'Sorry, just getting changed and sorting out a locker before we left.' She gave him directions to the childminder's house and looked around with a smile on her face.

'I didn't take you for a four-by-four guy. I thought you'd have something sleeker, more sporty.'

He raised his eyebrows. 'Really? Why on earth did you think that?'

She laughed. 'You've got that "I drive a flash car" look about you. Wouldn't have thought there'd be much call for a four-by-four in the city. I've been surprised by how many I've seen.'

'Haven't you heard? It's the latest fashion craze and I'm just following the crowd.'

She shook her head. 'Yeah, yeah. Somehow I get the distinct impression you've never been a crowd follower.'

He tried to hide his smile. 'I'm shocked. We've only just met and you're trying to tell me I'm not a people pleaser.'

She started laughing again. 'Seriously? You were a bit

grumpy this morning. The staff seem quite intimidated by you. Are you always like that?'

'You were late. That's why I was grumpy.' It was the best excuse he could give. The truth was he'd spent the last fourteen months being grumpy—and only a few select people knew why. Jacob had always been a completely hands-on kind of doctor. Some physicians who were Head of Department reduced their clinical time by a large amount. He'd never been that kind of doctor but had been grateful to use his position as an excuse for his lack of patient contact at times over the past fourteen months. That was the thing about some types of chemotherapy—at certain times in the cycle, patient contact just wasn't appropriate. Particularly when you had to deal with pregnant women and neonates—two of the most vulnerable groups around. Grumpy probably didn't even come close to covering his temperament and frustration these last fourteen months.

She shook her head as they turned into the childminder's street. 'I think you were grumpy long before I was late. I need to know these things. I need to know if staff won't want to approach you about things. I need to know the dynamics of the labour suite.'

He liked her already. She was astute. It wouldn't be easy to pull the wool over her eyes—exactly what he should want from the sister of his labour suite. He just wished she weren't using her astuteness on him.

'You haven't mentioned what happens with the special clients. Do I get involved with those?'

He raised his eyebrows. 'The special clients?'

She smiled. 'Cambridge Royal is known for attracting the rich and famous. I haven't had a chance to look over the plans for the general hospital. What happens if we get someone who wants a private delivery? It wouldn't seem safe to have them in another area.'

He was impressed. She'd obviously done a lot of background reading. 'You're right. It wouldn't be safe. It isn't public knowledge but there are six private rooms just outside the doors to the labour suite, only a few minutes from Theatre. We don't want anyone to know where our private patients are.'

She gave a little nod of her head. 'Makes sense. Privacy, that's what people want. Isn't it? I guess we'll need to talk about the midwifery staffing for those rooms.'

There was something so strange about all this. Everything about being around Bonnie made him feel out of sorts. He had looked at her CV and hadn't understood at all why Valerie Glencross had thought she would be a suitable replacement for their ward sister. Then she'd been late.

But from the second her eyes had sparked and she'd given him a dressing-down in front of the staff he'd liked her. She was different. She'd proved more than competent at the roadside delivery. She was asking all the right questions about the ward and she was making all the right observations. Bonnie Reid was proving to be the most interesting woman he'd come across in a while.

She opened the car door as they pulled up outside the childminder's. 'I'll only be two minutes, I promise, and Lynn will be able to give me a car seat for Freya. That's the beauty of having a friend who is a childminder. She has a garage full of these things.'

Car seat. It hadn't even crossed his mind. That was how far out of the loop he was when it came to children. He tried not to focus on her well-fitting jeans as she ran up the path towards the door with her auburn hair bouncing behind her.

What kind of crazy fool cheated on a woman like Bonnie? The guy must have rocks in his head. Jacob had never realised quite how much he liked that colour of hair.

He watched as she ran back down the path holding the hand of a little girl. She was like an identikit of her mother. Same colour hair and pale skin. It only took Bonnie a minute to arrange the car seat and strap her little girl into place. She was obviously a dab hand at these things.

'Who are you?' The voice came from the back seat.

The little pair of curious blue eyes was fixed on his in the mirror. She had a little furrow across her brow. It was like a staring contest. A Mexican stand-off. And Jacob had a feeling he was going to lose.

Bonnie answered as she climbed back in the car. 'This is Mummy's friend from work. His name is Jacob. He's going to give us a lift back to the motel.'

He glanced in the rear-view mirror in time to see her shrink back into her seat a little. Was he really that scary? Bonnie had already mentioned the staff might find him unapproachable. He'd never really given it much thought.

'Hmm…' came the voice from the back of the car. She really didn't seem too sure about it. Bonnie gave him directions to the motel and he flinched when it came into view. If this was the outside—what was the inside like?

'Do you need a hand?'

'No,' she said too quickly, then her voice wavered. 'Actually, could you give me a hand carrying the car seat in?' She jumped out and unstrapped Freya, leading the way inside.

He followed them in, waiting patiently while she unlocked the door of her room. The first thing that hit him was the smell of damp. The really obvious smell of damp. He winced. How on earth did the motel owner think this was acceptable?

He looked around. 'This will play havoc with Freya's asthma.' The words came out before he really thought about it.

Bonnie sucked in a deep breath and licked her lips. There was a sheen across her eyes, as if she was holding back tears.

She'd already told him how much this bothered her. But now, seeing it with his own eyes, he understood.

Bonnie's pretty face was marred by a frown. He liked her. He hardly knew her but he liked her already. What was more she obviously had the skills that the labour suite badly needed right now.

And after what he'd seen today? He didn't want to lose her from CRMU.

His brain was in overdrive. There was no way he could leave them here. Not now he'd seen it. Not now he'd smelled it.

This was about work. He was prioritising the needs of the labour suite above all others. That was what he was telling himself right now, but that was the only way he could make sense of the possibility that had just flown into his head.

'You have to get her out of here. A child with asthma can't possibly stay in an environment like this.'

This time she was blinking back tears. 'What choice do I have?' She sounded exasperated, her hand curled protectively around her daughter.

'You can stay with me.' The words were out before he even had a chance to think properly.

It made no sense. It made no sense whatsoever. He

was a bachelor. After the last fourteen months he liked his solitude. His home was his salvation.

'What?' Bonnie straightened up. 'What do you mean?'

'I mean, you and your daughter can stay with me—until you find something more suitable, of course. I have space in my house. You can stay with me.'

'No. No, we can't do that.' She was shaking her head. 'We don't even really know you.'

A wave of embarrassment came over him. After his behaviour this morning it was understandable that she was wary.

He took a deep breath. 'Look, Bonnie, I'm sorry about this morning. I know I came across as difficult.' He shook his head. 'But that's just me. It probably wasn't the ideal first meeting.' He held out his hands. 'But there's absolutely no way I'm letting you spend the next few days here with your daughter. Not while her health is at risk.'

It took a few seconds for the initial shocked expression on her face to disappear. Her tense shoulders gradually relaxed and she nodded slowly. Relief. That was what she was feeling now. It was palpable in the air all around them. The frown had disappeared from her brow and her blue eyes were focused clearly on him.

'You really mean it?' She seemed really hesitant.

It was clear she couldn't believe it. 'Freya and I can stay with you for a few days?' She glanced around her. 'We don't need to stay in this mouldy motel room?'

'Just until you find somewhere suitable.' From the expression on her face any minute now she would jump for joy.

'Of course.' Parts of his insides were doing strange twisting things. Making him think the word *no* but not letting it come out. This was work. They'd found a new temporary ward sister who needed a short-term solution for accommodation. It was logical. That was all.

'That's such a weight off my mind. Thank you, Jacob. Will your wife or partner be okay with this? The last thing I want to do is foist myself and a five-year-old on someone unexpectedly.'

Jacob gave the tiniest shake of his head. 'No wife. No partner.' He shrugged his shoulders. 'No time.' He squirmed a little saying those words out loud. Most single guys would probably be delighted to declare their freedom to the world. But for some reason it made him sound so isolated.

'And it won't be too much of an inconvenience to you?' Her voice rose a little at the end of the sentence, as if she were worried at any minute he might change his mind.

'How much trouble can a five-year-old be?' He was giving her a half smile as a whole surge of wariness swept over him. He had absolutely *no* experience with five-year-olds. He didn't even know how to have a conversation with one. He tried to rationalise things out loud. 'It makes sense. We need a ward sister to get on top of things in the labour ward. The last thing you need is for your daughter to be sick and to spend your time at work worrying about where you're staying. It's logical.'

She held out her hands. 'You'll need to give us a few minutes to pack. Thankfully we didn't really have a chance to unpack last night.'

It was almost as if Bonnie went into automatic pilot. She started pushing things haphazardly into a large blue case, then sat on it to close it. Now he'd made the offer it was clear she couldn't wait to get out of here—no matter how temporary the solution. And the truth was, he couldn't wait to get out of here either.

'Here,' he said, gesturing her to move. 'Let me. I'll push down and you can snap it shut.'

It did only take her a few minutes. But by the time she was finished there were four bulging suitcases for the car as well as the car seat. He gave her a wink. 'Just as well I brought my four-by-four and not my sports car. How on earth did you get down from the train with these?'

Something juddered through him. *Had he just winked at her?* What on earth was wrong with him? Since when did he do things like that?

This woman was having a strange effect on him.

But Bonnie didn't seem to notice. She just looked a little sheepish. 'It's a bit hard trying to ram all your worldly goods into some suitcases. Particularly when your five-year-old wants to bring all twenty of her favourite cuddly toys.' She sighed. 'I've got some stuff in storage as well at my mum and dad's. Once we find somewhere to stay I'll send for it.'

He picked up the first two cases and carried them out to the car. All of a sudden he felt as if he'd put his foot in his mouth. He wasn't trying to offend her. He'd spent the last year so focused on his treatment and keeping the department running that he hadn't bothered much with social niceties. Maybe it was time to start paying attention again.

Bonnie went to pay her bill as he loaded the last two cases into the car. 'You shouldn't have paid anything. That place is a disgrace.'

She strapped Freya back in and climbed into the passenger seat. 'Don't. He wanted me to pay for the whole week because we've left early.'

'I hope you refused.'

She gave him a wink. 'Of course I did.'

He started the car with a smile. Just as well he hadn't been driving. He'd have probably swerved off the road. She had seen the wink and had taken it as intended— in good humour. Thank goodness. He couldn't afford to tiptoe around someone who would be staying in his house. He must have been crazy inviting her to stay. *She* must have been crazy to accept. Either that, or she was desperate.

And he already knew that she was.

He had to keep remembering that. Otherwise his mind might start to drift in other directions. He'd never shared his house with a woman before. Let alone a woman and child. He was used to his own space. This had disaster written all over it.

His stomach started to churn a little. This was the craziest thing he'd ever done. He knew that his house was tidy—Monday was the day his housekeeper came. He'd texted her earlier and asked her to pick up some food for him. His fridge was currently bare. It was hardly hospitable to invite a mother and child back with not even a drop of milk in the fridge.

There. That was better. A mother and child seemed a much safer thought than anything that involved the name Bonnie.

He pulled up outside his Victorian town house. It had just started to rain and Bonnie pressed her nose up against the glass. 'Please tell me you only own part of that.'

He opened the car door. 'Nope. It's all mine. Including the ancient kennel in the back garden.'

He felt a little surge of pride in his heart that she liked

his house. It was very traditional for Cambridge. Set in a residential area, in the middle of the city, the three-storey town house was just moments away from the river and college boathouses.

'You have a dog?'

Freya. He'd almost forgotten she was there. She had that expression on her face again. The little frown line across her forehead. She was standing in the rain staring up at the bay window at the front of the house. He pulled her hood up over her head. 'No. Sorry, I don't. I just have a really old kennel.'

He popped the boot and lifted out the first two cases, then walked up the path and deposited them at the doorway while he fished for his keys. 'Give me a sec,' he said as he opened the door and turned off the alarm. 'Go inside. I'll get the other cases.'

The rain was getting heavier now and it only took a few seconds to wrestle the other cases from the back of the car and get inside. He closed the door behind him and breathed a sigh of relief.

Home was usually his sanctuary. The place he came back to after work or treatment, closed the blinds and ignored the world. Chances were, he wouldn't get to do that any time soon. Thank goodness his treatment was over. Now he just had to wait for his results.

Bonnie had picked Freya up and carried her through the long corridor and turned left into the main lounge. He heard the little suck in of breath. What did that mean?

He dumped the cases at the door and followed her into the lounge. She spun around to face him. 'Wow. This place is just yours? It's gorgeous.' She set Freya down on the floor and walked over to the fireplace. 'This is just amazing. Does it work? Do you have a real fire on a winter's night?' She crouched down and touched the tile work around the fireplace.

He'd always been proud of his home, but for the first time he felt a little regretful. He touched the marble surround. 'No. I've never had the chimney swept. It is apparently in working order. I just never got around to it.' He pointed to the walls. 'I do have the original cast-iron radiators. So don't worry. You won't be cold.'

She shook her head. 'Oh, I'm not worried about being cold.' She looked down. 'The floorboards are gorgeous too. Are they original?' She knelt down and ran her hand along the floor. He was learning quickly that Bonnie was a very tactile person.

'I sanded them down. It took about a year to do the whole house.'

She nodded in approval. 'I noticed the gorgeous geometric floor tiles on the way in too. I always wanted a hallway with those.' She looked a little lost in her own thoughts, then gave a little shrug. 'I'd be happy just to have a hallway right now.'

'Those tiles were hidden under the ugliest shag-pile carpet you've ever seen.'

She gasped. 'Really?' Then shuddered. 'What a crime to cover those up.'

'It probably saved them from being ruined. I've had them all coated now with something that should mean they last the next hundred years.'

She took a look around her. 'I'll never be able to afford a place like this. You're so lucky.'

Lucky. Now there was a word he'd never use to describe himself. Over the course of such an eventful day he'd realised how easy it was to be around Bonnie. Now it struck him how little she actually knew him. How little most of the staff at CRMU actually knew him. He could count on one hand the people he'd actually trusted with his secret. They knew how much he'd struggled this last year. How frustrated he'd been when he couldn't deal with patients because of the type of chemotherapy he was undergoing. How much he wanted just to get back to normal and do his job the way he always had.

Lucky. Maybe he was lucky. His cancer was treatable. Other types weren't. He'd managed to undergo his treatment quietly with only one day off work sick. Good planning had played a huge part in that. Having a cancer treatment team who were willing to allow him to start chemotherapy on a Thursday evening, which meant the after-effects didn't really hit until the Friday night, meant he could still work, then spend most weekends in bed to allow himself to recover.

But he still didn't feel lucky. His mother certainly hadn't been. She'd had the same type of cancer that he had—non-Hodgkin's lymphoma. It was generally thought that it wasn't an inherited disease. But tell that to the families where more than one person had it. There was just so much still to learn about these diseases. So many genes in the body where they still couldn't determine their purpose.

But his last treatment was finished now. In a few weeks' time he'd have his bloods rechecked to see if the treatment had worked and his cancer was finally gone. The whole black cloud that had been hanging over his head for the last fourteen months would finally be gone. Maybe. Hopefully.

Bonnie was still walking around. She had a little look of wonder on her face. As if she really did love the place. She stood with her back to the bay window and looked across the room. A smile lit up her face. She was obviously seeing something that he didn't.

'This place must be so gorgeous at Christmastime. I can just imagine it.' She spun around and held out her hands. 'A huge tree at this window that everyone out on the street can see.' She walked towards the fireplace again. 'One of those green and red garlands for the mantel, with some twinkling lights.' She turned back to the window. 'And some old-fashioned heavy-duty velvet curtains around the window.' She touched the white blinds that were currently in place and gave a little frown. 'Do you change these at Christmas? It's such a gorgeous bay window. You should make the most of it.'

He could almost hear the shutters clanging into place in his brain. He saw it. The pictures in her head that would never be in his. Never. He didn't do Christmas—hadn't since he was a young boy.

She couldn't possibly know. She couldn't possibly understand. He and his father had literally watched the life being sucked out of his mother. She'd died around Christmastime and the season celebrations had been a permanent reminder ever since. He hated Christmas. He'd always offered to work it, and since most of his colleagues had children they'd always been happy to accept his offer. He'd never hung a single decoration in his home. He didn't even own any.

He could see her gaze narrow ever so slightly as she looked more critically now around the whitewashed room with white window blinds. Apart from the wooden floor, the only thing that gave the room some colour was the dark leather suite.

He'd always loved his house. It suited his needs fine.

He didn't want to accommodate anyone else's opinions or tastes.

He walked back out to the hall. Away from the look of expectation on Bonnie's face. Away from her smiling, overactive imagination. 'I don't really have time for Christmas, or to decorate. There's not much point. I'm always on duty at the hospital anyway. Come on, I'll show you both where your rooms are.'

He didn't even wait to see if she was following him. Just picked up the first two cases and headed to the stairs. Bonnie still had that glazed expression on her face. She touched the banister. 'This must be beautiful with tinsel wound around it.'

He swept past her on the staircase. 'Not going to happen. Not in this house.' He was done being subtle. She hadn't picked up on the first clues. He was going to have to hang a sign saying 'No Christmas' above the mantelpiece. What did it matter anyway—by Christmas she wouldn't be here. Not in his house anyway.

He paused at the landing, ignoring her puzzled expression and cutting her off before she had the chance to speak. 'There's three bedrooms on this floor—one of which is mine—and two bedrooms and a bathroom on the floor above. I think you and Bonnie might be better up there. More privacy for you both.'

More privacy for me too. He didn't want to wander along the hall half dressed to find a little red-haired girl with her disapproving glare.

He started up the other flight of stairs before Bonnie really had a chance to reply. The housekeeper had definitely been in today. The doors of both rooms were open and he could smell the freshly laundered linen on the beds. He put the cases in the first room that had a double bed. 'I'm assuming you'll sleep in here and Freya next door. There's a single in there. Bathroom's at the end of the hall.' He walked along the corridor and flicked the light switch in the white-tiled bathroom. He hadn't really thought about it before. Just about everything in this house was white.

He watched as Freya walked suspiciously into the single room, her eyes flitting from side to side. She looked at the single bed covered in a white duvet, the chest of drawers, and then turned around and walked back to Bonnie, wrapping her arms around her waist and cuddling her tight.

Her actions gave Jacob a start. There was nothing wrong with this room. It was fine. Why didn't she like it? He took a few seconds and looked again. Maybe the room was a little stark. Maybe it wasn't exactly welcoming for a little girl. But how on earth would he know what a little girl would like? It wasn't as if he'd had any practice. The kids he was generally around were only a few days or hours old.

'Maybe you'd like to sleep in with your mum?' He had no idea where that had come from. Chances were, he'd just committed some huge parenting faux pas. He was just struggling to understand Freya's reaction to the perfectly acceptable room.

Bonnie looked up and shot him a grateful glance. 'We'll play it by ear. Thank you, Jacob.'

He gave a relieved nod. 'Sorry, I didn't show you the kitchen or the back sitting room. It has a more comfortable sofa—and another TV and DVD player.' A thought darted into his brain. 'The only place I'd prefer Freya stay out of is my office downstairs.' The place was full of research about non-Hodgkin's lymphoma. Statistics for everything, including the most successful forms of treatment. Freya wouldn't be able to read any of that but Bonnie would if she followed Freya in.

'Absolutely no problem.' Bonnie had wound her hand through Freya's hair and was stroking the back of her neck. Did she know she was doing it? Or was it just a subconscious act?

'There's some food in the kitchen. Help yourself to anything that's in the fridge, freezer or cupboards.' He glanced at Freya. 'I'm not quite sure what Freya will like but my housekeeper picked up some groceries for me today. Or you could have some toast if you prefer?'

He had absolutely no idea what he was doing. This had been his craziest idea yet. A woman who was practically a stranger and a child who was clearly uncomfortable around him—and he'd invited them to stay in his home.

For the first time in a long time, Jacob Layton felt well and truly out of his depth.

Jacob was waiting for an answer. He had that anxious look on his face again. The one that kept appearing every few minutes. It was clear he wasn't used to having people in his house and she realised just what an inconvenience this must be to him. Her stomach flip-flopped with guilt. He must have regretted his offer as soon as the words had left his mouth.

But he seemed so anxious to please. It was almost cute. And she could bet that Jacob Layton had never been described as cute before.

She swallowed. She'd kill for a cup of tea right now. But it just didn't seem right to walk into someone else's kitchen and make yourself at home. 'I didn't mean to put you to so much trouble, Jacob. Please apologise to your housekeeper for me. I didn't mean to give her additional work.'

He waved his hand. 'You haven't. She shops for me on occasion anyway. I'm just not sure how much she'll have got as I didn't know I'd have guests. Check the fridge. I'll go and get your other cases.' He disappeared down the stairs as she stared at the bulging cases in the white room. Her blue case looked ready to explode. It was so out of place in here. A huge splash of colour against the stark white room. Thank goodness for the wooden floorboards. They added a little warmth about the place.

She shuffled over to the case, Freya still attached to her waist. It was clear her little girl was feeling overwhelmed by the whole situation. And to be truthful— she was too.

He had no idea what he'd let himself in for. Once she opened those cases his beautiful, pristine house would never look the same again. It wasn't that she was messy—she would never be messy staying as a guest in someone's house. It was just—once she opened the cases—things would start to get everywhere, as if they had self-migrating powers. And she wasn't quite sure how Jacob would feel about that. She let out a sigh and sat down on the bed, pulling Freya along with her. The comfortable mattress almost swallowed them up.

This place was a thousand times better than the motel. Here, she wouldn't be worried about Freya's asthma flaring up. The house was warm without being too hot. It was clean. It was spacious. They had their own rooms—they almost had their own floor.

Money. The thought came out of nowhere and she sat bolt upright. She hadn't offered him any money. There was no way she could stay here rent-free. It was quite obvious that Jacob was putting himself out for them. She would have to find a way to bring it up. But she had a bad feeling about how it would go.

Jacob. It was strange being in his house. *His home.* But that was just it. It didn't really feel like a home.

The white everywhere made it seem almost clinical. She would have imagined him staying in some brand-new luxury penthouse flat—not an old Victorian town house. It was beautiful. There was no doubt about that, and she hadn't even seen the kitchen yet.

But there were no pictures. No family photos. He hadn't even mentioned his family yet. There was no little sign of 'him' anywhere in the house. Who was Jacob Layton?

She ran her fingers across the bedspread. That was what was wrong. This was a beautiful house. But it didn't feel like home. Why?

A house like this should exude warmth, character. And Jacob's house wasn't like that. She had the overwhelming urge to change the curtains in the lounge, to buy some different bedspreads for the white rooms and to add some accessories—some red towels in the white bathrooms, some pictures along the walls in the hall. A splash of colour was just what this place needed. She shook her head. This wasn't her home and she should just be grateful to have somewhere to stay. It was none of her business how Jacob chose to decorate his beautiful home.

'Come on, pumpkin. Let's leave the cases for now and go and find some dinner.' She took Freya's warm hand in hers and led her downstairs, blinking as she entered the kitchen. Just as she expected. White and chrome, all gleaming and sparkling.

But there was one nice little touch. The worktop wasn't

granite like most designer kitchens. The worktop was a thick wooden polished surface that led to a deep white Belfast sink. It offset the rest of the white and chrome, giving the kitchen a little more warmth.

There was no kitchen table, just a central island with high black bar-style stools. She positioned Freya carefully on one and looked in the freezer. No—not a single thing.

She frowned and opened the fridge. Two steaks. One steak pie, some bacon, some eggs and two carefully wrapped bundles from the fishmongers. One labelled as cod in breadcrumbs. Even the fish fingers were posh round here.

Jacob appeared at her back as she was hunting for some oven trays and baking foil. 'Are you getting on okay?'

She nodded and smiled. 'We decided to eat first and unpack later. We both had first days today and we're pretty wiped out.'

He opened a cupboard and took out some wine glasses, then glanced at Freya and swapped one for a tumbler. 'Would you like some wine?'

She shook her head. 'Honestly? I'm just too tired. I'd love a cup of tea though. And I still need to empty our cases. Could you show me where the washing machine is? I'd appreciate it if we could do some laundry.'

He stood up and opened a few cupboards. 'My house-keeper always buys some fruit and some biscuits—they're in here. Tea and coffee is here. If you turn the red button down on the tap you'll get boiling water.'

'From the tap?'

He nodded. 'Saves boiling the kettle—' he glanced sideways '—and it's too high up for Freya to reach. There's a proper cappuccino maker next to the oven if you prefer.' He gave a little smile. 'To be honest there's too many buttons. I've never used it. But the instructions are there—you're welcome to christen it if you wish.'

He pointed behind her as he ducked into a cupboard and pulled out a bottle of diet cola. 'Utility room is through there. There's a washing machine, tumble dryer and dishwasher, as well as another toilet and the door to the back garden. Freya's welcome to play out there if it's warm enough.' He gave a little grimace. 'I think the only thing you'll find out there is an old football.'

'Don't you have a dog kennel?'

They both turned to the unexpected little voice. Freya had been silent since she'd come downstairs. Jacob moved over next to her. 'I told you that in the car, didn't I? There is an old kennel out there. It must have belonged to the people who owned the house before I did. It still has the dog's name above the kennel.'

'What was his name?'

'How did you know it was a boy?' he answered quickly.

She shrugged. 'I guessed.' Bonnie was amazed. Freya had seemed a little overwhelmed earlier. But maybe she was starting to feel a little more comfortable in the house. She was glad that Jacob was making an effort with her daughter. She already felt as if they'd have to tiptoe round about him. Maybe it wouldn't be quite as awkward as she'd thought.

'Well, you were right. It was a boy. His name was Bones.'

Freya wrinkled her nose. 'Bones? That's a rubbish name for a dog.'

Bonnie couldn't help but laugh at her blunt response. Jacob leaned his elbow on the island. 'Really? That's what I thought too. What would you call a dog?'

Freya thought for a few seconds. 'Sandy. I'd like a little dog. One that's white and sandy coloured.' She leaned forwards and whispered conspiratorially. 'That's why I'd call him Sandy.'

Bonnie tapped Jacob on the shoulder as she poured the diet cola into Freya's tumbler. Not the ideal drink for a five-year-old—but she was just thankful that Jacob had anything at all that was suitable. She set about making a cup of tea for herself. 'Don't give her any ideas. One day it's a bichon frise, the next it's a terrier, the next a Havanese. Let's remember that most places we'll be renting won't accept pets. I keep trying to tell her that.'

He smiled conspiratorially at Freya and pretend whispered to her. 'I think you need to tell Mummy to find a house that takes dogs.' She almost fell over. She hadn't thought he had it in him. Jacob was full of surprises.

He walked over to the fridge and pulled out a silver tray. 'Do you want to have fish too? My housekeeper seems to have bought plenty. She seems to have decided to feed me up. It will only take fifteen minutes.' He slid the sea bass into the oven next to Freya's fish fingers, then grabbed an oven tray, covered it in silver foil and tipped something from a plastic tub into it. He gave a shrug, 'Mediterranean crushed potatoes. I'm rubbish at shopping and cooking. My housekeeper always makes a few back-up meals for me. She says it's the only time my kitchen is put to good use.'

She gave an awkward nod and sat up on one of the stools, warming her hands on her teacup. This was all a little strange.

Jacob looked at her as he poured himself some wine. 'You okay?'

She sighed. 'It's been a big day. This morning I dropped my daughter at a brand-new school, took a bus ride through an unfamiliar city, was late for my first day at work. Accepted a temporary promotion, helped at the scene of an accident and moved into my boss's home. All in one day.'

He sipped his wine. 'I think I've got this one covered for you.'

'What do you mean?' She was curious.

He gave a little smile. 'One of my good friends is Scottish. I think this could be the "I'm completely knackered" answer.'

She burst out laughing and Freya's mouth hung open. 'What a terrible accent!' She lifted her cup of tea towards him. 'But the word is perfect, and, yes, it is the one I would have chosen. I'm completely and utterly knackered. I can't wait to climb into bed with Freya and go to sleep. I can guarantee you—we won't wake up until the alarm goes off.'

Something flickered across his face. 'I'm just glad that Freya will sleep safely. You must have had nightmares last night.'

She hesitated and gave a grateful nod. 'Jacob, we can't stay here without giving you some money. Can I give you what we would have paid for the motel?'

'No.' His answer came out a bit sharply and she started.

'It only seems fair,' she said slowly. 'I know we're imposing and you've already gone to too much trouble for us.' She gestured towards the oven. 'The food that you bought. I'll feel really uncomfortable if you don't let me contribute.'

He took a sip of his wine. 'Then feel really uncomfortable—because I won't. It's only temporary. You'll find somewhere to stay soon. It's only a stopgap to give you some breathing space. We both know that. And anyway—you'll buy your own food for yourself and Freya. I just thought you wouldn't have had much opportunity between arriving last night and coming to work today.' He gave a shrug of his shoulders. 'I don't want the new sister of the labour suite passing out from hunger tomorrow.'

He was so matter-of-fact about it. He made it sound so reasonable. Even though she knew it really wasn't.

She held up her cup of tea towards his. 'Thank you. But you need to know—I won't let this go. I'll keep hounding you.'

He clinked his glass against her cup. 'I'll look forward to it.'

His eyes connected with Bonnie's. That was the difference between herself and her daughter. Bonnie's eyes were deep blue—almost hypnotising. Freya's were the more traditional pale blue.

From the second he'd offered her a place to stay he'd wanted to drag the words back. His stomach had churned and he'd conjured up a million different excuses to try to back out. But his integrity wouldn't let him—that, and the relieved expression on Bonnie's face when he'd made the offer. His guts had twisted at the thought of people in his home. His private place. But it wasn't quite as bad as he'd imagined. It was odd. The last person he'd shared a house with had been his father. It was amazing how long two people could live together while barely talking. Particularly when he'd told his father he wasn't the following the military family tradition and was going into medicine instead. His father had barely looked him in the eye after that.

Before dinner he led them through the rest of the house, showing them a dining room, the door to his study, the downstairs cloakroom and the back sitting room and conservatory.

'This house is just amazing, Jacob, and it's so close to the city centre. What do they call this street—millionaire row?' She was joking but he could see the weariness in her eyes. She'd been uprooted from a familiar home and ended up in a bad motel. Now she was going to be spending the next few weeks scouring around for houses to rent or buy, trying to work out if it was in an area she'd want her and Freya to stay in. All in the run-up to Christmas. Her brain must be currently whirring.

He laughed. 'No. Not quite. I bought it around ten years ago before the prices went crazy. It needed a lot of fixing up and I've just done a little bit at a time.'

'Well, I think you've done a good job. I hope I'll get a chance to have a walk around the area in the next few days. It would be good to get a bit more familiar with Cambridge.'

'If I get a chance, I'll show you and Freya around. Point out the places to visit and the places to avoid.' Where had that come from? It was so unlike him. He'd spent the last year living his life in a bubble. Hardly any interaction with friends and colleagues. The few people that he'd confided in about his condition had all offered to help in any way that they could. But offers of help made him feel vulnerable, at risk even.

Jacob had got through this life shutting off his feelings from the world. He hadn't even properly mourned the death of his mother. That wasn't the Layton way. Or so his father had told him. He'd very much instilled the stiff-upper-lip mentality into his son.

And even after all these years it was still there. It was partly the reason he'd never had a lasting relationship. He'd shuttered himself away for so long it felt normal now. And after a while his friends had stopped offering any assistance. Eventually even good friends got tired of being rebuffed.

Bonnie gave him a smile. 'Thanks, Jacob. That's really nice of you to offer.'

The timer on the oven sounded and Bonnie helped him to put the food onto plates. Instead of moving to the dining room, they stayed at the more informal island in the kitchen. By now, Freya was desperate to see the old kennel outside and invented an imaginary dog for her stay. But it was already dark and after she'd finished her fish fingers her little head started to nod.

Bonnie wrapped her arm around Freya's shoulders. 'I think it's time to get a little girl into her bath and into bed. To be honest, I could do with an early night myself. Once I've helped you clear up I think we'll both go to bed.' She stood up and gave him a wink. 'I don't want to be late for work tomorrow.' She gave a fake roll of her eyes. 'You've no idea what the boss is like.'

He let out a laugh and lifted the plates. 'Don't worry. I've heard about him. Forget about clearing up. I'll dump the dishes in the dishwasher and we're done.'

'You're sure?' She'd already picked up Freya and the little girl had snuggled into her shoulder.

'I'm sure. Goodnight, Bonnie. Goodnight, Freya.' It was odd—for the first time in a long time, Jacob actually felt at peace.

Then Bonnie spoiled it. She fixed on him with her unblinking blue eyes. 'Goodnight, Jacob, and thank you,' then turned and walked up the stairs.

There was nothing surer. The sight of Bonnie's backside in those jeans would stay with him well into the early hours of the morning.

CHAPTER FOUR

THERE WAS NO denying it. The labour suite had been in a complete muddle. Her mother would have called it a right guddle—a good Scots word. And she would have been right.

It seemed that in the few weeks since the sister had left, a new ordering system had come into place, and a new electronic system for recording staff working hours. No one on the labour suite had the time or motivation to learn how to use either and things were well behind.

Bonnie was lucky. There were other staff who offered to help. Isabel Delamere, an obstetrician on an exchange from Australia, was quick to give her the low-down on most members of staff. She wasn't a gossip. In fact, Bonnie got the impression that Isabel was quite the opposite. But she'd been new here herself and obviously wanted to help.

Hope Sanders, one of the other midwives, had been great. She'd quickly explained both new systems to Bonnie. It was strange. Bonnie had seen Hope talk to Jacob a few times. It was obvious they were friends. And the tall curly-haired blonde had already told her she was single. But Bonnie could tell there wasn't anything romantic between them.

If anything, Hope just seemed concerned about Jacob. She was always reminding him about the number of hours he worked and telling him to get out a bit more.

Things were a little awkward on the ward. Both of them had decided it wouldn't be wise if the rest of the staff knew Bonnie and her daughter were staying with Jacob. It meant that she tried to jump out of the car before they reached the car park and other members of staff would notice them together. For the last few days things had been fine.

Well. That wasn't entirely true. She'd spent every night poring over the Internet looking at rental properties and houses for sale. Jacob had tried to be helpful. But Jacob's helpful had been telling her that one area where a house was for sale was less than salubrious and three of the rental properties had been similar. There was nothing else suitable in her price range. Trouble was, she'd moved here at the wrong time of year. Cambridge had lots of properties for rent, but most were rented by students and visiting lecturers for a year at a time. If she'd arrived a few months earlier there would probably have been lots of properties to view. Arriving in November? Not a chance.

Kerry, one of the midwives in the unit, leaned over the desk towards her. 'Bonnie, we've just had a call to say that Hayley Dickson is coming in, query spontaneous rupture of membranes. She's twenty-seven, and is thirty-six weeks pregnant with twins. We're expecting her in around an hour and I'll need some assistance. Any chance you can go for your lunch now?'

Bonnie smiled and nodded. 'My first twin delivery at Cambridge? Love to. Have you had lunch?'

Kerry nodded. 'It's only you that's still to go. Better hurry before there's nothing left in the canteen.'

Bonnie stood up. 'No problem. I'll be back in half an hour to help you get set up.'

She washed her hands and grabbed her bag. She was glad that the staff found her approachable and were happy to ask for assistance. It gave a bit of reassurance that they were accepting her as temporary sister around here.

The canteen was quiet. She grabbed a tuna sandwich and walked over to a table to join one of the other midwives that she'd met. Jessica Black worked in the special care baby unit. Her blond straight hair hung in a ponytail but her pretty face was marred by a frown as she stared out of the window.

'Mind if I join you?'

Jess started but gave a smile and waved at the empty seats across from her. 'By all means. Try and cheer me up if you can.'

Bonnie pulled out a chair. 'What's wrong? Man trouble?'

Jess rolled her eyes. 'As if. I wish. That would be easy to sort out.' She picked at her lunch. 'Family troubles. It's my parents' thirtieth wedding anniversary in a few weeks. It's been arranged for near Cambridge so I can't make an excuse not to go and I'm looking forward to it like a hole in the head.'

Bonnie was puzzled. 'Shouldn't that be something to celebrate?'

Jess sighed. 'It should. I love my parents. But it's yet another family event where I'll spend the whole time being compared to my sister. And will, yet again, be found lacking.'

'I can't believe that for a second. You've got a great job

and career ahead of you. You're a gorgeous girl. What on earth does your sister have that you don't?'

Jess paused for a second and let out another big sigh. 'She's not just my sister. She's my twin. Abbie is perfect. She always has been. The sports star, top marks at school, the coolest boyfriend—you name it, Abbie's done it. I've spent most of my life living in her shadow. If Abbie preferred my Christmas presents to hers, she made such a scene she always got them. When I started midwifery training, she decided she wanted to do it too. Then, she decided she wanted the boyfriend I had.' She gave her head a shake. 'So, she got him. Along with the big white wedding and three perfect kids with another on the way.' She held out her hands. 'In fact, here is the only place where I'm known as anything other than "Abbie's sister".'

Bonnie was shocked by Jess's words. She reached over and squeezed her hand. 'Competitive siblings can be a nightmare. My ex-husband was like that with his brother. It made him even harder to live with.' She sucked in a breath. 'And if Cambridge Royal is like every other hospital I've worked in, you'll have heard that I found my ex-husband in bed with my best friend. So, I sympathise. At least I had the option of walking away. I don't need to look at them together.' She leaned back and took a sip of her coffee. 'It sucks that you have to do that.'

Jess burst out laughing and reached over towards Bonnie. 'Yes, the hospital grapevine is in full flow and I love that you just say it like it is.'

Bonnie shrugged. 'After thirty-two years there's not much point in changing the habit of a lifetime.'

Jess gave her a rueful stare. 'I might have heard that about you too. Men suck. Unfortunately, men are my biggest issue. Or namely the fact I don't have one. That's the reason I'm dreading the anniversary party so much. Everyone is just waiting for me to produce who is going to be Mr Jessica Black and create the two-point-four kids we're supposed to have.'

Bonnie took a bite of her tuna sandwich. 'Can't you take a friend?'

'Yeah, but the friend would need to reach my family's exacting standards. They would have to be devastatingly handsome, completely charming and totally unfazed by my sister trying to be the centre of attention.'

Bonnie gave a little smile. 'I have to say, there's more than a few handsome guys around here. Can't you ask one to accompany you?'

Jess frowned. 'Like who?'

Bonnie swallowed and tried to appear casual. 'What about Jacob Layton?'

Jess waved her hand. 'Oh, he's handsome enough but way too grumpy.'

Bonnie tried not to let the wave of relief sweeping over her be obvious. 'Aaron Cartwright, the infertility specialist? An American might go down well.'

She smiled and shook her head. 'He might. But he's not for me. He's too committed to his work. That's the problem with most of the guys around here.'

Bonnie thought again. She was just here. But she'd met most of the consultants in the last few days. 'I've got it. What about an Australian, then, Sean Anderson, the obstetrician that arrived just a few weeks before me?'

'Are you serious?' Jess laughed and wagged her finger. 'I'm going to forgive your observational skills, Nurse, because you've just started. But have you noticed how jumpy Isabel is since he got here?'

Bonnie racked her brains. Isabel was also an Australian obstetrician. Bonnie hadn't connected the two, but maybe there was something... She'd been warm and friendly towards Bonnie since she arrived. She shook her head and shrugged. 'I've never seen them together, so I can't say I've noticed.'

Jess raised her eyebrows. 'She's like a proverbial cat on a hot tin roof. Mark my words, there's some history there. I'm not getting embroiled in that.'

Bonnie took a final bite of her tuna sandwich. When she'd finished chewing she had the perfect answer. 'I've got it. Why didn't I think of him before? You've got the perfect answer right under your nose. Dean Edwards, the SCBU doctor.'

Something flickered across Jess's eyes. Bonnie was on it in an instant.

'What? Has something happened between you two already?'

Jess almost choked. 'No. Absolutely not. But I'll be the only one. He has a different lady for every day of the week. His phone goes off *constantly*.'

Bonnie took a sip of her tea and sat back in her chair. 'Dean's a ladies' man? Who has he dated at work?'

Jess was quick to shake her head. 'Oh, no. He doesn't date anyone at work.' She held out her hands. 'But that leaves the rest of the world wide open for him.'

'And you struck off his list?' Drat. That came out too bluntly. She'd only met Jess on a few occasions.

But it was just the two of them and Jess looked up from her coffee, her light brown eyes rueful. Maybe it was easier to open up to someone who was new?

She blew out a long, slow breath from her lips. 'I guess so. He wouldn't look at me anyway—and even if he did, once he met Wonder Sister he'd be entranced by her. They all are. It wears pretty thin.'

Bonnie reached out towards her again. 'You're a gorgeous girl, Jess. It would be wrong of me to say anything about your sister, but, to be honest, she seems like a piece of work. You've got much more integrity than that, and somewhere—' she held up her hands '—out there, is a man who is just waiting to find a woman like you. You'll probably find him when you least expect to.' She glanced at the clock. 'I'm sorry but I better go. We've got a woman expecting twins due in.' She put her plate and cup on the tray and winked at Jess. 'I gave you the option of three gorgeous men and you said no to all of them. Don't let it be said that you're picky.'

Jess winked back and put her plate on her tray, standing up and walking towards the catering trolleys. 'You gave me the option of *four*, Bonnie. Now I'm wondering if you're keeping one to yourself.'

And she left, before Bonnie could pick her chin off the floor and stop kicking herself.

By the time she reached the ward she could feel herself blushing like crazy. This was ridiculous. No one knew she was staying at Jacob's. Everything at work was entirely professional.

Everything at home was entirely professional too. But Jacob was surprising her. For a guy that acted as though he would run a million miles from kids, he'd been surprisingly good with Freya. Yes, he was still a bit awkward, but he was definitely making an effort. And that mattered. A lot.

It was a dangerous line. If he hadn't been friendly, they could have felt like trespassers in his home. Jacob still didn't give much away. He was obviously a private person. And that was fine. Except five-year-olds weren't always good at knowing when to stop asking questions.

He met her at the doors of the ward. 'You're helping with the twin delivery?'

She grinned. 'I am. Is she your patient? Anything I should know?'

In a labour unit some women would be classed as mid-wifery care and some as medical care. Any woman with a multiple pregnancy automatically fell under medical care as they were at higher risk of complications. An average woman, with a normal pregnancy, could come into the unit and not come into contact with a medic at all. She would be delivered by the midwives and her follow-up care carried out by them. Babies were different—they were always checked over by a paediatrician.

Bonnie dumped her bag as Jacob kept pace with her. 'Hayley Dickson has had a textbook pregnancy but her blood pressure has gone up a little in the last two weeks. I'm actually glad she's gone into spontaneous labour because I was considering inducing her. She's been scanned for the last few weeks. No problems with the babies. It's non-identical twins and both babies are around six pounds.'

'Does she know what she's having?'

He shook his head. 'She didn't want to know.'

Bonnie smiled. 'Do you?'

'I might do—' he tapped his mouth '—but my lips are sealed. Let's go and introduce Mum to these beautiful babies.' He put his hand on Bonnie's shoulder. 'If it's okay with you, I'd like to let you and Kerry take the lead. I'm only here if there are any issues. I'll set up the epidural I know she wants. But Hayley is keen to have a normal delivery.'

Bonnie gave a nod. 'No problem. I'll go and pick up the cots, be back with you in a minute.'

She was glad that Jacob didn't want to try and take over and respected the birthing plan his patient had decided on. Sometimes medics could be a bit overzealous. She hated when that happened.

She collected the cots and baby warmers and headed back into the room. Kerry gave her a nod as she entered. 'Hayley, this is Bonnie, our new ward sister. She'll be helping with the delivery. Bonnie, this is Hayley and her husband, Jordan.'

Bonnie walked straight to the sink to wash her hands. 'Pleasure to meet you, Hayley. I'm really looking forward to meeting these two new babies.' She nodded towards the cots. 'As soon as the babies are out we'll have one of our paediatricians check them over. After you've had a cuddle, of course.'

Hayley gave a nervous smile, then grimaced as another contraction hit. 'I didn't expect these to be coming so quickly.'

Kerry had already completed all the paperwork and hooked Hayley up to the monitors. One was monitoring her babies, the other checking her blood pressure.

Jacob appeared at Bonnie's back, pushing a trolley with the equipment for the epidural. He gave a nod to Kerry. 'Have you done a check yet?'

Kerry nodded. 'Yes, we're good to go. Hayley is five centimetres dilated and the first baby is head down and in a good position.'

Jacob smiled. 'Perfect.' He sat next to Hayley to explain the procedure. It only took him a few minutes. 'Once the catheter is in place it will only take twenty minutes for the full effect. We'll keep an eye to make sure it doesn't slow your labour, but I suspect everything will be fine.' He gave Bonnie a little nod to help position Hayley on her side.

He was an expert. He had the catheter safely slid into place easily and the medication started. Bonnie stayed in the room with Kerry and they monitored Hayley's contractions.

Things went smoothly. Around two hours later the first little baby delivered easily. Bonnie quickly checked over the baby's mouth and breathing before setting the naked little baby on his mother's chest. 'You have a beautiful boy. Do you have a name yet?'

Hayley's husband couldn't wipe the dopey new-dad smile from his face. 'Dillon. We're going to call him Dillon.'

Sean came into the room with a smile. 'Perfect. I'm just in time. I'm Dr Anderson. I'll check your little man over in a few seconds, folks.'

He spoke with Jacob for a few minutes, checked Dillon over and declared him well with perfect APGARs. He gave them a little nod. 'I'll be back again when your next baby arrives. Good luck, guys.'

Kerry stayed with the new baby for another few minutes while Bonnie checked over Hayley again. The labour progressed quickly with the next baby's head being delivered; however, within a few seconds Bonnie frowned as another contraction hit. She turned rapidly to Jacob, keeping her voice very calm.

'I think we've got a shoulder dystocia.' Jacob moved over to the bed immediately but Bonnie had things under control. 'Hayley, your second baby has got a little stuck—

their shoulder is stuck behind your pubic bone. Dr Layton and I are going to help you change position to try and get your baby out as soon as possible. I need you to stop pushing for a second until we help you into position.'

Jacob didn't interrupt at all. He just positioned himself at the side of the bed. Bonnie kept talking calmly and smoothly. 'We're going to do something called the McRoberts manoeuvre. I need you to lie on your back and pull up your legs as far as you can. Kerry will help on one side, and Dr Layton on the other. This will make it easier to get your baby out.' Kerry handed the little boy back over to his dad.

Bonnie gave a little nod to Jacob. 'Dr Layton is going to push down on your tummy when you have the next contraction. This should free your baby's shoulder. It might be a little uncomfortable.' Bonnie glanced at the clock. She had to keep watch. A baby's umbilical cord could become compressed with shoulder dystocia. If they didn't get the baby out in the next few minutes, Hayley would need to go for an emergency Caesarean section.

The contraction hit right on cue. Bonnie eased her hands in to give a gentle pull on the baby as Jacob attempted to press the pelvic bone and release the baby's shoulder. After a few tense seconds, Hayley gave a yelp and the baby slid into Bonnie's hands.

Kerry had already sounded the alarm and Sean was waiting with outstretched arms to check over the baby. He only took a few minutes. It was important. Babies who had shoulder dystocia could have damage to the nerves in their shoulder, arm and hand. Some could have breathing difficulties if their cord had been compressed. But after a few minutes Sean pronounced the baby well. 'Congratulations, Mum and Dad, here's your new baby girl.'

Hayley and Jordan beamed. Bonnie stayed in position. After a few minutes Hayley delivered her placenta and Bonnie did her further checks. 'Have you got a name for your daughter?'

Hayley nodded. 'Carly. We're going to call her Carly.'

Kerry came over with the other baby. 'Dillon and Carly. They're beautiful names for your children. Congratulations.' She handed Dillon back over to his dad. 'Dillon was six pounds twelve, and Carly six pounds four. Good weights. Sean said he'd be back to check them again later but there's no reason for them to go to Special Care.'

Hayley and Jordan smiled at each other. They were clearly in the new parenthood haze. Bonnie remembered it well.

Her heart sank a little—just as it always did at this stage. Robert, her ex, had never looked at her the way Jordan was looking at his wife. Robert had just looked permanently stunned. The same expression he'd had on his face when she'd found him in bed with her best friend. He hadn't been ready for marriage. With hindsight, they both hadn't.

Robert had been her boyfriend for barely a year when she'd fallen unexpectedly pregnant. His parents were traditionalists and had wanted them to get married. And now, Bonnie realised she'd been more swept away with the *idea* of being in love, rather than actually *being* in love. Maybe, at heart, she'd always known that Robert wasn't marriage material.

But what hurt most of all, despite her best efforts, was the fact he hadn't made any attempt at all to see Freya since they'd separated. It turned out Robert hadn't been father material either.

Cambridge was the chance of a new start. She didn't want to make the same mistakes again. She was determined not to get swept away in some ill-fated romance. Not when she had Freya to think about.

She loved her job. She always had. But sometimes, especially at an emotional delivery, she was struck by the connection between the parents of the new baby. Freya was everything to her. But sometimes it made her a tiny bit envious that she was missing out on something she'd never experienced.

It was pathetic really. Most people didn't get the fairy tale. Most people got relationships that were hard work—and she knew that. But it didn't stop her craving the impossible.

She tidied up in the room and got one of the domestics to make Hayley some tea and toast. Most women said that their post-delivery tea and toast was the best in the world.

Kerry tapped her on the shoulder. 'It's nearly your finishing time. I'm going to help Hayley with breastfeeding and will hand over to the next shift. Thanks for the help, Bonnie.'

Bonnie gave a smile. 'No problem, you're welcome.' She took the dirty laundry with her to the sluice, disposed of it and washed her hands again.

Jacob appeared at her back. 'I think that was one of the smoothest shoulder dystocia deliveries I've ever seen. Good call.'

Bonnie shook her head. 'That was pure luck. We both know things could have been different. I was actually breathing a sigh of relief as soon as that baby came out.'

Jacob rested his hand on the small of her back. 'Believe me, so was I. I didn't like the thought of a quick sprint down the corridor to Theatre.'

She could feel his warm hand through her thin scrubs. The warmth was radiating across the small of her back. When was the last time a man had touched her? She couldn't even remember.

She turned her shoulder just a little so she was looking up at him. She hadn't moved enough to let his hand fall. She didn't want it to break contact with her. 'Thank you, Jacob,' she said quietly.

'What for?' He tilted his head to the side. She was only inches away from those green eyes that sparkled with flecks of gold. This was the closest she'd ever been to him. She could see the tiny emerging shadow of stubble along his chin—even though she knew he'd shaved this morning. Her fingers itched to reach up and touch.

The weariness that had been on his face the first day she'd met him had seemed to gradually disperse. On occasion, Jacob still looked tired. But there had been something else that first day—a little despair? Jacob was still a mystery to her. The only thing she knew for sure was that he didn't have a woman in his life and for some reason that made her happy. Not that she'd ever admit that to anyone—not even Jessica.

'For not interfering,' she was whispering, even though there was no need. The rush and bustle of the ward was still going on in the corridor outside, but this seemed like a private conversation. 'For not coming over all "doctor" and trying to take over: For giving me a chance to do my job.'

He leaned forwards just a little. One inch. That was the space currently between them. She held her breath. If she breathed out right now, her warm breath would touch his skin.

But there was a problem. As she'd breathed in, she'd

breathed in *him*. Jacob. The faintest aroma of this morning's aftershave. The scent of his skin. She could almost swear she'd just breathed in a whole host of pheromones. What other explanation could there be for the fact she was feeling the slightest bit light-headed? She'd never been light-headed in her life.

'I'll always give you the space to do your job, Bonnie. From what I've seen you're excellent at it. I have faith you. The staff have faith in you. The patients have faith in you. You're a real asset to Cambridge Maternity. And I look after my staff.'

Her lungs were going to explode. She had to breathe out. She really did. Her insides were all over the place. It was the way he'd said it. The way he'd looked into her eyes and told her he had faith in her. She leaned back a little against his hand and tilted her chin up towards him. 'Thank you, Jacob.'

They froze. Neither of them moving. Their eyes locked together.

'Bonnie, can you just sign…? Oh, sorry.'

They sprang apart. It was stupid. They hadn't been doing anything but Bonnie could feel the colour rushing into her face.

Ellis, one of the midwives, was standing with a delivery note in her hand. Her eyes darted between them; it was quite obvious she was cringing and that made Bonnie do the same.

'That's fine, Ellis. I was just washing up after the twin delivery. Did you hear that things went well?' She was back into professional mode. She didn't even look back, just took long strides towards Ellis, taking the delivery note from her hand and walking over to the nurses' station, pulling a pen from her pocket.

She was trying to appear as calm and professional as possible. As if nothing at all had been going on between them. Because that was true. Nothing had been going on between them.

So why was her heart thudding against her chest and why did her cheeks feel as if they were on fire? And why was Ellis looking at her as if she would be the next topic of conversation on the hospital grapevine?

Ellis took the paperwork and disappeared back down the corridor. Bonnie sucked in a deep breath. What on earth was wrong with her? She'd almost wanted him to kiss her in the sluice at work. Even the thought of that sent a shiver down her spine—it was hardly the most romantic place in the world.

But it hadn't been about the place. It had been about the moment. The feel of Jacob's hand at the small of her back and the way she could see all the tiny lines around his perfect green eyes.

She squeezed her eyes shut. Even her thoughts were getting ridiculous. She had to speak to him. She had to try and understand what was going on. She had to draw a line here. She wasn't looking for any kind of romance. And definitely not with her new boss—no matter how much he just made her tingle. She spun around towards the sluice again.

But Jacob was gone.

CHAPTER FIVE

SOMETHING WAS DIFFERENT. Something had changed. And Jacob couldn't quite put his finger on what it was.

All he knew was he was currently sitting on his sofa watching an animated movie with a five-year-old. If someone had told him two weeks ago this was what he'd be doing he'd never have believed it.

'Who's your favourite dwarf?' whispered Freya. She'd insisted on the main light being turned off and eating ice cream as if they were at the movies. He'd never really developed a taste for ice cream but rocky road was hitting the spot.

'I like that one,' he said, pointing at the screen.

'He's my favourite too.' She jumped up and a big dollop of ice cream landed on his lap. 'Oops,' she said.

He shrugged and scooped the ice cream off his jeans with his fingers and dumped it in his mouth. Freya went into uncontrollable kinks of laughter.

All he knew for sure was that the big black cloud that felt as if it were permanently circling above his head had moved a little higher for the past two weeks. Maybe it was the fact that he was now in the waiting cycle. His treatment was over. He didn't feel quite so snappy. He certainly didn't feel so tired. And he was free to work with patients again the way he had before.

Something had definitely improved his mood. Even the junior doctors, who constantly got everything wrong and couldn't do the most basic of procedures, weren't annoying him as much as usual. He'd only thrown one out of Theatre the other day, instead of the usual four. People would think he was getting soft. He just wasn't quite sure if it was the treatment that had improved his mood or the home circumstances.

Living with Bonnie and Freya was certainly out of his normal experience. Freya had a way of winding him around her little finger. He wasn't quite sure if it was a five-year-old's mastermind plot, or if she did it purely unintentionally.

She jumped up from the sofa and over to her school bag, which was lying on the floor. 'Look at this!' she said as she pulled out a crumpled drawing. 'I made this for you at school today.' It was a painting of a man—with very big ears. He couldn't help it—he started to laugh.

She bounced back up on the sofa next to him. 'It's you. Do you like it?' Her little face was so expectant, just waiting for his approval.

He touched his ears. 'Are they really this big?'

'Yes,' she said without a moment's hesitation. 'Can we put it up on the fridge? That's where my mummy used to put my pictures.' She tugged at his hand and he let her pull him up and lead him through to the kitchen.

Bonnie was wiping a glass bowl clean as they walked through. 'Look what I made for Jacob,' Freya shouted as she waved the picture. 'We're going to put it up.'

Bonnie glanced at the picture and tried to stifle a laugh. 'I think that's lovely, honey,' she said. She raised

her eyebrows at Jacob. 'Wait and I'll find you something to put that up with.' She opened a nearby drawer
and pulled out a fridge magnet he didn't even know he
owned. It seemed impolite not to put it up so he stuck it
on the fridge.

Freya's little face was beaming. 'Come on,' she said,
tugging at his arm again. 'My favourite song's about to
start.'

He'd always loved his home. His sanctuary. His way
of getting away from the outside world. But although his
peace had been shattered, it was nowhere near as inva-
sive as he might have thought.

He almost looked forward to coming home to them at
night. And he couldn't work out why. Maybe it was the
distraction. He didn't have time to think about the stuff
hanging over his head. He didn't have time to consider
what he would do if the test results weren't good—if the
non-Hodgkin's lymphoma hadn't been halted in its tracks.

He didn't have time to remember how his mum had
died of the horrible disease and how he could have the
same future ahead of him. These were the things that
used to spin around his head every night when he went
to bed.

'Jacob, *come on.*' The little voice was impatient. He
hadn't even realised that he'd been staring at Bonnie's
backside in her snug jeans again. She spun around and
gave a little smile as she put some cutlery back in a
kitchen drawer.

She looked relaxed. She looked happy. She looked
comfortable in his home. Something flipped over inside.
He wasn't quite sure how he felt about all this.

She tilted her head to the side. 'Should I get us some

wine to see us through the rest of the movie?' She was smiling again.

He gave a nod as he let Freya lead him back through to the front room and he heard the clink of glasses being pulled from the cupboard.

Their *almost* kiss in the sluice would no doubt haunt his dreams tonight.

What had happened?

He knew it was something. It was definitely something.

There had been a tiny moment when...just *something* could have happened. He'd felt it. And he was pretty sure she'd felt it too. He'd seen it in her all too expressive eyes.

They'd spent the last week tiptoeing around each other. But that hadn't stopped the buzz in the air between them. It hadn't stopped the way their gazes kept connecting with each other.

He'd spent so long concentrating on his disease and trying to get well again that he was out of practice with all this. But even though it was winter, the temperature here was definitely rising.

It was official. Bonnie Reid was keeping him awake at night.

But why did that seem like a good thing and not a bad?

It was her day off and she was prowling around the house. She couldn't help it. This weekend she would be working on Saturday as part of her rota for the hospital. It was fine. Lynn was happy to have Freya for the day and planned to take her and her boys to London Zoo.

But Bonnie wasn't used to having time to herself. She'd cleaned what she could without offending the housekeeper. She'd learned very quickly what was unacceptable for her to do in the house. All her and Freya's laundry was washed and ironed and sitting in neat piles. The beds were made, the shopping done.

She gave a little shudder. The house was getting cold. There had been a dip in the temperature in the last few days and she wasn't quite sure how the heating worked in this house. She wasn't quite sure how Jacob would feel if he found out she was tampering with the settings on his heating. She walked across the front room, her footsteps echoing on the wooden floorboards, her hand running across the top of the mantelpiece.

There was an ornamental coal scuttle at her feet. She knelt down. It was filled with real coal. Jacob had said he hadn't got round to having the chimney swept.

She gave another shudder. Nothing would be nicer at this time of year than a real fire burning in this gorgeous fireplace.

She stood upright. That was what she could do. Jacob didn't seem to have any objections to a real fire. He'd just made it sound as if he hadn't got round to it. He wouldn't accept any money from her and, to be honest, it felt a little embarrassing. Maybe paying to have the chimney professionally swept would be a way to try and repay him a little for his kindness?

She didn't hesitate. This was the best idea she'd had in a while. She walked out to the hallway and dug around for the phone book. They were in the middle of Cambridge. There were lots of traditionally built houses around here. There must a local chimney sweep.

Jacob was on call. He might even not be home at all tonight. Sometimes he ended up just staying at the hospital if he was on call. As the consultant he would be called if there was any emergency with a patient. He'd already told her that he wasn't entirely sure that all the junior members of staff would page him. Some of them still seemed a little nervous around him. She'd tried not to laugh when he'd said that to her.

She picked up the phone and dialled. By the time Jacob got home tonight—or maybe tomorrow morning—she'd have a lovely fire burning in the fireplace, heating up the whole house and giving the place a more homely feel.

He'd love it. She was sure he would.

The first thing he'd noticed was the strange smell. Ever since Bonnie had arrived his house had smelled of those clean laundry candles that she insisted on lighting everywhere. They actually made his nose itch but he wasn't inclined to tell her.

She'd waved some red and green ones under his nose the other night and told him she'd bought some Christmas spice candles. If this was what they smelled like he'd be blowing them straight out.

She still hadn't picked up on his hints about Christmas. The main fact being he just didn't do it.

There was a strange noise to his left. It sounded like a sniffle. Or more like a sob.

He sneezed. Something was definitely irritating him.

'Jacob? Is that you?'

Bonnie. Her voice sounded panicked. He dropped his bag at the door and lengthened his stride, walking into his front room.

Or walking into the room that used to be his front room.

Bonnie was on her hands and knees on the floor, a basin next to her, scrubbing away at the floorboards.

Freya was sitting on a towel on the faraway leather sofa playing with her dolls.

He sucked in a breath at the sight of his perfect white walls.

They weren't perfect any more. There was a huge black streak that seemed to have puffed out from the fireplace and left an ugly, angry, giant-sized handprint on the wall.

Bonnie jumped up to speak to him. Soot was smudged across her cheeks and forehead, even discolouring her dark auburn hair. The front of her T-shirt was dirty, as were the knees of her trousers. 'Oh, Jacob. I'm so sorry. I thought I would have a chance to clean this up before you got home.'

He stepped forwards into the room and held out his hands. 'What on earth happened?'

Freya tutted from her sofa and shook her head. 'Naughty Mummy.' She fixed her eyes on Bonnie. 'Told you,' she said in the voice of someone at least fifty years older than her.

Tears streaked down Bonnie's face. 'I thought it might be a nice idea to get the chimney swept for you. You know—so you could come home to a nice warm fire. The house was so cold today. So I contacted a chimney sweep. And they seemed so professional. They even put a covering on the floor and some kind of plastic seal around the fireplace. But when he swept the chimney, there must have been a gap.' She turned to face the blighted wall again as her voice wobbled. 'And it just seemed to go everywhere. And they tried to clean up, they really did. And they've promised to come back tomorrow and re-paint the walls.'

He should be angry. But Bonnie was babbling. Just

as she had that first day he'd met her. Just as she did when she was really, really nervous and thought she'd just blown things.

It was kind of endearing. But he'd never tell her that. 'Okay,' he said quietly.

She looked confused. Another tear streaked down her smudged face. 'Go and get washed up. I'll finish the clean-up.'

He was too tired to be angry. He'd wanted to come home to a quiet house and rest. But the days of coming home to a quiet house were over. He could never imagine a house being quiet while Freya stayed there. She was questioning. She was curious. She was relentless.

Her head bobbed up from the menagerie of dolls she had accumulated on the other sofa. She shot him a smile. 'Hi, Jacob. How many babies did you see today?'

'Four,' he said promptly.

This had turned into a game. She asked every day. She frowned at him. 'Just four. Your record is six. You'll need to do better.'

'I agree.' He nodded towards Bonnie. 'On you go. Go and get showered. Freya will be fine.'

Bonnie still seemed surprised by his mediocre reaction. The truth was he was surprised by his reaction too. If he waited to see the chimney sweep tomorrow the reaction might not be quite so contained. But he wouldn't do that either.

He noticed the extra coal scuttle by the fire that contained wood-burning logs. Bonnie must have bought them to help light the fire.

When was the last time someone had done something like this for him? Sure, a few of his friends had offered help when they knew about his diagnosis. Hope and Isabel were the only two people—apart from his consultant—in the entire hospital who knew about his diagnosis. He'd worked with Hope for years and even though Isabel had only arrived a few months ago he'd known straight away she was completely trustworthy. When she'd caught him being sick in the sluice one day she'd just pulled the door closed and come over and asked what was wrong.

Both tried to help by feeding him various items of food. Hope had even tried to bake chocolate muffins for him and Isabel had handed him some tubs of beef casserole to stick in the freezer. Anything to get him to eat and keep his strength up. But he was embarrassed to say he'd only been minimally grateful. He was so focused on people not knowing what was wrong that he didn't really want to accept help.

This felt different. This was nothing about his illness. Bonnie knew nothing about that at all—and that was the way he liked it. The last thing he wanted to see on her face was pity.

This was something spontaneous. Something completely unique to him and her. Of course, she currently felt indebted to him. And that did kind of irk. But the fact she'd wanted to do something for *him*…just warmed him from the inside out.

He finished scrubbing the floor and carried the basin of dirty water back through to the kitchen, scrubbing his hands and turning the oven on for dinner. He put on the TV for Freya and headed upstairs into the shower. It only took two minutes to wash the smell of the hospital from his skin and hair, and pull on some jeans and a T-shirt.

As he headed back along the corridor Bonnie passed him on the stairs carrying Freya in her arms. 'Sorry,' she whispered. 'I made her dinner earlier and she's knackered. I'm just going to put her to bed. I didn't get a chance to put anything on for our dinner.'

Jacob noticed the circles under her eyes. He didn't want her to feel as if she had to do anything for him. 'How about I make it simple? Beans on toast?'

She smiled. It was the first genuine smile that he'd seen today. 'Perfect. Thank you.'

His culinary skills were just about up to beans on toast. He opened a bottle of white wine and spent a few minutes setting a new fire and lighting it. As his fingers touched the coal he was swamped by a whole host of memories. Last time he'd lit a fire he'd been trying to keep his shivering mother warm. She'd been at the stage when she'd been permanently cold, even though their house hadn't been cold.

Once she'd died, he'd never gone to the bother of cleaning out the fireplace and restocking it. Neither had his father.

The fire lit quickly. Probably due to the modern firelighters. By the time he'd finished the dinner in the kitchen and walked back through with them both on a tray, Bonnie was sitting on the leather sofa, mesmerised by the fire. She jumped when he set the tray down on the low wooden table. 'Give me a sec,' he said, before returning with the wine and two glasses.

Her freshly washed dark auburn hair was piled up in a loose knot on top of her head, with a few little curling strands escaping. She'd changed into her favourite jeans and a gold T-shirt with a few scattered sequins that caught the flickering flames from the fire. Her pale skin glowed in the light.

She sighed as he poured the wine and she settled the plate on her knees. 'I don't know if I deserve this.'

Jacob looked at her sideways. He couldn't hide the smile on his face. She seemed so despondent. 'I'm not sure you do either. But it's either we drink wine together, or we fight. Take your pick.' He held up his glass towards her.

She paused for a second before catching a glimpse of the laughter in his eyes, then lifted her glass and clinked it against his. 'I'm too tired to fight. I'll just drink the wine.'

They ate companionably together. Finishing the first glass of wine, then pouring another. Jacob hadn't bothered to put the TV or radio on. The only noise was the hiss and cracks coming from the fire.

Bonnie pulled her feet up onto the sofa, giving him a glimpse of her pink-painted toes.

'It's amazing, isn't it?'

He nodded. Watching the fire was quite mesmerising. He could easily lose a few hours a night doing this, particularly if he had a warm body lying next to him on the sofa. His guts twisted. Why hadn't he done this before?

'I'm sorry about the wall,' she whispered again.

His eyes fixed on hers in the flickering firelight. They gleamed in the orange and yellow light. He looked over to the black ugly mark on the wall and couldn't help but start to laugh.

It was hideous. But it could be fixed. By tomorrow it would be freshly painted and forgotten about. His shoulders started to shake, the wine in his glass swaying from side to side.

'What did you say when it happened?' He could barely get the words out for laughter.

She started to laugh too and shook her head. 'You've no idea. I was in the kitchen with Freya and I just heard this whooshing noise and a thump. The guy landed on his backside in the middle of the floor. He looked as if he was about to be sick.'

Now the laughter had finally started she seemed relieved to get it out. 'Then I came through and just burst into tears. I don't think that helped him.'

'I'll bet it didn't.'

He turned towards her on the sofa, his arm already stretched behind her head. It was only natural she turned towards him too.

'Please tell me you're not really mad with me.'

He shook his head and reached his finger up to touch her cheek. He didn't even think before he did it. It just seemed like the most natural act in the world. The act he'd wanted to do a few days before in the sluice room.

'I'm not mad at you. What you did was nice. It was thoughtful.' He gave a little shrug. 'I always meant to get around to it. It just never happened.' His voice tailed off a little. 'Other stuff got in the way.'

Her hand came up and rested on his bare arm. 'What other stuff?'

It was like a whole host of tiny electric shocks racing up his arm. He could feel the warmth of her skin next to his. All he wanted to do was grab her whole body and press it against his. Skin against skin.

'Nothing important. Work, that kind of stuff.' He didn't want to go there. Not with Bonnie. He didn't want to have any of those kinds of conversations with Bonnie. This thing between them. He didn't know what it was. But it seemed almost unreal. Not really acknowledged. Not really known by anyone but them.

She hesitated but didn't move her hand. She left it there in contact with his skin.

'I need some advice. I saw some other possible rentals today and one small flat that I could afford to buy. You need to tell me about the areas.'

The squeeze inside was so unexpected it made him jolt. He should be jumping for joy. But he strangely wasn't.

Sitting in the flickering firelight with Bonnie, watching the orange light glint off her auburn hair and light up her pale skin, giving her advice to leave seemed ridiculous.

It was just the two of them right now. In the glimmering light her bright blue eyes reflected off his. He was close enough to see the tiny freckles across the bridge of her nose.

But he wanted to be closer.

He licked his dry lips and watched as she mirrored his actions. This woman was going to drive him crazy.

'Where?' His voice was so low it was barely audible.

'One rental in Olderfield, one in Rancor and the flat is in Calderwood.' She named the prices for each.

He shook his head. 'Olderfield is not an area you want to stay in.' It was almost a relief to say those words. 'The price of the rental in Rancor is nearly three hundred pounds a month above any other. It sounds like a bit of a con. As for Calderwood—it's nice. It's fine. But it's the other side of the city. You'd need to change Freya's school again. Do you really want to do that?'

Everything he was saying was safe and rational. It was sensible.

But that wasn't how he was feeling right now.

He'd inched closer. And so had she.

It was almost as if an invisible force were drawing them together. Pushing them together. He could feel her warm breath dancing across his skin. The scent she'd put on after showering was pervading its way around him, wrapping round like a tentacle and reeling him in.

He had absolutely no wish or desire to resist it. None at all.

He was trying to read what was in her eyes. He was sure he could see passion burning there. She hadn't moved; she hadn't flinched. She just unobtrusively moved even closer, slotting under his arm as though she were meant to be there.

And for the first time it felt as if someone *was* meant to be there.

The flickering fire didn't just bathe the room and her skin in warm light. It made him feel different inside. It made him feel that the thing that was missing from this home might finally be there.

There was no time for talk.

He moved forwards, his lips against hers.

It was the lightest of touches. The merest hint of what was to come.

She let out a little sigh and her hand moved up to his shoulder, as if she was going to pull him closer.

The tiny voice came out of nowhere, cutting through the building heat in the room.

'Mummy?'

They sprang apart. Both of them realising what had almost happened. Bonnie was on her feet in an instant and out of the door, running up the stairs to the little voice at the top of them.

Jacob was left in the room. His breathing ragged and

his soul twisting like the ugly black mark on the wall. Was he mad?

What had he nearly done? She was a colleague. For a few minutes he'd completely forgotten about the little girl upstairs.

What could have happened next?

He stood up and flicked on the light, flooding the room with a bright white glare and dousing the flames in an instant.

It was time to pretend this had never happened.

CHAPTER SIX

'Wow, WHAT'S GOING on with Jacob Layton?' Kerry came through the theatre doors and walked to the sink, scrubbing her hands post-surgery.

Bonnie glanced over her shoulder as Isabel walked out of the theatre doors too, ripping off her gloves and gown and joining Kerry at the sink. 'I know.' The two of them exchanged glances and smiled at each other. 'I wonder what's changed his mood.'

Isabel's eyes met Bonnie's and an uncomfortable shiver went down her spine. 'What are you talking about?' she asked.

Kerry rolled her eyes. 'I dropped an instrument tray in Theatre. Usually, Jacob would have gone nuts and I'd have been flung out of Theatre.'

'Really?' Bonnie frowned. She'd heard of surgeons being extreme in Theatre. But she'd never experienced it herself. She certainly didn't like the thought of one of the obstetricians she worked with behaving like that. She wouldn't stand for it.

But Isabel and Kerry were still smiling at her as they finished drying their hands. 'What's that Scottish word you use to describe pcople who are grumpy or miserable?'

Bonnie was a bit unsure where this was going. 'Crabbit.' She used it quite a lot, along with a whole host of other Scottish words that were second nature to her, but seemed to leave the staff baffled.

Isabel and Kerry exchanged smiles again. Isabel deposited her paper towels in the bin. 'It's a good word. A very descriptive word.' She turned to her colleague. 'Kerry, would you say that Jacob's been crabbit lately?'

Kerry crossed the room. 'Nope. I'd say Jacob's had a whole new personality transplant. He didn't shout at all today. He just looked up and asked me to get him a new set of instruments. The whole Theatre was shocked.'

Bonnie frowned. 'Jacob normally behaved like that in Theatre?'

Isabel laughed. 'Not just Theatre. Labour suite, wards, clinics, the neonatal unit.' She held up her hand. 'Don't get me wrong, he would always switch on the charm for the patients, but for the staff?' She shook her head. 'Oh, no.'

Kerry put her hands on her hips. 'And both of you ladies haven't been here that long. A few years ago, Jacob was always Doctor Charming. But then just over a year ago he changed—practically overnight. He's been like a bear with a sore head ever since. Or he had been...' she turned to face Bonnie '...until a few weeks ago.'

Bonnie shifted uncomfortably on her feet. Two pairs of eyes were staring at her, smiling. 'I have no idea what you mean.'

Isabel walked past and tapped her on the shoulder. 'I don't know what it is you're doing. But all I can say is— keep doing it.'

Kerry nodded in agreement as the doors swung open again. It was Sean, the new obstetrician who'd arrived from Melbourne just a few weeks before Bonnie. 'Hi, ladies, sorry to interrupt. Isabel, can we talk?'

Something flickered across Isabel's face. It was the strangest look Bonnie had seen in a while. She couldn't quite put her finger on it. Something between complete avoidance and dread. It seemed that Jess Black had been right.

Isabel was super friendly and completely confident about the work she did. This was the first time that Bonnie had seen her look neither.

'It will only take a few minutes, Isabel.' Sean looked tired, but it seemed he wasn't going to be put off.

Her eyes flitted over to Bonnie. 'Didn't you want me to see a patient on the labour suite?'

'Eh...yes.' Bonnie knew avoidance tactics when she saw them. And there was no way she wasn't going to help out a colleague. Particularly when this might take the heat off her.

In a way it was good that people thought Jacob was more amenable. The question was—what had been wrong with him before? She had no idea. She and her daughter were living with a guy they hardly knew. She'd almost kissed him the other night! If Freya hadn't shouted...

She was crazy. She was plainly crazy. Jacob was her boss. Her brand-new boss. The last thing she should be doing on this planet was kissing the boss—no matter how much she'd wanted to.

She bit her lip. She was new here. She hadn't even had time to find her feet yet. Her new job was a big responsibility. *That* was where she should be focusing her attention.

She had Freya to think about. Her little girl had already been exposed to one disastrous relationship—there was no way she wanted to expose her to another. It was too soon. Far too soon.

It was time to focus on work—and only work. She wouldn't allow thoughts of Jacob to distract her from her job.

Sean disappeared back out of the doors, sighing loudly. Isabel's eyes flickered towards Bonnie. 'Thanks,' she said before putting her head down and disappearing out of another door.

Kerry folded her arms across her chest. 'This place just gets more interesting by the second.'

Bonnie gave a little smile and shake of her head as she headed to the door. 'Kerry, you have no idea.'

Jacob was feeling strangely nervous. One of the other obstetricians had been off sick for a few days and he'd covered their on-call rota. It meant that he and Bonnie hadn't really been alone together for the last few days.

The front room was back to normal. The walls freshly painted and bright white again. Except, the room wasn't back to normal. The room had changed. And the mood of the house had changed with it.

The temperature seemed to have dropped permanently in the last few days. It meant that every time he walked through the front door of his house, his feet turned automatically to the fireplace in the front room.

Bonnie was right. There was something about a fireplace. He was drawn to it like the proverbial moth to a flame. Last night he'd even contemplated buying a rug to put in front of it. He'd never really thought about soft furnishings before. He wasn't that kind of guy. He was all about the basics. The functional stuff.

Except that last night he'd spent an hour on the Internet wondering what colour rug to buy.

Now his fingers hovered over something else. Freya

had been really excited the other night when she'd seen the advert for the latest kids' Christmas film. It had been years since Jacob had gone to the movies. He'd still been in his early twenties.

He glanced at the film times before clicking to buy tickets. It was Tuesday night. Freya and Bonnie didn't do anything on a Tuesday. Monday was dancing, Wednesday was Rainbow Brownies. He couldn't believe that after a few weeks he actually knew this kind of stuff. It was all so alien to him.

Once he'd bought the tickets he looked for a restaurant. For the first time in his life, Jacob Layton picked up the phone to ask if his favourite place to eat had a children's menu. It had never crossed his mind before.

It was odd. This wasn't a date. This wasn't anything like that.

He just wanted to have some time away from the hospital, away from the house, and to spend a little time with Bonnie and Freya.

He was planning. He was being rational. But little voices in his brain were screaming at him. He didn't do this kind of stuff. Well, of course, he'd taken a woman to dinner before. The truth was he'd done that on *lots* of occasions. But incorporating a child into his plans? This was a whole new concept for him.

Bonnie appeared at the door. 'Jacob? Outpatients just phoned. Lisa Brennan, a thirty-three-year-old diabetic who is in for her twenty-week scan. They're having a few problems and wondered if you could go down. The sonographer is new and thinks there may be an anomaly but isn't quite sure.'

He stood up straight away. 'No problem. I'll go now.'

He paused in the doorway. 'I thought maybe we could do something tonight?'

A look of mild panic flickered across Bonnie's face and his stomach dropped. 'I mean, you, me and Freya. I was thinking about that new film she wanted to see. What do you think?'

He was babbling now. Doing the thing that he found so endearing in Bonnie. Why had she looked panicked? Did she really want to say no? Maybe he was reading things all wrong.

Her lips pressed together and after a few seconds the edges turned upwards. 'Freya would love that. It's a great idea.'

He brushed past her. 'Good. I'll book tickets and maybe we could grab some dinner first?'

He kept walking down the corridor as she gave the slightest nod of her head. He didn't want to tell her he'd already booked the tickets and the restaurant. That would seem presumptuous.

It was the oddest feeling. Jacob hadn't felt this nervous asking a girl out since he was a teenager. For a second, he'd thought she might actually say no.

As he turned the corner at the bottom of the corridor Bonnie was still standing at the office door with a smile on her face.

For a second he felt sixteen again. It was all he could do not to punch the air.

Bonnie was nervous—and that was ridiculous. She looked at the clothes laid out on her bed. Nothing seemed to suit.

'Wear the Christmas jumper, Mummy!' said Freya as she bounced in the room. 'We can match.'

Bonnie blinked. Freya hadn't been wearing that jumper a few minutes ago. She was going through a stage of changing her clothes constantly—and putting everything she'd worn for ten minutes in the washing basket.

She smiled. 'Well, I suppose it is officially December now.' She pulled the black jumper, adorned with a bright green Christmas tree and glittering red sequins for the Christmas baubles, over her head. As soon as she pulled it on she felt more comfortable.

That was what was wrong. She was fretting over what to wear as if this were actually a *date*. And it wasn't. But it had felt like that when Jacob had asked her. It had given her that warm, tingly feeling that spread throughout her body and stayed there all day.

Ridiculous. This was Jacob being polite and taking out his house guests. And if there hadn't been that soft, sizzling kiss a few nights ago that might have been a rational thought. It might have been brief but she couldn't get the feel of Jacob's lips out of her mind.

'Come on, Mummy.' Bonnie pulled on her favourite jeans and stuck her feet into her boots. She'd put makeup on this morning and had no wish to do it again, so just reapplied some lipstick. There. Ready.

Jacob was waiting for them at the bottom of the stairs as they walked down. The look of appreciation and smile he gave her made the little fire inside light up again.

'I can't wait to see this film,' chattered Freya. 'Three people at school have seen it already and they said it's brilliant. The princess dances on ice and the prince lives underneath the water.'

'Are you sure you're up for this?' Bonnie asked.

But he smiled. 'Oh, I'm sure. I'm sure in the next few days every adult will have seen this film too and it's all we'll hear about.' He opened the front door. 'I booked Paulette's Italian. Are you okay with that? I thought it would suit Freya since spaghetti bolognaise is her favourite food.'

She'd expected to go to the nearest fast-food restaurant. Jacob Layton was proving to be more than a little surprising.

It only took ten minutes to reach the cinema complex and the nearby restaurant. Dinner was almost a disaster. Freya was too excited to eat and ended up wearing most of her spaghetti rather than eating it. But the food was good and the company even better.

Jacob was careful not to talk shop in front of Freya—or ask Bonnie any difficult questions about being back in Scotland. He asked Freya about school and her friends, and Bonnie about her favourite things and how she was settling in.

She took a sip of her glass of wine. 'I love CRMU. The staff are really friendly. A few of them have invited me out—Isabel, Hope and Jessica. But it's difficult. If we were still at home I could ask my mum and dad to babysit. Going out in the evenings in Cambridge isn't really an option for me.'

Jacob hesitated. His fork poised just before his mouth. 'I could do it.'

She almost choked. 'What? No, I couldn't ask you to do that.'

'I mean, as long as I wasn't on call or anything. I mean, once Freya's had dinner and done her homework, there's really no problem. We could watch a film together and then it would be time for bed.'

Bonnie shook her head, glancing sideways at Freya, who seemed to have missed the conversation. 'That's so kind of you to offer. But no, Jacob, I wouldn't do that to you.' She paused for a second. 'I could always ask Lynn, the childminder. I'm sure she would say it was okay.' She put her hand around Freya's shoulder. 'But I'm just not ready to do that yet. We've had a lot of change in a short period of time. I'd like her to feel really settled before I start thinking about going out.'

Jacob nodded thoughtfully then shrugged. 'Okay. But the offer is there if you need it.'

'Is it time for the film yet?' cut in Freya, smiling, with her bolognaise-smeared face.

Bonnie glanced at her watch as she wiped Freya's face with a napkin. 'I think it is. Are you ready to go?'

Freya bounced out of her seat. 'I'm ready. Let's go and see the princess.'

Jacob paid their bill and helped Freya on with her jacket before they walked the short distance to the cinema. It was already busy, with numerous excitable children all waiting to see the film. The noise level was incredible.

Jacob winced. 'Is every kids' show like this?'

Bonnie nodded. 'Believe it or not, they do go quiet when the film starts.'

They collected their tickets and bought some popcorn, then filed into the cinema and found their seats. Freya changed seats three times. Sitting between them, then on one side of Bonnie, on one side of Jacob and back to the middle again. She leaned forwards as the film started.

In the darkness of the cinema something struck Bonnie. Freya had never been to the cinema with her father. Robert had always managed to find an excuse not to go on family outings with them and the cinema had rapidly become a treat for Bonnie and Freya on their own.

This was the first time she'd actually been at the cinema with a man since she'd been born. Regret twisted inside Bonnie. She should have chosen better. Robert had never lived up to the role of a father, and now here was Jacob, a single man with no experience of kids, bending over backwards to be accommodating towards them.

She wasn't sure what all this meant, but it was so nice to feel considered. She appreciated it more than she could ever say.

She reached over in the darkness, across the space where Freya leaned forwards, and slid her hand into Jacob's. He turned towards her, surprise on his face.

'Thank you for doing this,' she whispered.

He smiled and gave her hand a squeeze, circling his thumb in her palm.

He kept it that way for the whole ninety-minute film. And she let him.

CHAPTER SEVEN

THE HOUSE WAS looking truly magical. Freya was watching from the window, the excitement almost too much for her.

Today had been a quiet day. It was odd. It was a few days into December already and there were still no decorations in the house. Bonnie had always been the type to put her decorations up on the first of the month. Any later made her antsy.

Yesterday, a few tree decorations had arrived that she'd ordered online. Along with a personalised stocking for Freya and some Christmas candles.

This morning she'd had a look in some of the cupboards around the house, expecting to find a few cardboard boxes of decorations that she and Freya could put up. But there was nothing. Not even a single strand of tinsel.

Maybe Jacob hadn't bothered because he lived alone? He'd already told her he worked at the hospital most Christmases. He'd made a few fleeting remarks about not really doing Christmas. But nothing definite. Nothing that he'd actually explained.

So, this morning she and Freya had hatched the master plan. Jacob was working today. It was a Saturday and there were a few patients in the hospital that needed to be reviewed, so she was sure he would be kept busy.

It gave her and Freya time to visit the local hardware store and stock up on Christmas decorations. The kind that she'd always wanted to buy. Her credit card had trembled as she'd entered the store and fainted on the way out.

She'd never bought a real tree before. But the hardware store could deliver on the same day, and only an hour after they'd left the store the delivery driver arrived. He was great. He carried the tree up the front steps and into the front room. It had already been mounted for them and he made sure it was straight before he left.

Freya had been jumping for joy as they'd plugged the twinkling star lights in to check they worked before winding them around the tree. By four o'clock it was already starting to get dark. Bonnie pulled the blinds in the front room. She didn't want Jacob to see the tree from the street. She wanted him to come through the front door and get the full effect.

A thick green and red garland was wound up the banister on the stairs. Another, set with red twinkling lights, was adorning the mantelpiece in the front room. The fire was burning in the hearth and she'd switched off the main lights so only the twinkling lights and flickering flames warmed the room.

Freya wound her hands around Bonnie's neck. 'It's so beautiful, isn't it, Mummy?'

'Yes, honey, it is.'

She so wanted Christmas to be perfect for her daughter. It was beginning to look as if they wouldn't have found somewhere else to stay by then. Her ex hadn't even tried to make contact with his daughter—not even once—since they'd moved down here.

It was no real surprise. He hadn't bothered when they'd stayed in the same town. But she was worried about the effect on her little girl. How must it feel for Freya to know her daddy didn't love her? Not the way he should.

They finished unpacking the last of the deliveries. A carved wooden nativity scene that Freya helped set out on one of the side tables. Everything really did look perfect.

She heard a car door slam outside and Freya ran and peeked under the blinds. 'Jacob's coming. He's coming, Mummy.' She jumped up and down on the spot clapping her hands.

Bonnie couldn't wipe the smile off her face. She stood in the corridor, just at the entrance to the front room—waiting for him to appear.

It only took a few seconds. He walked through the front door, dropping his case and hanging his jacket on the coat stand.

'Hey, Jacob.' She smiled.

He smiled back. 'Hey, yourself,' then started to frown. He gave a little start, his eyes fixed on the banister behind her.

'We've got a surprise,' yelled Freya, running through the door.

Bonnie's skin prickled, her hairs standing on end. He didn't look happy. He didn't look anything *like* happy. Her blood felt as if it were running cold.

All of a sudden she got the feeling that she'd done something very wrong.

Jacob strode past her and into the front room, virtually ignoring Freya.

His face fell as soon as he walked into the middle of the floor, holding his hands out as he spun around, taking in the full effect of the room. She loved it. It was beautiful and really captured the spirit of Christmas with the flickering flames and twinkling festive lights.

Anyone would love it.

Anyone but Jacob, that was.

He looked as if he'd just been sat down in his worst possible nightmare. He walked over to the fireplace and tugged harshly on the beautiful green and red garland, pulling part of it free. 'What on earth have you done?' His voice was incredulous. 'Tell me you're joking. You've done this everywhere? This?'

He stared at the greenery in his hand, then dropped it to the floor. Freya's mouth was hanging open. She was stunned—as was Bonnie—but, what was more, she looked a little frightened.

He walked over and grabbed the tree, knocking some of the carefully hung red and green ornaments to the floor, one of them breaking with a crash. 'Who on earth said you could do this? What made you think you could decorate my house without my permission?' In a surge of anger he pushed the tree to the floor, scattering the decorations everywhere and making the lights flicker dangerously.

He was furious. Really furious. So angry he was trembling. Bonnie had never, ever seen Jacob like this. And although she was bewildered, she wasn't afraid; in fact, she was angry. But he wasn't finished. He leaned over the fallen Christmas tree and started yanking the tinsel from it. The harshness of his movements meant the sitting-room air and floor quickly filled with tiny ripped-off strands of multicoloured tinsel all around them. 'I hate this. I have to tolerate this stuff everywhere else—but not in my house!'

She walked over and put her arm around Freya's shoulder. 'What is wrong with you, Jacob? We wanted to do something nice for you—to surprise you.'

But it was almost as if he hadn't heard her. He was still shaking his head at the twinkling lights. He crossed the room and flicked the switch on one of the plugs, plunging that part of the room into darkness.

Almost as dark as your mood was her fleeting thought as he turned on her again.

'How dare you do this? Didn't I tell you I don't celebrate Christmas? I don't even *like* Christmas.' The words were said with such venom she actually found herself pulling back a little. But it only lasted a second. Because after that the red mist started to descend.

All the hours of work and preparation. The build-up of excitement between her and Freya all day. And he was ruining it all with some angry words and some hand movements. Destroying all their hard work.

She dropped her arm from around Freya's shoulder and stepped right up to his face. 'Oh, I get that. I get that you don't like Christmas. Enough, Jacob!' she snapped. 'You've made your point. You don't like Christmas. Well, pardon me for not being a mind reader. And pardon me, and my daughter, for trying to do something to say thank you for letting us stay. We won't make that mistake again!'

She turned at the sound of a little sob behind her and dropped to her knees, wrapping her arms around Freya's little body. She would kill him. She would kill him with her bare hands for his pathetic overreaction.

Jacob flinched. It was as if reality had just slapped him on the forehead and he realised the impact his reactions had had on Freya. For the tiniest second he seemed to hesitate, but Bonnie glared at him, furious with him for upsetting her daughter, and he spun on his heel and stalked back along the corridor, slamming the front door behind him.

The blood was pounding in her ears. She'd never been so angry with someone—not even her pathetic husband when she'd found him in bed with her so-called friend. Freya's shoulders were shaking and her head was buried into the nape of Bonnie's neck.

Over Christmas decorations? Really?

She didn't care that this was his house. She didn't care that on every other occasion Jacob had been a kind and hospitable housemate. This blew everything else out of the water.

He'd upset her daughter.

Jacob Layton was about to find out that hell hath no fury like an angry mother.

'Isn't it about time you went home?'

He lifted his head from the bar and the barman gestured his head towards the clock. The guy obviously wanted to close up.

The old guy shrugged. 'Can't be that bad.'

Jacob picked up the now-warm remnants of beer and washed them down. 'You have no idea.'

He looked out through the murky window. It had started to snow. He didn't even have a jacket. In his haste to leave the house he hadn't stopped to pick one up.

How far had he walked? He had no idea. He'd never even been in this pub before. Let alone nearly fallen asleep at the bar.

He gave the barman a little nod and shivered as he walked out of the door and the wind whistled around his thin jumper. With his suit trousers and business shoes it was hardly winter gear. But he hadn't stopped to think about much before he left.

That was the trouble. He *couldn't* think. He'd taken one look at all those Christmas decorations and a whole host of unwanted memories had come flooding back.

It was ridiculous. It was pathetic. He'd spent every year of his life around Christmas decorations.

But not in his space. Not in his home. In other places, they were bearable. In other places there were other things to do, other things to think about. At home, they would be right under his nose constantly—forcing him to think about things he'd long since pushed to the back of his mind.

The cold wind started to penetrate through his thin jumper, making him shiver. His insides were cringing.

Freya.

Her little face had crumpled and she'd started to cry.

He was ashamed of himself. Ashamed of his behaviour. He hadn't even stopped to think about her. And everything about that was wrong.

What embarrassed him even more was the fact that if it had been just Bonnie, he might not be feeling so ashamed. It had taken a five-year-old to teach him what acceptable behaviour was. What kind of human being did that make him?

The kind that had spent the last three hours in a bar, like some sad and lonely old drifter sitting on a bar stool alone, nursing one bottle of beer after another.

Pathetic. Was that really the kind of man he wanted to be? Was that the kind of man that would have made his mother proud?

All of a sudden he wasn't feeling the cold any more. All of sudden he was lost in distant memories as his feet trudged through the snow, his dress shoes getting damper by the second as the memories of his mother burned deep in his mind.

She had complemented his closed-off father beautifully with her calming good nature. She was always able to put a smile on his father's often grumpy face, or give a measured argument against his forceful opinions—skills that Jacob hadn't seemed to inherit.

If his mother had still been alive he would never have ended up at loggerheads with his father over his refusal to follow the family tradition into the military. His mother would have argued peacefully, but successfully, for his entry to medical school and the opportunity to pursue his own career options.

His father had never really accepted his decision—particularly when Jacob had opted to become an obstetrician. It wasn't heroic enough for his father. It wasn't front line enough, or pioneering enough. He didn't see the joy in bringing life into the world, compared with so many other specialities that frequently dealt with death. Just as well his mother had left him enough money, not only to put himself through medical school, but also to allow him the freedom to place a deposit on a house and have the option of being part of one of the finest universities and hospitals in the country.

She *would* be proud of him. She *should* be proud of him. She would love what her son had achieved.

But she would also expect him to treat everyone with the same respect he'd given her. With the love and compassion he'd given her.

The long street ahead was coated with snow. The orange streetlights cast a warm glow across the snow-topped cars. People spilled out of the pub ahead of him, laughing and joking. Full of cheer.

When was the last time he'd been in Cambridge city centre on a Saturday night? He couldn't even remember. Now he looked around him, Christmas was everywhere. Every shop window was decorated and a few of the flats on the main street had glistening trees in their windows.

He hung his head as the cold bit harder. Festive cheer. It should be spreading warmth through his soul. What on earth was he going home to?

His footsteps quickened as a horrible thought shot through his head. What if they'd left? What if they'd left because of his behaviour?

The beer sloshed around in his stomach. He hadn't eaten at all in the last few hours and that last thought made him feel physically sick.

The thought of going home to an empty house after a month wasn't at all appealing. It was strange how things had changed without him really noticing. *Please don't let them leave*. He would much prefer it if Bonnie was waiting at home ready to tell him exactly what she thought of him. He could take it.

He might even try and explain why he'd behaved like that—if, of course, she gave him a chance to speak.

The snow was getting heavier. It was kicking up under his feet and lying on his shoulders and eyelashes. His feet moved even quicker. How far had he walked?

It was a relief to finally turn into his street. Only a few windows were uncovered, letting their warm light spill out onto the snow-covered street. From a distance, he could see his tightly pulled white blinds.

He swallowed. His mouth had never felt so dry. Drinking beer certainly hadn't helped. More than anything right now he just wanted to know what lay behind his door.

He had to stop himself from breaking into a run. His brain was spinning. What would he do if they'd left? What would he say if they'd stayed? A thousand excuses and explanations were running through his brain. But somehow he knew they wouldn't wash with Bonnie.

Nothing but the truth would do for her.

He pulled his key from his pocket as he walked up the steps. He paused at the door. The house was silent. Not a single sound from inside.

The traditional door handle was icy cold. He pushed down on it and the door clicked open.

Relief. Pure and utter relief. If Bonnie had left, the door would have been locked.

He brushed the snow off his shoulders and hair and kicked it from his damp shoes.

Still nothing.

He walked silently down the corridor. The light was out in the kitchen and in the back sitting room. His stomach twisted. The green and red garland was gone from the stairs. There was no sign it had even been there.

He held his breath as he stepped into his front room. His completely bare front room.

All signs of Christmas were gone.

The tree. The lights. The garland. The nativity.

Just one small lamp was lit in the corner of the room, reflecting the bare white walls back at him. He'd never realised just how sparse this room was.

Bonnie was sitting on the sofa. She didn't even turn her head towards him. She was staring at the now unlit fire. Her jaw was set. In one hand she held a glass of wine, the fingers of the other hand running up and down the stem of the glass.

He braced himself, but she said nothing.

'Bonnie,' he acknowledged. An elephant had just decided to sit on his chest. At least that was what it felt like.

She didn't move, didn't flinch. It was almost as if he weren't even there.

He swallowed again. He really, really needed a drink of water. His mouth had never felt so dry. But he took a deep breath and sat down next to her on the sofa.

'Let me try and explain,' he said quietly.

'Oh, you'd better.' Her words dripped ice. Any minute now she was going to pick up the bottle of wine at her feet and launch it at his head.

Jacob had never really been lost for words before. This was a first for him. He didn't talk. He didn't share. Ever since his father had packed him off to boarding school once his mother died, there just hadn't been anyone to share with. Not like that. Not like the way he used to with her.

The truth was, he always felt that no one else had ever been that invested in him. Building walls around yourself as a child protected you as an adult. At least, that was what he'd always thought.

His behaviour tonight had been over the top. He had to explain. He hated what she might think of him right now. What Freya might think of him right now.

'I'm sorry I upset Freya tonight. I never meant to do that.'

'Well, you did. And it will be the first and last time.'

Bonnie's voice had no hesitation. The line was very clearly drawn in the sand.

'Let me be clear. Freya is my first and *only* priority. Every. Single. Day.'

He could feel prickles down his back. She was worse than mad.

'I know that.'

He leaned back against the sofa. This was going to take some work. He wasn't used to talking about himself. And he had no idea what Bonnie's response might be to his words.

For a tiny second he squeezed his eyes shut. They were still here. That must mean something.

He licked his dry lips. 'I haven't told you much about my past.'

Her fingers continued to stroke up and down the wineglass stem. It was almost as if she was using it as a measure of control. 'No. You haven't.'

She was wearing those jeans again and a soft woollen jumper. Right now he wanted to reach out and touch her. Right now he wanted to feel some comfort. Saying these words out loud wasn't easy.

'My mother died when I was ten.'

There. It was out there. The light in the corner flickered inexplicably and he heard her suck in a breath.

'She was the heart of our family. I was an only child and my father spent most of his life in the military. When my mother died it was almost as if all the life was just sucked out of us both.'

She turned a little towards him. 'What did you do?'

He shrugged. 'What could I do? I was ten. I'd spent most of my time with my mother. We'd shared everything. My relationship with my father had always been a little strained. I just think he didn't know how to relate to kids.'

As he was talking he'd moved to face her and as he finished his last sentence her eyebrows lifted. He knew exactly what she was thinking. Like father, like son. And he was struck by the realisation that was the last thing he wanted.

He fixed on her blue eyes. 'My dad sent me to boarding school.'

'Do those places even exist any more? I thought they only ever existed in Enid Blyton books.'

He shook his head. 'Oh, they exist all right. And they're just the place to send a ten-year-old whose mother's died.' He couldn't keep the irony or the bitterness out of his voice. 'I hated every second of it. The education part was fine. The school activity part was fine. But to go from living with your mother, to living there, with nothing really in between…' His voice tailed off.

'Why did he send you there?'

Jacob sighed. 'There was no one else to look after me. I'm an only child and so were my father and mother. Both sets of grandparents were already dead. My father had another posting abroad with the military and there was no question that he wouldn't go. He told me later that he'd always planned on sending me to boarding school.' He pushed up the sleeves of his wet jumper.

She tilted her head to one side. 'Had your mother stopped that?'

He shook his head. 'I have no idea.' He groaned and sagged back against the sofa. 'There were so many things that I wished I had asked her. So many conversations I wish I could remember. Most of it is just all caught up in here.' He waved his finger next to his head. 'Sometimes I think that things I remember I've just made up.'

'How did she die?'

Jacob hesitated, then took a deep breath. 'Cancer. Non-Hodgkin's lymphoma. It was brutal—it sucked the life right out of her.'

She licked her lips. 'Did you go to your mother's funeral?'

He nodded. 'It was full of people I didn't really know. No one really spoke to me. And because of the time of year it was bitter cold and lashing with rain. We were only at the graveside for around five minutes.'

A little spark of realisation shot across her face. 'When did your mother die, Jacob?'

This was it. This was the important part. He felt his eyes fill up and was instantly embarrassed. Men didn't cry. Men *shouldn't* cry.

But no matter how hard he tried not to, one tear escaped and slid down his cheek. His voice was hoarse. 'She died three days before Christmas. I came home to a house we'd decorated together, that would never feel the same again.'

'Oh, Jacob.' Bonnie's tears fell instantly, and she reached up to his cheek to brush his away. 'I can't even begin to imagine what that felt like.'

Now he'd started he couldn't stop. He felt safe. He felt safe talking to Bonnie. Someone he'd known only a month and invited into his home. There was nothing superficial about Bonnie Reid. She was all heart and soul. He'd never met anyone like her before. Or if he had, he'd never taken the time to get to know them.

It felt right to tell Bonnie about his mother and why his insides were so messed up about Christmas.

'I felt like when we buried my mother, we buried a little bit of ourselves. My father was never the same. I can't remember ever seeing my father smile once my mother died. Our relationship was non-existent. I'm embarrassed by it. I've no idea if he just couldn't cope. If it was all just grief. Or, if my mother had brought out another side of him, and when she died he just reverted back to how he normally was. All I know is that from the age of ten, happiness just didn't feature in our house.'

Bonnie's tears were free-flowing. 'That's awful. You had no one? No one else you could turn to?'

He shook his head. 'Christmas felt like a curse after that. That's why I hate it so much. I try not to be bitter. But it just doesn't evoke the happy memories in me that it does for others. I do have good memories of Christmases with my mother. But they were so long ago. Sometimes I wonder if they even existed.'

'Oh, Jacob.' Bonnie reached over, her hand stroking the top of his. She left it there and squeezed gently, the warm sleeve of her jumper touching his forearm.

It was the touch. The heat of her hand, coupled with the act of compassion. Something he hadn't felt in such a long time. Or maybe it was the relief?

The relief of reaching thirty-seven and finally being able to share with someone. It was as if a whole dark weight had lifted off his shoulders. He couldn't rationalise it. It didn't make any sense. But saying the words out loud, to someone who might actually understand, was a whole new concept for Jacob.

These last fourteen months had been so hard. The next few weeks probably the hardest while he waited for his results. The outcome of whether he'd come out the other side of non-Hodgkin's lymphoma, or he'd succumb like his mother. Bonnie and Freya had been good for him. They'd brought some light back into his life at a time when he needed it most.

Bonnie squeezed his hand again. 'You can't do that, Jacob. You can't take your feelings out on my little girl.'

He pulled his hand away and put them both up to his face, cringing. 'I know that. I'm so sorry. I wasn't thinking straight. I just came in, saw the decorations and it brought back a whole host of things I just wasn't ready for.' He put his head in his hands for a second. 'I overreacted. I *know* I overreacted. I'm sorry, I really am.' He turned to face her.

She was beautiful. Bonnie Reid was actually beautiful. Even with the harsh light in this stark white room, her dark red hair, bright blue eyes and pale skin made her the most beautiful woman he'd ever been close to. 'What can I do? What can I do to make it up to her? To make it up to you? I don't want her to hate me. I don't want her to be scared of me.'

Bonnie nodded slowly and met his gaze. There was a gentle smile on her lips. 'I can't tell you that, Jacob. You've got to figure that out for yourself. You're the adult—she's the child. You have to take some time to work through how you feel about everything.'

'How do I do that?' His voice was low. He couldn't tear his eyes away from her. All he wanted to do was reach out and touch her perfect skin—to join the invisible dots between the light sprinkling of freckles across her nose.

He wanted Bonnie and Freya to feel safe. To feel safe around him. Just as he'd felt safe to tell her about his past.

'What happened to your dad?'

He gave a little sigh. 'He died—two years ago of heart failure. Had a funeral with full military honours.' He raised his eyebrows. 'He would have been very proud.'

* * *

Bonnie bent down and lifted the bottle of wine. 'Why don't we have a drink together and just talk?'

He nodded, then smiled as he took the bottle from her hand and turned the label around. He raised his eyebrows. 'Did you open the most expensive bottle of wine that I had?'

She smiled and held up her phone. 'You bet your life I did. I looked it up online first. I was planning on finishing it before you got back. You're lucky I left you any.' She handed him a glass.

He poured the remaining wine into his glass and stopped for a minute, holding it between both hands. He was staring at the liquid in the glass. 'I'm just glad that you didn't leave,' he said quietly.

She reached over and put a hand on his back. 'I wanted to. I didn't even care that we had nowhere to go.' She shook her head, as if she couldn't quite understand herself. 'But I just couldn't, Jacob. Not like this.'

There was a silence for a few moments between them. Was she considering the same implications that he was? That what had started out as a temporary arrangement was becoming so much more?

He looked up through heavy lids. Now he'd come in from the cold, the heat of the house was hitting him in a big way. He'd gone from being frozen to the bone to feeling superheated in a matter of minutes.

Sensations of fatigue were sweeping over him. But his body was fighting it every step of the way. Fighting to hold on to the other sensations in his prickling skin. Those bright blue eyes were mesmerising. She didn't need to speak. It was almost as if he knew what she was thinking. Was he imagining this? He'd never felt a connection like this before.

'I guess not everyone leaves,' he whispered.

Bonnie took a long, slow breath and put her wine glass on the floor. Although her actions were slow and measured, he didn't doubt for a second that she knew exactly what she was doing.

As she turned to face him, one leg was pulled up on the sofa, tucking under her as she put her arms around his neck. 'No, Jacob,' she whispered. 'Not everyone leaves.'

His breath was stuck somewhere in his throat. He'd never told anyone what he'd just told Bonnie. Now she seemed connected to him—tied to him, and he didn't want that to end. The blood was roaring through his ears. The feel of the soft fluffy wool on the sleeves of her jumper pushed his temperature skyward.

But his self-defence mechanisms were still kicking into place. He'd lived his life too long like this for them to disappear instantly. 'But you did leave,' he murmured. 'You left your husband.'

He was fixed on her eyes. Fixed on the perfectness of her skin and beautiful auburn hair framing her face. She nodded. 'I did.' It was almost as if she sensed she had to tease him every part of the way. She gave a little smile, 'But I had exceptional circumstances—you know what they were.'

He reached over and touched her hair. 'Not really. Tell me about them. Tell me about Freya's dad.'

He could see her hesitation, see her sucking in a breath. He'd just shared with her. She now knew about one of the biggest influencing factors in his life. He'd barely scratched the surface with her.

Her eyes fixed on the floor. 'Robert was my boyfriend.

We were together about a year when I fell pregnant unexpectedly.' She threw up her hands. 'I know. Don't say
anything. A midwife accidentally falling pregnant. The
irony kills me.' Then she smiled. 'But Freya is the best
accident that will ever happen to me.' She bit her lip. 'It's
stupid really, and hindsight is a wonderful thing. Robert's parents were real traditionalists. So we got swept
along with their ideals and got married before Freya arrived. The truth was Robert was never really the mar-
rying kind.'

'But you married him anyway?' He gave a little smile.
It wasn't really a question, it was a more a sympathetic
observation. Bonnie didn't seem upset, just a little sad.

She started winding a strand of hair around her finger.
She nodded. 'I think I was more in love with the *idea* of
being in love, than actually *being* in love. In my heart of
hearts, I never really pictured us growing old together.'

'And?'

She shrugged her shoulders. 'I was busy with work and
juggling childcare for Freya. I kind of lost sight of being
married. Robert was distant—distracted. I suspected
something was going on. It made me mad. I came home
early from work one day and found another car in the
drive. I let myself into the house and found Freya playing downstairs. Robert was upstairs, in bed, with one of
my closest friends.' She shook her head and sagged back
a little. 'It wasn't my finest hour. The fact Freya was in
the house. The fact it was one of my friends...'

Jacob raised his eyebrows. 'Oh, no. What did you do?'

She rolled her eyes. 'My "friend" ended up naked in
my front garden after I'd marched her down the stairs.
Robert's clothes were deposited out of the bedroom window—so at least she found something to wear.' She shook

her head. 'After that, I just grabbed some things for me and Freya, packed up and went to my parents. I filed for divorce straight away.'

He was watching her closely. 'How did you feel?'

She paused for a second. 'It's probably a really awful thing to say—but I was more humiliated than anything else. Robert and I had been growing apart. I probably always thought we would come to a natural end. I just didn't expect it to be like that.' She gave a rueful smile. 'I wasn't exactly heartbroken about it. I might even have been secretly relieved it was over. But we lived in a small place. Every person in the town knew exactly what Robert had done to me. And pride is a terrible thing. I felt people staring at me wherever I went. I couldn't take it any longer.'

He nodded slowly. 'So you came to Cambridge?'

'I had to. I know you understand, Jacob. It's called self-preservation. It's the thing that makes you get out of bed for another day, even when you don't want to. I needed a change for Freya and me. I needed a chance of a new life for us both.'

He reached and brushed a thumb down her cheek. She was so wise. He'd never met anyone like this before. There was so much more to learn about Bonnie Reid.

He'd shared with her tonight, and now she'd shared with him.

'Thank you,' he whispered.

Her pretty brow furrowed. 'For what?'

'For not leaving tonight.' It was the thing that had bothered him every step of the way back home. It was the thing that he'd dreaded. That he'd expected. Because that was what he deserved. And he knew that. But Bonnie Reid had just surpassed all of his expectations.

His heart squeezed. If he'd left this room as she'd decorated it, things would have been perfect. The fire flickering in the fireplace, the tree lights twinkling all around them. But he'd destroyed all that and brought them back to his white, harsh, empty walls.

Bonnie Reid deserved better than that. Freya Reid deserved better than that.

She licked her lips. It was the tiniest movement—a subconscious movement—but it was all that he needed. He moved forwards, not hesitating, his lips connecting with hers.

She tasted of strawberries mixed with wine. The remnants of her perfume drifted up his nose, the feel of her jumper connecting with the delicate skin at the bottom of his throat. She didn't seem to mind his wet jumper. She didn't seem to care that wine sloshed from his glass as he wrapped one arm around her and tangled the other hand through her hair.

That hair. He'd wanted to touch it from the moment he'd seen it. It was silky, falling through his fingers easily. But he didn't want it to fall through. He wanted to catch it—just as he wanted to catch her. So he wrapped it around his fingers, anchoring his hand at the back of her head as the kissing increased.

She pulled back—and for a horrible second he thought she was going to say this was all a terrible mistake. But she didn't. Bonnie Reid was taking charge.

She moved, lifting the glass from his hand and sitting it on the side table, then, pushing his shoulders back against the sofa, she swung one leg over him, so she was sitting on top of him.

She put her arms around his shoulders again and looked him straight in the eye. 'There. That's better.'

'It certainly is.' He didn't hesitate. He pulled her closer, feeling the warm curves of her breasts against his chest. He slid his hands up and under her jumper. Her smooth, silky skin beneath his fingertips. Everything about this felt right.

Her smell. Her taste. Her touch. Her fingers skirted around his neck and shoulders, along the line of his jaw, scratching against his stubble, then through his hair, pulling his lips hard against her own.

His tongue played around the edges of her mouth as their kiss deepened. Suddenly, these clothes were too much; they were stopping him from feeling exactly what he wanted to.

He drew back and pulled his wet jumper and shirt over his head, then pulled her soft jumper off, throwing it on the floor with his own.

Her round full breasts were encased in a cream lace bra. She was breathing heavily now, her body weight on the most sensitive part of him.

He ran his fingers across her shoulder, reaching the pale skin at the bottom of her neck and then down, over her breastbone, between her breasts and down to her navel, resting just above the button of her jeans.

She sucked in her stomach—an automatic reaction but an unnecessary one. He loved every part of her soft curves.

His brain was screaming 'no' to him right now. But his body just wasn't listening.

He shouldn't be doing this. Bonnie and Freya were in a vulnerable position right now. This was only a temporary arrangement. Jacob Layton didn't form attachments. Not like this.

But everything about this felt right. Everything about

this had been simmering under the surface since his first meeting with Bonnie. Now it was exploding to the surface in volcanic proportions.

For his part, the attraction had just grown. The more he got to know her and Freya, the more he admired her. Her strength, her resilience, her determination to do a good job.

Her empathy with patients, her patience with staff. Her sense of humour, her stubborn streak and the way she answered back. Bonnie Reid was one of a kind.

And he was about to make the biggest mistake of his life.

Bonnie had already experienced one screwed-up partner. The last thing she needed was another. His hands stilled on her back.

Bonnie and Freya deserved a bright future. How could he give them one with his cancer history? That would always, permanently, hang over his head. He knew without asking that Bonnie would want more kids.

And he knew without thinking about it that he already believed the cancer was in his genes. He couldn't do that to a child. He couldn't do that to Bonnie and Freya.

'Jacob? Is everything okay?' She'd pulled back a little, a frown creasing her brow.

'Mummy?' The little voice cut through the emotions in the room.

Jacob froze. Bonnie did the opposite. She let out a little gasp, then flicked around, trying to locate her discarded jumper. She leapt off his lap and pulled the jumper over her head. Freya's voice hadn't sounded too close. She must be standing at the top of the stairs.

Jacob looked at his crumpled shirt and jumper, still

together, but lying at Bonnie's feet. 'Do you want me to come?'

She shook her head quickly as she started towards the door. 'No, no, it's fine. Let me deal with Freya.'

His last view was of the bottom he so admired in those jeans. He heard her padding up the stairs in her bare feet. 'Hi, honey. What's wrong? Let's get you back to bed.' He heard the noise of her sweeping Freya into her arms and the voices faded quickly.

Jacob leaned forwards and put his head in his hands. What was he thinking? How could he have explained to Bonnie why he'd stopped kissing her, without telling her about his diagnosis—the one part of himself he still wanted to remain private?

His stomach twisted. He knew none of this was right. But Jacob didn't share. It didn't feel normal to him; it didn't feel natural. Telling Bonnie about his mother had been the first time in his life he'd ever really shared.

But the cancer diagnosis? No. He didn't want her to look at him that way. With pity. With sympathy. With the 'I'm sorry there's a chance you'll die' expression on her face.

He never wanted anyone to look at him like that—let alone Bonnie. He'd only told two colleagues—ones he trusted explicitly—and that was only because he'd had to reduce his patient contact while undergoing his most intense treatments. If he could have got away with telling no one that was exactly what he'd have done.

He sighed and leaned back against the sofa, his bare back coming into contact with the leather surface. It wasn't comfortable, not against bare skin. Somehow he hadn't noticed with Bonnie on his lap.

He looked around the room. White, stark walls.

It had looked so much better before.

He could admit that now. He could try and be rational about things. It seemed a little easier now he'd told Bonnie about his mother dying at Christmas.

He winced as he remembered the look of their faces earlier when he'd started to tear the decorations back down. How stupid. How pathetic. How ungrateful.

He stood up and grabbed his shirt and jumper from the floor, walking through to the kitchen and dumping them in the laundry basket. He had a pile of clothes sitting on top of the tumble dryer. He grabbed a T-shirt and walked back through to the hall.

He had to find a way to make things up to Bonnie and Freya. He hated that Freya might be scared of him now. He had to do something to change that.

He pulled open the hall cupboard door and was nearly speared in the face with Christmas tree branch. A single red bauble rolled past his feet. She'd stripped the Christmas tree but obviously kept all the decorations.

He gave a smile of relief. That was where she'd stored them.

He glanced at the empty banister. He might not have got some things right tonight, but if he wanted to make it up to them he knew exactly where to start.

CHAPTER EIGHT

BONNIE RUBBED HER sleep-ridden eyes. She'd had trouble sleeping after last night's events. Freya had only woken up to go to the toilet and been a little disorientated. Once Bonnie had cuddled her back into bed she'd fallen asleep instantly.

But Bonnie's head had been spinning. She'd been shocked by Jacob earlier. But she'd also known there had to be a reason behind it. A deep-seated reason. And that was why she'd given him the tiniest bit of leeway.

Now she understood. It didn't excuse his actions, but she knew exactly how sorry he was—it had been written over every inch of his face. And when he'd shared about his mother she couldn't help but cry.

Her thoughts immediately went to Freya. She couldn't stand the thought of something happening to her and Freya being left alone. Who would love her the way she did? Certainly not her father. Something prickled down her spine. If anything ever happened to her, Freya would automatically go to her father. What kind of life would she have with him? The kind of life that Jacob had endured as a child?

Her skin tingled as Jacob entered her thoughts. Who

was she kidding? Had she just made the biggest mistake of her life?

Jacob had opened up to her. But there was still so much she didn't know about him—even though they were living under one roof. Maybe she was just being paranoid. But after living with an unfaithful, feckless husband, she wanted to go into any new relationship with her eyes wide open.

She'd been hurt. Freya had been hurt. She'd no intention of ever going down that road again. Self-preservation was a must. Even if any thought of him made her heart pitter-patter faster.

'Can we have breakfast, Mummy?' The little voice cut through her thoughts.

She turned and smiled at her little girl. She was blessed: Freya woke up each day in a good mood. She reached over and gave Bonnie a hug. 'I like it when you're in my bed, Mummy.'

She hugged back. 'I like it too. But it's only on special occasions. Now, what do you want for breakfast?'

'Toast and jam.'

'I think I can do that. Let's go to the toilet and wash our face and hands first.'

As they reached the top of the stairs she bent down to pick Freya up. It was just instinct—she'd done it most mornings since they'd got there. Freya wasn't used to stairs and Bonnie was always worried that she'd trip if she was still sleepy.

As she gathered Freya in her arms she realised something was a little off. It took her the first few steps to realise what it was. The red and green garland was wound back around the banister.

A smile started to edge around her lips. She kept

walking. Now she could hear, and smell, activity in the kitchen. Someone was cooking bacon and singing while they cooked.

As she reached the bottom of the stairs the twinkling lights from the front room attracted her like a magnet. She walked back into the front room.

Everything was back exactly where it should be. 'Look, Freya,' she whispered.

The tree lights were twinkling, the branches redecorated with tinsel and baubles. The nativity scene was back on the side table. The red and green garland for the mantelpiece was back in place. She'd no idea how he'd managed to patch it together—but she didn't really care.

The fact was, he'd done it.

'Mummy, our tree's back up,' said Freya. A smile had lit up her face. 'Does Jacob like it now?'

Bonnie nodded slowly. 'I think he must.' She couldn't stop smiling. He'd revealed part of himself last night but now he'd obviously made the decision to try and move on.

The house felt full of warmth. It was so much nicer with the Christmas decorations up; it felt much more like a home, rather than just a house.

She carried Freya through to the kitchen. Jacob was putting a pot of tea on the kitchen table. 'Oh, you're up, good.' His eyes skirted over to Freya; he looked wary. 'I've made breakfast. Sit down.'

Freya stared at the plate of bacon as Bonnie put her in one of the chairs. 'I don't want bacon. I want toast and jam.'

Jacob smiled at her. 'I thought you might say that.' He produced a toast rack stacked full of toast and a jar of jam.

Bonnie smiled as she sat down. Freya reached over and

grabbed a slice of toast. 'Can you butter this, Mummy?' Her eyes fixed on Jacob again. 'I like that the tree's back. I like the lights.'

A second of hesitation passed over Jacob's face before he pulled out a chair and sat down next to Freya. 'I do too. I think it was a good idea to get a tree for the house. Thank you very much. I'm sorry if I seemed angry last night. I was just a little surprised.'

Bonnie held her breath as she handed over the buttered toast to Freya and opened the jar of jam. She wasn't entirely sure how Freya would respond.

But Freya just shrugged. 'Can we watch cartoons today?'

It was that simple for a five-year-old. No stomach churning. No fretting. She just accepted what he said and was happy that the tree was back up.

Jacob and Freya continued to chat over breakfast. Today, it seemed, was going to be a quiet day in the house.

Jacob seemed more at ease. Maybe he was just getting used to having people in his house—or maybe talking about his mother last night had helped him a little.

She certainly hoped so.

It was so strange to see Freya chatting away with him. Even when they'd lived with her husband, breakfast had usually been their time together. Robert had rarely appeared at the breakfast table. And last night's events seemed to have been quickly forgotten.

They laughed together and something twisted inside her. She wasn't quite sure what it was. Fear? Envy? Confusion?

Jacob seemed comfortable this morning—but was she? She'd kissed him last night. If Freya hadn't interrupted it might have become a whole lot more. Bonnie didn't usually act on impulse—not when it came to men. But things with Jacob last night had just seemed so natural. So heated.

It made her want to catch her breath.

This was a new job. A new city. A new life.

Just how much change was she ready for?

Jacob felt as if he'd been holding his breath since last night. Ever since he'd kissed Bonnie and realised exactly the effect she had on him.

Part of him was sorry. Now he would always know exactly what he was missing. Part of him wasn't the least bit sorry. It had been a long time since he'd felt a connection to someone. The fact that Bonnie was a mother hadn't even entered his head.

If you'd asked him a few years ago if he'd ever have a relationship with someone who had children he would have said an overwhelming no. But he'd have been wrong. With the exception of last night, he'd liked being around Freya. It was surprising him—just as much as it was probably surprising Bonnie and Freya.

He'd noticed the way people were looking at him at work. For the last ten days he'd felt differently. He'd felt lighter. This morning he practically felt so light he could float away. The only thing that was still anchoring him to the ground was his test results.

Even if—and he prayed they would be—they were good results, it still wouldn't change other things for Jacob. The cancer would always lurk in the background, always a possibility of a recurrence. Always that uncertainty of whether it was familial and he could pass it on. Gene mapping wasn't quite there yet to give him that answer.

But these last few days at home had felt so much better. Putting up the decorations again last night had given him a lot of thinking time. It was time to put the negative associations that he had with Christmas to bed.

His mother would have hated him being like this. Feeling like this about a season that should be the happiest of times.

The look on Freya and Bonnie's faces this morning when they realised he'd put the decorations back up had been enough for him. He was sure he'd done the right thing. He'd also done something else. He was still to find out if it was right or not.

He pushed some tickets along the table to Freya. 'I found out about a little surprise. I was wondering if you and your mum would like to come.'

Freya stared down at the tickets. The words were obviously too complicated for a five-year-old, but the pictures told a good story. She pointed. 'Is that Rudolph? Can we go and see Rudolph?'

Jacob looked up at Bonnie. He was feeling hopeful, even though he should probably have run this by her first. She leaned over and spun the tickets around. 'Today? The Christmas lights, a visit to Santa *and* a chance to meet the reindeers?' Surprise and amusement, with a tiny bit of disbelief, mixed through her voice as her eyebrows rose.

He nodded carefully. 'What do you think? Would you like to go?'

Her face relaxed and she lifted her mug of tea to take

a sip. Her voice was quiet. 'I think that would be lovely. Thank you for thinking of us, Jacob.'

Her gaze met his. She was still thinking about last night.

He'd pulled back. She must be wondering why. Because the air between them still sizzled. It crackled. He still wanted to reach out and touch her cheek, kiss her lips. He just didn't want to be unfair.

He took a deep breath. 'I'll always think about you, Bonnie.'

Silence hung between them. It was probably the wrong thing to say. It almost seemed as if he were finishing something that had never started. Truth was, he didn't have a clue what he was doing right now. But the implication was clear. Bonnie was affecting him. He *did* feel something for her—even if he didn't know what it was.

But those words seemed enough for Bonnie; she gave a little smile and stood up. 'Come on, Freya, the Christmas lights and Santa visit aren't until three o'clock this afternoon. Let's have a lazy morning on the sofa.'

Freya jumped up in agreement and ran out of the kitchen towards the front room, leaving Jacob at the kitchen table, eyes fixed on Bonnie's backside in her pyjama trousers, trying to keep his thoughts in check.

'Is everyone ready?'

They were all practically standing in a line. Winter jackets, scarfs, gloves and wellington boots in place. Freya couldn't stand still. She had ants in her pants. She didn't care that the temperature had plummeted again and a mixture of sleet and snow was starting to fall. She just wanted to meet Rudolph.

'Will I get to sit on his back? Will Donner be there? And Blitzen? Is his nose really red?'

The questions had been never-ending since this morning.

Jacob smiled. 'I have no idea. This is all new to me.'

Freya frowned. 'Is it far? Are we going in the car?'

Bonnie shook her head. 'No. We're going to walk. That way, we'll get to have plenty of time to see all the Christmas lights.'

'Will Fraser from school be going to see Santa too?'

Jacob knelt in front of her. 'And who might Fraser be?'

Freya tossed her red hair over her shoulder. 'My friend,' she said matter-of-factly.

Bonnie suppressed a laugh. 'Welcome to my world, Jacob. Or rather the world of little girls—a new best friend every day. I just try and keep up.'

Jacob folded his arms across his chest and did his best to look severe. 'Fraser, eh? Well, if he's there you'll need to point him out. I'd like to meet this Fraser.'

Freya giggled. 'Can I get my picture with Santa?'

Bonnie nodded and bent to straighten Freya's hat. 'Yes, it's all arranged. Now, are you ready?'

She jumped up and down. 'I've been ready for hours, Mum. Let's go!'

It was the perfect afternoon. Cold without being *too* cold. A light dusting of snow everywhere. By three o'clock it was already getting dark.

Freya's little hand was in Jacob's. It was surprising how comfortable it felt. How comfortable *he* felt doing this. Bonnie had a cream woollen hat pulled over her auburn hair and a thick green wool coat. She looked perfect. Like something from a Christmas card.

He swung Freya up into his arms. 'Come on. Let's go and visit Santa and the reindeers. It won't be long until the lights get switched on.'

The prepaid tickets were the godsend. Thank goodness for one of the midwives in the special care unit. She'd mentioned buying the tickets last year and not having to wait in the freezing cold for hours with her young kids.

Freya only had to wait five minutes before she was able to jump on Santa's knee and tell him what she wanted for Christmas. She counted off things on her finger. 'I'd like a new baby doll, one that can eat and poop. I like to change nappies,' she said proudly.

Santa nodded in amusement. 'I think that can be arranged,' he said, nodding towards Bonnie.

She was leaning against Jacob. 'Thank goodness it isn't Christmas Eve,' she said. 'Last year Freya announced she wanted some board game when we visited Santa on Christmas Eve. It was the first time she'd mentioned it at all. And, of course, it was after five o'clock on Christmas Eve.'

He wrapped his arm around her waist. It was so easy to do that. 'What did you do?'

She shook her head. 'What do you think I did? I panicked!'

He watched Freya. She was saying to Santa Claus, 'We really need a house too. We've just moved down from Scotland and we still haven't found somewhere else to stay.' She looked up into the air. 'I mean, the house we're staying in right now is perfect. So, if we could have one just like it, that would be great.'

'You like where you stay?' Santa asked.

Freya sighed. 'It's the most beautiful house in the world.'

Something twisted inside Jacob. He'd always loved his house—even if he hadn't really made his mark on it. But to hear someone else say those words out loud? Say that they loved his house—that was special. It almost made him feel warm inside.

And for the strangest reason, it didn't send him into a mad panic. He wanted Bonnie and Freya to feel welcome in his home. He liked having them around.

Bonnie shifted a little as if she were uncomfortable. 'But it could be more perfect.'

Jacob turned at the sound of Freya's voice. She had his full attention.

'What would make it perfect, then?' asked Santa.

'A dog,' Freya said quickly.

Jacob burst out laughing. 'She doesn't seem to be letting this one go, does she?'

Bonnie laughed too. 'I'll have to buy her a stuffed one for Christmas. Or maybe one of those ones that bark? There's no way we could deal with a real dog. Not with me working full-time. It just wouldn't be fair.'

Jacob nodded. 'You're right. I've always considered getting a dog, but even with all the dog-walking companies, it just didn't seem fair to leave a dog by itself all day.'

She looked surprised. 'You've thought about getting a dog?'

'Of course.' He winked. 'I've heard they're not as complicated as women, or...' he looked over at Freya '...five-year-olds!'

Bonnie laughed as Freya jumped down from Santa's

lap and held out her hand towards him. 'Thanks, Santa, I'll let you know if I get what I asked for.'

Santa looked a little surprised and shot Bonnie and Jacob a smile as he shook Freya's outstretched hand. 'This is a very astute little girl. Merry Christmas to you all.'

They walked outside towards the reindeer pen and Bonnie pulled the bag of food they'd been given from her bag. One of the staff showed Freya how to hold the food in her hand and she screamed as a reindeer named Vixen slobbered all over her hand.

Without even thinking about it, Jacob stuck his hand in Bonnie's bag and pulled out the wipes that were sticking out, grabbing one out and wiping Freya's hand.

'Jacob?' He knelt down in front of her. 'Why don't the reindeers have red noses? Aren't they supposed to?'

He smiled. He loved the way Freya's mind worked. Her endless questions. Her five-year-old's logic. And her complete and utter belief in all things Christmas. This morning she'd shown him a website they'd been shown at school that would plot Santa's journey all the way around the world on Christmas Eve. They'd even been able to input the house address to let Santa know where they were.

He whispered in her ear. 'You've got to remember. It's not Christmas Eve yet. They don't fly until Christmas Eve, so they don't need their red noses until then.'

He could almost hear her thinking out loud. Finally she gave a little nod. 'Now I understand.'

His phone rang and he stood up and pulled it from his back pocket, looking to see who was calling. He glanced towards Bonnie and Freya and walked off to the side.

* * *

Bonnie looked up. It must be a work call. Jacob obviously didn't want to discuss a patient around them and that was fine.

Freya was still excited. In a few minutes' time it would be time for the countdown and switch-on of the Christmas lights. Bonnie held out her hand. 'Come on. The lights will be on in a few minutes. Let's find somewhere good to stand.'

The smells from the street vendors were wafting all around them. Roasting chestnuts, hot chocolate and mulled wine. The rich pine scents from the wreaths outside the nearby florist were mixing in with other aromas. Holly was intertwined amongst them and mistletoe hung from the door of the shop. Should she buy some?

Jacob was still talking. He looked worried; there were deep furrows across his brow. She crossed her fingers that there were no problems on the labour ward.

He caught her eye and turned away. Something twisted inside.

Now she was being stupid.

This was simple. This was just a nice day out between work colleagues—housemates. Because if she took that kiss out of the equation, there really wasn't anything else between them—was there?

In theory, no. But that wasn't the way she was feeling inside. And everything about that made her uncomfortable. After the nightmare of her ex-husband she'd vowed not to expose herself or Freya to anything like that again. She didn't need the hassle of the conflict.

Bonnie Reid fully intended to be a man-free zone. So what had gone wrong?

She hadn't even lasted a day. They'd moved in with Jacob their first day. How ridiculous was that?

From the initial grumpy meeting, Jacob had seemed to chill. She'd been nervous about staying there with Freya; the first few days she'd scoured the Internet for somewhere else.

But it was almost as if, after the first few days, he wasn't really in a hurry for them to move out. Anywhere she showed him he always had a reason for them not to move there. Too far out. Too rough. Not near a good school. And while it was helpful and informative, it wasn't actually inspiring her to move elsewhere.

She and Freya were getting a little too comfortable in Jacob's lovely house. It was almost starting to feel like home.

Jacob put the phone back in his pocket and spun around to face them. He walked over, picked up Freya and put her on his shoulders. 'This is where you'll get the best view,' he said, and she squealed with happiness as he swung her up.

But Bonnie's stomach was still churning. It was almost as if the phone call hadn't happened. It was almost as if he hadn't deliberately walked away from them and excluded them from his conversation.

A horrible chill crept down her spine. Jacob wasn't on call any more. His on-call duties finished at midday. Whoever had phoned him—it hadn't been about work. There were no patient confidentiality issues. So what didn't he want her to hear?

She didn't have time to think any further, because his arm was around her shoulders and he moved them forwards a little as Santa positioned himself on stage to make the announcement and turn on the lights.

Crowds had gathered all around them. They were

lucky Jacob had thought to buy them tickets. The area in front of the stage was crushed full of people. At the side, they could see the view all along the street. A perfect position to see the lights switched on.

Santa started cheering the crowd on. Some of the handlers had brought the reindeers out from the pen and positioned them behind him. The animals seemed completely unperturbed by the noise or the crowds. Freya, in the meantime, was clapping her hands with excitement.

'Ten, nine, eight, seven, six.' Bonnie joined in the countdown with the rest of the crowd. This was what she wanted for her little girl. To be full of the joys of Christmas and to enter into the spirit of things.

Moving down here had been hard. Emotionally hard. The separation in miles was the final nail in her divorce coffin, and one that she so badly needed. Everything down here was new. Everything down here was fresh.

Living in a town where Freya could have seen her father at any point, and been ignored by him, was too much for her. His lack of involvement hurt. It wasn't the issue of being both mum and dad to her little girl—that was without question. It was the carefully chosen words she had to find to explain why he didn't call—why he didn't visit.

And it didn't matter that moving to Cambridge gave Robert a perfect excuse for not visiting Freya. He hadn't needed one in Scotland. It just lessened the impact of him not being around. Freya was so caught up in her new home, her new school and her new friends that she hadn't even had a chance to miss him and that was a welcome relief.

Jacob looked over at her and squeezed her shoulder. 'Okay?'

'Yes.' She nodded, pushing away all the other little

doubts that had started to creep into her mind. It was one phone call. One. Nothing else.

Jacob wasn't Robert. And even if he was, it was none of her business. They were work colleagues—friends.

Santa finished the countdown, 'Three, two, one,' and flicked the switch.

It was magical. Like something from a movie. The Christmas lights started at the bottom of the street. Red, green and gold garlands strung across the road flickered to life.

It was like a Mexican wave. At points along the way there were bigger illuminations. A North Pole house, a multicoloured sleigh, a large pile of presents. The church halfway along the street had joined in. Multicoloured lights wrapped around the stained-glass windows and steeple lit up the dark night sky. A nativity scene in the churchyard, complete with shepherds and magi, was brought to life.

Freya loved every part of it. Every time another part lit she gasped with excitement. The lights were getting closer, finishing with the large Christmas tree in the middle of the square. The colours lit up one at a time, as if someone were stringing tinsel around the tree while they watched. First green, then red, then gold. Finally a large white twinkling star lit at the top of the tree as fireworks started to go off behind them. Cambridge really knew how to do Christmas.

One of the brass bands from the local schools started to play Christmas carols and Bonnie, Freya and Jacob joined in. By the time Jacob slid Freya off his shoulders an hour later her eyelids were heavy. Bonnie held out her arms to take her but Jacob shook his head. 'It's fine. We've still got quite a way to walk back.' She saw the tiniest flash of hesitation across his eyes, then he bent down and dropped a kiss on her lips.

Just when she thought she had things sorted in her head. Just when she'd convinced herself that what Jacob did was none of her business and she should forget their last kiss.

The kiss zapped everything back into his place. The taste of his lips and the feel of his hands sliding under her jumper and up her back.

'Come on.' He smiled at her. 'Let's get sleepyhead back home. It's getting cold out here.'

A few gentle flakes of snow started to fall around them. Freya had automatically snuggled into Jacob's neck and was already half asleep. Jacob kept his other arm around Bonnie and steered them both through the crowd and along the street.

Bonnie looked around. To everyone else, they must look like a regular family. Mum, Dad and little girl. Part of that terrified her. The other part pined for it.

She wanted Freya to be loved, to be part of a family. She wanted her little girl to have the relationship that she'd missed out on with her own father.

And Bonnie didn't want to grow old alone. She'd been stung by her cheating ex and it had made her wary. But it didn't stop her hoping that somewhere out there would be a man who would love and respect her the way she did him.

Would make her skin tingle and send pulses through her body from a mere look, a touch.

Trouble was, the only person who fitted the bill right now was Jacob Layton.

Could she really trust him with her heart? And with Freya's too?

CHAPTER NINE

JACOB STARED AT the letter in his hand.

This was it. The appointment he'd been waiting for. The one that could be the end of the big black cloud that had been hanging over his head for the last fifteen months.

His scheduled appointment was fourteen days away but he'd phoned and asked for a cancellation. He couldn't wait any longer to find out his results—good or bad.

Professional courtesy in the NHS went a long way. CT scan and blood tests tomorrow. Appointment with the specialist the day after.

His stomach twisted. Over the last few days he'd reverted to form and he knew it. He was snapping at people again, being grumpy at work.

All because of what was happening inside.

Something had hit him. Ever since he'd had that conversation with Bonnie and kissed her he couldn't think straight. His house was now full of Christmas decorations and happy, smiley people. And for the first time in his life he actually wanted to be a happy, smiley person too.

But he just couldn't be. Not with this hanging over his head.

The possibility of a real relationship—a real connection with someone—was there. But he felt as if it were slipping through his fingers like shifting sands.

Talking about his mother had been an enormous help. Sharing with Bonnie had given him a connection he hadn't felt since he was a young child. Bonnie was a woman he could trust. A woman he could love with his whole heart.

His grip tightened on the letter in his hand. So why hadn't he told her about this?

The truth was he wasn't ready. Cancer was a burden. Cancer was a relationship deal breaker. He was still at that uncertain stage with Bonnie. He didn't want to be a burden to her and Freya—particularly if the news he was about to receive was bad.

If it was, he would step back and fade into the background of their lives. He would probably stop making up reasons she shouldn't move to any of the properties that she'd shown him and help her and Freya take the next steps in their lives.

Above everything he didn't want Bonnie to feel sorry for him. To form a relationship with him out of sympathy or pity. He didn't want that kind of relationship.

He wanted the kind that had started to burn inside him already. The kind where she was his first thought in the morning and his last thought at night. The kind where he could walk into the labour suite and sense she was there without even seeing her.

The kind where her scent would drift across the room towards him and wrap itself around him like a magic spell. So the first face he would see would be hers and her smile would send him a thousand unspoken promises.

Bonnie and Freya had been badly let down before. He didn't want that for them again. And until he found out about his test results, he couldn't even begin to have the kind of conversations with Bonnie that he should be having.

Would she even consider their relationship progressing? How would she feel knowing that he'd had cancer? How would she feel about his position on children? She already had Freya, but Bonnie struck him as the kind of woman who'd want to expand her family. Could she be in a relationship with a man who didn't want to pass the risk of cancer—no matter how small—on to his kids?

So many unanswered questions. So many dangerous assumptions. Crabbit. That was how she'd good-naturedly described him the other day. It was a good Scottish word for him—because that was exactly how he felt.

Unsure. That was another word that described him right now.

He'd always spent his life knowing exactly who he was and what he wanted.

Bonnie—and Freya—had literally turned his world upside down.

'Jacob?'

He crumpled the paper in his hand and thrust it into his pocket. 'Yes?' Bonnie was standing at his office door. A furrow ran across her brow.

'Sean just phoned. Someone else phoned in sick for tomorrow. He wondered if you could cover the theatre list?'

Jacob hesitated. He'd never refused to cover for a fellow doctor before. His automatic default position was always to say yes.

But this was different. If he missed the tests tomorrow, he'd have to wait another two weeks before his routine appointment came up. There were another four obstetricians at CRMU. Sean had probably just asked him first as a matter of routine. He took a deep breath. 'No. Sorry, tell him I have obligations that I can't break. He'll need to ask someone else.'

Bonnie hesitated and took a little step towards him. 'Jacob?'

He shook his head. He couldn't have this conversation with her—not right now. He swept past her, before her light perfume started to invade his senses. 'Tell him to ask Isabel. I'm sure she'll oblige.'

He carried on down the corridor. One look from Bonnie's confused blue eyes was enough for him. He had to be so careful. She'd been hurt badly by her husband. He'd already done damage when he'd torn down the Christmas decorations. For the next two days it would be best if he could avoid her. He'd find a reason to work late tonight. And another reason to stay out of her way tomorrow. His tests were in the afternoon. Then he'd just have to wait twenty-four hours to find out his results.

He glanced at his watch. He needed to have a conversation with Dean Edwards about a baby in Special Care. He could go there. Bonnie would be tied up in the labour suite for the rest of the day.

He sucked in a breath as he pushed open the swing doors. Forty-eight hours. Forty-eight hours, then he'd know if his life was about to begin, or could be about to end.

CHAPTER TEN

SOMETHING WAS WRONG. She could feel it in her bones.

Jacob was avoiding her—and avoiding Freya. Last night he'd come home when they'd both been in bed. When she'd got up and gone downstairs to make a cup of tea and talk to him, it had been obvious he had other things on his mind.

It was painful. It was embarrassing to be around someone that had kissed her so passionately a few days before and now acted as though he didn't want her around.

Maybe it stung so much because she actually cared. She cared what Jacob thought about her.

And caring was the one thing she shouldn't be doing.

Jacob had told her about his mother. But there was something else he was keeping from her. And it made her uncomfortable.

She deserved better than that—Freya deserved better than that.

Worse than anything, she didn't even feel as if she could call him on it. They weren't even in a proper relationship. She had no right to ask where he was going, or what he was doing. She just had that horrible sensation of being taken for a fool.

It didn't help that she was staying in his house. In fact,

it made things ten times worse. If she'd met him through work and they'd maybe just shared a kiss, or gone on a date, she would be able to take a step back and distance herself.

Living under one roof made things a whole lot more complicated.

She tapped at the computer screen. It was only a few weeks until Christmas and the choices seemed even more limited than the last time she'd looked. Seven flats—all within her price range. All white, bland, soulless rooms in a range of buildings she wasn't sure she wanted to stay in.

Two in tower blocks. Three in areas that were less than salubrious. And that hadn't come from Jacob—a few of the other members of staff in the labour suite had recounted tales of staying in some of the surrounding areas. One looked in the same state as the motel she and Freya had stayed in, and another was nearer Freya's school but was a tiny one-bedroom flat.

She clicked on another that flashed by on the top of her screen. This time it was a beautiful two-bedroom flat well out of her price range. A large, spacious flat with original polished floorboards like Jacob's and the same bay-style windows dressed with the kind of curtains she'd imagined for his house.

She pressed the delete button quickly. She was being stupid. Even her house search reminded her of him.

She scribbled down the details of the tiny one-bedroom flat. She'd phone the agent later. How much space did she really need anyway? As long as the place was heated and didn't suffer from damp it would be fine. It had the essential ingredients. It was near Freya's school and it would be a place to call their own.

A tiny shiver crept down her spine. It had always been

her intention to find somewhere for her and Freya to stay. She'd allowed herself to be distracted by Jacob. She'd let herself be influenced by him when he'd told her everything she'd looked at was unsuitable. In a few short weeks, she and Freya had become comfortable in his home.

The sharp man she'd met on her first day had all but vanished. Once you scratched beneath the surface with Jacob Layton there was so much more. He was just good at hiding all the stuff that was really important. His sense of humour, his warmth, his vulnerability and his strength.

'Bonnie? Can you come and give us a hand? We've just been phoned. We've got a woman who is thirty-two weeks pregnant with twins coming in by ambulance. They think the babies are in distress.' Karen, one of the junior midwives, was at the door.

Bonnie clicked the window on the computer to close it and stood up quickly. 'No problem, Karen.' She walked out of the office and across to the treatment room to wash her hands and put on an apron. 'Which room are you preparing?'

Karen glanced over at the whiteboard. 'Room 3, I think. That's the biggest. I'll go and page the on-call obstetrician.'

Bonnie felt her stomach flip over. One of the obstetricians was off sick. There was every chance Jacob would now be on call.

She finished the final checks in the room just as the ambulance crew wheeled the patient in. 'Hi, Bonnie. This is Eleanor Brooks. She's thirty-two weeks pregnant with twins. Hasn't felt well the last few days and fainted in the street around thirty minutes ago.'

Bonnie moved over to the side of the bed and grabbed

the edge of the sheet as the paramedic pulled Eleanor over on the patient slide board.

'Hi, Eleanor, I'm Bonnie, the sister in the labour suite. Let me help you off with your jacket and we'll see how you're doing.'

Eleanor gave a nod and shrugged her shoulders out of her jacket, letting Bonnie pull it away as she lay back against the pillows. Her colour was poor and it only took Bonnie a few seconds to wind the blood-pressure cuff around her arm and start to inflate it.

Karen appeared again with the paperwork and spoke in a low voice for a few minutes with the ambulance crew.

'Eleanor, is there someone I can phone for you?'

Eleanor nodded towards her bag. 'My mobile is in there. My husband is John, but he works offshore on the rigs. You might not be able to get him. My mum's number is in there too. She lives in Cambridge.'

Karen glanced in Bonnie's direction; Bonnie gave her a silent nod. 'Is your husband up in Aberdeen?' She was calculating in her head how long it would take to helicopter him back from the rigs to the mainland, and then down to Cambridge. She blinked at the reading on the screen from the BP cuff. Karen's eyes widened.

'Have you seen your community midwife lately, Eleanor?'

Eleanor's blood pressure was unusually high. Any woman with a twin pregnancy was normally monitored quite closely. Eleanor shook her head. 'I had an appointment last week but she was off sick, and this week I wasn't feeling well enough to go, so I missed it.'

Karen scribbled a little note on the paperwork. 'I'll go and make these calls, chase up the obstetrician and arrange for Eleanor's notes.'

Bonnie gave a nod. 'Eleanor, can you tell me how you've been feeling this past week?'

'Awful.' The one-word answer said everything.

'Did you call your midwife for some advice?'

Eleanor sighed. Her eyes were half closed; it was obvious she was tired. Her legs and ankles were puffy. Bonnie bent over and gave the skin a gentle squeeze between her fingers, the imprint of her fingers clearly denting the skin.

'I didn't want to bother my midwife. I thought I'd feel better in a day or so. Everyone's had a viral thing lately. I was sure I had the same.'

Eleanor moved uncomfortably, ignoring Bonnie at her ankles and taking a little gasp of breath as she pressed her hand against her right-hand ribs.

'Eleanor? Are you having pain?'

Eleanor grimaced and nodded. The pain was too high up to be a labour pain, but it could indicate something else. The pain seemed to pass quickly and she relaxed a little. 'I've been tired. Really tired. But that's normal for twin pregnancies, isn't it? I've been feeling a bit sick too. I've had a headache for the last few days. I actually vomited twice yesterday—I've never done that before. And usually I'm peeing all the time, now I'm hardly peeing at all.'

Alarm bells were going off in Bonnie's head. Eleanor was showing some signs of pre-eclampsia. It wasn't that unusual in twin pregnancies, but Eleanor's condition seemed to be taking a dangerous turn.

She put her hand on Eleanor's arm. 'I know I've just got you into bed. But do you think you could manage to give me a urine sample? I know you said you're hardly peeing right now, but if you could squeeze something out that would be great.' She hesitated for a second. 'I'm also going to call the phlebotomist to take some bloods.'

Eleanor gave a little sigh and swung her legs around while Bonnie brought a commode into room. Right now, she didn't even want Eleanor walking into the separate bathroom. She wanted to monitor her at all times.

Karen came back into the room as Bonnie was helping Eleanor back into bed. She pressed the button on the blood-pressure monitor again. Karen held up some foetal monitors. 'I thought you might want me to attach these? And Sean is outside.'

Bonnie nodded as she wheeled the commode towards the door. 'Will you stay here until I get back?' Karen gave the tiniest nod of her head. They were both aware of the seriousness of the situation.

It only took Bonnie two minutes to dipstick the small sample of urine and put the rest in a collection bottle for the lab.

Once she'd washed her hands she went back outside. But Sean wasn't alone. He'd been joined at the desk by Jacob.

Her stomach flipped over. This was work. He couldn't avoid her—no matter how much he tried to.

Sean turned to face her. 'Can you give me an update?'

Bonnie nodded. Aware that Jacob still wasn't really looking at her.

'Eleanor Brooks is thirty-four. She's thirty-two weeks pregnant with twins. I've not seen her notes, but I'm assuming her pregnancy has been unremarkable up until now. She collapsed in the street earlier today. She has upper-right-quadrant pain, pitting oedema in her ankles, her blood pressure is one-sixty over one-ten. Pulse eighty-seven. I've just tested her urine and it's positive for protein.'

She watched as Sean scribbled some notes. 'There's more. She's had a headache the last few days, vomited twice yesterday and she's been very tircd.'

Jacob frowned. 'Hasn't she seen a midwife at any point?'

Bonnie felt automatically defensive. 'She should have. She was last seen three weeks ago. The week after that, her midwife was sick, and last week she felt too unwell to attend. She didn't call in to speak to the midwife as she thought she just had a virus.'

Jacob started to swear under his breath. 'This is looking like HELLP syndrome. Do you mind if I come with you, Sean? We might need to do an emergency twin delivery.'

'Glad of the help,' Sean said quickly. He handed some blood forms to Bonnie. 'Can you get these done as an emergency?'

'No problem.' She took them as Sean and Jacob walked into the room to assess Eleanor. Five minutes later the ward clerk arrived with the notes and the phlebotomist answered her page. Bonnie flicked through the notes. Nothing untoward. All Eleanor's previous appointments had shown a healthy developing pregnancy.

The missed appointments were unfortunate. She just wished Eleanor had phoned her midwife when she'd started to feel unwell. Maybe her condition could have been picked up sooner. HELLP was serious. It could be life-threatening for both mother and babies.

Symptoms could be vague but it always started with pre-eclampsia. One of the crucial tests was the blood work and the quickest turnaround time from the lab would be just over an hour. Eleanor was already showing some of the classic signs.

Sean and Jacob came out of the room, both talking in low voices. The phlebotomist arrived, picked up the blood forms and went to collect the samples that would be needed.

'I think we should prepare and contact the anaesthetist anyway. Give her an ace-inhibitor to try and bring her blood pressure down and don't leave her alone.' Those last words were aimed at Bonnie. It was the first time his eyes had connected with hers.

There was something wrong—which was stupid, because she knew that already. But the look in Jacob's eyes? It was almost blank. As if there had never been anything between them, and there never would be.

Focus. She sucked in her breath. There was a patient to deal with. But as soon as Eleanor's condition was under control, Bonnie was definitely calling the letting agency.

She'd become too attached to him. *They'd* become too attached to him, too quickly. It was time to take stock. To take a breath.

She'd made a massive mistake with Robert. She'd married a man she didn't really love. When it came to men— her previous choice hadn't been great. Could she really trust her own judgement now?

Her heart was telling her one thing and her head another. It was all too much.

The phlebotomist appeared and waved the blood bottles at them. 'I'll take these direct to the lab and ask for the results to be phoned direct.'

Sean gave a nod. 'Thanks.' He turned to face Jacob. 'If I speak to the anaesthetist now are you free to assist in Theatre if required?'

There was silence for a few seconds. The quiet made Bonnie look up. Jacob always responded immediately. He never hesitated over clinical care.

But this time he did. This time he glanced at his watch. She could see him swallow as if a million things were flashing through his brain. 'I'll need to make a call to try to delay something else.'

Sean looked just as surprised as Bonnie. 'No problem. I can always find Isabel. She's covering the other theatre list today—but we can cancel the routine procedures for an emergency.'

That was right. The other theatre list. The one that Jacob had refused to cover today because he had somewhere else to be. Where exactly was that?

A whole wash of memories flooded over her. Robert. Continually making excuses about where he was going or where he had been. The way he could never look her in the eye when he'd been telling her those lies. Her stomach was in knots. She hated that Jacob was following the same pattern. He could never know how much those memories and associations hurt.

Jacob wasn't Robert. He would never be Robert. But he was definitely hiding something. It made her question herself. It made her question her judgement. Her choices had been wrong before. It felt as if she could be walking down the same path.

Where on earth was he going? And why was he being so evasive about it?

Jacob waved his hand at Sean. 'It will be fine. Give me five minutes to make the call. Let's just try and make sure that if we need to take Eleanor to Theatre there are no delays and we're ready to go as soon as we get the blood results.'

Sean nodded towards Bonnie. His initial surprise had died away and now he just looked relieved that he didn't have to go and call Isabel. What was the deal with those two?

'I'm going to stay close by. Give me a shout if you need anything.'

Bonnie went back to the room to help Karen. It only took a few minutes to administer the blood-pressure drugs and start some IV fluids. Karen continued to monitor the babies and Bonnie set the blood-pressure cuff for every ten minutes.

Eleanor kept her eyes closed, occasionally wincing and touching her right side. It was a clear sign that her liver was affected.

Jacob seemed impatient. He was pacing up and down the corridor, and phoned the lab twice to harass them for the blood results. She'd never seen him quite so on edge.

On one hand, she knew that he was putting the care of Eleanor and her babies first. On the other, it was obvious he was anxious to still keep his other plans.

The anaesthetist, Laura, appeared and did a quick assessment. While Eleanor's current condition was serious she had no significant history that would cause any Theatre delays.

Laura was already dressed in theatre scrubs and tucked her hair into her hat as the phone rang. Jacob snatched it up, listening carefully before putting it back down. 'Her blood tests confirm thrombocytopenia and liver dysfunction.' These, combined with her other symptoms, meant that Eleanor could be at risk of liver rupture, uncontrolled bleeding or cerebral oedema.

'Let's go, then,' said Laura. 'I'll meet you in Theatre once you've spoken to Eleanor.'

Things moved quickly. Eleanor's mother arrived with news that her husband was already on the helicopter and had left the oil rig. It would still be hours before he arrived.

Eleanor's condition was worsening. She was beginning to get drowsy, so once Jacob had explained what was happening and consented her they prepared her for Theatre in a matter of minutes and whisked her down the corridor.

Jacob and Sean disappeared to scrub and Bonnie hurried back to the labour ward.

It was three long hours before she heard anything else.

Sean walked up to the nursing station and pulled his theatre hat off his head. His mussed-up hair and tired eyes said everything. She looked over his shoulder. 'Where's Jacob?'

Sean shrugged. 'As soon as we had stabilised Eleanor and the babies and everyone was happy he disappeared.'

She bit her lip to stop her saying what she actually thought. 'What about Eleanor and her babies?'

Sean nodded. 'Two girls. Both in SCBU. Three pounds, four ounces and three pounds, two ounces. Not bad for twins. One had to have a little support breathing and the other was fine.'

'And Eleanor?'

He sighed. 'She started bleeding out almost straight away. Her blood pressure plummeted and she had six units of blood and then some platelets. We caught her just in time.'

'What's happening now?'

'She's stable. Mainly thanks to Jacob. She's been transferred to ICU. They need to keep a careful watch for organ failure.'

Bonnie sighed. 'Poor woman. I hope she's going to be okay. Will you let me know how she is?'

Sean raised his eyebrow. 'Won't Jacob tell you?'

Bonnie felt colour rush into her cheeks. 'What do you mean?'

Sean seemed completely unperturbed. He leaned on the desk towards her, a cheeky grin on his face. 'You two had a fight? For a few weeks the world of CRMU thought you'd turned Jacob into Prince Charming. But now he's back to his usual lovely self. I take it Prince Charming has turned into a frog?'

Sean was good-natured. He was only teasing but she felt distinctly uncomfortable. She wagged her finger at him. 'If I find out you've been gossiping about me, Sean, I'll ban you from our tea room. Don't think I don't know who goes in there and eats all the biscuits and sweets.'

Sean pulled back in mock horror. 'Ouch. Tough sanctions.' He waved his hand as he started down the corridor. 'Don't worry, Bonnie. All your secrets are safe with me.'

She blushed again as one of the other midwives came out of a patient's room and raised her eyebrows at the comment. She pulled her phone from her pocket. Enough was enough. It was time to make that call to the letting agency.

'Mummy, where are we going?' Freya was looking at the photo on the laptop screen.

Bonnie took a deep breath. 'We're going to stay somewhere else, honey. This was only ever temporary. Jacob let us stay for a few weeks until we could find somewhere for ourselves.'

'But I like it here. I like staying with Jacob.' Freya stuck her chin out and folded her arms across her chest.

I like staying with Jacob too.

She knelt down in front of Freya. 'I know that, honey. But we have to find a home of our own.' She tucked Freya's hair behind her ear and turned the computer screen around to show her the flat she'd just reserved. 'It will be fine. Honestly, it's near to the school and you'll still get to see all your friends.'

Freya gave a nod and stared at the cases. 'Will we have a Christmas tree like Jacob's?'

No. Something tugged at her heartstrings. She didn't want to leave. She *really* didn't want to leave.

Jacob was being secretive. He'd kissed her, but never made any promises. He'd never even asked her and Freya to stay for Christmas. He hadn't asked them to leave either…in fact, he'd made lots of excuses for them not to leave. But it wasn't the same.

A distant, secretive man was not what she needed. No matter how much he made her heart flip over. It made her question herself all the time. She needed to protect her heart and her daughter's. They'd got too attached. Freya's reaction now just made her even more determined.

Tears were bristling in her eyes. 'We'll get another Christmas tree and I promise it will be just as gorgeous as the one we decorated here.' *Bang goes my limited budget.*

It was fine. She would make sure it was fine. Anything to keep Freya settled after all the disruption she'd exposed her to. She already had the ridiculously expensive doll and all her accessories that Freya wanted for Christmas. Blowing what little savings she had left on another set of Christmas decorations was an easy sacrifice.

The key turned in the lock and she heard footsteps coming towards the sitting room. Jacob. He opened the door and his face dropped as soon as he saw what they were doing. The flat was clearly visible on the laptop screen in front of them.

'Bonnie? Freya? What's going on?'

Bonnie could feel her heart beating against her chest. She hadn't expected Jacob to come home—not when he'd been avoiding them. She'd planned to write him a note, thanking him for his hospitality, but saying they'd found somewhere to stay and she'd see him at work.

She put her arm around Freya's shoulders. 'Oh, Jacob, I didn't expect to see you. It's just—' she held out her hand '—I think we might have outstayed our welcome. I've found somewhere for us to stay.' She met his confused gaze. 'I think it's time for Freya and I to move on.'

His mouth was slightly agape. He looked shocked. He looked a bit hurt. And everything about this was confusing her.

This was definitely the right thing to do. This was *absolutely* the right thing to do.

'I'll miss you, Jacob.' Freya's little voice cut through the silence. 'Thank you for letting us stay.'

Jacob knelt down opposite her. 'I'll miss you too, Freya.' His voice sounded hoarse. 'You...and your mother.' He didn't look up. He didn't look at Bonnie at all.

This was it. This was his chance to say something. To tell Bonnie that his feelings were every bit as strong as hers.

That he wanted to kiss her again—just as he had the other night.

That he wanted to spend more time with her and Freya. That he wanted to give this relationship a chance. That this actually *was* a relationship.

That she wasn't completely crazy, and he was as crazy about her as she was about him.

She held her breath. Waiting. Waiting. For something. For anything.

But nothing came. Jacob still couldn't look her in the eye.

'Freya, go and get your coat and shoes. We need to go to the shops.' Freya disappeared without a word.

He lifted his head. 'Why are you leaving? Why are you leaving *now*?'

It was the way he said the word. She stepped forwards, everything erupting to the surface. 'We can't be here any more. Freya's getting too used to being around you.' She lifted her eyes. 'And so am I.'

She gave her head a shake. 'This was a bad idea. You helped us out, thank you. But I have no idea what's happening between us, Jacob.' She held out her hands. 'I have no idea what *this* is.' She took a deep breath. 'I've found somewhere for us to go. We'll be out of your hair.'

'You have? Where? Is it one of those ones that you showed me?' He sounded automatically defensive—as if he were going to tell them not to go.

She shook her head. 'No, it's another. It's small, but in the area of Freya's school. It will suit us for the next few months until we can find something else.' She licked her lips. This was horrible. This was awkward.

There was a huge hand currently inside her chest, squeezing her heart hard.

Jacob looked at her again. There was a flash of something behind his eyes, which disappeared almost instantly. He looked down again.

'What's going on, Jacob? I know something's been bothering you the last few days. But you haven't said anything. You've been avoiding me. I thought we could talk about things.' Her voice was edged with hopefulness that he might actually respond.

He shook his head. 'There's nothing.' His voice was flat.

His dismissal made her mad. 'Don't say that. Don't say it's nothing. I know it is. Tell me. Tell me what's going on.' She was shouting now and she could almost see all his barriers being built up all around him. She bit her lip in anger and tried one last time. 'I thought we could share things. I told you about my past—and you told me about yours. At least I thought you had.'

She glanced towards the door, worried that Freya would reappear.

He sucked in a deep breath. It made him seem taller, his chest wider and more imposing. 'Not everything can be shared. Not everything is your business.' His words were clipped.

'Then we have to go,' she said quietly. 'I can't be around you, Jacob. I can't watch my little girl forming a closer attachment to you day by day when I feel as if you can't be honest with me.' She picked up her green coat. 'I've been down this road before.' Her eyes swept down to the floor and she gave a little shake of her head. 'I thought that this time I could trust my judgement.' She lifted her head and met his gaze. 'I guess I was wrong.'

There was silence for a few seconds.

'I hope you'll be happy,' he said quietly.

Something inside her died. That was it. Nothing else.

She'd been wrong. She'd been wrong about her and Jacob. There was nothing between them. A wave of humiliation washed over her.

She'd never felt like such a fool—not even when she'd found Robert in bed with her friend. Everything about this was different. With Robert, there had been no emotional investment left. With Jacob?

This hurt. This hurt so much it felt as if it could kill her.

Freya appeared at the door and she took her hand. 'Goodbye, Jacob.' Her voice was trembling. She just hoped he didn't notice.

She held herself straight and lifted her head before she opened the door and walked outside.

It was definitely time to go.

CHAPTER ELEVEN

JACOB TUGGED AT the collar of his shirt. It had never seemed tight before, but today it was cutting into him.

He hadn't slept a wink last night. Probably because everything about yesterday felt wrong and his house was…empty.

He shuffled on the seat and glanced at his watch for the hundredth time. He wasn't good at being a patient. Probably because he wasn't exactly that—patient. He watched as the door to the consultant's office opened and he sat up anxiously. The woman sitting next to him rustled her newspaper nervously as she was called in. He sighed and leaned back again.

That woman looked exactly the way he did—sick with worry. It was so strange being on the other side of the fence. This was exactly why he'd gone into obstetrics. He wanted to help life into the world. He wanted people to have joy in their lives.

Oncology services? Never. He hated having to give any expectant mother bad news. Imagine having to do this almost every day? He couldn't stomach that.

Right now he couldn't think about all the cancer success stories.

His insides clenched once again as he took some deep

breaths. Worst-case scenarios. That was all that was running through his head right now. Stepping back from colleagues, stepping back from the job that he loved so he could undergo another set of treatment. Feeling sick to his stomach for days on end. Forgetting completely about any chance of a relationship with Bonnie and Freya. Living the rest of his life alone.

It wasn't what he wanted. *None* of this was what he wanted.

But the way he felt right now? There was no way he could put this on Bonnie and Freya.

What he wanted was a fiery redhead and her adorable daughter.

The words he'd wanted to say yesterday had stuck in his throat. *Don't go. Stay with me, please—even though I'm not sure I can offer you a future.* He couldn't put himself out there—not until he really knew what he was offering.

But one thing she'd said had affected him more than others. Freya was becoming too attached. He felt it too. And it seemed entirely natural. As if that was the way it should be. Because the little part of his heart he hadn't blocked off *wanted* to feel like that. But right now, his brain couldn't even let himself go there.

He was finding it hard enough to deal with himself without having to worry about other people's feelings. He couldn't even begin to imagine forming a relationship with Freya, only for her to have to be told down the line that her parent figure had died.

He knew exactly what that did to a kid. He could never wish that on another.

His house had been hideously empty last night. It was

odd; it had never felt that way before. When he'd lived alone he'd never noticed the silence.

But last night he had. Every noise had seemed to echo through the empty rooms. Taking out one cup for coffee, or one glass for wine, had seemed pathetic. Finding Freya's plastic cup in the sink had made his hands shake and for a second he'd thought he might break down.

The pain he'd felt last night was familiar.

Bonnie had left. His mother had left. Not in the same way, of course. But he felt every bit as raw now as he had all those years ago.

The pressure of the waiting game was almost breaking him.

The hands on his watch moved oh-so-slowly. Ten minutes felt like two hours. He just wanted to know. Even if the test results were bad at least he could start making plans.

He jumped as the door opened and the woman came back out, a stunned expression on her pale face. Did she get good news, or bad?

'Jacob Layton?'

He was on his feet in an instant.

'Come in, please.'

For a second his feet were stuck to the floor, but he was too determined to get this part over with to let anything hold him back. He took long strides into the room, not waiting to be offered a seat, his eyes scanning the notes upside down on the desk. Trying to see if they would reveal anything.

The oncology consultant closed the door and took his seat opposite Jacob. Desmond Carter had looked after Jacob throughout his treatment. As soon as he'd been diagnosed, Jacob had looked for the best. Someone who would understand his need to continue to work and be able to tailor his treatment to his needs.

Desmond should probably have retired years ago. His hair was grey, his face deeply lined. But it appeared he loved his job as much as Jacob loved his.

He gave Jacob a little nod of acknowledgement. Another thing Jacob liked about Desmond Carter—he was a straight talker. He didn't give false platitudes and he told it like it was.

He glanced down at the notes in front of him. 'Jacob, let's talk about these test results.'

Bonnie was on edge. She was nervous about having moved to the new tiny flat just before Christmas. Nervous about the impact on Freya. Nervous about how she felt now she was out from under Jacob's roof.

It's temporary. She kept repeating the words in her head—hoping she might start to believe them.

She'd had to do it. Had to. She couldn't go on like this. Her insides had been so screwed up last night, praying, just praying Jacob might say something to her about how he felt. When it hadn't happened she'd spent the rest of the night crying into her pillow. Pathetic.

This was about her. This wasn't really about Jacob.

She was scared. Scared of putting herself out there and getting into a relationship with another man. She'd vowed to herself that if she ever got involved again, she would be absolutely sure. There wouldn't be a hint of doubt in her head.

But if Jacob couldn't tell her how he felt about her and Freya…then she was right. She was right to move out and give herself some headspace. Some time to make sure she could trust her judgement when it came to men.

The labour suite was busy today. All the staff kept joking about a power cut in Cambridge nine months before. And it certainly felt like that—she'd been catching babies all day.

But she hadn't caught sight of Jacob all day. It was probably just as well. He was bound to be avoiding her again. The further she pushed Jacob Layton from her mind, the better.

She finished stripping a bed in one of the rooms and walked along the corridor to the sluice. It was all hands on deck today; they even had a few midwives from some of the other areas helping out.

As she walked past the treatment room she glimpsed Isabel in a conversation with Hope.

Both had always been warm and friendly towards her—even inviting her to join them for dinner—and Jacob had mentioned that he was friends with both women. It struck her as a little strange. He seemed to hold them both in high regard, but she hadn't really seen him talking with either one.

'What's going on with Jacob?' Bonnie's footsteps stilled as Isabel's Australian accent floated out towards her.

They were drawing up a controlled drug for a pregnant woman in labour.

'How would I know?' answered Hope. 'I can barely get him to talk to me these days. It's a shame, but for a while we started to see the old Jacob again.'

Bonnie walked into the sluice and pushed the laundry into one of the baskets. She wasn't trying to overhear, but the two rooms were right next to each other with only a thin corridor leading to the sister's office separating them. She could still hear every word. She walked over to the sink to wash her hands.

'Do you think it's the cancer again?'

She froze. *What?*

Hope sounded serious. 'Do you think it's back? Oh, no. Don't say that. Not after everything he's been through.'

'Wouldn't he be due to get reassessed again? Some tests to see if the treatment's worked?'

The water was trickling in front of her but she hadn't moved.

Jacob. Jacob had cancer. *Her* Jacob had cancer and hadn't told her.

No. He couldn't possibly have. This couldn't be right. She held out her hands automatically, going through the motions of washing and drying them.

He hadn't lost his hair. It was short. But not missing. She hadn't noticed any marks on his skin for IV chemotherapy. He hadn't been sick around her. He didn't look sickly.

Really? Jacob had cancer? She finished drying her hands.

She couldn't help it. Her legs took her straight to the door of the treatment room.

'Jacob has cancer?' Her voice cracked. She could barely get the words out; her eyes were already filling with tears.

Hope and Isabel's heads shot around—a look of horror on both of their faces. They exchanged shocked glances.

Isabel took a step forward. 'Bonnie, I'm sorry. We didn't see you there.' She looked panicked. 'We should never have said anything.'

Her head was spinning. This almost felt as if it were happening to someone else.

Under any other circumstances she might think they were gossiping. But these women were Jacob's friends. They'd known him longer than she had and it was likely he'd taken them into his confidence.

'But you said it because you care—because Jacob is your friend.' Her heart was thudding against her chest.

Hope stepped forward too. She shook her head. 'Please understand, this happened long before you got here. We were both sworn to secrecy. No one else knows. Jacob didn't want anyone to know he had non-Hodgkin's lymphoma, or that he was undergoing treatment.'

Bonnie felt her blood run cold. Non-Hodgkin's lymphoma. The same type of cancer that his mother had died from. Oh, no. Poor Jacob.

She could be sick, right now, all over the treatment-room floor.

Hope touched her arm. 'Are you okay? You look terrible, Bonnie. I'm so sorry. I knew something was going on between you and Jacob. I just didn't know what. I guess I thought he might tell you.'

She started to shake, but whether it was from shock or disbelief she just didn't know. She took a long, slow breath.

Pieces in her brain started to slot into place. Now she knew why he'd been evasive. Now she knew exactly why he'd been acting the way he had. Everything made sense to her.

But he hadn't told her. And that hurt. It hurt so much she wanted to grab him and shake him.

Isabel stepped over next to them both. 'Bonnie,' she said carefully, 'I can see you're upset. I have no idea what's going on with you two—but I want you to know. You're good for Jacob. Up until a few days ago he was the happiest I've ever seen him. If you can help him, then please do.' She glanced at Hope. 'He's our friend. Above everything, we want him to be happy and well. Things that we've got no control over.'

She squeezed Bonnie's arm. 'I think you may be an influencing factor over one of those things.'

The tears welled in Bonnie's eyes. 'But he didn't tell me. He told me some things, but he never mentioned this at all.'

A worried glance shot between Hope and Isabel and Bonnie took another deep breath, trying to calm her frantic brain. 'But I think I know why.'

She turned on her heel and walked out of the door. The labour suite might be busy, but she wasn't looking after a patient right now and there were more than enough staff on shift.

Jacob had to be her priority.

Her footsteps halted a little on the way down the corridor. She'd spent the last two days fretting over herself. Thinking only about herself and Freya. She hadn't actually stopped to think that something might be wrong with Jacob. She'd challenged him. She'd asked him to tell her what was wrong. But not in a loving, compassionate way. She'd asked him in an angry, recriminatory kind of way. No wonder he hadn't told her.

She'd been too busy worrying about making a mistake again—focusing on the past instead of the future. How wrong she'd been. News like this put everything into perspective and made her realise exactly how precious life was.

She stalked past the midwives' station and opened the door of his office. He hadn't been around all day, but he was here now, sitting behind his desk.

Was he paler than normal? Were those dark circles under his eyes?

He jumped to his feet as soon as he saw her.

Now she could see him standing in front of her she could feel the adrenaline course through her. He could have told her. He could have told her the truth, couldn't he? Why hadn't he told her?

She'd been thinking a whole host of other things—she'd thought the worst of him. When she'd had no right to. Jacob had been nothing but kind and supportive to her and Freya. And she'd pushed him away with her own insecurities. But instead of reaching out to her, he'd pushed her away too. What were the reasons for that?

This man had wound his way around her heart. She'd seen another side to him, a warm and loving side. A side that showed her, even if he didn't know it, he was ready to move on with his life.

He'd lit something inside her that she hadn't felt in years.

'Bonnie? Is there an emergency? Is something wrong with a patient?'

He was ready to run to the attention of any patient that needed him. But what about her?

She closed the door quietly behind her and folded her arms across her chest. She would not cry. *She would not cry.*

But her heart was squeezing in her chest. Jacob had cancer. Jacob had the same cancer that he'd watched his mother die from. She already knew the damage that had inflicted on him as a child, and in turn as an adult. But she'd only known half the story.

What had the test results shown?

'Nothing's wrong with a patient, Jacob.'

Confusion flooded his face. 'Then, what is it?'

'Something's wrong with me.' She pointed her finger. 'Something's wrong with you.' Frustration was building in her chest. 'Why didn't you tell me you had non-Hodgkin's? Why didn't you tell me you had the same type of cancer as your mother?'

This not-crying thing wasn't going to work. The tears were threatening to fall any second.

His mouth opened but no words came out. He sagged down into his chair as if she'd just knocked the wind from his sails. 'Who told you?'

She pulled out the chair opposite and sat down. 'It doesn't matter who told me, Jacob. What matters is why *you* didn't?'

He still couldn't speak. He just shook his head for a few seconds, then put up his hands. 'How could I tell you, Bonnie? We've just met. I never expected this. I never expected to meet someone who would just—'

'Just what?'

His eyes met hers. There were no barriers in place. No shields to hide behind. 'Who would make me want to love again—to be part of a family again.'

She couldn't speak. A wave of emotion welled up inside her. This time a tear did escape, sliding down her cheek.

'I'm so sorry. I'm sorry I didn't stop to think what was wrong.' She shook her head. 'I just thought I was making a mistake again, that I didn't really know you that well.' She lifted her head and looked into his eyes. 'I felt as if I couldn't trust my judgement,' was all she could say. 'When all the time I knew what kind of man you were. I just didn't realise. I didn't think you might actually be sick.'

He stood up, walking around the desk and crouching down in front of her. He reached up and touched her hand, enveloping it with his. 'I had to wait, Bonnie. I had to know for sure. I couldn't put you and Freya through what I experienced as a kid. We'd only just met. I couldn't possibly expect you to sign up for that.'

She reached over and touched his cheeks. 'But you can, Jacob. I'm here for you. We're here for you. I don't care that you're sick. All I care about is that we're together.'

He reached up and brushed the tear from her cheek, taking one of her hands again. 'But why would I put someone that I love through that?' His face was serious. 'Two people that I love?'

The heat from his hand was rushing around her body. A whole host of tingles shooting straight towards her heart. 'You do?'

She couldn't help but smile. She hadn't been wrong. She hadn't imagined the connection between them. On one hand it was pure relief, on the other, she still couldn't understand why he wouldn't share with her.

'I do,' he said sincerely. 'I really do.'

She was fixed on his intense green eyes. 'Then why didn't you tell me, Jacob? You told me about your mum—why didn't you tell me about you?'

He ran one hand through his hair, giving his head a shake again. 'How could I tell you that, Bonnie? How can I declare love one minute, then tell you I've got a potential death sentence the next? What kind of man would do that to you? What kind of a man would do that to Freya?'

She held her breath. She understood. She understood exactly what he was saying but it still wasn't what she wanted to hear.

'So why couldn't we have that discussion, Jacob? I thought you didn't care about us at all. Why do you think I arranged to move out? Did you really think I wanted to?' She reached over and touched his jawline, feeling his smooth skin under her fingertips. 'Did you really think I would want to walk away if things were going to be tough? Because I wouldn't, Jacob. Not in a heartbeat. I love you. I don't care if it gets tough. I want to be the person by your side, holding your hand.'

His voice was quiet. 'But I don't want that for Freya. I don't want that for you. I watched my mother waste away before my eyes, the life just drained out of her. In the end, it wasn't a life at all. I could never do that to Freya. You've been through enough already.' He paused for a second then met her gaze again as he pulled his hand away from hers. 'I still can't.'

Bonnie leaned forwards; her face was inches from his. He could see fire spark behind her bright blue eyes. 'You don't get to make that choice any more, Jacob.' She pushed her hand up to her heart. '*I* do.'

He opened his mouth to speak again but she held up her hand. 'You've told me that you love me. You told me that you love Freya too. That's enough, Jacob. That's enough for me. I left because I doubted myself. I doubted my judgement. My past experience has made me untrusting, and I'm sorry for that.'

He pulled back. 'I can't do this. I can't let you do this. My mother had this cancer. I've had this cancer. I've got to assume that it's somehow in my genes. I can't make you any guarantees. I can't offer you what you want, Bonnie. Not when there's such a high risk.'

She stood up from the chair and faced him. 'What is it that I want?'

He frowned. 'Children. You'll want more children. This has to be in my genes. I could never, ever live with myself if I passed this disease on to our children.'

Bonnie looked furious. 'Have you asked me that? Have we had that conversation? What about what I think?'

He shook his head again. 'Look at you, Bonnie. You thrive on being a mother. You *love* being a mother—and you're fantastic at it. You were born to be a mother. I know that you want a whole house full of children. Don't pretend otherwise.' He pointed to his chest. 'And I can't give you that. I just can't.'

She blinked and he could see more unshed tears behind her eyes. 'I want you, Jacob. You and Freya. That's what I want. That's who I want my family to be. Can't we just work on that? Can't we just work on making a life together with what we have between us?' She stepped forwards, reaching up and cupping his cheek in her hand. 'Tell me about your test results. Tell me what happened. Good news or bad, I'm here for you. We're here for you. Just trust me enough to tell me.'

It was the first thing he'd noticed about her. Those bright blue eyes. And they were fixed on him with such an intensity right now that it felt as if a fist had closed around his heart and squeezed tight. He'd never felt like this. He'd never loved someone as he loved Bonnie. He'd never wanted to put himself on the line before. But Bonnie was everything. She didn't know. She didn't know he'd had good results. She didn't care. She still wanted to be with him.

For the first time he stopped to think straight. To let his heart rule his head. Every rational part of his brain had told him to back away. Every part of him that loved her didn't want her to be hurt.

But, for the first time, he could see himself building a life with Bonnie and Freya. A life that wasn't overshadowed with the thought of cancer recurring. A life that might actually be filled with love and hope.

And from the determined look in Bonnie's eyes it was exactly what she wanted.

His hand covered hers. 'My results were good, Bonnie. The non-Hodgkin's is in remission—for now. I'll need to keep having checks every six months for the next five years. There's always a chance it could recur.' As he said the words out loud he felt relief flood through him. He hadn't let that happen yet. He hadn't stopped to take a breath. The big black cloud that had been hanging over him for the last fourteen months had finally gone.

She didn't hesitate. She flung her arms around his neck. 'Oh, Jacob. That's fantastic.'

Her body was pressed against his. The warm angles familiar. The feeling of warmth, the feeling of love, the feeling of compassion were all here. All his for the taking. Could he really walk away from Bonnie now? When she'd told him no matter what his results she wanted to be by his side?

He stopped and pulled back, running his hand through her auburn hair. 'It is, isn't it?'

He was feeling lighter. And it wasn't just the diagnosis. It was the feeling of sharing. The feeling of having someone else invested in him. Of not having to face the future alone.

Bonnie's grin reached from ear to ear. 'It's better than fantastic.' She jumped up on him, her hands already around his neck, her legs now around his waist. The force sent him backwards against the wall and he started to laugh. Really laugh. Laugh as he hadn't in the last few years.

'Get rid of me now, Dr Layton,' she joked, her eyes gleaming.

This. This was what he wanted. This was what he'd wanted from the moment he'd seen her. Was he brave enough to reach out and grab it—just the way Bonnie had?

He was still smiling but he put on his most serious voice. 'Sister Reid, you seem to have put me in a compromising position.'

She tilted her head to one side. 'I have, haven't I? So, what are you going to do about it?' There was a challenge in her voice. 'I've already told you. Your choices are limited.' She uncoiled one hand from his neck and stroked her finger down his cheek. 'I think it's my job, and Freya's, to make sure that this year you have the happiest Christmas ever—*we* have the happiest Christmas ever.' The seriousness left her voice. 'So, what are you going to do, then?'

'Oh, that's easy,' he said as he adjusted her in his arms. 'I'm going to kiss you.'

And he did. Over and over again.

EPILOGUE

One year later

'ARE YOU READY, MUMMY?' Freya was bouncing up and down in her calf-length emerald-green bridesmaid dress.

Bonnie picked up her Christmas-themed bouquet and smiled. 'Oh, I've never been more ready. Let's go, gorgeous.'

They held hands and walked out of the hotel room to the top of the stairs. Jacob was standing at the bottom, waiting for them. In her honour, he'd dressed in a kilt. And she'd never seen a more handsome honorary Scotsman.

Her steps had never been surer as she picked up the skirts of her wedding dress and walked down the stairs to meet the man who made her complete.

Her last wedding hadn't felt anything like this. It had been beautiful, but she hadn't felt love in her heart and soul the way she did today. Jacob hadn't taken his eyes off her on her whole way down the stairs.

Her friends from the hospital applauded as she reached the bottom and she let out a nervous laugh. Jacob leaned over to kiss her. 'You look gorgeous,' he whispered.

'I don't think you're supposed to do that until after the ceremony,' she murmured back.

He smiled. 'Well, don't tell anyone. But I've got a really take-charge wife-to-be. She's taught me just to seize the moment.'

And she had. They'd spent the last year growing together as a family. Taking steps that she'd never have even considered a few years ago.

The celebrant gave them a nod towards the room where the wedding was to take place. The whole hotel was decorated for Christmas. A large Christmas tree was next to them at the bottom of the stairs and dark green and red garlands decorated the stairs. Twinkling lights glistened all around them. It really was the perfect setting.

'I'm not finished yet.' Jacob smiled.

'What do you mean?' she asked. This wasn't in the plans. But her tiny wave of panic disappeared in an instant. Whatever it was that Jacob wanted to do—she was sure she would love it.

'Before we start,' he said to their surrounding guests, 'I'd like to let you into a little secret.' He glanced at her. 'Bonnie and I have been keeping secrets from you—but even my future wife doesn't know this one.'

Her stomach flip-flopped. What was he talking about?

He pulled an envelope from inside his highland dress jacket. 'This morning, we received the news that we've been waiting for.' He gave her a smile that made her toes tingle. 'I haven't even had a chance to tell Bonnie yet, because I've been keeping with the wedding tradition of not seeing the bride before the ceremony.'

He held up the envelope. 'We got news this morning that Bonnie and I have been approved as adoptive parents.'

He bent down and picked up Freya. 'Do you know that little brother or sister we've been talking about?'

She nodded solemnly. 'Well, some time next year you'll get to be a big sister.'

'I will?'

'We will?' Bonnie could hardly contain her excitement. They'd been waiting for the final verdict. And this just made the whole day even more perfect.

A number of waiters appeared with trays of champagne that were quickly dispersed amongst the guests. Jacob handed one to Bonnie. He held his aloft. 'So, we've not even made it to the altar yet. But I guess I decided to seize the moment.' She could see the glint in his eyes as he spoke.

'Can I ask you all to raise your glasses? To the best Christmas ever and to families.'

Bonnie clinked her glass with his and took a sip, then wrapped her arms around him and Freya. 'You're going to make me cry.' She laughed. 'And we're not even married yet.' She gave her head a little shake. 'This couldn't be more perfect.'

His green eyes fixed on hers. 'Oh, yes, it could,' he said as he bent to kiss her. 'Happy Christmas, Mrs Layton.'

* * * * *

HER CHRISTMAS BABY BUMP

BY
ROBIN GIANNA

Published in Great Britain 2015
by Mills & Boon, an imprint of Harlequin (UK) Limited,
Eton House, 18-24 Paradise Road, Richmond, Surrey, TW9 1SR

© 2015 Harlequin Books S.A.

Special thanks and acknowledgement are given to Robin Gianna
for her contribution to the Midwives On-Call at Christmas series.

ISBN: 978-0-263-24741-1

Dear Reader,

This book is the first I've written as part of a continuity, and it was fun and challenging. I really enjoyed the way the editors came up with story ideas and connected the different books. It would have been hard to choose which hunky hero I wanted to write about, so I'm thrilled I was given sexy Aaron Cartwright to fall in love with in my story.

The other authors in the series set up an online chat so we could discuss the storylines and ask questions of each other. A thank-you shout-out to Louisa George, Scarlet Wilson and Tina Beckett for their help—particularly Scarlet who, as the only author in our group currently living in the UK, was always happy to answer the numerous questions I had about medicine and midwives in England as compared to the US…and there were plenty of surprising differences.

Aaron and Hope share an attraction they've felt just from noticing one another in the hospital corridors even before they officially meet. When they finally do, it's *zing* with a capital Z! But both have baggage from their pasts that make a relationship impossible. Not to mention Hope's secret plans to have a baby on her own through IVF very soon—a decision that rips open Aaron's old wounds when he finds out. But a fling isn't a relationship, right? Or so they think…! :)

I hope you enjoy Hope and Aaron's story, and the way they both come to see that the things they've always believed about themselves aren't necessarily true. Learning this isn't easy, and it takes falling in love with one another to see it.

I'd love to know what you think of this story! You can email me at Robin@RobinGianna.com, find me on my website, RobinGianna.com, or look me up on Facebook.

I look forward to hearing from you!

Robin xoxo

This one is for you, Flora Torralba!

Thanks so much for your steady willingness to help
in any way, for tolerating my nuttiness,
and for keeping me sane.

I don't know what I'd do without you—
you're the best! xoxo

After completing a degree in journalism, working
in the advertising industry, then becoming a stay-at-
home mum, **Robin Gianna** had what she calls her
'mid-life awakening'. She decided she wanted to write
the romance novels she'd loved since her teens, and
embarked on that quest by joining RWA, Central Ohio
Fiction Writers, and working hard at learning the craft.
She loves sharing the journey with her characters,
helping them through obstacles and problems to find
their own happily-ever-afters. When not writing, Robin
likes to create in her kitchen, dig in the dirt, and enjoy
life with her tolerant husband, three great kids, drooling
bulldog and grouchy Siamese cat. To learn more about
her work visit her website: RobinGianna.com.

Books by Robin Gianna

Mills & Boon Medical Romance

Changed by His Son's Smile
The Last Temptation of Dr Dalton
Flirting with Dr Off-Limits
It Happened in Paris…
Her Greek Doctor's Proposal

Visit the Author Profile page at
millsandboon.co.uk for more titles.

CHAPTER ONE

"HELLO, KATE? IT'S just me." Hope Sanders gently knocked on the door and stepped inside her patient's room. "Let's check and see how it's going, shall we?"

Kate kept sucking on her ice cube and just stared, apparently so exhausted she couldn't conjure up any kind of response. Hope gave her a positive smile, sending up a silent prayer that, this time, the poor woman would finally be ready to deliver. After thirty-six hours of labor, any soon-to-be mother was beyond ready, mentally and emotionally, but sometimes her body and her baby just wouldn't cooperate the way everyone wished they would.

"Are you feeling all right?" Hope asked as she washed her hands and snapped on green examination gloves. "Contractions any worse or more frequent?"

"I'm not sure. I just want the baby out. Why can't you get it out?" Kate asked in a tearful voice.

"I know. It's been a long time, hasn't it?" Hope gave Kate's huge belly a gentle pat. "And you've been so tough throughout all these hours. But you're making good progress, so the doctor and I are pretty positive we can avoid a C-section. Maybe you're there now, so let's see."

"I'm sorry," Kate said, sniffing back her tears as Hope began an internal exam. "I shouldn't snap at you like that.

Why on earth did you want to become a midwife and have to deal with cranky women like me?"

"First, you're not cranky, believe me. You've been very brave and stoic all this time." And the truth of that made Hope smile as she thought of the many mums who'd been so far past cranky during labor that there wasn't a word for it. "I enjoy helping mums through the difficulty of labor and delivery, and on to the joy of getting to hold their newborns for the first time. There's nothing as beautiful as a baby, is there? That's exactly why I became a midwife."

As she said the words the truth of that statement, and the emotion that came with it, closed her throat. Was she really, hopefully, about to have a baby of her very own? What she'd dreamed of when she'd first studied midwifery? When she'd thought she had all the time in the world to establish her career before having children, never imagining she'd still be alone at thirty-four?

"Well, you've been great, Hope, helping make all these hours more bearable," Kate's husband said. "We really appreciate it."

"Thank you. That means a lot to me." Hope's findings from the internal exam sent a huge sigh of relief from her lungs. She gave Kate a big smile she didn't have to force this time. "Guess what? Great news! You're there, Kate! Fully dilated at ten centimeters. Baby has decided she's ready to come into the world."

Kate kept licking her ice cube, almost as if she hadn't heard Hope, but her husband practically leaped out of his chair and came to stand by the bed. The poor man had dark circles all around his eyes and was about as disheveled as a person could look, but his beaming smile banished his obvious fatigue.

"You mean the baby's coming? It's time?"

"It's time. I'm putting a heart-rate monitor around your belly, Kate, so we can see how baby is doing during delivery," Hope said as she strapped it on, praying this final stage went a lot more smoothly and quickly than the previous hours. "We need to get pushing. Can you give me a push next time you feel a contraction? I know you aren't feeling them as strongly because of your epidural, but tell me when you do."

"I... I'm having one," she said, sitting up straighter and looking alert now.

"Then give me a push. That's it. Well done. Again." Hope kept giving her gentle encouragement and checking her progress, pleased the fetal monitor showed the baby's heart rate was normal. Maybe after the long ordeal, this delivery really would be quick and easy. "Wonderful! Nice job."

Kate moaned and pushed as her husband clutched her hand. "Breathe now, love. Breathe."

"Yes, Kate," Hope said. "Take a breath between contractions. Puff, puff, puff. Then during a push, tuck your chin down, hold your breath and give it all you've got."

Kate worked hard, and Hope kept her tone soothing and encouraging, knowing if she exuded a relaxed composure it helped the mother in labor stay composed, too. After only a few more contractions, the top of baby's head was suddenly there, visible, and Hope sent mum another huge grin. "She's crowning! Almost here, Kate. Give me a push. You're doing a great job. Okay, I've got her head. One more push now. One more. Yes! You did it!" She wrapped her hands around the baby's shoulders and helped her slide out into her new world.

Hope's heart leaped into her throat as she held the

slippery infant. No matter how many times she did this, the wonder of it, the miracle, hit her every single time, filling her chest with elation.

"Here she is, Mum! Perfect and beautiful. Congratulations." She laid the infant on Kate's chest, letting them marvel over their new little one for just a moment. "You were wonderful, even after being so tired. I'm so proud of you!"

Kate held her baby close, murmuring and cooing, and Hope hated to disturb the sweet moment. "I'm sorry, but I need to take her, as we don't want her to get chilled. We'll get her cleaned up and warm, then I promise I'll have her back to you in a jiffy."

As she lifted the baby from her mother's chest and placed her on the cloth her assistant held, Hope saw tears sliding down the new father's cheeks as he leaned down to kiss his wife.

A pang of something sharp stabbed at Hope's heart. Regret, maybe, that she'd never experience that? That her own baby, if she was blessed with one soon, wouldn't have a daddy who wept at its birth and was there as he or she grew up? And all because of Hope's physical and emotional inadequacies?

She sucked in a calming breath and attended to Kate as the nurse assistant placed the baby in the bassinet beneath the heat lamp. She rubbed her all over until she was clean and rosy, slid a little knit cap onto her tiny head, then swaddled her in blankets. Hope lifted the infant into her arms, pausing for a moment before taking her to her daddy.

Serious blue-gray eyes stared up at her with a frown furrowing her tiny brows, as though she was asking Hope where in the world she was and why she was there. As

Hope looked at the tiny, vulnerable new life she pictured her very own baby in her arms. The thought sent a thrill surging through her veins, warring with an icy fear that seemed to freeze her blood at the very same time.

She was close, so close, to that dream if she went through with her plans. But would her own child look to her with those same questions in its eyes? Who am I, and why am I here? Would she be able to answer, *You're here because I love you*? Would she be the kind of mother she wanted to be?

She tore her gaze from the precious one staring accusingly at her and took the baby to her parents, placing her gently into her father's arms.

"Your new daughter. Congratulations again."

Both stared at their newborn in awe as Hope swiped her cold hands down her scrubs. Terrifying doubt choked her. Would making a baby of her own be the right decision, or would it be a horrible mistake?

She fiercely shook off the sudden and disturbing doubts. She'd wanted a baby forever. Adored babies. Adored children, too. She was running out of time for that dream to come true, and despite her history, despite what her old boyfriend had said, there was no reason on earth to fear that she might not be capable of being the loving mother she so wanted to be.

Prayed she could be. Would be.

"She's so beautiful." Kate's husband looked at his wife. "She looks like you, I think."

Kate laughed. "Am I that pink and puffy right now? Probably, yes." She reached to stroke the baby's cheek, her voice becoming a whisper. "You were an awful lot of effort, but you were worth it, sweetest one."

She and her husband shared a long, intimate smile,

and Hope felt that irritating pang jab her again. What was wrong with her? Why the sudden sadness over not having a man in her life, when she clearly had never wanted one? Why the ridiculous doubt when she'd been happy and confident before?

"Have you picked out a name for her?" Hope asked, busying herself with the final things that needed to be done for Kate post-delivery. Distracting herself with small talk was sure to banish these peculiar and unwelcome feelings swirling around her belly.

"Nine months didn't seem like long enough to decide," Kate said with a grin. "But we finally whittled it down to either Emily or Rachel."

"I'm fond of the more traditional names, and those are both very pretty."

"Here, love, you hold her for a bit." Her husband placed the baby in Kate's arms and stared at the infant with his brows creased. "She's...she looks like a—"

"Rachel," they both said simultaneously, then laughed.

"Perfect," Hope said, her throat absurdly clogging up at this scene that could have come straight from a chick flick. Lord, you'd think she hadn't delivered hundreds of babies in her career. Or that she'd already received the upcoming hormone injections, with these kinds of silly emotions pinging all over the place.

Probably should buy some stock in a handkerchief company right now. If this kept up, for the next nine months she'd be sobbing all over her patients with every healthy delivery.

"You're all set now, Kate." She stripped off her gloves and managed to smile at the giddy new parents. "I'll be back in a bit to see how you're doing."

Hope headed down the hospital corridor to write up

her notes on Kate and baby Rachel and glanced at her watch, glad to see her shift was almost over. And for once her Friday night would be filled with something more than just a casual dinner with friends.

Tonight was the big gala fund-raiser organized by one of the hunkiest doctors at Cambridge Royal Hospital. Not only was the man absurdly good-looking, Aaron Cartwright apparently cared about children, too, creating the foundation that promoted adoption in and around Cambridge. Plus, he'd been nice enough to invite several midwives and obstetricians from the hospital to share a few adoption stories their patients had experienced, knowing some financial donors might be interested in hearing them.

Hope had long admired Aaron Cartwright from afar, starting the very first day she'd spotted him in the hospital three years ago, stopping mid-step to do a double take at the man. He might be a man with a bit of a playboy reputation, but who cared? A woman didn't have to be in the market for a relationship to enjoy looking at a heartthrob.

Tonight she'd finally get to meet the dreamy doc, who half the women in the hospital swooned over. While enjoying champagne and yummy food and dancing, before the start of her new life.

The bounce began to come back to her step as she walked into her office. What could possibly be a more perfect Friday-night distraction to get her mind back on the right track?

"You're going to be late if you don't finish up soon."

Aaron Cartwright looked up from the pamphlets he'd been grabbing from a drawer outside an exam room to see Sue Calloway frowning at him. Her lips were pursed and her hands held several clothes hangers filled with his tux, shirt, bow tie and cummerbund. "Isn't organizing my wardrobe outside an office manager's job description?"

"Nothing's outside my job description and you know it," she said. "You've been with your patients almost an hour already, and everyone's going to be wondering where you are."

"No one will be wondering about me. They'll all be happily eating and drinking and won't even notice when I show up." He gently tapped the top of her head with the brochures. "Don't worry, though, we're almost done. This couple is nervous, and need a little more TLC before they're ready to go home. I'm giving them loads of stuff to read to keep them occupied, even though I already gave them plenty."

"When is their IVF procedure scheduled?"

"This Tuesday. And now I'm going back in there, unless you want to give me more grief and make me even later."

"Well, hurry, then," she said in a testy voice, her twinkling eyes belying her tone. "I'd give you a little shove to get you going if I could, except my arms aren't free. Don't keep me standing here holding your finery forever."

He chuckled, shaking his head as he headed back into the room. Not too many other doctors were lucky enough to have someone like Sue to run the office—and his schedule—like a drill sergeant.

The anxious expressions on the couple sitting in the consulting room showed Aaron he hadn't alleviated their worries. But with the latest advances in fertility techniques and a little luck, the procedure he'd proposed could work for them.

He sat and put on his most reassuring smile, handing

them the additional brochures on in vitro fertilization and the newest technique he was recommending. "I understand this has been a stressful and difficult struggle for both of you, but now that we know exactly what's going on there's a better than good chance you'll be able to conceive."

"How many times have you done this ICSI procedure, Dr. Cartwright?" John Walters asked.

"More times than I can count. And the success rate of ICSI is a solid ninety percent. In fact, my success rate has been even higher than that, if I can toot my own horn a little." He smiled again. "As I told you before, I'm a big believer in this procedure. Under circumstances like yours, it's much better than the shotgun approach of traditional IVF."

John's lips were pressed into a grim line, and Aaron reached to squeeze his shoulder. Infertility issues were hard on everyone, but many men had a more difficult time dealing with it when it was due to their physical issues, as opposed to their wives'. As though it made someone less of a man, which of course it didn't. There were all too many men who made babies only to abandon them, and plenty of others who were donors but in no way could be considered fathers. Whose children would never know where they came from.

"I know you said you will only implant two eggs, but I still think we should implant more than that," Angela said, clutching her husband's hand. "I mean, it gives us a better chance of having one take, right? And if we ended up having multiple babies, we'd be more than happy about that."

"You think now that you would, but multiples are harder on the mother's body. More likely to lead to preterm birth with complications resulting from that, as well as serious birth defects. Not to mention that caring for triplets or quads can be harder than anyone imagines."

Harder than his own biological mother ever imagined. Even harder on her children, ending with tough consequences for all of them.

"I know, but still. I feel like this could be our last chance. So why not, when we're ready to accept whatever happens?"

The dormant emotion that occasionally surged to the surface and threatened his cool at times like this always took him by surprise. It had all happened so long ago, so why? Maybe he was like a sapling that had seeded next to barbed wire. He'd still managed to grow strong, absorbing it inside until it was invisible, but the sharp pain could still deeply stab when he least expected it.

He drew a long breath, battling to keep his voice calm. Firm and authoritative without verging on dictatorial. But he believed it was an important part of his job, a critical part, to help patients make responsible decisions, no matter how desperate they were for a baby.

"I appreciate that this has been a long and difficult process for both of you, Angela. And as I said before, if you want to work with another specialist who feels differently than I do on this subject, I will completely understand if you prefer to do that. You wouldn't have to start all over again—there are several doctors in this hospital I can refer you to, giving them your history and information on the meds you've been taking. I would guess someone else would be available to do the ICSI procedure soon."

"No," Angela said, shaking her head. "Everyone has told us you're the best at the ICSI procedure, Dr. Cartwright. I'm just… I'm worried that with only two eggs, none will take."

"And I'm not going to deny that that's possible, but we can try again, remember? One healthy, full-term baby, two at the most, is the goal."

"Yes. A healthy baby is all we want." She gave her husband a tremulous smile. "How long is nine months from next week? I better make sure everything's ready."

"Early August. A good birthday month, since it's yours, too." The return smile he gave her was strained. "Though everything's been ready for a long time, hasn't it?"

"A long time."

Her voice quavered, and tears filled her eyes. Aaron handed her a tissue he pulled from the box he always kept next to him. The pain and depression, grief and failure that couples struggling with fertility problems felt was often profound. He'd do the best he could to help these two people have the baby they longed for.

And pray they'd be mentally and emotionally prepared for that baby when it came.

He resolutely shoved down the old, faded memories that for some damn reason insisted on resurfacing today and refocused on his patients. He was pretty confident that the ICSI procedure would work for them. That he wouldn't need to nudge them to think about adoption, the way he did with couples unable to conceive even after medical science had tried everything.

Adoption. The word reminded him that Sue was waiting with his tux, and that, even though he was sure nobody would be worrying about his late arrival, he did want to speak earlier at the adoption fund-raiser he'd organized, rather than later. People loved seeing his slide

presentation that showed foster kids becoming a permanent part of happy families, and were even more generous
with their donations to plump the foundation's coffers.

Aaron resisted the urge to glance at his watch. As he'd
told Sue, he'd never cut short a meeting with any patient
for any reason. Every one of them deserved to be able to
ask as many questions as they needed to feel comfortable
prior to any procedure. Questions he always answered
honestly, even it if was an opinion patients weren't always ready to hear.

"Thanks so much, Dr. Cartwright." John stood and
shook Aaron's hand, he and his wife now smiling real
smiles. "We'll see you next week for the big day."

"Which will hopefully result in an even bigger day
next August," Angela said.

"See you Tuesday morning at eight-thirty." Aaron
opened his office door, and as soon as the patients began
walking down the short hall to the office exit Sue appeared again.

"Better get spiffed up fast. You might think none of
the highbrow folks at your fund-raiser will wonder why
dynamic fertility expert and adoption advocate Dr. Aaron
Cartwright is the last to arrive, but I know you want
plenty of time to pass the hat. Expert though you are at
squeezing cash from the most miserly turnip."

"Is that a criticism or a compliment?" He had to laugh,
at the same time hoping it was true, since every dona-
tion helped. "I appreciate you sticking around and getting everything ready. So have you changed your mind
about attending?"

"Too rich for my blood at three hundred quid a ticket.
Six hundred if I bring Paul."

"You know you're both on my guest list. You just like

to play the poor, hard-working office manager who isn't paid enough to look after me."

She grinned at him. "And how do you know me so well after only three years?"

"Maybe because those exact words come out of your mouth almost daily." He grinned back. "Come on. Grab a dress and your husband and come have fun. You handled all the details for the thing practically single-handedly. Thanks to you, the band and the food will be great. Besides, you can keep me out of trouble."

"Another job that's too hard." Her eyes twinkled as she patted his arm. "Thanks for putting me on the guest list. And the OBs and midwives who have adoption stories to share, too—that's so smart of you. But Paul doesn't enjoy things like that, and I don't want to go without him. I'm sure it'll be a huge success just like last year, though. I hope you get lots of new donors and enjoy yourself."

"Fine. Don't be jealous when I'm in the newspaper photos of the gala and you're not."

"As if I'd be in them anyway. They just want pics of the handsome American doctor who helps patients conceive the baby they want, advocates for adoption of adorable children and who just might be dancing with a beautiful woman."

"They're destined for disappointment, then. There'll be too many people to talk into donating more for me to be distracted by a woman."

"Unless the right woman is there to distract you. Which I know does happen periodically, though you never let them hang around long, poor things. You're the most uncatchable doctor in this entire hospital." She winked. "Hurry and get dressed now. You're already past late."

"Yes, Mom." He took the clothes she shoved into his arms and had to smile at the way she mothered him. Not unlike the way his adoptive mother had, despite how messed up he'd been as a kid, which was challenging as hell for both his parents.

Thankfully, traffic wasn't quite as bad as usual, and he made it to the hotel quicker than he'd expected. He took a second to catch his breath, surveying the elegantly appointed ballroom.

It was decorated for Christmas with tasteful table decorations of silver and gold balls in sleigh-shaped containers. Shiny twigs and sparkly something-or-others were tucked between them, and red, pink and white poinsettias sat everywhere in eye-catching groups. Big-band music filled the room, the fifteen-piece orchestra he'd hired in full swing. Glittery Christmas trees stood here and there on the edges of the room, flanking the equally glittery women and tuxedo-clad men.

Aaron smiled. Sue had outdone herself. Might just be a record crowd of well-heeled guests, most of them smiling, talking and nibbling on hors d'oeuvres, clearly enjoying themselves.

Opening their wallets, too, which was the whole reason for this event. November was a little early for a Christmas party, but it was better not to compete with all the December holiday stuff going on out there. He had to admit he was proud that, in just three years, this event had become the must-go-to social extravaganza of Cambridge, with people coming from quite a few places well beyond the city. Paying for top-notch entertainment and food was necessary to attract the kind of attendees he needed to reach his fund-raising goals.

His stomach growled as he watched someone take a

bite of chicken on a stick. Better grab some food before his belly embarrassed him as he tried to talk to guests. He took a little of everything so he could eliminate any mediocre items from next year's gala menu. Even if he'd moved on to a different hospital and city by then, he'd have a thick file to pass on to whoever took over after he left.

Aaron had just stuck a bite in his mouth when his gaze was drawn to the doorway. He nearly swallowed a shrimp whole when he saw the vision standing there.

She was tall and graceful, and the cascade of golden blond hair that had caught his eye the first time he'd seen her long ago was instead elegantly piled on top of her head. Wispy tendrils touched her cheeks and the long, slender curve of her neck. Her slim frame was accentuated by a long, pale blue dress that he would guess probably cost a tenth of what most of the women in this room had spent on their clothes, but she looked more gorgeous than any of them. Pretty much every time he'd passed by her in the hospital, he'd been struck by how amazingly good she managed to look in shapeless scrubs. But this woman?

This woman knocked his socks off.

He didn't know anything about her, except that she was one of the midwives at the hospital. He'd taken a second and third glance at her every time he'd seen her in a hallway, and who wouldn't? The woman was pure eye candy and obviously smart, too, but since his work didn't involve delivering the babies he helped parents create, he'd never had the pleasure of her acquaintance.

Maybe tonight was the night to change that. To tell her he was glad that at least a few of the midwives he'd invited had decided to come. To find out over a glass of champagne what adoption stories of patients whose babies she'd delivered she was planning to share with some of the donors. To casually see if there was a wedding ring on her finger...

He went to the lectern standing in front of a retractable screen that had been set up opposite the band to give his presentation. Applause met his speech and the slides he showed of the other Christmas party the foundation hosted each year, where children wanting a home met parents considering adoption. Then more pictures of happy families newly bonded together.

The nods of approval and glowing smiles around the room made him smile, too. A good sign that quite a few folks would give even more than the price their tickets had provided to the charity named after his adoptive parents, The Tom and Caroline Cartwright Foundation. When he was finished speaking he worked the crowd, shaking hands and answering questions.

The music started up again, and as people moved to the dance floor he took advantage of the break to grab a cold sparkling water. He scanned the crowd, hoping to catch another look at the beautiful blonde midwife and maybe introduce himself.

"Nice party you've got going here, Aaron."

He turned to see Sean Anderson standing next to him, holding a plate piled high with shrimp and crab cakes. The Aussie obstetrician had been at Cambridge Royal Maternity Unit for only a month or so, but Aaron had already seen the guy was both dedicated and talented.

"Thanks, but I can't take credit for all of it. Or any of it, if you ask my office manager. She spent months pulling this together."

"Deserving or not, take credit when you can. That's

my motto." Sean grinned. "Even if you didn't plan the menu or send the invitations, I know you're the brains behind the whole idea, so kudos to you for that. Placing children with potential adoptive parents, especially older kids, is something anybody can get behind."

"I hope so. I also hope you and the other OBs will talk to folks about some of your patients who've found good homes for their babies, and parents who adopted. Those kinds of personal connections help a lot."

The man seemed to be looking past Aaron now, and when his response finally came, he sounded distracted. "Uh, yes. Will do."

Aaron looked over his shoulder and saw Isabel Delamere, another talented Australian OB. It didn't take much in the way of observation skills to see that her eyes met Sean's for a long moment. Her usual warm and friendly smile faded, and she turned away.

What was that all about? Sean hadn't been at CRMU long—surely he didn't have something going on with beautiful Isabel already? Could there be a professional rift between them? "You and Isabel have some kind of problem?"

"Problem?" Sean's attention came back to him slowly. "No, of course not."

But then it was Aaron's turn to be distracted as the knock-out blonde midwife left the dance floor, leaving her dance partner with a smile before she moved toward the bar next to them.

"Hope!" Sean called out, and she turned. "Great job today on those twins."

She smiled and stepped closer to them. "Thank you, Dr. Anderson. They were both little peanuts, but I'm relieved they seem to be perfectly healthy."

Hope. So that was her name. It was the first time he'd been so close to the woman, and he couldn't help but stare. To notice that her eyes were a mesmerizing dark blue, her skin luminous, her lips full and rosy, and just looking at them made him decide right then and there that he wanted to kiss her.

"I don't think we've ever actually met," he said, holding out his hand. "I'm Aaron Cartwright."

Sean looked at him in surprise. "Sorry, I didn't realize. But of course, you probably haven't worked together. Aaron, this is Hope Sanders, a midwife at CRMU, and a darned good one. Hope, Dr. Aaron Cartwright. OB and fertility specialist."

"We may not have met, but I know who you are, Dr. Cartwright. I've had more than one patient able to have the baby she's longed for, thanks to you." Her smile lit the room more than the glittering chandeliers as her slender hand shook his. "This is a wonderful party for a wonderful cause. Thanks so much for inviting us. I've already talked with a few donors about how your organization helps adoptive parents and children find one another."

"I appreciate that. I'm glad you were able to make it. Have you—"

"You know, I'll talk with you later, Aaron," Sean said, clapping Aaron on the shoulder. "I see someone I need to speak with. Congrats again on the crowd you've got here tonight."

He watched Sean move quickly across the room toward Isabel. He wondered again if they had something going, but whatever might be between them wasn't any of his business, and he had more interesting things to think about.

Like the very beautiful Hope Sanders.

"I think Sean and I interrupted your trek to the bar. Can I get you something?" He let his gaze roam over her face, fascinated by the exquisite shape of it, her silky brows, a pert nose above the delicately chiseled bow of her lip that tempted a man to explore its shape with his tongue.

"Just water, please. I was thirsty after dancing. The band you have here is fabulous, though I have to admit I'm a little surprised. Doesn't a party like this take a big chunk of the donations you're getting?"

"Seems like it would, doesn't it?" Interesting that she was tuned into that, when most people just enjoyed the extravaganza. "Some people donate generously simply because they understand the need. But I volunteered with a similar foundation in the States, and learned a lot that I've applied to this one. For better or worse, a great party with a high cost of admission has an exclusive aura to it. Foundations that spend big money on a fund-raising event like this reach people with the means to donate the most. They feel special, have a good time, and write checks."

"That seems...wrong."

"It's just human nature, which I know you understand well, working with patients all day." The little pucker over her eyes was cute as hell. "Think of it as a win-win. Everyone has a good time, and the foundation makes money to help families."

"I guess so." The pucker vanished as she smiled. "And I admit I'm having a very good time, so thank you again for inviting me."

"Glad you came." He tore his gaze from her appealing face, ratcheting back the libido that kept sending his thoughts places they shouldn't go with a woman he barely knew. "How about water with a glass of champagne on the side? In celebration of the party going off without a hitch."

"You do know saying something like that is tempting fate? The minute you're sure there's not a hitch, some disaster is sure to follow."

"You think?" Tempting fate? Her teasing smile was tempting all right, and who knew? Maybe fate was involved in that. Bringing her to this party so he could finally meet the woman who consistently grabbed his attention even from a distance.

"Dr. Cartwright. We just wanted to say you've put together another wonderful party."

He turned to the couple at his elbow and recognized them as big donors from last year. Spinning through his brain, he was relieved to come up with their names. "Mr. Adams. Mrs. Adams. Thank you, but my office manager organized it. I just show up. I'm glad you decided to come again this year."

"Wouldn't miss it," Mr. Adams said.

"Yes, we had a lovely time last Christmas and your foundation is doing such good things. We had a nice talk with Hope, here, who shared a few adoption stories that made us want to contribute even more. What a challenging job being a midwife must be."

"It can be," Hope said. "But of course it's tremendously rewarding to help bring new life into the world, and help the parents as well." She looked up at Aaron, and the admiration in her eyes surprised him. "Dr. Cartwright's work is both challenging and impressive. He helps parents have children who didn't think they could, and this wonderful foundation brings new families together in other ways."

Aaron nearly fidgeted under the admiring gazes of all three of them. It was the school of hard knocks, not heroism, that motivated the work he did.

"Well, we're very impressed with it," Mrs. Adams said. "And now we're going to enjoy the decadent things on that dessert table."

After another handshake, they wandered off and Aaron turned to Hope. "Thanks for talking with them. Maybe you've veered onto the wrong career path, and sales and marketing are your real calling."

"Selling things I'm excited about? Easy. Selling itchy socks or bad-tasting toothpaste just because it was my job? I'm pretty sure I'd be an utter failure at that." The humor in her gaze, the sheer intelligence, drew him closer without even realizing he'd gone there.

He shoved his hands into his pockets, resisting a sudden urge to reach out and sweep away a tendril of hair that had slipped across her eye. Maybe she'd seen him staring at its silkiness, as her slender fingers lifted to her face, shoving it aside. Fingers that weren't wearing anything resembling a wedding ring.

And that knowledge kindled the hot spark of interest he'd felt the second she'd walked into the room. "I'd suggest again we share some champagne to eliminate all thoughts of bad-tasting toothpaste, but don't want to be pushy about drinking if you don't want to." Champagne was nice, but holding Hope Sanders close in his arms? An entire case of Dom Pérignon couldn't begin to compare to that kind of ambrosia. "So how about dancing with me instead?"

"Perhaps you haven't noticed they've just finished up a swing tune and aren't playing at the moment."

"That's funny, I hear music. Don't you?" That fate she'd talked about played right into his hand as a slow song began to echo around the room. She dazzled him with another smile as he reached for her hand, folding its soft warmth within his. He led her onto the floor, and the number of people crowding it made holding her fairly close a necessity he was more than happy about. "This kind of music is more my speed anyway, when it comes to dancing. Which for me mostly consists of rocking from one foot to the other, I'm sorry to say. Not my best talent."

"So what is your best talent?"

There was almost a seductive quality to her voice and the amazing blue of her eyes looking into his robbed him of breath. He was pretty sure she didn't realize the way she'd asked the question, and he fought down the desire to press her body even closer to his, along with an offer to show her one of them.

"Hmm, that's a tough one. I'm good at my job, but I'm not sure that qualifies as a talent. I can kick a mean soccer ball and used to throw a damn good football spiral, too." He lowered his head close to her ear, and her soft hair tickled his temple. "But probably my best talent?"

"I think I'm sorry I asked." Her voice was a little breathy, and the sexy sound of it sent him sliding his palm from between her shoulder blades down to just above the curve of her shapely behind, bringing her body closer to his.

"Sorry, why?"

"Afraid that maybe your talent is something my innocent ears can't handle."

"Are your ears innocent?" He studied her, amused and curious. Innocent, no, as she clearly was used to sophisticated banter. But there was something guileless about her, a sweetness and sincerity that went beyond appealing. "Don't worry, I'm a gentleman. Your ears are safe."

Their bodies swaying together in a fit so perfect it was hard to tell where his body began and hers ended, they danced in silence for long minutes. Her sweet scent filled his nose, and he closed his eyes and breathed her in, holding her close enough to feel the brush of her breasts against his chest. Her forehead grazed his chin and her hand was tucked into his and pressed to his sternum as if they knew each other much better than two people who had met only ten minutes ago.

Aaron had been with quite a few women in his life, and he found himself studying the curve of her ear, the smoothness of her skin, trying to figure out what, exactly, made this feel somehow different. Had he ever felt a connection this instant and intense with anyone before? Or was he just not remembering?

The music drew to a close and they slowly separated, their eyes meeting. Her lips were parted, her skin seemed a little flushed, and it took every ounce of willpower for Aaron to remember they were in a public place in the middle of a hundred people. To remember he couldn't pull her back into his arms and kiss her until neither of them could breathe.

"You still haven't told me," Hope said, apparently trying to bring normalcy back to the moment, replacing the chemistry that was pinging hot and fast between them.

"Told you what?"

"What your best talent is."

Damn if the curve of her lips wasn't pure temptation. Temptation to try to impress her by showing her at least one answer to that question.

CHAPTER TWO

HOPE'S HEART KEPT doing an uncontrollable little dance of its own as she looked up at Aaron Cartwright. At the smile in his rich brown eyes as they stared into hers. She wasn't sure what had prompted her to ask that question. Again. She might not be a shy belle, but neither was she a flirtatious siren. Yet here she was, saying things that couldn't be interpreted as anything but suggestive.

She'd hoped she might meet Aaron at this party. But she hadn't expected to dance with the tall, ridiculously good-looking fertility specialist that practically every nurse and midwife at the hospital swooned over when he passed through the hallways.

She'd never have dreamed it possible, but the man was even more swoon-worthy in his tuxedo. And here she was, being held in his strong arms, dancing so closely they could have kissed by moving their faces barely an inch.

His deliciously male body radiating heat like a furnace, the way his big hand caught and held hers against his muscular chest, the deep, sexy rumble of his voice in her ear, all had combined to steal every molecule of breath from her lungs and, apparently, all sense from her brain as well. How else could she explain asking him—a second time, as though she really needed to know—what his best talent was?

Lord. She swallowed, embarrassment seeping through her body, adding to the heat that had nearly sent her up in flames. She stepped off the dance floor with him fluidly moving next to her and opened her mouth to say something, anything, that could possibly make him forget her last question, when he spoke.

"Punting."

She stared up at him blankly. "Punting?"

"Maybe not my best talent, but yes, I'm very good at it."

A nervous and relieved laugh escaped her throat. Thank heavens he wasn't going to take her up on her unfortunate innuendo. "You already told me you're good at kicking a football…er…soccer ball to Americans. Unless you mean gambling?"

"I never gamble. At least, not with money." He slid her a teasing look, and the way his eyes crinkled at the corners messed with her breathing all over again. "The punting I'm referring to is in a boat. You may think only Cambridge residents and tourists enjoy lazily shoving themselves down a river, but we've been doing it back home for centuries, too."

"And where is back home?" Since the midwives liked to talk about the various handsome men in the hospital, she knew he was American and from California, but not much other than that.

"Northern California. Wine country."

"Wine country? And here I'd assumed being from California that you were a surfer dude."

His eyes twinkled as the crinkles around them got deeper. "I've surfed, but I don't think that moniker fits me. And do you have any idea how adorable the words 'surfer dude' sound in your wonderful British accent?"

"I don't have an accent. You're the one with an accent." Which she found incredibly sexy, she had to admit, but wasn't about to say that and embarrass herself all over again.

"If you say so." He leaned closer. "But please let me hear you say 'surfer dude' one more time."

She laughed and felt her face heat again, but this time she had a feeling it was from his closeness, and how wonderful he smelled and looked, and how it all made her heart beat a little faster. "So people punt in wine country? Are there little canals between the vineyards?" she joked.

"Yes. They're filled with grape juice." His wink and grin were so charming, she had a bad feeling she might swoon for real next time she saw him at the hospital, requiring a hefty dose of smelling salts. "The punting I did back home was in Denver, Colorado, where I went to med school. Learned on Cherry Creek, and eventually raced. All the punting here is one of the reasons I liked the idea of working in Cambridge for a while."

"I find it hard to believe you consider punting a talent. I mean, how difficult could it be to shove a boat down a river with a pole?"

"You live here and don't know the answer to that?" He stared at her. "Punting takes a lot of practice. And it's excellent exercise. Surely you've tried it?"

"Well, no actually. I've been on the River Cam many times in the punts, but always had someone else manning the pole. Should I be embarrassed to admit that, since I was born and raised here?"

"This is shocking. And also unacceptable." He shook his head as his warm palm slid down her arm to grasp her elbow, propelling her across the room. "I assume you have a coat checked?"

"Yes, but—"

"Do you have a car here?"

"No, I came with another midwife from the hospital. I—"

"Good." They stopped at the coat check closet and he held out his hand. "May I have your ticket?"

She fumbled in her evening bag for it, wondering what in the world he was up to, and why she was getting out the ticket and giving it to him when she had no idea as to the answer. "The party's only half over. Are you throwing me out because I'm a shame to the CRMU and the entire city of Cambridge?"

He flashed her a devastating smile. "You, Hope Sanders, are obviously a shining star. Which is also why we have to fix this problem immediately. I'm taking you to the River Cam for a little punting lesson."

"What? Surely you can't leave this early? Besides, it's freezing outside! I can't believe you did your punting in November."

"I can leave whenever I want. I've given my talk and the guests are all happy. And it's not freezing." He slid her coat on before donning his own. "Fifty degrees Fahrenheit is downright balmy. We punted year round, just like people do here, in much colder temps than that."

"But I'm wearing a long gown! And you're in a tuxedo, for heaven's sake." Was the man out of his mind? No way was she getting on that river tonight, but she couldn't deny feeling a thrill of excitement at the idea of going out with Aaron Cartwright. Which was utterly crazy, since now was definitely not the time to get involved with a man. Not with her life about to change forever. "I'm not punting tonight and that's that."

"I'm about to gamble that you might change your mind about that, Ms. Sanders. Let's hit a pub by the river and decide from there." The humor in his eyes and the feel of his warm hand closing around hers left her with zero ability to protest again. "Come on."

Hope was still a little disbelieving that she was now sitting intimately close to Aaron Cartwright as he drove his purring sports car through the city. They talked about the hospital and work, but the bland conversation didn't slow her heart rate to normal. Probably because he smelled amazingly good, looked even better and kept glancing at her with unmistakable interest in his eyes.

No use in pretending to herself that she didn't share that interest. But from what she'd heard, the man was one of those love-'em-and-leave-'em types, involved with a woman for just a few months before moving on. Of course, her own history had proven she wasn't relationship material anyway. Not to mention that, scary though it was, she was about to give herself the gift of a child very soon. The child she'd dreamed of forever.

Since neither one of them was into relationships, this odd excursion wasn't a big deal, then, right? Why not just go along for the ride and enjoy herself?

He parked the car, then walked around the front of it to open her door. The moment she stepped out, a chilly wind whipped her hair, dipped inside her coat collar and fluttered the skirt of her dress. She hugged herself and cocked her head at him. "Still think it's downright balmy out here?"

"Maybe it's not quite as balmy as I thought." He

wrapped his long arm around her shoulders and pulled her against his side as they walked to the path lining the river. The glow of electric lamps warmly illuminated the stony path and the dark water as it flowed hypnotically beside them. The brick exteriors of several pubs were lit, too, as they strolled past rows of empty punts bobbing shoulder to shoulder in the water. "A glass of brandy might warm us up, then we'll decide if maybe this was a harebrained idea after all."

"No maybe about it." Then again, without his harebrained idea, she wouldn't be standing here in the curve of his arm being held close to his big, warm body, which felt absurdly cozy and nice. "But I admit it's beautiful outside tonight. And I also hate to admit that I rarely come here to enjoy it."

"Too busy working? Or playing?"

"Working." She was past her playing days. Though at that moment, the pleasure she felt just walking with Aaron in the crisp, starry night made her wonder if that was as true as she'd believed it was.

The thought brought her to a sudden standstill. Of course she was done with her playing days. Hadn't wanted them for years anyway. She'd gone out on the town because there'd been no one special in her life, and no child of her own to keep her home. Enjoying this night out with Aaron didn't mean she wasn't capable of being a loving, dedicated mother.

She glanced up at Aaron and could tell he wondered why she'd stopped walking. She forced a smile at him and started moving again. "Plus, I live on the outskirts of town, so I just don't get into the city center very often."

"You said you were born and raised here?"

"Yes. Been here forever. Went to university here, too,

except when I did my advanced midwife training in London." He was looking at her a little quizzically. "I take it you think that's a little strange, since you lived in California, went to university in Denver and now you're here."

"I've traveled to a lot of other places over the years. Been accused many times of being the stone that refuses to gather moss." His teeth flashed in a white smile. "I don't think it's strange that you've dug roots in here, but I admit moving around is more my style. That I've been here three years is a surprise to me, to be honest. I'm sure the travel bug will bite me one of these days and I'll move on."

The utter opposite of Hope. She couldn't imagine how he didn't feel a need to put down roots somewhere. Cambridge felt like a part of her, deeply entwined with her heart and her soul, and settling in there forever like a broody hen with her job and a family was all she'd ever wanted.

The patio of the pub they came to held a few hardy souls sitting at a table, but most were cozy inside. Cheerful music somehow penetrated beyond the thick brick to where they stood, and through the windows Hope could see a crowd of people mingling and laughing. Those days would be completely behind her very soon, and she closed her eyes and smiled, visualizing her new future.

Motherhood.

Despite the chill, she wasn't ready to go inside. She wanted to breathe in the fresh air and take in the surprising pleasure of walking with a man holding her close before there would be no possibility of that happening anytime soon.

She looked up at Aaron, surprised to see his eyes were on her and not the pub, his expression inscrutable. "Shall we walk just a bit farther?" she asked, wanting the moment to last a little longer. "That bridge up ahead is spectacular."

"The whole city is beautiful. I've been impressed with its architecture since the day I got here." He tugged her closer as they resumed their walk. "The path ends at the bridge, so we'll have to double back or climb the stairs from the riverbank to the restaurants and pubs up there."

The glow of lights faded behind them as they neared the dead end just before the old gothic-style bridge, where one lone punt disappeared on the water beyond it. Aaron dropped his arm from her shoulders, sliding it down to grasp her hand again as he turned to look at her. "I enjoy walking along here often," he said, his voice quiet. "But tonight it's especially beautiful. Thanks for coming with me, even though you didn't really want to."

"It was punting in an evening dress that was the problem, Dr. Cartwright. And the cold air. And the threat of exercise." Though she wasn't feeling at all cold. In fact, an intense warmth seemed to be creeping across every inch of her skin beneath her coat. "Who knew I'd be glad you dragged me here?"

He laughed, the sound a soft rumble in his chest as he drew her close. "So my gamble paid off." Then he lowered his mouth to hers.

For one split second, she was stunned with surprise. Then it was quickly gone, replaced by a punch of desire the likes of which she hadn't felt for a long, long time. Her eyelids flickered closed as his mouth moved oh-so-skillfully on hers. Teasing and tasting, sweet then intense, with a hunger that made her dizzy. She gasped into his mouth as her heart pounded and her knees wobbled, and she blindly lifted her hands to grip his wide shoulders so she wouldn't sink straight to the stone path.

His mouth moved from hers to caress the sensitive spot beneath her ear before warmly sliding across her jawline and up her cold cheek to rest at the corner of her lips. "You taste better than anything on that buffet dessert table, Hope," he whispered. "Better than champagne. Better than the finest vintage in Napa Valley."

"Have you had every fine vintage in Napa?" she breathed.

"No." She could feel him smile against her mouth. "Not necessary to know with absolute certainty that it's true, though I've had my share."

His share of wine or his share of women? Women for sure, if rumor was to be believed. And she did believe, because there was no doubt other women found him as completely irresistible as she did, considering she'd barely spent an hour with the man and was kissing him as she hadn't kissed anyone in pretty much forever.

His mouth covered hers again in another kiss that left her quivering. When their lips finally separated, quick breaths came hard and fast against each other's cold skin.

Moonlight gleamed on his dark brown hair, creating shadows beneath his prominent cheekbones and highlighting a stubborn jaw. His brown eyes no longer seemed warmly chocolatey, but instead glittered like molten onyx, hot and dangerous. Her insides quivered and she tried to think of something to say, but couldn't come up with a single, rational thought.

"I've decided you were right," he said in a low voice.

"Right?"

"About punting tonight. Staying inside where it's

warm and showing you another of my talents is a much better idea."

That startled a laugh out of her. "Mmm-hmm. And I can guess what those talents might be, Dr. Has-A-Big-Ego. I can also guess that showing me those talents was your plan all along."

"Plan, no. But hoping to get to know the beautiful Hope I've noticed so often in the hospital? That I'm delighted to learn is single?" His hand slipped down to grasp hers, his thumb stroking across her empty ring finger. "Oh, yeah. I freely admit I'd hoped for that."

"That's a lot of hope in one sentence," she said, trying for a little humor so she could catch her breath and banish thoughts of those talents he boasted, which, based on his amazing kissing skills, she was more than ready to believe on a scale of one to ten were probably a twenty.

As for being single, that was true. The way she was wired, apparently. Something sadly missing in her DNA. The other reason she wasn't really available despite her single status would doubtless surprise him. Maybe even shock him.

"I guess it is. But one thing I never thought to hope for is this unbelievable chemistry between us. Unless it's only me who feels like a nuclear bomb just went off in my head from kissing you. Is it?"

She stared into the gaze searching hers, the question hanging in their dark depths. She opened her mouth to answer, but found her throat all closed up at the heat she saw there, at the dangerous current swirling around as if the two of them were standing in some electrified tornado.

"Is it, Hope?"

Her name on his lips, spoken in a deep voice that

promised a delicious pleasure she hadn't had in so long, and definitely wouldn't have for even longer, maybe even ever, sent her closing the gap between them. Shocking her. Speaking her surprising answer against his lips. "No. It's not just you."

The kiss was excruciatingly soft and sweet and went on so long, she felt dizzy. When their lips separated, they just stared at one another until he spoke in a rough voice.

"I live just a block away." His warm lips pressed softly against one chilled cheek, then the other. Feathered against each eyelid before his gaze met hers again. "I want you, which I'm sure doesn't come as a surprise. Will you come home with me to see where our undeniable chemistry leads? And if you decide it leads to just a glass of wine or brandy, that's okay."

Oh. My. God. He wanted her. The sexy man she'd have to confess she'd had more than one fantasy about wanted *her*.

Not that she was completely taken aback, after his comment about nuclear explosions and those knee-melting kisses they'd shared. And after hearing the stories of his lifestyle. Her heart pounded so hard in her chest, she was sure he could probably hear it.

Did she really want to be another notch in his bedpost?

Her gaze took in how his dark hair blew across his forehead, how his lips were curved in a small smile, how his brown eyes gleamed with an unmistakable desire and, for the first time in her life, she wanted to say *Oh, yes!* to a one-night fling.

As she looked at him she thought about her new life right there on the horizon. A new life which would be all about changes to her body and sleepless nights and new responsibilities. Didn't she pride herself on knowing what she wanted and making it happen? What would be wrong with enjoying one, doubtless delectable night with Aaron Cartwright? She never worked with the man, and a one-night fling wasn't any kind of real relationship anyway, right?

"I…um…" She licked her lips and tried again. "I'm not in a place in my life where I want a relationship."

"I'm never in a place in my life where I want a relationship." His smile widened. "At least not one that's long-term. I don't stay put in one place long enough for that. But time with you, getting to know all about Hope Sanders and who she is and what she likes? That I'd like very much."

His hand dropped hers to cup her cheek, warm against her cool skin, and his thumb slipped across her cheekbone with the same feathery touch he'd used on her fingers. Hope quivered as her thoughts suddenly turned to how those fingers might feel against other parts of her body.

"I meant I'm not in a place where we could spend any time together other than tonight."

"Other than tonight?" His dark brows raised slightly, his eyes now looking both perplexed and slightly amused. "Got to say, a woman saying she wants to kick me out the door after one night together is a first."

"Wouldn't be kicking you out, because it's your own house." She managed a breathless laugh. "I admit it's a first for me, too. But that's all I can offer and…and…"

As she struggled to figure out what to say he touched his lips gently to hers. "And what?"

"And I'm offering it." She gulped in disbelief that the words had actually come out of her mouth. But as his lips sweetly, softly pressed against hers, warm and tender and oh-so-delicious, her disbelief and uncertainty faded. She lifted her hands to the sides of his strong neck as heat radiated from him, warming her even through her coat. It all felt so good, so wonderful, so right, she knew she wouldn't regret being with him tonight. Just one evening of excitement and passion with a strong, sexy man before everything in her life changed.

He pulled back, and the eyes staring into hers were that smoldering, dark onyx again. "You might not believe it, but I'm not normally a one-night-stand guy. If that's all you're willing to offer, though, I find it's damned impossible for me to say no. We'll go to my apartment and have that nightcap, and you can decide then where, if anywhere, you'd like the rest of the evening to go before I take you home."

His hand wrapped around hers again, and he led her up the stone steps. He was moving fast, and she nearly tripped in her heels. He looked at her feet and slowed down as his hot gaze lifted to hers again. "Sorry. I forgot you had those things on. Very sexy," he said, leaning down to brush his warm lips against her cheek. "But not so great for walking, hmm? Thankfully, we don't have to go far."

They didn't speak again on the short trek, and Hope's breath was short, but not from the walk. Her chest was filled with a crazy excitement that completely overwhelmed the nervous butterflies in her stomach.

They trotted up short steps to a gorgeous Victorian-style stone building with two ornate front doors, and Hope had to pause to admire it.

"Is this a semi? Do you own this one side?"

"Yes, it's a duplex and my neighbor is a nice, quiet, older lady. But since I move around a lot, renting is always the way to go."

Apparently it was true that the man wanted nothing to tie him down, but it wasn't any of her business why he felt that way. His hand palmed her back as she stepped inside the door on the right, the butterflies now flapping a little more insistently. He shut the door behind them, and his eyes met hers for the briefest moment before he wrapped his arms around her, pulled her close and kissed her.

There was nothing sweet or gentle or teasing about this one. It went from zero to sixty in a split second, hot and intense, his tongue exploring her mouth with a thoroughness that weakened her knees and melted every brain cell. She let her hands slip up his chest and the sides of his neck into his soft thick hair, mussing it even more than the breeze had, and found herself pressing his mouth somehow even closer to hers, deepening the kiss until she was quivering from head to toe.

"I keep my home pretty chilly. But kissing you has definitely warmed me up." The dark hunger in his eyes as he pulled back made it hard to breathe. Even harder when he reached to flick her coat buttons open one by one. He tossed the coat on a chair behind him, then took off his own. "You warmer now, too? Would you like that brandy we talked about? Or a glass of wine?"

His voice was husky, and Hope was surprised at the sincerity in it, considering the gleam in his eyes and the shortness of his breath that mirrored her own. He clearly had truly meant what he'd said about giving her time to decide what she wanted from the evening. It added one more layer to his already delicious appeal, and every last vestige of doubt slid away as she tugged at the bow of his tie until it lay loose around his neck.

"Would you be surprised if I told you that every time I saw you at the hospital, fantasies of kissing you and being with you usually followed? So even though we don't really know each other, somehow I feel like we do. Like those fantasies were real." It was true, and she was surprised she didn't feel embarrassed to tell him. To help him understand why she felt good about being here with him tonight. "So right now I don't want a drink. What I want is for those fantasies to truly become real."

His gaze slid to her mouth, to the beading on her dress above her breasts, before slowly meeting hers again. "You can be sure you've starred in my fantasies as well, Hope Sanders. I always assumed a woman like you would already be taken by some lucky guy, and I'm more than glad to learn that's not the case." His lips tilted in a slow smile. "But I know it must be because you dump all the men eager to be with you as soon as you've had your way with them."

That hadn't been her failing, but she was glad he didn't know what was. "Not quite accurate, but I'm finding it rather fun to pretend to be that woman tonight."

He grasped her shoulders and turned her around. Cool air swept her hot skin as he tugged on the tab of her zipper, his soft, moist mouth pressing against the side of her neck.

His lips crept along her skin as he lowered the zipper inch by inch, his hands trailing after in a slow, shivery path so heart-poundingly delicious she feared she might pass out from the intense pleasure of it. Over her shoulder blade, her spine, sliding the dress off as he went, ending with his hands grasping her hips and his tongue caressing the indentations above each buttock.

"Your skin feels so soft," he whispered. "Tastes so good."

Trembling, she could have stood there for ever savoring the feel of his hands and mouth, the rumble of his low voice against her flesh. Except she didn't want to be the only one standing there half-naked, and she turned. Trembling even more when she realized he'd crouched down to kiss her back, and that his mouth was now just above her panties. Slowly, excruciatingly, kissing all across the lacy top before lazily licking her skin beneath.

Part of her wanted him to just keep going with all the licking and kissing that was short-circuiting all thoughts except how incredibly good it felt. But the part of her brain that somehow still worked had her grasping his arms to tug him upright before she just lay down on the floor and begged him to make love to her.

"Not fair for me to be standing here freezing while you're still dressed." Though freezing was about the last word to describe how she really felt. "I'd undo your shirt, except I don't know what to do with those little pearl buttons."

"I'm perfectly happy with things staying unfair, but if you insist."

He stood to tower over her—something she wasn't used to at five feet eight inches. "How tall are you, anyway?" she asked absently, staring with fascination as his fingers flicked open his buttons one by one, slowly revealing dark brown hair in the center of his chest that tapered down to a taut stomach.

"Six foot three or so."

His shirt slipped off him completely, showing smooth, broad shoulders and a torso that was thickly muscled and masculine and so sexy, her mouth watered. She'd thought the man swoon-worthy in a suit and tie, scrubs, or tux. None of that had prepared her for the sheer, male beauty that was Aaron Cartwright.

Speechless, she stared at him as he kicked off his shoes and tossed his belt on the floor. The brown eyes that met hers glittered with the same crazy desire she felt, but he had that appealing little smile on his lips, too, as he wrapped one arm around her and kissed her. Without the intensity of the deep kiss they'd shared the minute they'd stepped inside his door. This one was sweet, and slow, tasting like a promise, and she couldn't help but melt right into him. The kiss stayed mind-blowingly tender as his fingers moved to trace the lace of her bra, then slipped inside to caress her nipple. It felt so good, so wonderful, she moved back a smidge to give him better access.

"I guess…this is that talent you were talking about," she managed to whisper as they kissed. "You weren't lying about being good at it."

"Did I say I wanted to show you just one talent?" She felt him smile against her mouth. "I have more."

She smiled, too, since, holy wow, that was beyond true. His kisses and caresses were pretty much the best things she'd enjoyed in forever. "Does that big ego count as a talent?"

"No." His fingers moved to trace where his tongue had gone inside the lace of her panties, and her amusement faded with a gasp as they moved south to stroke her moist folds. "My big ego is a failing of mine, so if you can help me with doing better, I'd appreciate it."

She bit back a moan. "Having an orgasm right this second probably wouldn't help you with that."

"No. But it would make me very happy." His hot breath mingled with hers as their tongues continued a gentle dance. The feel of the hard muscle of his chest with its soft hair beneath her hands, his low voice, and the ex-cruciatingly wonderful touch of his fingers expertly moving on her most sensitive part sent her over the edge she hadn't wanted to go over, and she shuddered and moaned.

"I didn't mean for that to happen." Gasping, she slumped against him feeling slightly embarrassed. But mostly she felt incredibly, amazingly, quiveringly good. From just his touch and nothing else.

He held her tightly against him, and his hand slipped from her wetness to cup her rear inside her panties. His lips touched her cheek, her ear, her forehead. "I did." His voice sounded breathless, too, and rough, and also very satisfied, damn it.

"I guess I failed in my assignment to help keep that ego of yours in check."

"I'm probably a hopeless case, anyway." He chuckled as his lips pressed the corner of her mouth. "Let's go somewhere more comfortable, hmm?"

She didn't care where they went, so long as it was for more of the bliss he'd just given her. The floor would be fine with her, but he led her to a room with a big, wide bed. He yanked back the covers before he picked her up and deposited her into the middle of it. He stared at her, and the fire in his eyes scorched every inch of her body they perused, making her tremble all over again. Had any man ever looked at her like that before?

"You are a beautiful woman, Hope." He yanked off his trousers and socks and she had a heart-stopping moment to admire his gorgeous nakedness and the clear evidence that he was every bit as aroused as she was. "Even more beautiful than my fantasies."

"My fantasies about you had you being pretty god-like, Dr. Cartwright. And let me say you've met those expectations quite well. Except, oops, there I go forgetting about that ego assignment again."

Another chuckle rumbled from his chest into hers as he lay next to her on the bed and pulled her close, kissing her and touching her until she'd have been hard pressed to come up with her own name. Dimly, she realized her underwear was now off and every inch of her body was quivering from the touch of his mouth and talented fingers. She tried to return the favor as much as she possibly could in the state of sexual intoxication he'd driven her to, but found every sense focused on the intense pleasure he was giving her.

Finally, he rose above her and sheathed himself with a condom before he slid inside her more-than-ready body. Their eyes met and held in a spellbinding connection she couldn't remember ever experiencing while making love with a man. They moved together, their bodies fitting perfectly just as they had at the dance. Even as Hope absorbed the rhythmic pleasure of it all, the feel of his skin against hers, the look in his eyes and the taste of his mouth, the foggy edge of her mind was aware of a twinge of regret that they could share this moment only once. Aware of a sense of confusion over how all this couldn't be new to her experience, and yet it was.

But there was one thing she wasn't confused about. Once was far, far better than never.

CHAPTER THREE

AARON HEADED DOWN the hospital corridor to begin his first procedure of the day and stopped dead when he glimpsed a tall, slender woman dressed in scrubs walking toward one of the labor suites at the end of the hall. A tidy ponytail tamed the silky golden hair he could still feel tickling his skin as it had loosened from its elegant knot, and her face in profile reminded him of a stunning, alabaster cameo of a goddess.

Hope Sanders.

His heart kicked hard in his chest and he stood stock still, mesmerized by the smile she gave a nurse as she paused outside the door. A smile so dazzling it had seemed to light the entire ballroom the moment she'd directed it at him, making him smile back and want another one. A smile that had changed from interestingly intelligent, to fun and flirty, to filled with a deeply sensuous bliss he'd been incredibly lucky to put there.

Damn. He realized his breath was a little fast, and his heart rate, too, and it was a good thing she disappeared into the labor suite or he might have found his feet heading her way before he'd even thought about it.

The attraction he'd felt for her before, just from seeing her in the hospital, was nothing compared to the attraction he felt now that he knew a little more about how smart and charming she was. How good she tasted, how soft her skin felt, how beautiful every inch of her body was. How well her body fit his, and how he hadn't been able to stop thinking about all that since the moment he'd kissed her goodbye.

That kiss had been sweet and hot and intense like all the others they'd shared. A kiss that had felt as if it held plenty of promise, until she'd broken it and taken a step back and he'd known the promise wasn't there at all. Something about the look on her face at that moment had shown she wanted to bring a distance between them that wasn't just physical. A determined look that said she'd meant it when she'd stated there was no possibility of them spending any more time together, and he had to wonder why.

Also wonder if, maybe, he could convince her otherwise.

Or maybe karma was catching up with him, and he was getting served with the "it's been fun but gotta run" that he'd ended relationships with many a time. Except she wanted to end this one a whole lot sooner than he'd ever done. He knew he should just enjoy the memory of their one night and move on. He also knew he damn well couldn't forget all about Hope Sanders, even though she'd said and shown loud and clear that he had no choice about it.

Could all these unsettling feelings be a sign he'd been in Cambridge long enough? A sign that it was time to move on? He didn't want or need to get entwined with any one woman or any one place. Maybe he should start thinking of where in the world he'd like to live next.

With that thought, he went into the procedure room

to see his patients, John and Angela Walters. Resolutely refocusing his attention on his job and what they all hoped to achieve.

"Good morning," Aaron said as he sat in front of Angela. "The big day is here. Are you two ready?"

"More than ready, Dr. Cartwright. You know we've been waiting for this for a long time," John said through his surgical mask, reaching to grip his wife's hand as she lay in the hospital bed, gowned and ready. While they were understandably on edge, the couple seemed slightly more relaxed than they had been in his office last Friday, and Aaron was glad to see it. Hopefully that meant they'd listened to all he'd talked to them about and had read the extra literature. Knew the risks, and also that the odds were in their favor for achieving what they hoped for, which was a successful pregnancy and healthy baby.

"Dr. Miller told me your part went well, John." Next came a little light humor, which always helped everyone relax. "I hope it wasn't miserable—Dr. Miller and I both dread being on people's hate list. Makes it hard to sleep."

"Guess your sleep is safe enough," John said, his eyes smiling over his mask. "Not something I want to do every day, but it wasn't too terrible."

"Glad to hear it. And we shouldn't have to do it again, even if we need to try the ICSI once more. Freezing the fertilized embryos in case we need them will make things easier next time, though I have every hope that won't be necessary."

"I still can't believe freezing doesn't hurt them, Dr. Cartwright," Angela said, the anxious look forming on her face again.

"It is a little hard to imagine, isn't it? But they're still really just cells at that point so it's true, I promise."

"I, um, know I already said this." Angela nervously licked her lips, and Aaron prepared himself for whatever misgivings she might be having. "But I'm worried about implanting only two eggs. We've been through so much, and I know John and I can handle multiples, if that should happen."

"Two implanted eggs should result in a baby," he said, trying to keep his voice gentle and understanding, but it was an effort to battle down his frustration. If only would-be parents fully believed and understood the challenges he tried to educate them about. The kinds of challenges and terrible consequences that the stress of multiple births sometimes put parents through.

Your mother just couldn't handle so many babies on her own, Aaron. I'm sorry we came all this way and she didn't want to see you. But everyone's hoping she can get better and leave the hospital sometime soon. We'll visit another time, okay? Maybe she'll want to see you then.

Aaron squeezed his eyes shut for a second, willing away the unwelcome memory of one of his foster parents' words. One foster parent out of several, whose names he couldn't remember anymore. One of many memories, some the same, some different, but always disturbing. Always painful. Hating that they invaded his brain when he least wanted them.

He opened his eyes to focus on Angela, somehow giving her a smile. Forcing his voice to a lighter tone. "A woman isn't a Golden Retriever, you know. Your very human uterus wasn't designed to carry a litter of pups, was it?"

"Okay, point taken." Aaron was relieved to see her smile, glad it wasn't going to become an issue just before the procedure was to begin. "I never thought I'd say this to anyone except John, but—are you ready to make a baby?"

"Oh, yeah, I'm ready," Aaron said. They all chuckled, and he looked around for the nurse to get this show on the road. The quicker they got Angela sedated and her eggs retrieved, the better.

Except only the ultrasound technician and the patient care specialist were there, not his nurse. "Where's Kathy?"

"I don't know, Doctor. She hasn't been here since I brought the Walters in."

Strange. Kathy was as reliable as an atomic clock. "Would you mind finding her? I—"

"Dr. Cartwright." A nurse poked her head through the doorway. "Wanted to let you know Kathy's come down with a nasty bug, and she's had to go home."

"Can you assist me, then?"

"Sorry." Her face twisted in apology. "I'm helping one of the midwives with a delivery. And baby's coming soon so I need to get back in there."

"All right. Thanks." Well, damn. He pulled down his mask to give another reassuring smile to the couple. "Sorry, but you'll have to hang on just a few more minutes. I'll find a nurse and be right back."

He strode toward the labor and delivery suite, figuring he could find a midwife whose patient wouldn't be delivering for a while, and who would be quite safe in the hands of the midwife's assistant until later. Refusing to admit that the assistant he really wanted to find had long blonde hair and sweet lips and a body that was beyond seductive, even in shapeless green scrubs.

Then, as though he'd willed it, the woman on his mind

stepped out of the doorway he'd seen her go into not much earlier.

"Hope." He picked up the pace until he stood next to her. Close enough to see the fascinating green and black flecks within the blue of her eyes. "I'm about to retrieve a patient's eggs, then do ICSI, except my nurse has gone home sick. Any chance you're free to assist?"

"Assist?" Her blue eyes stared up at him, and the zing that had happened the second he'd met her at the party crackled the air between them. Against his will, he found his gaze dropping to her full pink lips as she licked them. Nervously? Because she felt the same electric current he did?

He couldn't help but smile at that thought, but the hospital corridor wasn't exactly the place to see where all that electricity might lead, since he was pretty sure it would be similar to a high-voltage lightning strike like before. He schooled his expression into a professional cool. "Yes. I'll need you to do an IV sedation and monitor her as I retrieve the eggs. Should only take about ten minutes. Twenty tops."

"All right." Her face relaxed into a smile. "I've never seen this procedure, so it should be interesting."

"Good. The patient is a little nervous, so I appreciate your helping before she gets too worried."

As he'd expected, Mr. and Mrs. Walters were looking anxious again. "Nurse Midwife Hope Sanders is here to help, Angela. Hope, this is Angela and John Walters. Right after we retrieve the eggs, I'm going to do the ICSI procedure to fertilize them and see which ones want to develop into a baby."

"Thank you for coming, Hope." Angela was gripping her husband's hand like a lifeline. "We were getting worried we'd have to wait until another time, and that would be torture."

"I'm happy to help," Hope said, her smile friendly and sincere as she scrubbed and put on a gown and mask. "The CRMU prides itself on avoiding patient torture whenever possible."

The couple chuckled, and Aaron marveled at how easily she put them at ease—much more easily than he'd managed to do. "Time for you to go to sleep for a little while, Angela. Hope, will you please get her IV sedation going?"

Aaron watched her place the IV in Angela's arm, impressed at how quickly and painlessly she had it ready. The woman was obviously an excellent nurse, which didn't surprise him. He'd bet she was a great midwife, too, chatting with birthing mothers in the same soothing tone she was using with Angela, having the woman more relaxed than he'd ever seen her.

"Nicely done, Hope. Obviously an expert."

Her eyes smiled at him over her mask before she administered the drug and in moments the patient was sedated. The ultrasound tech placed the monitor just above Angela's pelvis to give Aaron a good picture of her ovaries.

"John, you're welcome to stay, but it may make you uncomfortable to watch. If you decide you want to wait outside, we all completely understand and will take good care of Angela."

John nodded, and the way his face paled just from the ultrasound told Aaron the man would probably have to leave when the needle was inserted to retrieve his wife's eggs. He knew the man wanted to be there though, and tried to distract him by explaining what was going on, to keep his attention on the monitor instead of the needle that tended to freak out husbands.

"Watch the monitor, John," he said as he worked. "You're looking at Angela's ovary. We've got some good-sized follicles here, which should give us a nice number of eggs."

"Yes. Good."

Aaron glanced at John, who'd gone a pasty gray and was leaning a little sideways in his chair. He sent a quick look to the patient care specialist and nodded toward John before turning his attention back to the monitor again. "Don't want you to pass out, John. How about going out to the waiting room? We'll be done here in no time, then you can come back to support Angela when she wakes up. Okay?"

The patient care specialist had obviously gotten the hint and was already taking John's arm and leading him from the room. As Aaron studied the monitor while he worked he was aware of Hope intently watching the procedure.

"Glad you noticed he wasn't looking too well. I was about to say the exact same thing, though it wouldn't really have been my place to do that."

"Keeping someone from fainting and cracking their head open on the floor is anyone's job." Their eyes met, and being able to just see her eyes and not the rest of her pretty face made him notice how long her lashes were. How expressive her gaze was.

"How many eggs do you usually get?" she asked.

"Eight to ten is a good number, but the number might be a lot smaller if the woman is older. Angela thankfully has quite a few eggs, considering she's going on forty. Shouldn't have any problem getting some very viable ones."

"That's good news for them, I assume?"

"Hopefully. But the next part of the equation might be the trickiest one."

"What part?"

Since she was a member of the medical team helping with the procedure, it was perfectly ethical to share their history with her, and he explained the details of the ICSI procedure.

She nodded, a thoughtful crease between her brows as she stared at the monitor. "So what happens now?"

"In just a few more minutes, I'll be done retrieving the fluid and eggs, then they'll be sent to the IVF lab. They'll be rinsed in a culture media and put in a dish for about four hours, then they'll be ready for fertilization. I'll study the eggs to see which look the most viable and choose two."

"Amazing. I've been told all this but—"

She abruptly stopped speaking, and the strange, alarmed look in her eyes caught his attention. As did the fact that what he could see of her face not covered by her mask had flushed scarlet. What was all that about?

"Told all this?" he prompted.

"Nothing. I mean, in nursing school I'd been told it. Learned about it."

She turned away, busying herself with checking Angela's vital signs. Aaron studied her another moment, then dismissed his thought that she'd suddenly acted strange. Probably imagining it.

"So that's it," he said, leaning back and gathering the dishes he'd placed the fluids in as the ultrasound technician cleaned up her things and left the room. "Do you need to check on your patient, or do you have time to wake Angela? If you can, I'll check on her and prescribe some pain meds, then have someone keep an eye on her for about an hour before she's discharged."

"Let me check on my patient, then I'll let you know one way or another, though I expect she's still far from ready to deliver." Hope stood and placed her hand on his shoulder. "I want to tell you that what you do is so impressive. So wonderful that doctors like you can give people who can't have babies the family they want. It's… You have to feel great about that."

"All doctors train to help people in different ways. I like what I do, but it probably isn't quite as important as brain surgery or treating someone's cancer." He didn't add that in addition to helping people create the baby they desperately wanted, his mission was to help prevent the kind of tragedy his own family had suffered.

"Those are important, yes. But believe me when I say that what you do is incredibly important too." To his surprise, she leaned down and pressed her lips to his forehead, and, even though she still had on her paper mask, it felt nice. Nice enough that he wanted to stand up and press his own mouth to hers to see if a paper-mask kiss with her might almost be better than a real kiss with anyone else.

He shook his head at the stupid thought. After only one night, the woman had bewitched him, and he knew at that moment he couldn't just accept her telling him more time together was out of the question without understanding why. Without pursuing her a little more to see if, maybe, she didn't really mean it after all.

"Since you're so interested in the procedure, could you find time around one p.m. today to come watch the fertilization process? It's pretty incredible to see. I think you'd be fascinated."

"I'd love that, and I'll be off work by then." Her eyes shone at him over her mask, then the glow faded. "I do have an appointment though, and I'm not sure how long it will take. But if I can be there, I will. I'll go check on my patient and be right back."

He watched her leave the room, and it was hard to imagine there could be anything sexy about her loose scrubs, her golden hair tucked into a paper hat, or the flapping paper gown concealing any curves. But he knew what that beautiful body of hers looked like underneath all that, and his heart stepped up its pace as he remembered.

He pressed his fingers to his own pulse and shook his head at himself, wondering what the heck it was about Hope Sanders that had him feeling like an adolescent with his first crush.

Whatever it was, he had no idea. And, yeah, this strange preoccupation and restlessness clearly showed that he needed to think hard about what his next job might look like. He didn't belong in Cambridge. He didn't belong anywhere.

But until he moved on, changing her mind about the two of them spending time together just became his priority. What better way to celebrate the Christmas season?

CHAPTER FOUR

How in the world had it not occurred to her what a massive and embarrassing problem this could be? As if she weren't already a bit nervous anyway, and this situation compounded the jitter of her nerves tenfold.

With her heart fluttering in her throat, Hope practically tiptoed into the offices the IVF physicians at CRMU shared. She peeked through the fingers she held up to the side of her face to see if Dr. Aaron Cartwright would be inopportunely standing there. As though her hand would somehow, magically, make her unrecognizable even if he was.

An invisibility potion was what she really needed. Or a new brain.

The only people in sight were the receptionist behind the front desk and one patient sitting in the small waiting room. She huffed out a relieved breath and, with her legs feeling a little jelly-like, stepped to the glass window. The receptionist slid it open with a smile.

"May I help you?"

Help her with that new brain thing, maybe. "I'm Hope Sanders." Would the woman think it odd that she was whispering, or just assume she had laryngitis? She glanced all around behind the receptionist, praying she didn't see a tall, brown-haired hunk of a doctor back there. "I have a noon appointment with Dr. Devor."

"Ah. Well." The woman's face lost its smile, instead turning somehow frowning and apologetic at the same time, which seemed a little odd to Hope. But then again, Hope's tentative steps, whispering and furtive looks probably seemed even more odd. "Come with me, please."

Hope followed her down a hallway until she was ushered into a small room. "Make yourself comfortable. The office manager, Sue Calloway, will be right with you."

Trying to occupy herself and forget the possibility of seeing Aaron Cartwright, and what in the world she'd say if she did, she picked up literature invitingly placed in cardboard holders on a side table. She tried to flip through it, but couldn't focus on the illustrations and information. And really didn't need to, because after all she'd seen the amazing egg-retrieval procedure on that monitor today very clearly. Calmly and oh-so-skillfully done by Aaron, his dark eyes focused and intent on the monitor. Not a single hesitation in his movements throughout the entire thing, he was obviously supremely confident in his work.

Supremely confident as a lover, as well.

Sighing, Hope closed her eyes, and images of their evening together filled her mind. The carved planes of his handsome face, his brown eyes looking at her with humor and heat. The heart-stopping beauty of his muscular physique, lying over her, pressed against her.

The sensations, too. The deep, hot, mind-blowing kisses that nearly melted her to the floor. The shivery feel of his fingers stroking her skin. The masculine scent of him in her nostrils as she kissed and licked his strong jaw, his throat, his chest. She breathed through her nose, imagining it all, sinking into thoughts of him and what they'd done together until her heart was tripping as though he really were there.

The thought had her flinging her eyelids open and sitting bolt upright to stare at the door, then slumping back into the chair when she saw it was still closed. Lord, the memory of his scent had seemed so vivid, she'd been suddenly terrified he'd be standing right there. Asking what in the world she was doing there.

And why did it seem terrifying, anyway?

She stood and paced the small room. A one-night fling with a super-sexy man was just that. It had no impact or influence on the decision she'd made to have a baby now while she still could. She knew what she wanted and wasn't ashamed of it. Hadn't made the decision hastily. Her mother fully supported her. Which were the only things that mattered. Certainly not the briefest of relationships, so she shouldn't have even the slightest funny feeling about it.

At the same time, it was a very private thing, wasn't it? She didn't want to share it with the world yet, especially since she had no idea whether things would go as she planned or not. Despite wanting to keep it to herself for now, she feared lying wouldn't work if Aaron saw her there. It had never come easily to her and he'd probably see through it anyway. So what could be her excuse, then? *Oh, I'm doing research on IVF just because I'm interested in it.*

Not because I'm planning to get pregnant that way in just a couple of weeks.

She sighed again. At some point, he'd probably see her at work with her belly swollen. But by then, their amazing evening together would be a distant memory, wouldn't it? It was the "right now," just days after they'd made love, that must be making her feel so strange about him finding out her plans.

She tensed as the door opened, but it was a short, middle-aged woman, and not, thankfully, Aaron. Presumably the office manager she'd been told to expect.

"Hello!" The woman held out her hand. "I'm Sue Calloway. I run this place, and don't let any of the doctors tell you otherwise."

Hope liked her cheerful smile immediately. "My mother always says that women run the world and men take the credit for it."

"True. Very true." Sue nodded and chuckled, then her mirth faded and she gestured for Hope to sit down. "Part of running this place is giving patients unfortunate news. Which is that Dr. Devor has had to leave Cambridge to tend to a family emergency and won't be back until probably next week, or possibly longer."

"Oh no!" Hope stared at her, heart sinking. Next week? What a disappointing delay!

But the peculiar feeling that instantly rolled around in her gut at the news had her wondering about that thought. Because the feeling seemed just as much relief as dismay, and how could that be? Yes, she was a little scared. But from the time she was a teen, she'd pictured two things in her life. Becoming a certified midwife, and holding her own baby in her arms.

Anger joined the other confusing emotions churning in her chest. Why had she listened to her parents' insistence that she couldn't do both at the same time, just because they hadn't been able to? Just because they'd gotten married too young because her mum was pregnant, and didn't even like each other much?

Their battles eventually became a cold, distant silence between the two of them, and between her and her dad, too. Doubtless all that had scarred her in some way. She knew it must be part of the reason why she'd never been able to commit to a man. Never truly loved a man.

Never truly loved George, and hoped and prayed that he was wrong. That there wasn't something utterly lacking inside her heart that would make it impossible to love anyone, including this baby she so wanted.

Her throat closed as fear clutched at her again, but she fiercely shook it off. She could love her child. She knew she could.

"You have several options, though," Sue said.

"Options?"

"Obviously, you can simply wait until Dr. Devor returns, and we'll put you at the top of his schedule then. Or you can see another of our IVF consultants to discuss the treatment options and get the necessary tests done. If you decide to go on with it, you could already be getting started on the course of hormones to stimulate your ovaries before Dr. Devor even returns."

About the only thing Hope heard the woman say was "you can see another of our IVF consultants," which sent a cold shiver down her spine, and not the good kind Aaron had sent through her whole body the other night. Imagining just running into him here was bad enough, but having him as her consultant? After they'd slept together?

Not only disturbing, but also highly unethical. What could she say to Sue, though? *Oh, well, another doctor would be fine, except not sexy Dr. Cartwright because he's already seen me completely and intimately naked.*

Sue was regarding her a bit oddly, and she wondered

what she looked like, other than very, very flushed at the embarrassing thought. She cleared her throat. "Thank you for giving me some options. Since it sounds like Dr. Devor will likely return fairly soon, I think I'll just wait until then."

"Fine. I'll call you to schedule another appointment when he's back."

"That sounds perfect. Thank you."

They both stood and Sue opened the door, gesturing for her to lead the way. Hope took a few tentative steps down a short hall and into the waiting room, her nerves jangling all over again as she furtively glanced around, then practically ran out of the door, not caring if Sue thought she was a nutcase or not.

She kept going until she was a good distance from the office before she finally slowed down, annoyed with herself that she was being such a Nervous Nellie, but unable to stop feeling that way. She pressed her hands to her hot cheeks, not paying much attention to where she was walking, until she realized she was outside the swinging doors to the hospital wing where Aaron would be fertilizing Mrs. Walters's eggs at 1:00 p.m. The ICSI procedure.

It wasn't the procedure she would be using, since traditional IVF was an easier method if the ICSI procedure wasn't necessary for success. But she'd been fascinated to see the egg retrieval today, and knew getting to see firsthand this fairly new procedure would be too. Fascinating because she was a nurse and a midwife, and because she'd be having her own IVF procedure soon.

She stared at the door, feeling indecisive and uncomfortable all over again, which was completely unlike her. Aaron had suggested she join him there for educational reasons, right? It had nothing to do with the undeniable chemistry between them that zapped in the air every time their eyes met.

Right. She shook her head and forced herself to move on down the hall and out of the door. The last thing she should do was encourage the man to think she was interested in him. She had big plans, wonderful plans, and shoving aside and trying to forget about her ridiculous attraction to Aaron Cartwright was the only sensible choice.

Aaron grabbed his briefcase of patient files to study later and took a few steps down the office hallway, poking his head into Sue's office. "My last patient canceled, so I'm heading home."

"Early for you. Hot date tonight?"

He had to chuckle at Sue's exaggerated eyebrow waggling as she asked. "Why do you want to know? Jealous?"

"I live for gossip. You know that."

"Well, I'm sorry to disappoint you, but I'm just going to take advantage of what's left of the daylight to go for a run, then do some paperwork. Excitement is my middle name."

"Hmm. Either you're not telling me the truth, or you've decided you don't want to break any more hearts right now and ruin a girl's holiday."

The truth? Truth was, the only woman he was interested in at the moment had clearly meant it when she'd said one night was all she could offer. He'd been disappointed when she hadn't shown up to see the ICSI procedure she'd seemed so interested in, and while it was possible she'd just gotten stuck at whatever her appointment was, he had a feeling it was more that she'd decided to keep her distance.

Then the past few days, when he'd found reasons to stop into the labor and delivery ward and seen Hope at a distance, she'd given him a quick smile and wave of her fingers before practically tearing off in the other direction.

Which was a very clear message—*keep your distance, buddy.* A message that should have left him shrugging his shoulders and moving on. Problem was, he didn't want to move on right then. He wanted to spend more time enjoying her lively mind and her beautiful body. He just had to figure out a way to charm her into it.

If he ever had a chance to be near her and spend time with her again, that was. Which was looking less promising by the day.

"I don't know where you got this idea that I'm a heartbreaker," he said. "The women I date don't expect anything long-term."

"Maybe don't expect it, but definitely want it. And why you're so determined to stay footloose and fancy-free, I don't know."

Didn't take a rocket scientist, or a shrink, to figure it out. Abandonment in childhood created adults who didn't want to risk that happening again. Moving from place to place and not getting too close to anyone or anything was the solution. Pathetic? Probably, but he'd been just fine living his life that way. "Why you're so determined to see me tied down, I don't know either. Probably so I can be as miserable as Paul is."

She tossed a wadded-up ball of paper at his head and he laughed that he'd gotten the reaction he'd wanted, and a change of subject. "See you tomorrow."

"After that insult, you'll be lucky if I'm here."

"You'll be here. Not being able to bug me every day

would drive you crazy." Chuckling at the second ball of paper launched at his head and the faux outrage on her face, he ducked out of the office, only to practically knock down the receptionist.

"Sorry, Liz!" He grabbed her plump shoulders to steady her. "Sue's in a bad mood, trying to hurt me, and I wasn't looking where I was going."

"Well, this will cheer her up, but probably not you," Liz said, grinning broadly as she held up a newspaper. "She said there would be a photo of you with a woman at the gala, and she'll be happy to be right."

He sighed and put his briefcase by his feet to reach for the paper. Hopefully, the article concentrated mostly on the adoption foundation, and not on him. For whatever reason though, after the past few galas, the reporters had seemed to love to include tidbits about his background and his single status along with the important information. He didn't care much for it, but could put up with undesirable attention if it helped get the foundation the attention he worked for.

"Let me see," Sue said, practically chortling as she came to stand next to him.

"I have it folded to the photo. Page seven, on the other side." Liz tapped the paper with her finger. "He's dancing with a gorgeous blonde, and the picture practically looks like an advertisement for Valentine's Day, the way they're making eyes at one another."

The only woman he'd danced with had been Hope, and gorgeous blonde was just a small part of the way he'd describe her. He frowned and turned the paper over. Sure enough, amid other photos of various attendees, there they were, dancing so closely their bodies were touching, and looking into one another's eyes as if there weren't another soul in the room.

Well, damn. Part of him felt a little embarrassed at what the photo revealed. But staring at the picture reminded him how stunning she'd looked that night. Her sweet smile. Her intelligent, amused eyes. The beautiful curve of her lips.

The memory of it all hit him almost as though she were in his arms again. The feel of the smooth skin of her back against his palm, the way her curves fit his body as they danced, the scent of her in his nose and the mesmerizing blue of her eyes as they met his.

His memories moved on to the incredible bliss they'd shared later that night in glorious Technicolor, and his damned mindless body actually started to physically react. He folded the paper with a snap. "I'll read it later. Make a note, Sue, to get the newspaper reporter and photographer to the Christmas adoption party, so they can get more important photos of adoptable kids meeting potential parents."

"I already have, and you know it. It's not my fault they took this kind of pic, which I know you hate." She tugged at the paper. "Might as well let me see it, because I get it at home anyway."

"You live for gossip, all right. Especially when it involves me." He grimaced at her and handed it over. If he didn't, it would make it seem suspiciously an even bigger deal. He braced himself, knowing Sue would tease him about the way he and Hope were looking all starstruck at one another. How had she managed to make him forget everything in the room but her? "Fine. But I don't want to hear anything more about it."

"Oh, you two *are* making goo-goo eyes at one another! She—"

To his surprise, Sue stopped in mid-sentence, and the mirth in her face disappeared as she stared at the photo, then slowly moved her gaze up to Aaron. Her expression was so oddly, well, *stunned* was the word that came to mind, it was downright strange. "What? What's with the weird face? You're looking at me like it's a picture of me dancing with the queen. Or the devil."

"No. I just—she's a midwife here at CRMU, right?"

"Right. She's one of several that came to share a few adoption stories with donors, which I appreciated. Then we danced, and that photo is ridiculous, because we weren't making goo-goo eyes at each other at all. So don't act like there's some big meaning behind it." He wasn't about to share anything else, or admit that the picture captured exactly how he'd been feeling at that moment.

Captivated and aroused.

"I won't. Of course it's just a meaningless picture of a brief moment. You don't have any real interest in her, do you?"

She sounded almost hopeful, which was also very strange, since she was always nagging him about finding the right woman and settling down, despite him always responding that he had zero interest in that. "No. We were just dancing." And that was a lie, but his interest in Hope wasn't anyone's business.

Sue put on a smile that seemed oddly forced as she folded the newspaper and gave it back to Liz. Which was one more bizarre thing, since in the past when things like this had happened she'd loved parading it around the office to show everyone. What in the world was making her act so strange?

Not that he was unhappy about closing the newspaper and the subject. "I'm heading out. See you in the morning."

The photo of him and Hope swam in his mind, and damned if part of him wanted to swing through Labor and Delivery again just to look at her in person. Maybe see if she'd be off work soon.

Then reminded himself about her not wanting any more contact between them. Since when had he wanted to be an annoyance to a woman? If she wasn't interested, there were others who were. And yeah, maybe this strange preoccupation with her really was a sign he'd been in Cambridge too long.

He strode down the hall toward the parking garage and glanced at the weather report on his phone, glad to see it was warm enough outside that he could take his run wearing a single layer of clothes. Running hard and building up a sweat would both relax his tight muscles after doing procedures all day, and get his one-track mind off Hope Sanders.

"Help! I have an emergency!" a woman's voice shouted. "I need a delivery doctor right away! Can anyone help?"

CHAPTER FIVE

AARON TURNED TOWARD the loud, anxious voice, astonished to see Hope Sanders literally running down the hall full steam, pushing a patient on a cart and craning her neck to look in various open doors as she shouted. A nurse followed just as fast, and he pivoted in their direction, then strode beside her as she kept up her fast pace.

"What's wrong?" He glanced at the moaning woman on the cart. "What do you need?"

"I have a shoulder dystocia. Can't move the baby into position. The doctors on call are busy with at-risk births and there's no time to lose. I'm getting her to the OR now."

"Why do you think it's shoulder dystocia?" he asked, tossing his briefcase on a nurse's desk as they hurried by.

"The head crowned, then turtled back against the perineum and the baby's cheeks bulged out," she continued in a tight, breathless voice as she swung the cart through the OR doors with remarkable precision, considering she'd barely slowed down.

Damn. Definitely dystocia, which had to be dealt with immediately, or the baby could be either seriously injured or die. And Aaron hadn't dealt with one since his obstetrics training in the United States, and then only a few times.

"I thought the dad was going to faint, so he's been taken to the waiting room," Hope said.

"All right." He quickly scrubbed, then snapped on gloves as Hope and the nurse got the patient set up in the room. The moaning, obviously terrified mother stared at him as he stood in front of her, Hope beside him.

"Is it okay? Oh, my God," she cried, her moan morphing into a wail.

"Let's see what's going on," Aaron said. Keeping his voice calm and soothing was an effort when he saw what he and Hope were dealing with here. Every muscle tensed and he took a deep breath, working to keep his calm and remember his training. "How long do you think it's been since the baby's head crowned?"

"Probably only a minute. I knew I had to get help immediately." Hope pressed the microphone around her neck. "I'll get Neonatal on the line now."

"Good. Anesthesia, too, in case we have to C-section. Nurse, I need you to keep track of the time, and call out every thirty seconds that pass. Mom, what's happening here is that the baby's shoulder is stuck on your pelvis. I'm going to try to release it, okay?"

Her answer was another wail as he used the various maneuvers that sometimes worked in a situation like this. "Sorry. Hang in there. Big baby we've got here."

Hope anticipated every action as they worked together to release the baby's shoulder, but it was still jammed tight like a branch in a river rock.

"Thirty seconds," the nurse said.

Sweat pricked Aaron's skin as Hope's intense eyes met his, and he knew she was thinking exactly what he was. That if they couldn't get the baby out within moments, the chances of it being healthy and undamaged were damned unlikely.

"Is anesthesia on the way? No choice but to do the Zavanelli maneuver. Get her prepped for C-section. Make it a flash and dash to get the Betadine on in a hurry. Not low transverse, classical. You know time is critical. Then get scrubbed to assist."

She gave him a quick nod. "Got it."

Aaron sucked in another calming breath as he worked to maneuver the baby back to a position they could deliver it with a C-section. Hope quickly swabbed the woman's belly with antiseptic. Anesthesia ran in, and Aaron sent up a silent prayer of thanks that the troops had arrived. Except they were far from out of the woods.

"Need general anesthesia, and some Versed too. Hang in there for us, Mom."

"Oh, God," the mother said again, gasping, her eyes already closing, her words slurred. "My baby. Is it going… to be…all right?"

"Doing the best we can." He didn't know the answer to her question, but he damned well was going to get the baby out as fast as possible to increase the odds of it surviving. Aaron tensely watched the anesthesia team get the patient intubated. "Is she ready?"

"She's out. Good to go."

"I'm ready, too, Doctor," Hope said next to him.

"Good. Nurse, hand me the knife. Hope, I'm going to need you to help me from below."

"I'm getting baby moved up a little more," Hope said, her eyes fierce with concentration. "It's…it's fully back in her uterus now."

"Good. I'm going to get started. Neonatal here yet?"

"Not yet," Hope answered, her voice tense and worried.

"I need you to assist. Get ready to resuscitate baby and run it to the special care baby unit if Neonatal's not here in time."

"I'm ready."

Aaron began the section and got the baby exposed as quickly as possible. He reached to lift the baby boy out, gritting his teeth at the infant's dangerously deep purple color. If they didn't get him breathing in short order, he either wouldn't make it, or there'd be damage to his brain.

He quickly wiped the baby's face, but knew Hope and the nurse would do a better job with cleaning the baby and getting it breathing than he would remember how to do.

As he passed the infant to Hope his eyes briefly met hers. Intense blue eyes that reflected back the same concern he had about the baby's chances before she quickly focused with deep concentration on the infant.

"Is the Ambu bag ready?" Hope asked the nurse without looking up as she swiftly and efficiently suctioned the baby's mouth and nose.

"Right here."

Hope reached for it, placing the oxygen mask over the child's nose and mouth as she instructed the nurse to rub the baby with a towel to dry and warm him. Just as Aaron was about to turn to the mother the rest of the cavalry ran into the room. He huffed out a giant breath of relief. Had to be the neonatal team, ready to assist Hope and take over. Then it was time to pray like hell for the little guy.

He watched for a second to see Hope pass the baby to the neonatal team. They wasted no time getting the baby resuscitated and stabilized as they checked his heart rate.

Aaron sent up a silent prayer of thanks that the infant's color already seemed a little better.

He refocused on the still-unconscious mother, who'd been through quite an ordeal, and got started repairing her incision. He could hear Hope briefing the neonatal team. Calm, composed information and questions, which was impressive, since he knew she had to be feeling the same adrenaline rush and stress he did.

"Baby's in good hands, Dr. Cartwright," Hope said from across the room. "I'll scrub again, then I'll help you close."

"Good." He wasn't about to say, *I can use all the help I can get* and let everyone in the room know he was a little rusty at surgery, but had a feeling Hope already knew that.

Hope stood next to him, her arm pressing against his as they worked together. He glanced down at her and their eyes met again. This time, hers were smiling. "Impressive work, Dr. Cartwright. No one would ever guess you didn't deliver babies every day, especially tough ones like this."

"Doubt that's true, but thanks. And you were pretty impressive yourself, diagnosing the problem instantly, getting her down to the OR and getting big baby pushed back up in time for me to get him out fast. We made a pretty good team, I think."

"Yeah. We did." Their eyes met again, held, and this time there was an odd, serious note in her eyes along with that smile and a clear admiration that made him feel pretty damned happy he'd been in the right place at the right time.

"Did Neonatal get cord blood to check baby's gases?"

"Yes. They sent it to the lab stat, so we should know his PH soon. I'm praying he's okay."

So was Aaron. He'd almost forgotten how amazing it was to help bring a baby into the world and felt an attachment to the little guy. "How's his anterior shoulder and arm?"

"Not moving it quite as well as he should, but the pediatrician said she thinks it's going to be fine."

"Good."

They finished the repair in silence, Hope again working efficiently, anticipating everything he needed before he had to ask. "Okay." He sat back and snapped off his gloves. "We can slow down her meds now and get Mom waking up," he said to the anesthesiologist. "Nurse, can you take care of Mom and get her to Recovery while Hope and I go talk to the family?"

"Yes, Doctor."

The two of them walked together toward the waiting room, and the same sense of connection he'd felt with Hope from the moment they'd first spent time together was there, but magnified times ten. He knew it was probably because they'd gone through such an intense procedure together with a baby's life on the line, but it was a sensation he wasn't familiar with. Didn't know what to do with, either.

"Let's see if we can get the PH test results before we talk to family. If he's healthy we can pass that good news on, but if we're not sure yet it would make sense to gently prepare them for the possibility that he'd gone without oxygen a little too long and will have to be evaluated."

"I agree." She talked into the little microphone around her neck, then looked up at him, her blue eyes lit with joy. "PH was seven point four! Clearly no brain damage. He's going to be just fine."

"Thank God." The relief that swept through him was surprisingly intense. Despite the stress of it all, he realized he was glad he'd had this experience today. Helping people conceive, being there for them for both success and failure, was what he did every day. Bringing that baby into the world was an entirely different kind of important. A reminder, really, that when he helped a couple get pregnant the end result was an incredible miracle. "You did it, Hope. You got him to the OR, then stabilized and bagged in the nick of time."

"No, we did it. And Mum is all right, too, thanks to you." Her elated and admiring gaze met his, and just as his chest began to fill with the same emotion she surprised him by practically launching herself at him, flinging her arms around his neck. A laugh bubbled from her lips as his arms wrapped around her, too. As if they belonged there. "Thank God you were in the hall when I came looking for help. You were amazing."

"Like we said before, it was a team effort, Hope." He couldn't stop his hand from gently smoothing back strands of hair on her forehead that had escaped her ponytail. "You were more than amazing, and have a lot to be proud of today."

"We do." To his shock and utter pleasure, she gave him a big, smacking kiss on the lips, and he had to force himself to not go back for one less celebratory and a lot more sensual.

"I have to tell you though, for a minute there I was really worried," she said. "When you couldn't get him loose, even after you tried to turn him several different ways, and his color was so ghastly, I really thought it might be too late."

"For the record, I was a little worried, too." He pressed his mouth to her ear. "Don't tell anybody, but I've never delivered a shoulder dystocia by myself before."

"What? That makes it even more amazing!" Her eyes widened. "I guess I should have realized. You help people make babies, you don't deliver them. When was the last time you did?"

"Obviously, during my obstetrics training I delivered a lot of babies, but not since then. And dystocia is pretty rare, as you know, though I hear it's getting more common with bigger babies being born."

"He was a big one, wasn't he? I hope I don't have to go through that again any time soon." Unfortunately, she seemed to realize she was clinging to his neck and drew back. While Aaron liked her just where she was, her body pressed all warm and soft against his, he figured the hospital hallway didn't provide the kind of privacy he found himself wishing for at that moment.

A man leaped up the second they stepped into the waiting room, and Hope approached him with a smile. "First, Mum and baby are doing fine, Mr. Smith. And second, it's a boy! Congratulations."

"Oh, thank God. Thank you. Thank you so much."

The man's voice was choked, and his eyes puddled up as he pumped Hope's hand. Aaron felt relieved all over again that they were able to give him good news, when it had been too damned close to being the opposite.

"This is Dr. Cartwright, who delivered your son. I'll let him explain what had to happen."

"Hope probably told you the baby's shoulder was lodged into your wife's pubic bone. We did what we could to get him loose, but in the end had to do a Cesarean section. Being stuck in the birth canal like that is traumatizing to a baby, and we had to deliver him fast. But as Hope told you, your wife is fine and your son is fine. Quite a bruiser, too—I predict he'll be a damn good rugby player someday."

The man laughed and swiped at his eyes. "Can I see them?"

"Baby is in the SCBU, on the second floor," Hope said. "I'll meet you there in a few minutes, then take you, and baby, too, if I get the green light, to see your wife."

The man again profusely thanked them and left, leaving Aaron to enjoy the smiling blue of Hope's eyes for another minute. And he realized that, despite telling himself he needed to be, he wasn't ready to accept her insistence that one evening together was all they could have.

Why he wanted to convince a woman to be with him if she didn't want to be, he didn't know, but he wasn't going to waste time wondering. And with any luck, today's events just might have provided him with a damned good bargaining tool.

"I think a celebration is in order, don't you?" he asked, looking down into Hope's glowing eyes. "How about we do that punting you're dying to learn how to do, then have a drink in honor of Mom and big bruiser? I checked the weather just a little while ago, and it really is balmy right now. Honest."

"I... I..."

He hated to see her joyous smile fade, her face turn away from him slightly to look over his shoulder at the wall. He grasped her chin in his fingers to bring her gaze back to him, and the troubled expression on her face made it difficult to keep his tone light. "Are you saying

'Aye-aye, Captain,' in anticipation of our boating expedition? What time are you off?"

"I'm working late, actually. Sorry."

Well, damned if her voice and expression weren't both equally stiff now. The part of him that knew he should go right back to what he'd decided earlier, which was to forget about her and whatever reason she had for not wanting to spend time with him, was overwhelmed by the chemistry between them. An attraction that sizzled every bit as much as it had the other night whether she liked it or not.

He dropped his hand from her chin and glanced around. The few people nearby were doing their jobs, and didn't seem particularly interested in watching the two of them. "Is that true, or an excuse because you don't want to go out with me?"

"Okay." Her gaze met his squarely. "I'm not working late. It's just that, like I said before, we can't date."

Those blue eyes might be trying to look decisive and firm, but he was pretty sure the little pucker between her brows showed confusion. And he knew damned well the heat sparking between them didn't go just one way. Did it?

"That you would fib about that gouges right into my heart, you know."

"Uh-huh. As though I could hurt Dr. Aaron Cartwright's feelings." The eye roll she gave didn't completely conceal the flicker of worry on her face that maybe she actually had, and he had to smile at how sweet she was.

"You might be surprised." He didn't share his feelings easily, but he sure as hell had them. Especially around her. At the moment, those feelings were pushing him to coerce her into saying "yes" to a little more time together, good idea or not. "All I'm suggesting is a little celebration of our success, and for one of Cambridge's lifelong citizens to learn punting so she doesn't embarrass her hometown. But if you won't join me, I'll just go home and celebrate with a beer all by my lonesome, even though I did come to your rescue."

"Not my rescue, the mum and baby's rescue." She folded her arms across her chest, but the amusement in her eyes that suddenly replaced the worry had him hopeful that she just might cave and forget whatever concerns she had. "Why I'm letting you twist my arm this way, I don't know," she said, shaking her head. "After I take Mr. Smith to see his wife and possibly bring baby to her as well, I'll get cleaned up. I'll meet you at the dock by that pub we went by the…the other night."

Her face flushed as soon as she finished the sentence. The last thing he wanted was for memories of that night to make her change her mind, though how that could happen, he couldn't imagine. Lord knew those memories were part of what made him determined to be with her again. "Listen, I rode my bike to work, but how about I ride it home now to get my car and pick you up here in, say, an hour instead of meeting you there?"

"You rode your bike?" Those pretty pink lips of hers parted in surprise. "I rode my bike, too, since it was such a nice day."

"See there? It was meant to be." And it was. He'd felt that way the minute he'd met her, and this was more proof they were destined to spend some time together for a while. "We can enjoy the warm, late afternoon sun by riding along the river, have our punting lesson, then eat pub food. I'll meet you at the north bike racks in an hour."

He almost turned to walk away, not wanting to give

her the chance to say no, but knew that would be rude. So he waited, his chest feeling a little tighter with each long beat that passed, wondering why her answer mattered so much. Why he felt nearly weak with relief when she finally nodded. "All right. An hour."

"Good." He headed back toward the nurses' station where he'd left his briefcase, resisting the urge to look back at her. Wishing she'd been smiling when she'd answered, instead of so serious-looking, but he'd take what he could get.

With any luck, Hope really did want to be with him this evening and didn't just feel obligated after he'd been so pushy about it. That kind of question had never entered his mind before on past dates, and he didn't like it that he had to wonder about it now. But however their evening together went, for better or for worse, it was more than worth finding the answer.

CHAPTER SIX

THE EVENING SUN glowed low on the horizon, casting fingers of brilliant gold through the barren trees and across the landscape, turning the still green grass to a cheerful chartreuse. Hope breathed in the clear air, her chest somehow light and energized at the same time her tummy tightened with misgiving, wondering what in the world she was doing.

She dared to glance at the man riding beside her, the sun gleaming on his chestnut hair and movie-star-handsome face. Sunglasses covered his eyes, and he wore a fairly tight-fitting, long-sleeved athletic shirt that molded itself to the contours of his muscular arms and torso, and *whoo, boy*, were those contours very, very sexy.

He must have felt her looking at him, as he turned to her and smiled. The curve of his lips was sexy, too, and why was she out here tempting herself with this *über*-attractive man when any kind of relationship was out of the question?

The rapid beat of her heart gave her the unwelcome answer, and it wasn't because she was riding the bicycle. The pace they kept was pretty modest, and as she focused her attention on the river path she couldn't deny the truth.

She was out here with him because she wanted to be.

Which made her one confused woman. Then again, he wasn't a man who was looking for anything long-term, so her inadequacy in that arena didn't matter, right? She didn't have to understand love and relationships to get all hot and bothered just by looking at him. To want to sink into his kisses and enjoy the feel of his arms around her holding her close one more time.

She stole another glance at him, and darn it if he wasn't still smiling at her, looking as though he was thoroughly enjoying this ride with her. And if he was, that made it okay, didn't it? Enjoy a little harmless fun together just once more, with no expectations for anything more, like lots of singles did all the time.

The thought reassured and relaxed her, and she inwardly laughed at herself for making all of this a bigger thing than it was.

"There's a bike rack down here. Follow me," Aaron said, speeding up to take the lead.

They rode single file down a small incline to a rack filled with bicycles. Aaron slowed to a stop and shoved his front wheel into a slot before coming to grasp the handlebars of hers as she balanced on it. The path was shadowed here, and he slipped off his sunglasses, tucking them into the neck of his shirt before he reached for the clip of her helmet.

"Instead of messing with my helmet, maybe you should try wearing one of your own," she said, brushing aside his fingers to undo the clip herself, at the same time hoping to also brush aside the tingles that simple touch had sent down her throat. "I would think every doctor was well acquainted with the dangers of a head injury."

He smiled, and as she stared at the curve of his lips she nearly forgot to remove her helmet after she'd unclipped it. Her hair tangled a little inside it as she pulled it off, and she was trying to shake it loose when his fingers set it free, gently combing through it.

"If I'm racing, or skiing fast, I wear one. But meandering down a river trail? I'd rather feel the wind on my head."

"You can fall and hit your head on cement just straddling a bike," she said, intentionally sounding like a scolding schoolmarm in the hopes that he wouldn't notice how his touch made her heart go into a near arrhythmia. Trying not to think about how hunky he looked in his athletic clothes with his thick hair all tousled from said wind. With a five o'clock shadow darkening his sculpted jaw.

She asked herself why she'd wanted to come out with him again. The clear, gorgeous answer was right in front of her, enough to tempt any woman with a beating heart. Which hers was currently doing in double time.

Those chocolatey brown eyes of his crinkled at the corners as his gaze captured hers. "Well, all of life's a risk, isn't it?"

Yes, it sure was. She had a very big feeling that being here with him tonight posed some kind of serious risk, but what exactly that risk was she didn't know. Consequences, maybe, too?

She definitely hoped not. But it was her last chance for a little pre-baby, pre-changed-life fun, right? Before she devoted herself to loving her baby, proving she was as capable of that as anyone who'd always wanted a child. Proving George wrong.

Gulping in some courage, Hope got off her bike. Surely she'd look back on this evening and mock herself about silly thoughts of risks and consequences from a simple night out with a man.

Aaron's big hand engulfed hers as they walked to the punts. "Are you ready for your first lesson?"

"Not sure. Will I embarrass myself?"

"The only possible way you could embarrass yourself is if you get so frustrated you throw the pole overboard. Which I've seen happen. If you just plan to have fun learning, you'll be fine."

She had to laugh. "I admit I like to be good at whatever I do, but I think I'm mature enough to know that everything takes practice. So I'll go for the fun, and shove the competitive Hope under the punt."

"I admit I'd enjoy seeing the competitive Hope some time. Very intriguing to wonder what she would be like," he said with a teasing look.

"She can be scary. Especially in sports. In school once, I was so intent on getting the netball in the hoop I cracked heads with another girl and nearly knocked both of us out."

"Now I understand your nagging about the bike helmet," he said, laughing. "The good news is you're not likely to crack your head open punting even if you fall out, so you can forgo the helmet. Though you do look very cute in it."

He'd leaned close as he spoke, his voice a sexy deep rumble in her ear that gave her bad thoughts. Thoughts of ditching this punting lesson to suggest something a lot more fun.

She yanked her thoughts back to what they'd been talking about before. If she could remember what it was. Oh, yes. Helmets and punting.

"Helmets are not cute, but they are practical," she said, conjuring the schoolmarm voice again in the hopes that he didn't notice her slight breathlessness.

"And you're a very practical woman. Sometimes." That teasing glint was back in his eyes, and she tried to ignore its appeal. "I assume you swim, but if you go overboard I promise I'll come rescue you."

"I swim very well, thank you. And I'm quite certain I won't go overboard."

"Don't be so certain. Especially if you, as a Cambridge native, insist on punting Cambridge style."

"Cambridge style?"

They'd reached the dock and Aaron answered as he arranged to rent the boat. "Standing on the till—the flat part at the stern. In Oxford, punters stand inside the boat and punt with the till forward. Both groups think their way is the right way, and are sure anyone who does it different is all wrong."

"And how does an American know all this when I've never heard it?"

He flashed her that quick grin again, more dazzling than the evening sun. "Because I've punted plenty of times with both groups in both places. Pretty amusing to sit back and hear them argue about it, because in Colorado we use both techniques, depending on how fast the water is. And I also know this because I'm an expert at many, many things."

Which she already knew. "There's that ego thing again," she said lightly, hoping he didn't know that memories of his expertise instantly came to mind in glorious detail.

He grinned and reached for her hand again as she stepped into the punt, then followed her as the boat gently rocked. "We'll do it Cambridge style, since we don't want fingers pointing at us, do we? How about I go first so you can watch, then you can take over?"

"Sounds like a good plan." She'd watched plenty of punting in her life without paying much attention to the technique. But watching his muscular physique in that tight shirt of his as he did? Thinking about his various techniques at everything from doctoring to lovemaking? Not something she was going to argue with or complain about.

She settled onto the bench seat, more than happy to be facing him because, as she'd suspected, the moment he pushed the pole into the water his biceps bulged and his pectorals flexed and she wondered if she could convince him to forget the teaching part of it all so she could just keep admiring him.

The boat slid smoothly across the water, away from the other boats cruising the river. Aaron's gaze moved from the river to her and back, and she was struck all over again at how beautiful he truly was, with his chiseled features relaxed, his hair all messy, a smile of pure pleasure on his face. Yes, this man was very different from the busy, serious doctor she'd noticed from afar at the hospital.

This man was testosterone on a stick, and pure fun to boot.

"I don't know, you haven't convinced me it's hard. Slide the pole in and push, then do it again. Easy." The second the words came out of her mouth she sat up straight, blushing from head to toe. Hoping against hope that he hadn't really been listening.

How ridiculous and…and horrifying that her comment had instantly made her think of sex. Was it because she'd said it to Aaron? She glanced away at the water so he couldn't see her eyes. And prayed he wasn't a mind reader.

"Sometimes easy, sometimes...hard."

His eyes gleamed wickedly at her, and she felt beyond thankful for the cool air against her hot cheeks. Lord, she had to be more careful when she talked, and, if at all possible, careful with her thoughts, too. Clearly a challenge in the company of Aaron Cartwright.

"Something a Cambridge native will be interested to know?" he said as he smoothly sent the boat downstream. "Most of the punts we used in Denver were fiberglass and made right here in your fair city."

"Really? I find that hard to believe. I would think all kinds of American boat companies would make them."

"There's not really a lot of punting in the States, to be honest. It's more of a niche thing for boaters. Plus those of us who do punt bow to England's long tradition and expertise."

They glided on in a silence that was peaceful and quiet and yet still that zing she inexplicably couldn't help but feel around him seemed to be right there in the boat, swirling in the air around them as their eyes met. As they smiled at one another, the pleasure of it seeped into every cell in her body, making her feel relaxed and energized at the same time. If she'd ever felt this way around George, maybe she would have agreed to marry him.

She sat bolt upright, shocked at the thought. She hadn't been able to marry George, couldn't love him, because there was something missing inside her. She knew that, knew the distance and near dislike between her parents, the distance between her and her dad, too, had frozen that ability somehow. Made it impossible for her to know how to love someone.

George had been right about that. But not about loving

the baby she'd wanted for so long. That he was wrong about. Had to be.

The long, peaceful glide of the punt down the river eased the tightness that had squeezed her chest. Helped release the unwelcome worries that surely happened to anyone making a big life decision. By the time Aaron nosed the boat to a part of the river where there wasn't a soul in sight, she felt relaxed again. Back to normal and able to enjoy the beautiful evening. He pulled the pole close to the side of the little boat, somehow bringing it to a standstill.

"A nice, empty place to practice. Come on. Your turn."

She didn't particularly want a turn, but he held out his hand and she stood, placing hers in his as the boat rocked a little. He drew her close and just as she thought he might kiss her, her heart thumping hard as she tried to decide what she wanted to do if he did, he turned her around to face the bow. One strong arm came around her stomach, and his pelvis bumped into her lower back, which did nothing to bring her heart rate back to normal.

"Spread your legs a bit for balance. Take the pole in both hands. I was lucky to get the spruce wood one, even though the rental places always have a lot more that are aluminum. The wood ones are warmer to hold, and more responsive, too."

Maybe she was made of wood. Since she was feeling very warm and responsive to the closeness of his body, the rumble of his voice, the brush of his breath against her cheek. *Concentrate*, she scolded herself.

"Okay." She grasped the pole and knew her voice was about as shallow as the river, but what could she do?

"So thrust the pole downward, close to the side of the punt. Let it drop to the bottom, then use both hands to bring it up to your chest, which will propel the boat forward in a nice, long stroke. Like this."

He kept his arm around her waist, and one hand below hers on the pole. Together they drew it in, her hands ending up against her breasts and his, warm and firm, against her abdomen. So intensely aware of every one of those tingly sensations, she hardly noticed the punt glide forward.

"After the stroke, just relax and let the pole float up, then we'll do it again."

Okay, enough. She relaxed her hold on the pole and sucked in a calming breath at the same time a laugh bubbled in her throat. She fisted her free hand on her hip and turned her head to look up at his face, so intimately close to hers. "Now I know why you wanted to teach me this. Is this sport always full of sexual innuendo, or just when you're the instructor?"

"What do you mean?" His fingers opened on the pole as he held it out, his expression the picture of innocence. At the same time the brown eyes crinkling at the corners held a superheated gleam. "If you were taking lessons at a club, those would be the official instructions."

"Maybe so. But you have to admit that talking about spreading legs, warm and responsive poles, and stroking then relaxing is about as sexual a conversation as a person can have."

"Maybe it's your interpretation of it, and not the conversation itself." His head dipped to touch his mouth to her cheek, slipping it over to her ear and making her shiver. "Could it be that, unconsciously, you want it to be sexual? And maybe I'm subconsciously wanting the same thing."

She had a feeling there was no maybe about it for

either of them. Hope let her head tip back against his collarbone and closed her eyes, giving herself up to the pleasure of his warm mouth on her skin. Trailing along her jaw in a breathlessly slow journey to eventually rest against the corner of her mouth.

She turned, his arm sliding along her belly around to her back, and their eyes met for a long, hungry moment before he kissed her. Her eyes slid closed as she sank into the intoxicating taste of Aaron. She let go of the pole completely, wanting to wrap her arms around his neck and pull him even closer, wanting to feel the solid strength of him pressed tightly against her body.

Perfection. Wasn't it? Warm and heady perfection. Just as she'd thought when they'd swayed together on that dance floor, and as they'd made love, their bodies seemed to be designed to fit together.

The arm that had been wrapped around her so tightly loosened, then dropped away for a split second until she could feel the heat from his palm through her shirt as it tracked to her side. Across her belly and up to cup her breast through her clothes. It felt so good, a little inarticulate sound formed in the middle of their kiss, and he pulled back an inch. The eyes staring into hers were half-mast and rich as the darkest Belgian chocolate. "You're so damn soft, so beautiful. I love to touch you. Love the feel of you."

His touch, his words, his mouth devouring hers again sent flames licking across her skin. When he lifted his hand from her breast, she opened her mouth to protest, but she thought, *Why?* His fingers slipped under her shirt to gently caress her quivering stomach then slide inside her bra to thumb her nipple.

This time, the sound she made was more like a moan.

Which quickly changed to a yelp as the boat jerked with a solid thud, jolting loose the lovely warm palm cupping her breast and making her take a stumbling side step. The pole in Aaron's hand jabbed hard into her spine before clattering to the side of the boat and diving straight into the water.

"Well, hell! Sit down for a sec."

Aaron grasped her shoulders to steady her, then jumped into action. Her legs shaky, she lowered herself to the seat and watched Aaron kneel and try in vain to reach the pole, finally sticking both arms all the way into the water, sweeping them as if he were doing the breaststroke.

A different version of which he'd just been doing to her, the enjoyment of which had left the punt without a captain.

Hope had to giggle at the whole situation with the punt still knocking against the bank and the pole still escaping. "Are you going to have to jump in to get it?"

"I hope not." He kept paddling, slowly moving the punt away from the bank and toward the middle of the river in chase. "You said you're a good swimmer. Feel like practicing?"

"No way. The only water I swim in is either a heated pool or the Mediterranean. Besides, you're in charge of this excursion."

"Unfortunately true. Almost…there. Aha! Got…it!" He leaned way over, dangerously tipping the punt in the process, and managed to grab the pole, which disappointed Hope slightly. She wouldn't have minded seeing his clothes clinging to him if he'd had to get soaking wet.

With a triumphant whoop, he twisted to sit on the floor of the boat and raised the pole over his head like a victorious gladiator. That grin of his flashed wide as water dripped over his eyebrows and down his temples from the hair above his forehead, which had apparently gotten dipped into the river during the pursuit. Water dripped from his wet sleeves, too, and he looked so adorably boyish at that moment, her heart got disturbingly squishy.

"Impressed?" he asked as he rested the pole on his knees to wipe water from his face.

"Impressed that we whacked into the bank, nearly knocking us off our feet? That you might have had to swim for the pole or we'd be trapped in the middle of the river for days?"

"No." He moved to sit beside her. A few drops of water dripped on her shirt when he moved to wrap his arm around her shoulder, until he must have realized how wet he was and rested it on his lap instead. He leaned close, his eyes gleaming. "Impressed that I managed to stop kissing you and touching you long enough to deal with the problem. Would have thought only a ten-magnitude earthquake would shake me out of that kind of trance."

"Oh." Apparently, he'd put her in a similar trance. And apparently she still was, since "oh" was the only word that came to mind.

"Besides, if we'd gotten stuck in the middle of the river, I would have gone into the water and towed you to safety. Just like Humphrey Bogart in *The African Queen*."

"I'd like to see that." The image had her giggling again. "Maybe I'll come punting with you again sometime after all."

"No maybe about it." He pressed his lips to hers and her humor faded as she clutched his wet sleeves, a part of her mind vaguely thinking that it wouldn't be such a bad thing to be trapped on a boat with him for days on end. Not a bad thing at all.

The boat lurched again, banging their mouths together. "Ouch!" Hope pressed her fingers to her lips, and he pulled them away, peering with a frown.

"You okay?"

"Yes. You?" She pressed her fingers to his lips and he smiled against them before kissing each one.

"No blood. Which is unfortunate, since a man like me enjoys bragging about sporting injuries." He stood and grabbed the pole, pushing them from the bank. "Even so, I'd better get this boat under control before we hit some wild rapids."

"There are no wild rapids on the River Cam."

"Are you sure? Because just being on it with you has felt like a wild ride, and I'm ready for more of it."

A wild ride. Being with Aaron was definitely that. Even as he steered the boat, his eyes kept returning to hers, holding so much heat that her skin warmed without even his touch. She didn't have to be a mind reader to know exactly what the man had "more of" in mind, and her breath caught.

Should she let herself have one more wild ride with him?

She watched his muscles bunch as he pushed the pole into the water, his wet sleeves outlining his forearms and biceps with every steady stroke. His gaze collided with hers, and she knew the answer.

Yes. This crazy attraction between them was like nothing she'd felt before. Aaron didn't want a relationship, and she didn't either. She'd spent her life being confident in what she wanted and acting on it, including her decision to get pregnant and start a family. She felt good about that. She did, except for those times she let the negative voices of her past drown out her optimism.

And right now, she felt good about Aaron Cartwright, too. She wanted him, and couldn't think of a single reason why she shouldn't act on it for one more doubtless amazing time.

Her future plans weren't a factor. They weren't his business or anyone else's. He'd move on and she'd have her new life and all would be wonderful.

"You still have that brandy in your apartment you offered me before?"

"I do." His brow arched over the super-heated gleam in his eyes. "You needing to be warmed up?"

"I am," she said softly, resolutely throwing all caution overboard. "I find I'm needing it very much."

CHAPTER SEVEN

"HERE." AARON WRAPPED Hope's slender fingers around the snifter, his mouth already watering just thinking about how it would taste on her tongue when he kissed her. "Liquid warmth."

"Mmm. Liquid warmth sounds nice."

It sure did. His breath backed up in his lungs at the way she looked up at him beneath her lashes, a sexy smile on her lips as she sipped the brandy. The kind of liquid warmth he wanted to get his fingers on—her own special brand of liquid warmth that another part of his body couldn't wait to enjoy again. A part currently throbbing so hard he could barely think.

He remembered to take a swallow of his own drink, thinking maybe he should chug it instead of sip it so they could move on fast to the next part of their evening together. It would burn his throat, but would doubtless be preferable to this burning desire for her that he could barely bank down.

"So tell me," he asked, partly because he wanted to know, and partly because he needed to ratchet back his libido before he pounced on her like a Rottweiler on a filet mignon. "Why did you decide you wanted to come here tonight, when you told me after the gala that you could only offer me one time together?"

"Because I realized short-term fun doesn't have to be limited to once." She set her glass on the bar and stepped close to wrap her arms around his neck, a smile in her beautiful eyes. "Twice seems like a good plan when it's you, which is why I decided to seduce you one last time."

"Was that you seducing me?" A short laugh came from his chest, despite the disturbing feeling her words "one last time" gave him. And why they felt disturbing was a complete mystery, since women who didn't want anything from him were exactly the kind he preferred to date. "Insulting a man's skill at sport is how you seduce him?"

"Well, honestly, I don't have a lot of experience in seduction, so I'm sorry if my technique was lacking." Her lips came against his in a featherlight touch. "Asking to come here for brandy was about as forward as I get."

"You don't need a single seduction technique, Hope," he whispered against the sweet lips touching his. "You seduced me the second I saw you at the gala. Hell, you seduced me every time I saw you at the hospital when we'd never even met."

"Sounds like we're on the same page, then. Mutual seduction for one more memorable night."

He looked deep into the sincere blue of her eyes, realizing she really meant that she wanted this to be it for them, and wondered if the peculiar, off-balance sensation that gave him was from the shoe being on the other foot this time, or from something else.

He carefully set his snifter on the bar, but before he could analyze what he was feeling Hope pressed her soft breasts to his chest and kissed him.

His eyes closed as her tongue licked across his lower

lip, then swept inside to dance with his. Just as he'd guessed, the taste of the brandy in both their mouths added one more layer of tingling heat to their kiss. A kiss that held the same intense chemistry he'd felt with her that very first night roared through his blood, leaving him feeling dazed and crazed and more than a little out of control.

He grasped her shapely butt cheeks in his palms and lifted her, achingly sliding her body up his until it was right where he needed it to be. At first, he felt beyond grateful she responded by wrapping her legs tightly around his waist, until the pressure of her pelvis against his rock-hard body nearly undid him. He groaned into her mouth, and took a few steps to his biggest armchair before his legs buckled under him, sitting with her knees on either side of his hips.

"Time to enjoy some more of that liquid warmth," he managed to say as he found the elastic waist of her sweat pants and slid his hand inside.

"I left my brandy on the bar. I—oh, Aaron..."

He slipped his fingers farther inside her panties, loving the sound of his name on her lips. The sound of her moan. "This is the liquid warmth I've wanted all night. You, too?"

Her answer was unintelligible against his mouth, her breathing growing as ragged as his own. The soft slide of her mouth and tongue against his, the feel of her wet heat, was about to make him lose control, and he pulled his mouth from hers. Forced his hazy mind to focus on how he was touching her, on bringing her the pleasure she deserved. The pleasure he wanted so much to give.

The problem with that plan was that he was looking at her now. At her eyes, staring at him, slightly glassy but filled with desire, too. At her lips, moist, parted as she breathed. Just like that first night when he'd touched her like this, as his blood pounded through his veins and his heart drummed in his ears he was certain he'd never seen anything as beautiful as Hope Sanders about to climax.

He brought his other hand from her back to tunnel beneath her shirt and her bra, cupping her breast and caressing her nipple softly with his palm. "Come for me, Hope," he whispered, because he wanted to see her face when it happened, and because he was afraid if she didn't he damned well might and completely embarrass himself. "I want to be inside you, and—"

"I...we...oh..." Her voice trembled and shook with her body, and when she finally opened her eyes again, he expected that she might look a little self-conscious, just as she had their first night together. Instead she gave him a slow smile, then reached to press both palms to his beating heart, filling him with that sense of connection he kept feeling with her. Of belonging, which made no sense because he'd never really belonged anywhere. Had always known he never would.

"Aaron." She leaned forward to kiss him and he sank into the pleasure of it, surprised that after the intense heat of the past minutes the sensation felt more sweet and intimate than lustful. He held her face between his hands and made love to her mouth. Tunneled his fingers into the silky soft, golden waves that had been the very first thing he'd noticed about her long ago.

He had a feeling they would have sat that way for a long, blissful, strangely content moment if Hope hadn't broken the kiss to pull her shirt over her head. Slid from his lap to wriggle out of her athletic pants. She reached for his pants as she stood there, gorgeous and tantalizing, in only her bra and panties, and his breath got stuck in his lungs. "Time for these to come off, Dr. Cartwright. Ecstasy Street doesn't go only one way."

"You're the driver." Only too happy to strip fast, he had his clothes off in record time and pulled her underwear off, too. Picking her up to sit straddling his lap once more, he got distracted by the view. Her pink nipples on pert breasts, her smooth, pale shoulders, the slender curve of her waist and the moist triangle between her legs he'd had the privilege to touch only moments ago.

"You are so beautiful. I could look at you all night. Kiss you all night." It was true, and the first thing he wanted to kiss was that taut bit of pink candy right in front of him. He lowered his head to take her nipple into his mouth, but to his surprise she jerked back.

"Uh-uh. You gave me the driver's seat, remember?"

"Yeah. But the passenger's allowed to touch the music dial, right?"

Her eyes laughed at the same time they smoldered. "Maybe later." Her warm palms cupped his cheeks as she kissed him, then slid down to his chest and stomach, and every inch they traveled sent sparks across his flesh. He lifted his hands to her breasts, hoping like hell she wouldn't object, because he wanted to touch her, too, wanted to feel every inch of her soft skin.

After long minutes of kissing and touching until both were more than ready to move to the next step, he stood, carrying her in his arms as he strode to the bathroom to grab a condom. She took it from him with a smile so sensuous, it stole what little breath he had left. He realized at that moment there was nothing in the world more seductive than a sweet, smart woman who knew what she wanted both outside and inside the bedroom.

He dropped back down into the chair and groaned as she took charge of the condom, then lifted herself onto him. They moved slowly together, and the connection between them changed. More intimate, more overwhelming, as she moved on him. The look that had been on her face when he'd touched her was there again, her eyes intensely fixed on his as they moved in a rhythm as perfect and fulfilling as what they'd shared before. As he grasped her hips and made her one with him. As they moved together, building speed, until they peaked and crested and rounded the corner, flying across the finish line together.

Her silky hair spreading across his chest, her breath came hot against his chest as she collapsed onto him. He slowly stroked her back and beautiful round bottom, trying to get his breathing under control, feeling as blissed-out as he'd ever felt in his life. Then a peculiar sensation permeated the fog and his eyes sprang open in horror.

"Jesus, Hope." She lifted her head to look at him, clearly hearing the panic in his voice. "I think the condom broke."

Hope practically fell off his lap, all post-lovemaking deliciousness obliterated as Aaron jumped up, and the truth of his statement was instantly all too obvious. She looked up from the offending condom to see alarm all over Aaron's face.

"I'm so sorry. Damn it, this is…" He stopped and shook his head, his voice tight as he strode off to the bathroom to take care of the problem.

She wished she could reassure him that he didn't need to worry, but was afraid any conversation about her fertility issues would lead to things she didn't want to talk about. Like her plans for IVF and why, which were no one's business but hers.

But she could tell him she was at the wrong time of her cycle, which was the truth. Except standing there naked with the bloom completely off the rose, so to speak, wasn't the time to have a conversation about anything. She grabbed up her underwear and bra, getting them on in record time before Aaron came back. He'd somehow donned his sweatpants again, and had a big navy blue robe in his hands that he held open for her.

"I don't know what to say," he said, a deep frown between his brows. "I just bought the damned things, so how that could have happened, I don't know."

She slipped into the robe and tugged it tightly around her, figuring she'd feel better if she covered up now and finished dressing later in private. "Well, the good news is I keep careful track of my cycle, and this isn't the time for anything to happen, so I'm positive we don't need to be worried about that."

"You're sure?" He looked at her from his bar where he'd picked up their brandy snifters again, placing them on a table next to the chair.

"I'm sure." Poor man was finally looking more normal, thank goodness. He'd blanched so white she'd thought he might pass out. Obviously, he was a man who had zero interest in being a father, but then again, nobody wanted an unexpected pregnancy from a fling, anyway, right? But his distress was the perfect reason to emphasize again that they couldn't go out anymore, and she had a feeling that this time he'd agree.

She couldn't allow that thought to make her feel slightly blue.

"I probably should head on home now. I assume you're

willing to give me a lift? Or do I need to ride my bike home?" she said jokingly, resolutely squashing the inconvenient regret suddenly poking at her heart over never seeing him again.

"Funny." He closed the gap between them to grasp her elbows. A fairly loud breath of obvious relief whooshed from his lungs as he kissed her forehead. "Sorry I freaked out, but I figured you'd be upset, too. If you're not worried, though, that's good."

Not worried about the broken condom, but about him finding out about her IVF plans? For whatever reason, the thought still made her very uncomfortable, no matter how confident and good she felt about that decision.

"No worries. Honest." She tugged loose from his hold and leaned over to pick up her clothes again, squeaking in surprise when he swept her up into his arms and sat back down in the chair.

"I'll take you home soon, but I want to feel your warm body curved in my lap just a little longer," he said, touching his lips to her forehead and folding her close against him. "All right?"

"All right." And it was. More than all right. His firm chest and soft skin felt like the perfect place to rest her head, and she let herself relax into the rare comfort of being held like this. "So tell me more about your adoption foundation," Hope murmured, since she'd been wondering but hadn't asked yet. Apparently too distracted by all the kissing and lovemaking they'd done since practically the moment they'd met. "I heard you've got another Christmas party scheduled for it?"

"Next Wednesday. The hotel where we held the fundraising gala is giving me a good price on one of their meeting rooms, and my office staff is decorating it."

"More fund-raising with a different crowd?"

"No. This one is to give parents wanting to adopt a chance to meet children in a casual, fun environment. And for the kids to meet them, too, without the pressure and nervousness that can come with one-on-one introductions."

His hands slowly moved on her, up and down her arm, stroking her neck, cupping her jaw, twining his fingers with hers, and a fuzzy tenderness filled her heart. She'd been touched before. She was thirty-four-years old, for heaven's sake. Why did it feel so different, so overwhelming, with this man?

Probably because her plans to have a baby, to change her life, had given her a reason to relax around him. To not worry about what she could or couldn't give. A sense of freedom, she supposed, since all the usual dynamics of dating didn't apply anymore.

"That's such a great idea," she said, trying to focus on the conversation without getting distracted. Impressed all over again at how caring he was, how multifaceted. "Really wonderful—I can just picture all the children and adults enjoying spending time together, but with an important purpose, too."

"It works well. Everyone eats together and plays games, and with any luck find a good fit they want to pursue."

"Do you need some help? I did a lot of babysitting as a teen—babies are so adorable, it's what made me decide to become a midwife. But I enjoy all children, and I know quite a few games that would be fun to play."

"That would be great." He smiled down at her, pressing his lips to her nose. "I'm jealous I never had a babysitter like you. I can easily picture you as the cutest, most popular babysitter a kid could want."

Why did everything he said make her heart feel absurdly warm and squishy? They were just words, the kind a man like Aaron flirted and teased with, but she couldn't help but like hearing them anyway. "I'll plan on it, then."

The second the words were out of her mouth, she froze. Tonight was clear evidence that she couldn't resist his charms whenever they spent time together, even when she planned to. What was she thinking? She was about to start her fertility treatments. Any more time with him was out of the question.

Panic welled up as her mind spun, trying to find a plausible excuse to back out of her ill-thought-out commitment, at the same time wishing she could help such a great cause. Then grinned at the "eureka" solution that struck her. Unwitting chaperones.

"I'll ask one or two of the midwives at the hospital if they'd like to come along, too," she said. Surely that would help both of them stay at arm's length, wouldn't it?

"Any and all help is welcome."

He didn't seem to interpret her suggestion for what it really was, and she relaxed. "So, I've been wondering what made you decide to start the foundation. I know it had to have taken a lot of work."

He focused his attention on her hair, lazily twirling it between his fingers for so long, she wondered if he'd even heard her question. She was about to open her mouth to ask again, when he finally spoke.

"I was adopted, and my parents gave me a good home and upbringing. In California, I did a little volunteering with a great organization that helps children become permanently placed with families, instead of moving around for years from one home to another in foster care. When I came to Cambridge and saw the same challenges older children had in finding real homes, I decided I'd like to bring that model here."

"How old were you when you were adopted?"

Again the silence. Since it didn't seem like a particularly troubling question, she had to wonder what, exactly, his history was that he clearly didn't like to talk about. Finally, he gave her a short answer. "It wasn't an issue for me, but it is for a lot of kids."

Another oddly evasive response. She swiveled in his arms a little, trying to see his eyes, which were still focused on her hair. "Not an issue for you?"

Finally, his eyes met hers again. She couldn't interpret what was in them, exactly, but was that pain she saw deep inside?

She cupped his cheek in her hand. "You can tell me, you know. Just between us, I promise."

He stared at her a long moment, his face impassive, and just when she'd become sure he wouldn't share anything with her, he spoke. "I was almost two when I went into foster care. My biological mother was...unstable. Children's Services gives a parent as much time as they can to get healthy, but it didn't happen. My parents adopted me when I was seven."

"Oh, Aaron." Her heart hurt for the little boy he used to be, having to leave his mother then moving from home to home for years until he found a family. "That sounds... very hard. But you do know, don't you, how impressive it is that you've taken a difficult experience and turned it into a positive? Starting your foundation to help children and parents find one another is a wonderful thing."

He pulled her close and pressed his lips to hers, mak-

ing it very obvious he didn't want to talk about it anymore. That the subject was over. The pinch in her heart
from learning about the past pain in his life faded as his
mouth moved on hers. Kissing her with such softness,
such unbearable sweetness, she found herself unable to
think about anything but the way he made her feel as she
melted into him all over again.

"How about your issues?" he whispered against her
lips. "Why are you so damned determined to have a spe-
cific, preplanned expiration date for us, starting tomorrow?"

She opened her eyes to look into the brown ones meeting hers again, no longer seemingly evasive, but very,
very serious. And that seriousness nearly pulled the truth
out of her. Nearly made her want to come clean, and that
would be that and she wouldn't have to worry about him
finding out, worry about how he'd react, any more.

But she couldn't, even though she probably should.
Didn't want to see whatever his reaction would be. He'd
given her only the bare bones of his own history though,
right? She could give him the same thing. Not the painful
distance between her parents that had made their home
life uncomfortable. Not her father's obvious resentment
of being stuck with her and her mum, which was doubtless part of her inability to love a man.

She'd share some of her history. But her future? That,
she'd keep to herself. The future she both worried about
and couldn't wait for.

"I dated a man for a long time. Eight years, and I still
didn't want to commit. Just couldn't. So he broke it off.
Never met anyone afterward I wanted anything permanent with, either, so I realized I must just not be cut out
for something like that."

"That answers the question that's been bothering me, which is how the amazing Hope Sanders could possibly still be single." He placed his fingers beneath her chin, bringing her gaze back to his, which she hadn't even realized she'd moved to the wall behind him. "But I don't get what that has to do with us dating a little while. Two people, neither wanting a permanent relationship, who have enough electricity between them to light the entire city of Cambridge. Sounds pretty perfect to me."

Well, darn. She should have realized her answer wouldn't work, because he'd already said he had no interest in permanency, either.

"My life just isn't in a place where I can date you or anyone." She forced a light tone to her voice to banish the serious turn the conversation had taken. "But for what it's worth, if it was, you'd be at the top of the list. And I'd like to leave it at that, okay?"

Solemn brown eyes studied her face for what seemed like long minutes before he nodded.

"Still interested in helping with the party? If not, I won't hold you to it."

"Of course I'll still help with the party. What better way to celebrate the Christmas season than helping children find good homes?"

"Thank you." He leaned forward to press his lips to hers, and she soaked in their sweetness, trying to ignore the sharp sting in her chest that it had to be their very last kiss. "I'll leave the agenda on the front desk at the office so you can see what we already have planned."

"Okay." She set down her glass and slid off his lap, grabbing up her clothes. "I'd better be going. I have an early day at the hospital tomorrow."

She didn't look back as she hurried to the bathroom,

but knew he watched her go. Could feel his eyes on her every bit as painfully as she could feel the tight pinch in her heart that this was really goodbye.

CHAPTER EIGHT

"So the party is tomorrow, Bonnie, and I was wondering if you had any interest in helping me conduct some games for the children and potential parents," Hope said over the tea she and the energetic new midwife were sharing in the hospital cafeteria. "A few other people from the hospital will be there, and some of the parents coming have other children. I thought it might be a fun way for you to meet people."

"Sounds really nice, Hope. How sweet of you to think of me!" Bonnie smiled. "What a wonderful thing, a Christmas party to bring children together with people looking to adopt. I don't know Dr. Cartwright, other than that he's dreamily good-looking, but he's now high on my list of wonderful people at CRMU."

On Hope's, too, but she wasn't about to say so. Also had to stop thinking about the dreamily good-looking man. The man who wasn't only dreamy, but an amazing doctor, a caring man. With eyes like warm fudge and a crooked smile you couldn't help but smile back at.

How could she have fallen under the man's spell after spending mere hours with him? Clearly she wasn't cut out to have quick flings, if she couldn't stop feeling all gooey about him when it was over with. Who would have known she was even capable of that? But since that was the undeniable truth, she so wished she hadn't agreed to help with his party.

Somehow, she'd have to avoid him as much as possible by concentrating on the children and talking with Bonnie and the other CRMU staff instead of gazing like a schoolgirl at Dr. Aaron Cartwright.

"Yes, his adoption foundation is doing a lot of good." She tried to keep her voice professional, without a hint that thinking of the way the man kissed and made love kept invading her brain every time she mentioned him, sending unwelcome heat across her skin. Which instantly turned icy when she thought of her appointment this afternoon, and how she'd have to make sure she stealthily avoided Aaron Cartwright like a cat burglar while she was there. "I'll be picking up the party agenda from his office, and you and I can see what might fit into it."

"Could I bring my daughter, Freya?"

"I don't see why not. She'd probably have lots of fun. How old is she?"

"Just five. But fun is her middle name, believe me."

"Five is such an adorable age. I can't wait to meet her. And since I'm sure you have lots of experience playing games with Freya, it'll be wonderful to have you play with the children her age at the party, too. I'm so glad you can come." Hope drank the last of her tea, swallowing down the sick feeling in the pit of her stomach at the thought of heading to the offices the IVF doctors shared. "Got to go. Thanks for helping. See you tomorrow."

Hands sweating, she hurried down the hallway to meet with Dr. Devor. She stood outside the closed door, thinking the heavy, dark wood looked grimly ominous, then nearly laughed slightly hysterically at the ridiculous

thought. Was she being overdramatic or what? She sucked
in a great gulp of fortifying air and stepped inside.

The receptionist took her promptly back to a different
waiting room, and she dropped into the chair, her knees
a little weak with relief. How could she have gotten so
lucky to have been whisked out of the waiting room so
fast? Hidden from brown eyes that would doubtless have
held a very big question.

Stop this right now, she scolded herself. She was more
than ready to begin the IVF treatments. She could not
allow herself to worry about anything, or what anyone
thought, especially a man she'd simply slept with and
was now not going to see ever again except at one little
Christmas party and from afar at the hospital. If he found
out, so be it. She'd hold her head up proudly and be the
person she'd always been, a woman who knew what she
wanted and went for it.

Despite her big, brave pep talk, her heart leaped into
her throat at the short knock on the door before it opened.
"Dr. Devor!" She knew her voice sounded overly en-
thused, the relieved smile on her face so wide the man
probably thought she was slightly nutty.

"Hope. Good to see you," he said with a smile as he
shut the door behind him. "I'm sorry I wasn't here for
your appointment last week. My son at university was
in a car accident, and my wife and I had to go see him
in the hospital."

"Oh, no. Is he all right?"

"Thankfully, yes. Banged his noggin pretty good,
though. I told him he was lucky to be so hardheaded."

"That sounds like the kind of thing my father likes
to say to me, too. Stubbornness is a virtue, as far as I'm
concerned."

He chuckled as he sat in a chair in front of hers. "I agree, along with determination, which I've seen that you have in abundance. Did you go through all the literature I sent home with you?"

"I did. I've been thoroughly educating myself on all of it." The procedure didn't scare her. It was everything else twisting her stomach in a knot.

"Good." He nodded. "It's unfortunate we weren't successful with intrauterine insemination. It's likely due to your endometriosis, though I'd hoped it would still work. Have you thought about all we discussed regarding IVF and single parenting? The pros and cons?"

"I've thought about it very carefully and discussed everything at length with my parents." Her mum, at least, and she was fully behind Hope's decision. "I know what I'm getting into, and my family will help me as needed. I've wanted to be a mother forever, and I'm ready to do this."

"All right, then." He smiled. "I have every reason to believe that IVF will give you the baby you want."

The baby she wanted. A lump stuck in her throat as she had an instant vision of a cherub-faced infant, gurgling and cooing. A toddler running through her small house, eventually tired enough to snuggle in her lap. Growing into a child happily playing and reading books and giving abundant love and hugs, and it all filled her chest with such an overwhelming joy, she knew she had to be making the right decision. Having a job she adored and, when she wasn't working, holding a baby of her own in her arms? Perfect and wonderful.

She clasped her hands and drew a fortifying breath. "So let's get started."

"Here's the schedule we'll follow." He handed her a

calendar. "Today we'll draw your blood to do some necessary tests. When you come back next week, you'll receive an injection of FSH, which is a hormone that will stimulate your ovaries to produce more than one egg. The following week, we'll do some more blood tests and use ultrasound to determine if the eggs are ready for collection. If not, we'll need to give the FSH a little more time to work, usually just another day or two, then you'll get an injection of a medication that will help the eggs ripen."

"And then you'll retrieve the eggs?"

"Timing is important. We can't take them out too soon, or too late, or they won't develop normally." Maybe he saw the worry she couldn't help feel, because he smiled and leaned forward to pat her knee. "I've got it down to a science, I promise. And you'll be sedated when I retrieve the eggs at the perfect time."

"I know. I got to see Dr. Cartwright retrieving a patient's eggs and it was pretty amazing." Saying his name brought that awful twisting feeling to her belly again, which was beyond irritating. Why did that keep happening? He had nothing to do with her life or her goals or her future.

"Dr. Cartwright is very good at his job, and I am, too. You saw there's nothing to be scared about." Another smile from Dr. Devor. "So as we discussed on your first appointment, the eggs I retrieve will meet the donor sperm right away. We'll keep an eye on them while they spend a few days together, then I'll look to see which three seem the most viable, and freeze the rest that look good. Then we'll be ready for the IVF."

"You said that's done pretty quickly, right?"

He nodded. "Usually takes only about half an hour. Most women find it virtually painless. Resuming your normal activity is absolutely fine, just no vigorous exercise. Then we wait to see if one or more of the three eggs implants into the uterine wall."

Nervous and excited butterflies flapped around in her belly. "We'll know in about a week and a half, then?"

"Hopefully, though if we don't have a positive pregnancy test at that time we give it another few days and check again."

"Okay." She expelled a big breath and smiled. "I'd like to get started on the stimulating hormones as soon as possible."

"I got a little backed up from being gone, and I apologize for that. But the receptionist will fit you into my schedule as early as possible next week, and we'll have all the lab results in plenty of time before you come."

"All right." Next week suddenly seemed like an eternity, but she stuffed down her impatience. She did a quick mental calculation of the timing for taking the meds and the time needed after the procedure and had to smile. Maybe this delay was meant to be. Maybe learning she was pregnant was going to be the best Christmas present she'd ever had.

As she scheduled her next appointment her mind spun with the thrill of it all. A large envelope with her name on it caught her eye at the receptionist desk, and she remembered Aaron had said he'd leave the party agenda at the front desk for her.

Which brought her to earth with a hard thud, and started those nerves flapping all over again. She furtively glanced around the office, praying she wouldn't see him. Yes, she was as confident as she could be under the circumstances, beyond happy about this next phase of her life, but she didn't feel like talking about it with anyone yet, least of all the man she'd had hot sex with just days ago.

"So you're all set for next Thursday," the receptionist said, looking at her a little quizzically. "We'll see you then."

She flushed, wondering what her expression had been as the thought of Aaron and hot sex and the fear of seeing him had swept through her brain. "Great. Thanks. And I think that envelope is for me."

"Oh. So it is."

She handed it to Hope, who hightailed it out of there, beyond relieved that she'd again dodged running into Aaron. Their time together was too fresh for that, but surely, after enough months had passed for her pregnancy to show, their brief fling would seem very distant, long ago and unimportant.

Except it felt all too disturbingly important right then, and she had a bad feeling it would for a long time.

The sight of silky blond waves tumbling down the back of a tall, slender woman had Aaron doing a double take as he stepped from his office to the front desk, and his heart kicked sharply in his chest. He didn't have to see her sweet face to recognize every gentle curve of Hope Sanders. The door to the hallway closed behind her, and he had a sudden urge to run after her.

But of course he wouldn't. Their relationship had been a brief and memorable moment in time. Fantastic while it lasted, but over with whether he liked it or not.

She must have come into the office to get the party agenda. He looked down at the desktop and, sure enough, the envelope was gone.

The odd weight in his chest lifted a little that he'd at

least get to see her at the party. He knew whatever she came up with for the kids to do would be a big hit. Also knew he had to stop thinking about her, but the good news was his work didn't bring him to the labor and delivery suites very often. His memories of her would fade, and this disturbing preoccupation would fade along with them.

Looking for a new job should probably happen soon. If he decided to move on, his memories of Hope would surely fade even faster, and the thought held both appeal and melancholy. He realized he'd miss Cambridge and the CRMU, which took him a little by surprise.

"When is my next patient scheduled?" he asked Sue as she sent the receptionist on her break and settled herself in the desk chair.

"Um…" she responded, peering at the computer screen. "In fifteen minutes. Plenty of time for you to grab more coffee."

"Just had a cup. I'll stay here and bother you instead."

"Or you could man the desk while I file these and go grab a quick nap," she said, picking up the stack of patient folders on the desk.

"Right. Whirling tornados don't nap, which is why the staff gets out of your way when you barrel through. You—" He stopped mid-word when he saw the folder at the top of Sue's stack. A folder with the name Hope Sanders on it.

"What is that file?" he asked, tapping it with his finger. "She's single. A midwife here."

"I know." Sue glanced at him, then quickly stacked some more files on top of the pile. "She's the woman you were dancing with in the newspaper photo. The one you denied you had any interest in."

Yeah, and he was still going to. And didn't have any interest, really, because she didn't and it was over. "I don't. I'm just confused why there would be a file for her here unless she's a patient."

"Well, you're a doctor in this office. You want to look at the file, you have the right to, but I'm staying out of it."

The frown between her brows, the way she was warily looking at him like the bearer of bad news, sent alarm bells clanging in his brain. Which was stupid, since he didn't have a relationship with Hope Sanders. But as he was trying to convince himself of that, he dug through the stack for it, slid it out and flipped it open.

There was the usual column with the dates patients were in the office, then the next column listing the doctor they'd seen. Two appointments with Tom Devor were noted. The most recent being today. Along with Tom's summary notes on her visit, and the scheduled hormone injections to begin next week, preparing her for IVF.

He blinked, feeling as if the room were tilting a little, then somehow refocused on the page. The scrawled notes practically jumped off the page, loud and clear and unbelievable.

Hope was going to have IVF. The woman he'd kissed and touched and made unforgettable love with just days ago wanted to get pregnant and have a baby from some anonymous sperm donor who wouldn't have one damned thing to do with his child's life. The kid would forever wonder who he was and where he came from and why.

At first utterly numb, his whole body started to feel as if a million little needles were jabbing it, from his feet to the prickle of his scalp, and it got a little hard to breathe. His gaze moved from the file in his hand to Sue. To see the twist of her lips and concern in her eyes that told him she knew all about it, and also knew his claims to not be interested in the woman had been a damned lie.

"Maybe you should sit down for a minute," Sue said, her frown deepening as she stood. "Use this chair."

"I'm fine." And he damned well would be, as soon as he told Hope exactly what he thought about a single woman becoming a parent through IVF, risking multiple births and the potential terrible consequences of that. Yeah, he knew it was none of his business. He wasn't her doctor and he wasn't her boyfriend, and now he saw loud and clear why she'd insisted they couldn't go out again.

Because she'd likely be pregnant very soon.

How was it possible that a beautiful woman like Hope Sanders wanted to have a baby, or multiple babies, all alone? Surely, there was a line of men who'd love nothing more than to have a permanent relationship with her and have a family.

He sucked in a shaky breath, trying to wrap his brain around the whole thing as he seriously pondered heading to her house the second he was off work to talk to her about it.

Sticking his nose in her business probably wouldn't be welcomed, because he was sure she believed she'd carefully thought about it all before deciding on this path. Nearly everyone always did. But he had personal experience with the subject, personal knowledge of how negatively the challenges could affect both her and her children. Challenges that sometimes brought terrible consequences and lifelong pain.

Your mother has given up her parental rights, Aaron. And you know, of course, that we don't know who your father is. I understand all this might make you feel sad, but it's for the best. It means you can find a permanent family to live with, just like your brother and sister have. It's going to be okay.

His fingers tightened on the folder until they were white. Didn't he have an obligation to warn Hope that there was no way she was fully aware of what she and her babies could be facing? Wasn't that why he'd decided to become a fertility specialist to begin with, so he could make sure patients wanting a family truly knew all the pros and cons of IVF? Especially when the doctor performing the procedure was perfectly okay with implanting more than two eggs?

He hated that his hand was shaking as he carefully set Hope's file with the others. "I'll be in my office when my patient arrives."

"I'm sorry this is upsetting to you, Aaron," Sue said, reaching to touch his forearm.

"It's not upsetting. Just surprising. I barely know the woman." Which was obviously true, since he never would have dreamed she had anything like this in mind.

He dropped into his desk chair, wishing he still had paperwork left to do. Hoped like hell his patients came early. Focusing on them would be the distraction he needed to shove down the shock and disbelief he knew he shouldn't be feeling so intensely. Probably talking to Hope about it would be wrong. Probably by the end of the day his intense desire to run to her house that minute would fade away, and he'd be feeling more normal.

Which unfortunately didn't happen. By the end of the work day his shock had faded, but his need to talk to her about it hadn't. He tried to convince himself that the only interest he had in Hope's decision was professional but knew that was a lie.

He'd wondered why she'd been so adamant about them

not going out more than once or twice. Now that he knew the reason, he should be glad it didn't have anything to do with him. Shrug, and let it go. But the truth was, the thought of her getting pregnant through IVF without any support, without a man in her life, without a father for her children, twisted him up in knots.

But as he'd reminded himself ten times in the past few hours, her life was none of his business. He couldn't let it be, and forcefully stuffed down his consuming urge to show up at her door to talk to her, which would be completely inappropriate.

If she ended up coming to the Christmas adoption party to help, he'd be friendly but distant. After that, he'd rarely run into her, unless he was unlucky enough to be in the office the same time she saw Tom Devor. It would be easy to not notice the blue of her eyes. Not notice that gorgeous hair cascading down her back or tamed into a ponytail. Not notice her appealing body in the hallway at the hospital, a body that would change as it carried multiple babies. To not take a second look at her in the cafeteria, smiling and laughing with coworkers, or be aware of her absence when she was on maternity leave.

He grabbed up his briefcase and headed out of the door, deciding the longest run he'd ever taken might be the cure to this jittery, unsettled feeling that wouldn't leave his gut.

Hope Sanders had her life and the decisions she'd made for it, and he had his, which would never include a family. It would be easy to forget all about her.

It would.

CHAPTER NINE

It was scheduled. It was going to happen.

The thought fluttered around Hope's head and heart, taking center stage every time there was a lull at work. Nervousness warred with the excitement in her belly every time she thought of her meeting with Dr. Devor, wondering how the hormones would feel, how they might affect her, what it would be like to have her eggs retrieved once they were ready. Thinking about the fertilization, and how long the week or two would drag on as the cells grew. Thinking about having them implanted into her uterus.

Thinking about really and truly becoming pregnant.

"Congratulations. What a beauty," she said to the awestruck new parents of the baby she'd just helped bring into the world as she placed it, warm and swaddled, into its mother's arms. She hoped her smile showed only her sincerity and didn't at all reveal how antsy she felt about her own life now that she had a moment to think about it all again. "I'll leave the three of you alone for a bit, then I'll be back."

She left the labor and delivery room, wiping her suddenly sweaty hands against her scrubs, wanting to give the thrilled couple some privacy to enjoy their incredibly special first moment with their newborn baby. Maybe a nice, hot cup of tea would calm the restlessness she felt that was more than uncomfortable.

Almost every woman pregnant, or expecting to become pregnant, for the first time felt as she did, didn't they? Elated at the thought of becoming a mother, but a little worried about the rest of it? Wondering about how her body would change, about how the delivery would go, about whether she'd have an infant that slept through the night in just weeks, or one that had colic and cried all the time, even one who might have some developmental difficulty?

Regardless, it didn't matter. The baby or babies she'd be blessed to mother would be all hers, for better or worse, easy or difficult or anywhere in between. She was absolutely sure she could handle whatever came her way, and the thought helped her relax. As did picturing her mum as a very happy grandma, coddling the little ones they'd been blessed with.

The vision brought a smile and she drew a deep breath, shaking her head at herself. Her mother might have had Hope far before she was ready, but she did love children. That kind of love had nothing to do with sensual love, the love between a man and woman. Hope might not have grown up seeing that, or personally experienced it, but knew they were totally separate things, and shoved down the fears and doubts that kept surfacing.

It would be fine. It would be wonderful, and the days until she saw Dr. Devor again to begin the process were going to seem very long indeed.

A distraction was in order, and the best distraction she could think of was checking on the babies she'd delivered that week, and their mothers. All were doing well, and she enjoyed the satisfaction of seeing thriving babies and happy families.

She made her way to the room where Mrs. Smith was recovering from her emergency C-section, pleased to see that her baby was there with her, too. The woman looked tired, and no wonder, considering everything she'd been through, but her smile was happy. "You look like you're getting along pretty well, Mrs. Smith! And so is baby. What did you name him?"

"Patrick. After his grandfather. Dr. Cartwright told my Ted that our Patrick was such a 'bruiser' he was sure to play rugby someday. Since his granddad played rugby, we decided it was perfect. Except now, his granddad is proudly calling him 'Bruiser' instead, so I'm afraid it just might stick."

"Patrick is a lovely name, but Bruiser is unique, that's for sure." Hope had to chuckle, and for a moment she saw not the mother and baby, but Aaron. His eyes crinkling at the corners as he spoke to Mr. Smith, coining that name for the big baby who'd been very difficult to deliver. Aaron had been incredibly calm and efficient during the crisis delivery, especially considering he hadn't done it for a long time. And never alone, which she was surprised he'd admitted, and which showed his utter confidence in himself. The whole thing was amazing, really, and she wondered if the parents had any idea how lucky they'd all been that Aaron had been in the right place at the right time.

"Thank you for helping me and Patrick, Hope." Mrs. Smith reached to squeeze her hand. "I was terrified, so scared for the baby and for myself, too, I admit it. Dr. Cartwright told me the reason he's all right is because you knew right away what the problem was and got immediate help. We owe you a lot for that."

"You don't owe me anything. I'm so lucky my job gives me a chance to help mums and babies. And we're all lucky Dr. Cartwright was there to take charge and get Patrick delivered fast—he did an amazing job with a difficult situation. It's too bad you had to have a C-section, but I know having a healthy baby is well worth the pain you're going through recovering from it." Something she very well might have to experience, too, if more than one baby implanted from the IVF.

"More than worth it." She looked down at Patrick and smiled. "I understand that the kind of C-section I had to have means any more babies would have to be delivered the same way, but I'm okay with that as well. Babies are worth anything we have to go through, don't you think?"

"Yes, Mrs. Smith. I do." And she was about to go through quite a bit for hers, knowing her upcoming pregnancy would be her only pregnancy. She reached to stroke Patrick's downy head, getting another lump in her throat as she pictured holding her own in her arms in the not too distant future.

A quick knock came just before the sound of a familiar voice. "How are you and Bruiser doing today, Mrs. Smith?"

Hope stiffened and turned, knowing without a doubt who'd come in. Willing herself to act and feel normal, and not at all breathless and starry-eyed as she always seemed to be whenever he was near.

Aaron stopped dead in his tracks as their eyes met, his brows lowering in a deep frown. There was something about his expression that sent her heart pounding, and not in a good way. Something about the way his lips had thinned, the way his eyes narrowed slightly as he stared at her. Something about his stiff posture combined with all the rest of it seemed to be sending serious anger vibes directly at her, and her throat suddenly felt a little dry.

What had she done that had obviously disturbed him? Could he...? Surely he hadn't found out about her IVF plans? It must be something else. Something she couldn't think of at that moment. Or maybe she was completely imagining it.

Except the anxious quivers inside her gut didn't think she was imagining it at all.

"Ms. Sanders," he said in a voice that was tight and cool and unlike anything she'd heard from him before. "Nice to see you checking on our patients. If you have a minute, there's something I'd like to talk to you about after I've visited with the Smiths."

She nearly said, *Sorry, I can't*, because the alarm in her brain was ringing loud and clear that whatever he wanted to talk about wouldn't be a pleasant conversation. But avoiding it wouldn't be very mature or professional, and if it was something to do with her work she needed to know. Besides, she was a grown woman who could deal with anything thrown at her. "All right. I'll meet you in the hallway."

She turned to Mrs. Smith and forced a smile. "I'll come back tomorrow to see how you're doing, and with any luck you can take Patrick home soon."

Hope barely heard Mrs. Smith's response as she walked past Aaron to the door. He didn't even look at her as she did, moving to the side of the bed to talk to their patient, as though Hope were suddenly invisible.

What in the world? Out in the hallway, she sucked in a breath as the cowardly part of her urged her to leave, pointing out that if what Aaron wanted to talk about was important he'd find her later. But the perplexed and un-nerved part of her wanted to know what was going on with him and get it over with.

She stood immobile for what was probably only min-utes but seemed like an eternity, when the door finally swung open and Aaron was there. With the same con-fusing and disturbing expression on his face.

"Is there somewhere on this floor we can talk pri-vately?"

Privately. Because of patient confidentiality, or be-cause he was going to let loose on her for something? "There's a meeting room down this hall," she said, mov-ing toward it, proud that her voice sounded pretty normal.

He followed, silent, closing the meeting room door behind them. Last thing she wanted to do was sit at the table for some long chat, so she stopped just a few steps into the room. Curls of foreboding rolled in her stomach as she faced him. "What did you want to talk about?"

Standing maybe three feet from her, he stared at her, folding his arms across his wide chest. The lights in the room were fluorescent, unforgiving, and seemed to em-phasize the tension in his face, the harsh planes of it. "Yesterday, I was at the front desk at my office. Imagine my surprise when I saw a file there with your name on it."

So he did know. That was what this was about. She wiped her sweaty hands down her scrubs, fiercely re-minding herself it didn't matter. He'd have learned about it sooner or later, and she didn't owe him a thing anyway. She tipped up her chin and waited.

"Why the hell are you going to do IVF? With Tom Devor, who doesn't worry about the possible ramifica-tions of multiple births? Don't you realize the serious problems you could be bringing to both yourself and your children?"

"First, I've thought this through very carefully and am well aware of all the pluses and potential minuses. Second, I don't see how this is any of your business. Our relationship was brief, and now it's over."

"And now I know why." His eyes flashed at her. "What I don't know is why you're doing this. It may not be any of my business, but, since it's what I do for a living, I'm making it my business. You have plenty of time to find someone who would be a real father to your children and conceive naturally."

"Sorry, my reasons are not your concern, no matter what you do for a living." She didn't have to explain her mother's infertility from endometriosis when she was only in her twenties. Didn't have to tell him about her own early stages of the disease that would likely make conceiving harder as she got older. Didn't have to share her private inadequacies as a woman.

"Hope." He closed the gap between them to grasp her arms. "Believe me when I say I've been down this road too often, seeing single mothers without support who end up with twins or triplets or even more and can't handle it. They suffer and their babies suffer. Not to mention that many children who never had a father always, always wonder who he was. Always feel an emptiness, a deep longing to know where they came from and who they really are. Is that what you want for your children?"

She stared at him. At what could only be described as anguish along with the anger on his face. Obviously, he must have experienced the heartache he described because of his adoption history. Knowing he must carry some kind of deep pain about it, she felt her own anger at his attitude, at his apparent belief that he had a right to lecture her and tell her what to do, fade a little.

She pressed her palm against his chest and could feel his heart pounding. "I have good support, Aaron. My mum is excited about being a grandmother. She'll be there for me and my baby. Close ties with grandparents will fill any small gap a child feels—I'm sure of it. After all, there are millions of children with only one parent."

"And so many children with no parents, looking for a home." His voice had lowered, the angry tone tempered, but his eyes were still sharp, hard. "You can't count on your mother being here to help. Life has a way of destroying the things you count on. My own parents died just a year apart, both unexpectedly. Did it ever occur to you that you're being selfish? What if you were juggling your job and three babies, and the people helping were gone in an instant? What would you do then?"

"I'd figure it out." She pulled away from his hands, wanting to be done. Wanting to get away from his anger and deep disapproval, which painfully stabbed at her even though she shouldn't let it. "I appreciate that you must know patients who have had difficult problems. But a person can't just stop living because they might experience some challenges they didn't expect."

"I want you to cancel your appointment. Take more time to think about it. If you end up still wanting a child, you should consider adopting. Most already have abandonment issues, and they need a loving home they can call their own. And having one child wouldn't overwhelm you. A single parent."

"So you think I just couldn't handle more than one, is that it? That I'm being *selfish*, thinking only about myself until the going gets tough?" Her own anger was back now, times ten. He'd said so many beautiful things to her, complimentary things, things that she'd thought meant he truly respected her. It had obviously just been part of the have-a-fling game she wasn't experienced with. But now she sure was and would never make that mistake again. "Who do you think you are, telling me what to do and what not to do? You don't even know me. And this conversation is over."

"Hope, listen, I—"

She shouldered past him, ignoring the way his voice had softened, ignoring the confusion and maybe even remorse in it. "Goodbye, Dr. Cartwright. Please stay out of my life."

Aaron parked his car, then just sat there with his head against the seat back. He always looked forward to the adoption party. Enjoyed talking with everyone having a nice time, observing and encouraging good fits between kids and adults that looked very promising for a future together.

But not this one. Feeling like an ass and a jerk, and having to face the person he'd been an ass and jerk to, had him seriously considering skipping it this year.

Which of course he couldn't do. He owed it to the children hoping for a real family to show up and help them feel at ease. He owed it to the parents who'd been invited to talk with him about various ways the foundation supported them before and after adoption. And damn it, he owed it to Hope Sanders to show up and apologize to her.

He sat there a few more minutes, gathering the guts to walk inside. Hope was probably still mad as hell about the way he'd confronted her and lectured her, and who wouldn't be?

How had it happened, anyway? For the hundredth time, he inwardly thrashed himself about his loss of control. After his initial shock of learning Hope's plans had passed, he'd been sure he'd shoved it aside as none of his business. Yes, he liked Hope, but what she did with her life wasn't his concern. His own history didn't give him the right to lecture people on their choices, and even being a fertility doctor only gave him the right to give advice to his own patients. Not try to dictate their decisions.

But in spite of knowing all that, what had happened? The moment he'd walked into Mrs. Smith's room to see Hope's tender smile as she touched the baby's head, the reality that she was about to have the IVF procedure and get pregnant had punched him in the gut all over again, nearly knocking him flat.

Anger and frustration had welled up in his chest, consuming and overpowering. All common sense had been completely smothered out by bad memories. By the pain of his mother's mental illness. The pain of her abandonment. The pain of never knowing anything about his biological father and what kind of man he was.

It had fueled a burning need to tell her she was being crazy, that she had no idea of the horrible things that might happen, that she didn't understand the suffering she might unknowingly cause herself and her offspring.

So he'd blasted her with both barrels. And her reaction had been predictable. The way he would have reacted if someone had butted uninvited into his business and told him something he planned to do, wanted to do, would completely mess up his life and others along with it.

He heaved a deep sigh. He'd made plenty of mistakes in his life, done a few embarrassing things over the years, but this one was without a doubt one of the biggest. Hope probably assumed he was some macho man who believed he could boss women around, and her thinking of him that way sent a sick feeling to his gut.

He had to apologize. Probably, though, the only way she'd accept it, understand why he'd unleashed his verbal fury on her, was if he told her all of his history.

Which wasn't going to happen. His late parents were the only ones who'd known, and it was just as well that information had died with them.

He shoved open his car door and headed into the hotel, his legs feeling a little lead-like. No choice but to accept that Hope doubtless couldn't stand him now, and do what he had to do at the party to make it a success.

The room at the hotel was about a third of the size of the ballroom he'd used for the fund-raiser. He made a mental note to thank his office staff for the great job they'd done with the tinsel and garland draped everywhere. A few of the trees they'd used at the other party lit several corners, and various other Christmas decorations made it all look merry and festive for the guests.

Merry and festive. Not a chance he'd feel even a twinge of that.

He tried hard to get into party mode, smiling at several women dressed as elves, complete with pointy hats and curled slippers with bells, who were handing out small wrapped gifts to excited children. Other folks from the hospital were setting up games or already in the middle of one, and more volunteers were unveiling cupcakes and fruits and other treats that had been placed on a long table covered by a cheerful red tablecloth.

What he didn't see anywhere was Hope Sanders.

Could she have decided not to come? He sure couldn't blame her if she had.

He scanned the room again, and to his shock realized the tightness in his chest wasn't about hating to see disgust or dislike or anger in Hope's eyes. Or some kind of weird manifestation of relief that he apparently didn't have to face it. The squeezing sensation that made it a little hard to breathe was instead a deep and heavy disappointment that she hadn't come.

And how messed up was that? Despite everything, he'd wanted to look at her, talk with her, spend just a little more time with her, no matter if he stood on the lowest rung of her opinion now or not.

Then a flash of golden hair caught his peripheral vision, and he turned, hardly believing it was her emerging from behind one of the Christmas trees with a ball in her hand, holding it up with a beautiful smile on her sweet face. "Here it is! Hiding!"

"Thanks, Miss Hope! I can't believe it rolled all the way back there," a little girl said, giggling as she took the ball and ran back to whatever game she'd been playing.

The hard thump in his chest seemed to obliterate that nasty, squeezing sensation, and he found himself walking toward her before he'd even thought about what he could say. Should say. Or even if he should approach her at all.

But before he got close she was swept away by some other children to play what looked like musical chairs. A game like that wasn't his thing, so he decided to just stand back and watch her. To enjoy the way the light caught in her hair, making it gleam. To see her enthusiasm and laughter and the patient way she explained the game to those who didn't know it. To take in the heartfelt hugs she gave the children when they won or lost, encouraging them to try again.

He shook his head, upset with himself all over again.

How could he have thought for one second this woman might struggle with having children on her own? No matter his own dark history, he should have realized that warm, sweet, upbeat Hope Sanders had plenty of resilience, love and caring to handle it.

With a toddler propped on her hip, Hope headed toward the snack table and handed the child over to a smiling auburn-haired woman he was pretty sure was a midwife new to the CRMU. As Hope turned back to the game their eyes met across the room. She stood very still for a moment, and Aaron's heart about stopped with her. His brain spun through the ways he might approach starting a conversation.

A conversation and an apology.

But before he came up with anything that felt right, that he thought Hope might be willing to hear, she'd begun to move across the room. His heart started back up again, thumping hard with every step she took, and he couldn't take his eyes off the way her skirt swayed gently on her slim hips. The way her hair, too, moved with the same rhythm and suddenly he was struck right between the eyes with another bizarre and awkward revelation.

He felt jealous of the damned anonymous sperm donor that would father Hope's children.

Crazy, idiotic and ridiculous, yes, but he couldn't deny that emotion, stunning though it was. Couldn't pretend it hadn't been part of the reason he'd been unable to keep his opinion to himself instead of confronting and lecturing her.

Which maybe meant he should schedule an appointment with a damned shrink.

He'd never wanted to be committed to one place or one person, and sure as hell had no idea what it took to be a father. Yes, his adoptive dad had been a good role model, though Aaron hadn't been able to see or appreciate that for a long time. But his sperm-donor biological father? He'd gotten half of his genes from that man and didn't want to think about the kind of person he might have been. And the genes from his poor, unstable biological mother?

Not something he wanted to pass on to any child.

But that kind of introspection was disturbing, unwelcome and pointless. He moved to talk to some of the party guests, shoving it all aside, trying very hard to concentrate on everyone he was speaking with and not looking at Hope. But when he did, she seemed clearly focused on a similar goal of not looking at him.

"Nice party you've got here," one of the adoptive dads said to him as they stood by a table of children and adults enjoying the various snacks together. "My wife and I have met quite a few kids the past few months, but this has been hands-down the best environment to talk with them and see them in action. They're a lot more relaxed, you know? And I guess we are, too."

Aaron smiled. "That's the goal, so I'm glad to hear it. Have you—"

The sound of a metal chair toppling over with a clatter interrupted him. He glanced over to see a boy, probably about six years old, pretty much underneath it and kind of rolling around on the floor.

A woman sitting next to the toppled chair shook her head and grinned. "I think that's the fourth boy who's tripped over a chair to get some attention. Guess they don't need to play a game to be silly."

But the blood-curdling shriek that came from the child instantly wiped the humor from everyone's face. Aaron quickly strode over and pulled the chair off the child, setting it upright, and adrenaline rushed through his veins at what was more than obvious.

CHAPTER TEN

AARON CROUCHED DOWN, putting his hands on the boy to try to keep him from writhing around so much and hurting himself worse. "It's all right. You're going to be fine. I'm Dr. Cartwright. Take a breath and tell me where it hurts."

The boy stared up at him with tearful, terrified eyes. "It's my arm. It hurts. My arm hurts."

"I thought so. Let me see if I can help." He turned to the crowd gathering around. "Someone call the emergency squad. Everybody back off, please, so he can breathe."

He gently put his fingers on the child's arm, gritting his teeth at the shriek his barest touch had elicited. Even if he hadn't been a medical professional, he'd have known the kid's arm was broken pretty badly. His forearm was curved at such an odd angle a compound fracture was likely, but thankfully the bone hadn't torn through the skin.

"Oh, my heavens, Aaron, what happened?"

He glanced up to see Hope's worried face just before she crouched down next to him. He hadn't said anything to the boy yet, so he addressed him first, hoping to keep him from getting more scared. "Looks like you've probably got a broken arm, buddy. We're going to have to take you to a hospital to get it fixed up. How do you feel?"

"It hurts. I feel…sick."

He glanced at Hope, who leaped up to grab a small trash pail, just in case. Aaron pressed his fingers to the wrist of the child's uninjured arm to check his pulse as Hope crouched next to him again.

"He looks clammy," she said in a near whisper.

"Yeah. His pulse is a little thready, too." They didn't want the boy fainting on them or going into shock, and he turned to the child again. "We're going to get you a little more comfortable, okay?" He raised his voice to the crowd. "Can somebody find us a tablecloth, or a few coats? And I need one or two of those cupcake boxes emptied and brought over here, and some sturdy twine or a rag I can tear into strips."

Numerous adults sprang into action, and in no time several coats were dropped onto the floor by their feet. Obviously knowing why he'd asked for them, Hope quickly folded the coats as Aaron tried to barely move the boy into position, doing it as gently as possible. Just enough to get his feet up, being careful to not jostle the broken bone. The child cried out and moaned again, clutching his arm close to his body.

Damn. "Try not to move your hurt arm at all, okay?" The boy nodded, but Aaron knew that might be difficult for him and decided he had to get it stabilized fast to make sure he didn't. Last thing the kid needed was to move in such a way that the bone broke through the skin.

"Anybody able to get those cupcake boxes to me?"

"Working on it," someone answered.

Hope slid the jackets under the boy's feet before he'd had to ask her to, then placed a folded tablecloth under his head to keep it from pressing on the hard floor.

"Better, buddy?" he asked the boy, glad that he nodded in answer.

"His name's Ethan," a woman's tremulous voice said.

"Ethan." He patted the child's chest. "You're doing a good job staying still, Ethan."

"I'm trying. But it hurts so much."

"I know. I'm sorry it hurts." He took the kid's good hand and pinched the nail bed of several fingers.

"Checking his capillary refill?" Hope asked.

"Yes. Want to make sure the break hasn't impinged on his arteries. But the nail bed's pinking back up nicely, so it doesn't look like that's happened."

"Good." Hope clasped the boy's hand after Aaron let go of the child's fingers. "You're being so brave, Ethan. Hang in there just a little while longer, okay? The ambulance will be here soon."

Aaron marveled at her soothing and reassuring tone. So reassuring, the boy actually managed to give her a wan smile in return. The warm, sweet smile she sent back, the way she held his hand gently between both of hers, would make anybody feel better. CRMU was damned lucky to have this woman as a nurse and midwife, and so were her patients.

And he'd been lucky to get to spend even one day with her. Which made him want to kick himself all over again that he'd lost control and said things he shouldn't have.

Reassured a little though he seemed to be, the child's worried brown eyes kept moving from Hope to Aaron and back again. He'd fidget then cry out in pain, but in another minute he'd be fidgeting again. Injury or not, expecting a young child to stay completely still was probably asking the impossible, and Aaron knew he had to get the arm stabilized fast.

The EMTs would have the right equipment, and he wished he could wait for them to get there. But all it might take to damage the arm worse would be for the boy to slide it down his belly or clutch it to his chest.

"Is this how you want the empty boxes?" a man asked, holding them out. "Or is there something else you need me to do with them?"

"We'll take them just like that," Aaron said. "Thanks. We'll need that twine, too, or rags. Anybody find something like that?"

"I'm on it," the man said.

Aaron set the boxes on the floor and Hope's eyes met his. "Are you planning to use those as a splint?"

"You're one smart woman, you know that?" He had to believe not many people would have realized that, including plenty of doctors and nurses.

"I know." Her lips curved. "How do you want to do this?"

"That's the tricky part. I don't know exactly, because obviously I'm trying to avoid moving his arm and don't want trying to splint it to end up making it worse instead of better." The boy was looking more scared again, and he gave him a smile. "We want to splint your arm, using a kind of field medicine, like soldiers might do. Maybe you can pretend you're in the army and you've got a battle wound we have to fix up."

"I don't want to be in the army," the boy said, his lip quivering as tears filled his eyes again.

Well, damn. That strategy hadn't worked too well. Aaron looked to Hope. Maybe she had a better idea.

"What kinds of toys do you like to play with?" she asked.

"I don't know." Ethan sniffed back the tears. "Dinosaurs. Cars."

"Do you play with those cars that transform into giant robots? Maybe when we put the splint on your arm, we can pretend you're a car that's out of gas and can't move and the bad guys are after you. But after the splint's on, you'll transform into the giant robot to fight off the bad guys."

"O...Okay." He gave her a smile and looked a little starstruck.

Aaron figured that was probably the way he always looked at Hope, too. He leaned close to her ear. "Did I say smart? Brilliant's more like it."

"You're just now realizing this?"

"As you've already learned, I'm not too bright." Her eyes were on his again, and he hoped she knew what he was saying. Giving her an apology before he was able to apologize for real.

"Got this from the hotel," the helpful man said, handing him what looked like thick kitchen twine.

"This is perfect. Thank you. Robot time, Ethan. Remember, you can't move at all until I've transformed you, okay?" He turned to Hope. "I'm going to slide the cardboard under his arm, and with any luck I'll barely move it from where it's resting on his belly. Why don't you try to gently hold his arm as steady as possible while I do?"

She nodded. "Got it."

Hope held Ethan's hand with hers, and cupped the boy's elbow with her other hand. Aaron carefully slid the cardboard between his arm and stomach, glad the child wasn't shrieking again, just giving the occasional little gasp of pain. "You're doing great, Ethan. Only a little more and I'll have it all the way under your arm."

Sweating a little now, Aaron finally got it in place, sucking in a relieved breath. "Okay. I'm going to fold this sort of tube around his arm and you tie it in place, Hope."

"Already have some pieces cut. I hope they're the right size."

He held the cardboard curved around the boy's arm and watched Hope tie it on with the string loops about an inch apart. As he watched her work he found himself looking at her, the picture of avid concentration. Her lashes were lowered, as she watched herself work. Her brows were knit, and her white teeth sank into her bottom lip.

He could look at her for hours and never tire of the view.

"That's it, I think. Have a look, Dr. Cartwright."

"Perfect." He turned to smile at the boy. "Your transformation is complete, Ethan."

"You know, if you weren't a robot, I'd say you look an awful lot like a trussed roast, Ethan," Hope said with a grin, giving his nose a gentle flick.

The child actually managed a little laugh. "A roasted robot, that's what I am."

Hope looked at Aaron as their eyes met and held, and they both chuckled. The woman was downright magical with kids.

And to think that instead of admiring that about her, he'd insulted her, saying she might not be able to handle being a single mother.

What a damned idiot.

Just as Aaron was trying to figure out what to say or do next the EMTs came in with a cart and equipment.

"Well, you've battled off the bad guys, and now the

good guys have arrived, Ethan," he said. "They're going to get you all fixed up and take good care of you, okay?" Ethan nodded, and Aaron stood, reaching for Hope's hand to help her to her feet. They moved out of the way to give the emergency medical team a chance to work, checking Ethan's vital signs and getting him ready to transfer.

He studied Hope's elegant profile as she watched the EMTs, trying to decide if he should dive into his apology right then, in case he didn't have a chance later. But first, he had to make a point of something else. "You were great with Ethan tonight, Hope. Don't know what I would have done without you."

"You were wonderful, too, Aaron. And all the others who helped, as well. I guess it took a bit of a village, didn't it?" She waved her hand around the room, and he captured it in his again, because he wanted to hold it. Wanted to see if she'd pull it away. Realized, when she didn't, that he'd never in his life cared so much about something as simple as holding a woman's hand.

"I have a feeling if not another soul had been here, you would have done just fine all by yourself." In fact, he was sure that statement was absolutely true. The woman was softness and steel. A gentle nurse and a fearless warrior. He drew her closer, and, when she didn't step back or pull away, the discomfort he'd been feeling since their last, ill-fated meeting eased just a little. He leaned closer. "Can it be our secret again that I haven't seen a broken arm since med school?"

"No. Makes you all the more heroic." She cutely tilted her head. "Just think. When the story hits the local papers about this happening at the wonderful party designed to help children find parents, and the founder of the program who happens to be an OB managed to help a child with a seriously broken arm, people will be impressed. And donations will pour in. The end."

"Well, if that's the angle, I guess I have to go along with it." He had to grin. "What did I say before about you being a PR genius?"

"Did you say that? I don't remember." The way her kissable mouth and beautiful eyes were smiling at him took away a few more of the bruises from the self-bashing he'd given himself after lambasting her, and that he well deserved. "But I do remember other things you said to me just recently that were not so nice."

Her smile completely disappeared and her eyes got all serious. Damn it. But who could blame her? Calling his words "not nice" was an understatement. Seeing the change in her brought the ache about what he'd said surging back into his chest, but that wasn't important. What was important was that he'd hurt *her*. Had shocked and wounded her with his autocratic attitude and judgment, and now was the time to tell her how bad he felt about it. "Listen, I—"

"Is there a parent or guardian who can sign for the patient? And who wants to come to the hospital with us?"

Aaron realized the social worker who had brought a number of children to the party was looking to him with a question in her eyes. Damn. He hesitated for a split second, then gave her a quick nod before he turned back to Hope. "I really need to talk with you, but I have to take care of this first. Can I call you later?"

"All right." Her eyes were still oh-so-serious when he turned to the EMTs.

Aaron wished like hell he could apologize and somehow try to explain a little to Hope right now, but this had to be his top priority. "I'll come." He looked at the social worker. "I know you have to stay here with the other kids and get them back after the party's over. I'll take care of Ethan and keep you posted on whether or not they want to keep him overnight."

"I'm sorry this had to happen to take you from the party, but the rest of the children are having a lot of fun," she said.

"It's fine." He stepped to the gurney and placed his hand on the boy's leg, giving him a smile, hoping he felt at least a little reassured. "I'm coming with you to the hospital. The doctors and nurses will take good care of you, and I will, too, until we can get hold of your foster parents. Okay?"

Ethan nodded, looking grave but thankfully not too afraid. Aaron turned to look at Hope, glad to see she was still standing there. He couldn't tell exactly what expression was on her face, but at least it seemed she wasn't furious with him anymore. He gave her a twisted smile, hoping she'd interpret it the way he wanted her to. Which was that he knew he'd been an ass and owed her an apology.

He turned to the EMTs. "I'll sign everything on the way."

"Wait!" A woman rushed toward them with a man following behind. "Wait, please. We want to come to the hospital with Ethan. To...to get to know him better." She reached for the child's hand with a tender smile, and Aaron was surprised but happy to see Ethan smile back. "Would that be okay with you, Ethan?"

The boy nodded, still smiling, and the man turned to Aaron. "Would we be allowed to do that? We're very interested in spending more time with him now and over Christmas and all."

Well, how about that? Maybe Ethan's mishap would end up being a good thing in the end, giving them all more time to spend together. "Looks like he'd like that. I'll have to sign the medical release papers, and one of the social workers will catch up with you at the hospital to make various arrangements, but otherwise it sounds like a good plan."

With the paperwork signed and Ethan and crew gone, the party resumed, slightly subdued but still festive and fun for the kids. People kept coming up to talk to him and pump his hand, and, while their praise felt a little uncomfortable, maybe Hope was right. Maybe an unfortunate event like Ethan's could turn out to be a good thing. The child might have a new family, and the foundation might get some new donors.

Between conversations, Aaron's attention kept going straight to Hope. To see her sitting at a table with rambunctious children, smashing and squeezing modeling clay to make some kind of creatures. Laughing as she dove toward a chair when the music stopped, pretending to get bumped out of it by a giggling child. Helping little ones, too small to reach everything on the table, fill their plates with goodies.

Accomplished at her job, great with kids, warm, stable, caring and beautiful beyond belief—was there a woman on the planet more perfect than Hope Sanders?

He turned to shake hands with someone else who'd approached him, wondering why thinking about Hope and how amazing she was brought a stab of something uncomfortable to his chest. Probably because he hadn't had the chance to say he was sorry.

Past time for that to happen, and when he was done with his conversation he scanned the room. His gut tightened when he didn't see her. Surely she hadn't left without saying goodbye? Then again, just because they'd helped little Ethan together didn't mean she had any interest in further interaction.

It was clear she was no longer around all the games the children were playing. He had to talk to her. Had to apologize. If she'd just left, maybe he could still catch her in the parking lot. He was about to ask one of the midwives accompanying Hope, but he somehow felt her presence a moment before her golden hair appeared at his shoulder.

Mussed golden hair, with glitter sparkling in it he didn't think was an intentional festive accessory. "All partied out?" he asked, feeling stupidly happy that she was still here, and wondering how any woman could look sweet and adorable and sinfully sexy all at the same time.

"It's been exhausting, I admit, but fun. How about you?"

"Definitely partied out." He grasped a strand of her hair and slid his thumb and forefinger slowly down it. "I like the fashion statement. Though I wouldn't have thought you were a glitter kind of girl."

She laughed softly. "Maybe you don't know the real me."

"Maybe I don't." Which was a good segue to his overdue apology. Except he hated to see the relaxed, happy look she was giving him turn into anger, disgust or dislike or whatever she'd been feeling toward him before tonight. He steeled himself, knowing he had to take whatever lumps were coming regardless. "Hope, I want to apologize for all the things I said to you about your IVF plans. How upset I got about it. I have no right to judge you or lecture you. I was totally out of line."

"Yes, you were."

He waited silently, thinking there must be more coming, like her berating him right back. But she just kept looking at him, and for once her face didn't reveal anything of what she was thinking or feeling. "So." His planned-out apology and explanation seemed to have disappeared from his brain, leaving him floundering a little. "I hope you'll accept my apology. I've seen how smart and competent you are at your job, and now I've seen how great you are with children. If you're sure IVF is what you want, I wish you the best of luck."

He still felt pinned by that blue, impassive gaze of hers and started sweating almost as much as he had getting Ethan's splint on. "You know, you're making me nervous," he said. "Is this your payback for me being rude? You aren't rude back, just an expert at making people feel uncomfortable?"

"I don't try to make people feel uncomfortable. Maybe there's some other reason you do. Maybe it's because you owe me a little more of an explanation for why you went off on me like you did."

Maybe he did. But he wasn't going to go there. "I've just seen a lot of families, and particularly single parents, struggle with multiple births and the problems that can come with that. Preterm and low-birthweight babies, and infants with birth defects, all of which have special needs on top of the normal stress of parenting multiples. That's all. But I know you feel you have support and you're prepared, and I apologize again for saying otherwise."

Those blue eyes still seemed to be looking right through him, seeing things he didn't want her to see, when she finally spoke. "You want to come to the Mill Road Winter Fair with me this weekend?"

He blinked. Of all the things she might possibly have

said just then, inviting him on a date wouldn't have crossed his mind as one of them. He wanted to shout, *Hell, yes,* but had to wonder why she'd asked. "Aren't you the woman who said our fling was over and done with?"

"It is. But now you know why, which also means you understand and accept that we're just friends. Plus I have an ulterior motive."

"I'm guessing this could be some kind of payback for my being unpleasant to you?" Her eyes were gleaming with mischief, and he wondered what she had up her sleeve.

"You would guess right. I'm volunteering at one of the food stalls selling smoothies. Proceeds go to a literacy foundation, and we're shorthanded. Seeing you do emergency surgery the other day tells me you'll be excellent at cutting various fruits to make the smoothies."

That surprised a laugh out of him. The little smirk on her face told him she knew full well he couldn't say no, that he owed her after his prior idiocy. Funny thing was, standing in some food stall all day slicing fruit with her somehow sounded pretty good to him, just as friends or more than that.

More than that couldn't happen now anyway, though, remember? Even if she wasn't planning on IVF, she was obviously a woman who wanted a forever after with kids and a homestead with a picket fence, and he just wasn't that kind of guy.

Being just friends, though? He wasn't sure he could handle that, either, since his thoughts turned to kissing that beautiful mouth and touching her soft skin every time he was anywhere near her. Had to admit, too, that being friends with her while she was pregnant probably would be difficult for him to deal with for all kinds of reasons. Not the least of which had been the extent of his surprising reaction, and his complete inability to control it, when he'd first learned her baby plans.

Her blue eyes were looking at him expectantly, and the smile in them had him feeling good for the first time all day. And that feeling had him wanting to join Hope for one more, no-strings-attached encounter before she moved on with her life, even though it was a bad idea.

"Slicing fruit with you sounds like the best offer I've had all week."

CHAPTER ELEVEN

HOPE DUMPED WHAT seemed like the hundredth batch of cut fruit into the electric blender to join the yogurt, milk and juice and gave it good long zap before pouring it into a cup. "A Mill Road smoothie, made just for you," she said, handing it to the young man who'd ordered it.

"That sounds like an advertising slogan," Aaron said, standing next to her chopping away as he had been for two hours without a complaint. She'd never have guessed when she'd admired him from afar at the hospital how multifaceted the man was, chopping fruit like a trained chef. Devoting all kinds of time to charity causes. "I still think you're fibbing about not moonlighting in the advertising business when you're not working at the hospital."

"Ah, you have no idea what I moonlight at. Maybe I'm a punt-boat operator." She sent him a glance meant to be teasing, since he knew from experience she was not at all adept at punting.

But the brown eyes that met hers weren't laughing, they were…heated? Maybe even hungry, but not in a let's-eat-some-of-this-fruit kind of way. Instantly, she realized her words had sent his mind back to their time on the punt, to all that kissing and touching and maybe even to what came after they were back on dry land, snug in his apartment.

And then her mind went there as well, which made her notice all over again the width of his shoulders, the rippling muscles in his forearms as he chopped, the handsome planes of his face. How he looked far more deliciously edible than any fruit ever could.

He leaned close, his lips inches from her cheek. "If the moonlighting punt-boat operator doesn't stop looking at me like that, I might have to pull you into my arms and kiss you, forgetting we're just friends and that I have fruit and juice all over my hands." His voice was low and sexy, and the eyes meeting hers shined dark and hot.

"I'm not looking at you any way, except to wonder why you're so slow at chopping," she said, quickly turning her face to dump more stuff in the blender. "Don't you see the line we have here?"

"Mmm-hmm. If you say so."

Okay, it was true, darn it. Her heart had fluttered and her breathing went a little haywire just from admiring him. The question was, why? Yes, they'd steamed up the sheets together, which had been admittedly very, very nice. Incredible, really.

But what about the fact that he'd been an insulting jerk, too? His words still stung if she let herself think about them, and the only reason she'd invited him to join her today was because she'd realized at the party that, unbelievable as it seemed, he'd looked surprisingly vulnerable when he'd apologized for that.

Seeing that briefly unguarded moment had made her caregiving instincts jump up to step in. Could talented, confident Aaron Cartwright have something in his history, some kind of demon that haunted him? Something from his days in foster care that would be good for him to talk about?

Holding pain deep inside, refusing to share it, was hard on anyone, which was why she'd impulsively invited him here today. Thinking that perhaps spending time at the merry, entertaining atmosphere of the festival might relax him enough to unburden himself.

Only problem was, she'd thought his anger with her, and hers with him, would have smothered all that chemistry between them, leaving behind just a cordial friendship. Clearly she'd been utterly wrong, and how could that be, considering everything?

Somehow, she'd have to tamp it down when she tried to coax answers out of him. Then, whether he did or didn't talk about himself to her, this absolutely had to be their last day together as she started her new life.

The life he didn't approve of at all, which was odd as heck considering what he did for a living.

Remembering that helped cool the heat she'd been feeling a minute ago, and she concentrated on selling and making as many smoothies as possible. Finally, their shift was over, and none too soon, because her back was starting to ache and she figured his had to be, too.

"You've been a trouper, Aaron." She tugged at her apron strings as the next shift took over, then stopped to stare at Aaron's hands as he wiped them on a towel. "Oh, my gosh, your poor fingers are all pruney! I'm sorry—you should have asked to switch with me and let me take over the chopping for a while."

"I'd rather my hands get pruney than your pretty ones," he said. "Besides, I'm hoping that seeing me suffer like this for you will put me back in your good graces."

"You don't have to suffer to get back in my good

graces," she said, surprised that, even though his lips were curved, his eyes looked serious. "You apologized and also helped here. Forgiven."

"Thank you. Not sure I deserve it, but I appreciate it." He lifted her apron over her head then smoothed back her hair, his gaze still on hers. "So what now? Do I have to cut up smelly fish for a couple more hours to make fish smoothies?"

"Oh, yuck. No!" A laugh bubbled from her throat. "I think you just might have ruined my appetite for the rest of the day." How had she not realized before what a good sense of humor he had? Maybe because she'd been noticing everything else about him. Like his good looks, and how wonderful it had felt to touch the softness of his skin over all those hard muscles of his. Sensuously shaped lips that had made her utterly mindless when he'd kissed her.

No. Not going to think about any of that ever again. "Let's just walk for a bit, see what we find to do," she said a little breathlessly. She moved into the flow of the crowd, trying to think of what he might enjoy, and when the time might be right to pry into his life to play therapist. Then had to stop for a second to bend to each side, trying to loosen her tight muscles. "How come my back hurts standing in one place for two hours, when it never hurts running around the hospital, even after a ten-hour shift?"

"Because when you're moving around the hospital, you're using all your back muscles. Standing still in one position too long strains the extensor muscles at the back of your spine that help you stand straight, making them feel stiff." His eyes were fixed on her body as she stretched, and his voice went lower. "I'd be happy to give you a back massage. I'm pretty good at it."

She'd bet he was. Also good at turning that back massage into something more, no doubt. "It was a rhetorical question, Dr. Cartwright. I did have to study anatomy, you know."

"I do know. And I liked it a lot when you studied my anatomy."

That wicked glint was back in his eyes and she folded her arms across her chest and glared at him in the hopes that he wouldn't know her thoughts had gone straight to his deliciously awesome anatomy, and that he made her want to laugh again. "Ground rules. Amusing though you are, the suggestive remarks need to stop. Just friends, remember? And for obvious reasons, after today we won't even be that."

"Sorry. Something about you makes me want to tease like a teenager, but I'll be good."

Yes, the darned man was good all right. Very, very good.

She cleared her throat. "So, what would you like to do? There are art exhibits and all kinds of musicians and bands here and there, which we'll see as we walk around. Lots of restaurants have foods out on the pavement, usually their specialties, and other food stalls like ours are everywhere, if you're hungry. And then there's dancing."

"I think I already told you moving from one foot to the other is about the extent of my dancing skills. But if there's dancing you like to watch, I'm good with that."

"Something you'd probably enjoy is the belly dancing. Might even want to give it a try."

He laughed. "Me belly dancing is such a horrifying visual I don't want to even think about it. But you?" He might have been talking about belly dancing, but his gaze was on her mouth, which sent her heart into that ridiculous pit-a-pat it kept doing around him, in spite of everything. "Seeing you belly dance would probably give me a heart attack."

"Wouldn't want that. But since it's not on my list of talents, nor do I keep a jewel in my belly button, I'm pretty sure your heart is safe."

He didn't answer, just stood there looking at her, oddly still and suddenly serious, as though she'd said something important instead of silly.

Then he turned away to scan the crowd of people, stuffing his hands into the pockets of his jeans. "What do you usually like to do here?"

The change from teasing camaraderie to the kind of slightly distant demeanor he would have engaged her with at the hospital before they'd met was a little unnerving. But him putting distance between them was a good thing, right? So she wouldn't have to.

As if she'd been doing a very good job of it anyway.

"Let's eat first. Smelling that fruit for so long made my stomach a little gurgly, wanting some real food."

"Anything but fish smoothies sounds good to me."

She laughed, relieved to see his normal teasing look was back, though why that seemed so important, she wasn't sure.

Both were silent as they made their way down streets crowded with all kinds of people, some dressed in period clothing, some wearing wild colors, their faces painted in bright blues, greens and reds, others wearing fairy wings and crazy hats and everything else imaginable. Aaron still hadn't spoken again, and she looked up at him, wondering what he thought of it all. The look on his face as he studied the crowd could only be described as dumbfounded, and she had to chuckle.

"Crazy, huh? And you haven't even seen what people dress up in for the parade."

"Do these people live in Cambridge?" he asked in a tone that showed he found it hard to believe, and maybe a little alarming.

"A lot do. But plenty come from other places, even other countries. I think something like ten thousand people came to last year's festival."

"I'd always thought folks here seemed pretty normal."

"Don't be a fuddy-duddy. Dressing up and having fun is normal. Maybe you should try it." Though she had to admit she couldn't imagine it. The man practically exuded a level of testosterone that made it impossible to picture him in a silly costume.

"No, thanks. Unless wearing scrubs and pretending to be a doctor counts."

"Don't think it counts when you *are* a doctor, unless there's something you want to confess? Like you printed out your own medical degree from a six-week Internet course on fertility?"

"Ah, damn. You've found me out." His brown eyes twinkled at her. "Can we keep that just between the two of us? I need next week's paycheck."

"Our secret." She made an X across her heart. "You know, maybe being horrified by the idea of dressing up in a costume and having fun makes you the abnormal one," she joked, aware of a little happy feeling in her chest that they seemed to be back to enjoying the day the same way they had when they'd punted together, which was what she'd hoped for when she first suggested it.

Well, not exactly like that, since their boating trip had ended in lots of knee-melting kisses, not to mention a crashed boat and unforgettable lovemaking. Which she scolded herself for thinking of when he was standing right next to her, since he might see in her eyes exactly how those memories affected her.

"You know, I used to think I was pretty normal, but I'm beginning to wonder about that."

And there it was. That odd seriousness when he'd looked at her earlier. What was that about? Could it be a sign that the time was right to ask him more about his life, which she kept forgetting had been her ultimate goal for the day?

Just as she was pondering how to start that conversation, enticing scents from a grill set up outside a Middle Eastern restaurant wafted their way, apparently grabbing both their attention at the same time. Like tin soldiers winding down, they stopped mid-step, and the brown eyes that met hers were no longer serious but lit with anticipation.

"Are you feeling the same excitement my stomach is feeling? Because that smells incredibly good."

She pressed her palms to her suddenly growling belly, and blushed slightly at his chuckle, since he'd obviously heard. "Well, since we haven't come across any fish smoothies, we can settle for this, I guess."

"If we have to." He grinned at her, and insisted on paying as chicken kabobs and rice pilaf were piled onto paper plates and covered with some kind of thick yogurt sauce. Hope balanced the wobbly dish in her hands, wondering how she could manage to eat without spilling it all over her shirt, when one of the tables on the pavement was vacated at just the right moment.

"Come on." Aaron's long strides got there well before anyone else who'd been eyeing it could, and he set his plate down before pulling out a chair for her.

"This is perfect," she said. "Know why?"

"Because we don't have to balance our plates on one hand and eat standing up?"

"Because the parade will be coming down this street in about—" she glanced at her watch "—one minute. Believe me, you're going to be amazed at all the costumes and music."

Distant drumming, then accordion music and off-key singing drifted through the air, along with something that sounded like bells. Hope craned her neck, and, sure enough, dancers with outrageous costumes that looked like something from a bad outer-space movie appeared at the end of the street and headed their way as jesters hula-hooped their way through the crowd in front of them. Behind the accordions, a tall, tree-shaped thing appeared, wrapped in a mishmash of fabrics with flags fluttering all over it. A woman stuck out of the top, a massive silver ball of something on her head, as the whole thing rolled down the street toward them.

Hope glanced at Aaron. He was holding his kabob stick between his thumb and forefinger, and it hung suspended in the air as he stared. His expression was so comical, she burst out laughing.

"I wondered why you'd invited me here after you were mad at me for being so irritating." He turned that stunned look to her. "Now I know. You're torturing me for it. This is payback, isn't it?"

She nearly choked, laughing. "No. I swear. There really are a lot of fun things to do and see, and I find the costumes and silliness entertaining."

"You honestly like the costumes and…" he waved his kabob around "…all this?"

"I do." Maybe she should be irritated that he didn't

get the Mill Road scene, but the almost little-boy baf-
flement on his face was adorable. "It didn't occur to me
you'd be horrified. I thought you'd be amused. When
we're done eating, we'll move on to other things you'll
like. I promise."

"I'm not horrified. Just…confused." He lifted his free
hand to her face and stroked a strand of hair from her
eyes, his lips curving a little now. "But if you enjoy it,
that's all that matters."

And wasn't that a sweet thing to say? His perplexed
expression had melted away, and she could tell he really
meant it. Her heart got a little squishy again, thinking
about the giving, generous side of this man she'd already
seen a number of times. Not at all like some of the doctors she'd worked with who were surprisingly arrogant,
everything always having to revolve around what they
wanted and how they wanted it.

It occurred to her that right then was the perfect time
to talk to him. Instead of one-on-one with her where he
might feel under a microscope, being in the middle of
the crowd and loud performance seemed more casual
somehow.

She set down her kabob, then hesitated, suddenly feeling doubtful about her plan. Probably because she didn't
have any more right to ask him personal questions than
he'd had lecturing her about her life. Could she just be
being nosy? Just wanting to know more about super-sexy
Aaron Cartwright and who he was before they didn't see
each other again?

Maybe. But they were here now, and she might as well
ask. If he didn't want to answer, he wouldn't.

She drew a breath then jumped in. "Can I ask you a
personal question?"

The eyes that turned to her were instantly wary. "What kind of personal question?"

"I can't help but wonder why a fertility specialist would have such…surprising opinions about IVF and single women and multiple births. Isn't that all a part of what you do?"

He looked at her for a long moment before he spoke, his expression inscrutable. "I can't help but wonder why a beautiful woman, who any man would fall over himself to marry and have children with, wouldn't look for that instead of doing a procedure that leaves her with no help at home and her children without a father."

Her lips tightened. Here she'd wanted to have a conversation that might help him unburden himself about something, and instead it was leading right back to the argument they'd had before. "Any man? Pretty sure you said you were a man who wasn't interested in forever after, so does that mean there's something wrong with you?"

"Most men." A muscle ticked in his jaw as he modified that statement. "Not wanting that for myself doesn't mean there's something wrong with me."

"But me not wanting it for myself *does* mean there's something wrong with *me*?" Her heart slammed into her chest, because, yes, there might be something wrong with her, but since he didn't know that, his attitude was insulting. "A double standard for women and men? Wow, that's real fair, isn't it?"

"Never mind." He huffed out a breath and shook his head. "I don't want to get into another argument with you, and before I stick my foot in my mouth again, I'm shutting it."

"I already told you I'm apparently incapable of committing to a man. But I do want children, have always wanted children, and neither of those things means there's something wrong with me. But you know what is wrong with me?"

God, she was shaking. She sucked in a breath to control it, and tried to hold the words inside, just be quiet and get a grip on herself and walk away, but they burst out before she could stop them. "I have endometriosis. My parents had me when they were very young and insisted I not make the same mistake they did, having a baby before they were financially ready, then struggling to make ends meet. Things weren't good at home. Having a career before starting a family seemed best, that it would work for me. It never occurred to any of us that my mother being infertile from endometriosis in just her twenties might be genetic. But I'm thirty-four and, yeah, I have it. Does not being able to love a man, to want that kind of commitment in my life, destine me to be childless? I don't think it has to. And if I don't start a family now, it may be too late."

She jabbed her finger into his chest. "You don't want children, so you can't understand how I feel, how important it is to me. How I've pictured having a baby ever since I can remember. The truth? Yes, I'm scared I might not be a good mother. I'm afraid that my child will suffer not having a father, and that maybe it makes me selfish to have one anyway, just like you said. It worries me, but I'm trying hard to push that aside. To believe in myself and make my dream come true. And here you are, piling more weight on top of my fears." She dragged in a shaky breath. "No, you don't want children so you can't possibly understand my dream to have a baby that's mine. And since you don't understand, maybe don't even care to understand, you should keep your judgments and self-righteous opinions to yourself."

Unexpected tears stung her eyes and, horrified, she leaped from the chair and blindly made her way down the pavement, pushing her way through the crowd.

Where had all that come from? She swiped at her cheeks and kept going. Here she'd wanted him to unburden himself, and it ended up being her pouring her anxiety and pain all over him. Setting free all the emotion, the worry, the fear that had lodged deep inside after the failed artificial insemination attempts. Fear that she'd never have a child. Fears she hadn't even acknowledged—that maybe there really was something wrong with her that she couldn't say "yes" to George, that she was incapable of any kind of love. Fear that she'd be forever alone the rest of her life. With no one to love and care for. No one to love her in return.

"Hope! Hope, wait!"

She walked faster, not wanting to talk to him, to hear any more questions or criticism, to expose more of herself in such a public place.

"Hope, please stop."

A hand grasped her upper arm, effectively slowing her down. She tried to yank it loose, to no avail. His grip wasn't tight, but it was firm enough that she wasn't going anywhere, and he led her off the pavement, between two buildings and into the shadows.

"Hope, I'm sorry. I'm sorry." He turned her toward him and pulled her against his wide chest, his palm splayed on her back, holding her close. "I'm so sorry."

She stood stiffly in his arms, not wanting him to offer comfort. Not wanting to accept it. Not from a man who'd slammed her twice now for how she'd decided to live her life, and yes, she might be flawed as a woman, physically and emotionally flawed, but, if she was blessed enough to have the IVF work and have a beautiful baby that was all hers, she'd do everything in her power to be the kind of mother she wanted to be. The last thing she needed or wanted was for a man like Aaron to doubt that she could.

"Please let me go," she said, keeping her eyes level to stare at his coat button. "I'm going to get my bike and ride home."

"Hope." His big hand moved to her chin, lifting her gaze to his. It seemed there was shame in those brown eyes, a pain and remorse she thought she'd seen there before when he'd apologized, but it clearly meant nothing. It was lip service, nothing more, since he'd questioned her reasons, her choices, all over again. Probably, his "I'm sorry" were just words from a man who'd hoped to get her into bed one more time.

"Pretty sure we already had this conversation once. Let me go."

"Hope, please listen." His hand moved, gently cupping her cheek, and the intensity in his eyes pinned her with such fierceness she couldn't turn away from it. "I'm an idiot. A colossal one. I didn't have a right to question your choices before, and I sure as hell don't now. Instead of opening my big mouth the way I did, sounding like I disapproved all over again, I should have asked you to share with me how you're feeling about the IVF, if you're worried or if there was something I could help you with."

"I'm not worried about the IVF."

"No, but your medical condition worries you. And I'm sorry I upset you enough to tell me how hard this has been for you when you hadn't intended to share that. But while I am sorry, I'm also glad I know. I'm glad because,

even though you might not believe it, I care about you."
His hand slid across the side of her neck to tangle in her
hair, cradling the back of her head, his eyes and voice
softening as he drew her close. "That's really what this
has all been about, even though I've shown it in a completely ass-backward way. I care about you and I can't
help but worry about you, but because I'm a stupid man,
I don't seem to be able to show that in the right way."

She stared into his eyes. Troubled, tender, full of that
vulnerability she thought she'd seen before—all that
emotion seemed to be right there in their brown depths.
But she'd kidded herself about that before, hadn't she?
She didn't know this man, not really, other than that he
sometimes had a good sense of humor, was a great kisser
and lovemaker, a caring person when it came to children
without homes, and a great doctor.

And a man who didn't approve of single women having IVF, no matter what he was saying now.

Before she could pull away, his mouth lowered to hers,
as soft and sweet as his words. Maybe it was because her
emotions were already raw, or maybe it was because there
was just something about him that reached inside her,
touching her in good ways and bad. But she realized she
didn't want to resist the kiss, to end it before it started,
even though there were so many reasons she should. Her
eyes drifted closed, and she gave herself up one last time
to how he made her feel. Angry? Yes, that. But also wonderful. Deliciously aroused. Intoxicated with a kind of
longing she'd never experienced in her life. A longing
she'd believed she wasn't capable of.

His hands tightened, smashing her against his chest,
and she clutched his shoulders and hung on. Let her fingers stroke his neck, slide up to curl into his thick soft

hair, imprinting the feeling of every bit of it into her memory. Held his head still as she deepened the kiss, pulling a moan from his chest that seemed to reverberate through her own, shaking her heart. Until, somehow, she drew strength enough to separate her lips from his and pull away.

"So," he said, his voice rough, "is that a better way to show you, at least a little, how much I care about you? Help you forget all the wrong things I've said and forgive me?"

She tried for a light answer, something that would end the moment on a good note. A truce. Something that would close this brief time they'd spent together with a smile before the wave goodbye.

But she came up empty. As she let herself take in his features—his strong jaw, sensual lips, dark eyes she seemed to fall right into, all of the beautiful package that was Aaron Cartwright—the truth hit her like a blow to the solar plexus.

The tingle of her lips, the pounding of her heart, the way it felt perfectly right to be held close against his big body, were all proof that what she'd worried about for years was true.

There *was* something wrong with her. Really wrong. In all the years with George, in all the dates she'd experienced since, she'd never once felt the way she did with Aaron. Never had felt tempted to enjoy a fling the very first night she'd met someone. Never thought about a man all the time, never felt a heady, sexual pull every time he was near, never had a vision of a forever after that somehow felt absolutely right.

And the only time in her life she did? It was for a man who was a self-proclaimed rolling stone. A man who never stayed in one place very long, and who had zero interest in any kind of long-term relationship, especially a wife and children that would tie him down.

Was she the kind of woman only interested in a man she couldn't have? She'd never have dreamed that, but clearly she'd been deluding herself.

"I care about you, too. And while the things you've said hurt me, I figure some of it must come from your own pain. Your childhood in foster homes, even though you haven't said much about that. So I forgive you." She sucked in a fortifying breath, pressed her hands against his chest and took a firm step back, and the arms holding her close fell away. "Now we can close the chapter on our fling as friends. Thanks again for helping with the fruit. Goodbye, Aaron."

Somehow, she managed to put on a smile and stuck out her hand. Without returning her smile, Aaron looked at her hand for a long moment before he slowly engulfed it with his own. The smoky heat in his eyes faded to the seriousness she'd seen an awful lot of that day, and she found she couldn't look at it for another second.

She yanked her hand loose and practically ran out of the shadowy crevice they'd been standing in, praying he wouldn't follow her as she hurried the few blocks to her bicycle. But apparently he knew there was nothing else to say, because there was no voice behind her, calling her name this time. No hand grasping her arm to stop her.

Time to get her life back to its safe, steady track. Incomplete in many ways, yes, but hopefully a new addition would bring it closer to complete. Her heart and life would be filled to overflowing, which would be a very good thing, since right at that moment it felt all too sadly hollow.

CHAPTER TWELVE

"CONGRATULATIONS," AARON SAID, shaking the new father's hand. "Those are two beautiful baby girls you have there."

"Aren't they?" The man beamed. "Thank you for everything, Dr. Cartwright. We…we wouldn't have our daughters if not for you and can't tell you how much we appreciate it."

"Yes, thank you," the mother said with a smile overflowing in joy. "I'd shake your hand, too, except mine are a little full right now."

Aaron managed to smile back, but it was an effort. Looking at the blonde woman in the hospital bed, cradling a baby in each arm, made him think of Hope. Wonder about the babies she'd have, and if they'd favor her or their unknown sperm donor. Thinking how beautiful she'd look holding them in nine months if her own IVF treatment went well.

Her treatments that were about to start later that afternoon.

His gut tightened, feeling a little queasy, and he barely managed to eke out another smile as he gave his best wishes to the family and left the room, heading to his office for the rest of the day.

"What time is my first appointment?" he asked Sue, who was manning the front desk. He could have looked at the schedule himself, but didn't want to see Hope's name on Tom Devor's patient list.

Except he'd already snooped days ago. Maybe it verged on unethical, but he'd had to know. Then wished he hadn't looked, because the damned date had stuck in his brain, disturbingly nagging at him all week as it grew closer.

And now the day was here.

"One-fifteen," Sue said.

When she looked up at him, her smile turned to a small frown and he turned away. The woman seemed to have a sixth sense, and he sure as hell didn't need it boring into his brain today. "I'll be in my office."

He couldn't focus on paperwork and restlessly paced the room, finally stopping to stare out of the window at the heavy gray clouds in the overcast December sky. He'd kept asking himself all week if there was something different he could have said to Hope, something that might have made her rethink her plans, and every time he wondered, he asked himself why.

His inappropriate criticism and his apologies to Hope, his sincere praise that she'd be a wonderful mother, were all utterly irrelevant to her life. What he thought or had to say didn't matter. She wanted a baby and didn't have a man in her life to give her one. IVF was a perfectly reasonable choice for someone like her who deserved children, and any children she had would deserve her. She'd been a short interlude in his life, and he in hers. Nothing more.

But it felt like more.

He had to get over it. Get over it, and be happy for her.

It wasn't as though he could give her what she wanted, no matter how attracted they were to one another.

A soft knock at the door preceded Sue sticking her head in. "Mind if I come in?"

"Sure. What's up?"

"Your patient just called to say she's running about ten minutes late." She stepped in and closed the door behind her, which Aaron took as a bad sign. "I can tell something's bothering you, and I'm guessing it's because Hope Sanders is starting her hormone treatments today."

Well, hell. He folded his arms across his chest. "Why would that bother me?"

"I don't know, you tell me." She mirrored his pose, standing there staring at him like a stern schoolmarm asking who threw the spitball.

Why *was* it bothering him so much? Good damned question, except he knew the answer. "Fine. I know you won't leave until I say something to make you leave. I like her. I'd like to date her, but she wants kids, and yeah, I guess that bothers me a little. But you know as well as anyone I'm not a home and hearth guy. In fact, I've been thinking it's time to move on."

As soon as he said it the idea again seemed painful and appealing at the same time. Not having to see Hope pregnant, not having to see her bring her babies to the hospital. Start fresh somewhere he would feel like his old self again.

"I charge my therapist fees by the minute so listen carefully." Sue stepped closer, resting her hand on his forearm, and the warm look in her eyes reminded him of his mother. His real one, who'd put up with so much from him. Not the crazy one he barely remembered. "You're a good man, Aaron. Maybe it's time you asked yourself why you move from place to place every few years. Why you avoid commitment like an infectious disease. Why the idea of a family of your own has you running the other way as fast as you can, when making families for others—for your patients and through your adoption foundation—is the one thing you *have* committed your life to."

"Helping people make families or become a family has nothing to do with my avoidance of one for myself," he said. Probably a damned lie, but he didn't feel like digging too deep into his psyche right then. "But I appreciate you caring about me enough to give advice."

Which was the reason he'd given to Hope for why he'd lectured her about having IVF as a single woman. Because he cared about her.

More than he could remember caring about any other woman.

"Just think about it," Sue said with another pat on his arm. "I'll bring your patient when she gets here."

Being busy seeing patients the rest of the afternoon helped Aaron push thoughts of Hope to the side. He knew her appointment with Devor was scheduled at 4:00 p.m. and was glad he had a very nervous couple to talk to at that time, taking one hundred percent of his focus. After they'd left at four-thirty, he expected the knock at his door to be a nurse bringing his next patients in, leaving no time for anything but work.

Except it was Sue again, sans patients. "Your four-thirty canceled, and Dr. Krantz has some delay with the procedure he's doing. Would you mind talking to his patients for a few minutes? I've done what I can, but they're practically pacing a hole in the waiting room carpet. I'm thinking you can answer general questions to calm them down until Dr. Krantz can get here and take over."

"All right." Calming down nervous couples was something he thought he was fairly good at, and keeping busy was the goal. "You want to bring them in here, or to Krantz's office?"

"His, I think, so the patients can just stay there when he takes over. How about I introduce you in the waiting room, and you can take them there?"

A horribly uncomfortable feeling swirled in his gut just like he'd felt earlier in the day as he followed Sue down the hall past Devor's closed office door. That it was happening again really started to tick him off, and just as he was welcoming some good self-disgust for being like some overemotional woman Devor's door swung open and out stumbled Hope.

And stumbled wasn't an overstatement. Two staggering steps, then her hand slapped against the doorjamb, hanging onto it like a lifeline. Her face was white as chalk, her eyes wide and a little glassy, and when they looked up and latched onto his she let out a short, distressed cry.

"Hope." He grabbed her arms to steady her. "Are you all right?"

"I... I..."

Damned if she didn't actually blanch even more, and her lips seemed to tremble when she stopped trying to talk. But her eyes, filled with something akin to panic, stayed focused on his. Had she somehow had some unusual, bad reaction to the hormones? It did happen sometimes, but never in his years of practice had he seen it occur that fast. He looked past her to Tom. "What happened?"

"She'll be fine." Tom's face was unreadable. "She needs to sit down for a few more minutes, that's all. Hope, come back in and catch your breath, okay?"

"No. I... I need to go home. I need to think."

Something about the way her eyes were fixed on his scared the hell out of Aaron, though he couldn't say exactly why. "Hope, listen," he said, having no clue what he wanted her to listen to. He just knew he had to somehow wipe whatever that was—shock maybe?—off her face.

"No. I have to go." She managed to pull out of Aaron's hold and, for a woman who'd looked as if she was going to faint just seconds ago, practically left skid marks on the floor as she left.

He wanted to chase after her, but he didn't have the right, damn it. Standing still and watching her leave took a Herculean effort, but she was Devor's patient. Sue managed the office; she was the one who took care of non-medical problems. And as for him?

He knew Hope didn't even count him as a friend anymore.

Hope wasn't sure exactly how she'd made it home, as it was a bit of a blur, but she was there, somehow, snug in her flannel pajamas. Or she would be snug, if her whole body didn't still feel icy cold from shock.

She scrubbed her cheeks with soap, hoping the everyday routine would bring a feeling of normalcy after every bit of it had gone straight out of the window an hour ago. Bring a little circulation back to her skin's current numbness as she tried to come to grips with this unbelievable reality.

A reality that felt totally unreal and impossible. A

reality that in some ways was a dream come true. In other ways?

A total, unbelievable nightmare.

She toweled off her face then, like an automaton, walked into her living room. Slowly lowered herself onto the sofa to stare, unseeing, at the wall.

What in the world was she going to do?

Her hands went to her belly, instinctively. Protectively. And somehow, the simple movement calmed her.

The question her brain had asked in its panicked state wasn't the right one, was it? Obviously, without question, what she was going to do was have this baby she'd been blessed with. Not the way she'd planned, but things didn't always go to plan, did they?

She sat quietly, trying to process it, letting the truth of the situation seep through her body. Waited for the fear to jab at her again. The doubts that had plagued her as she'd tried to ready herself for the IVF and for having a baby.

But it didn't. Shock though it was, ideal situation though it wasn't, Hope found herself slowly filled with a quiet and deep gratitude. A warmth that spread through her being, chasing away her chill.

She was going to have a baby to love and care for and raise as best she could. Her dream, her wish, had been granted, and her heart suddenly bloomed with happiness, so full she thought it might burst right out of her chest with the joy of it all. Already being pregnant took all decisions out of the equation, didn't it? The questions of whether she should or shouldn't have IVF, be a single parent. Questions of whether or not she'd be able to love her baby the way it deserved to be loved.

The intense love already overflowing in her heart gave

her that answer, and her throat closed with the relief of it, the joy of it.

So now, the only real question was, should she tell Aaron? Or let him assume she'd had the IVF procedure to get pregnant, and leave him out of their baby's life?

She closed her eyes and pictured the father of her baby. His handsome features, his teasing smile. His focused commitment to his patients, his caring for children.

Then there were his kisses. His touch. The way he made her feel like no one else ever had. Just thinking of it left her breathing shallow, made her heart flutter, made her long to hold him in her arms and have him hold her in return.

No. Oh, no. Her eyes flew open as she faced the incredible and terrifying truth.

She loved him. She was totally, absurdly, ridiculously in love with a man who didn't want that in his life. It wasn't some crazy thing where she just wanted a man she couldn't have.

No. She wasn't crazy. But she was crazy in love with Aaron.

She pressed her hands to her eyes, absorbing the truth of how she felt. Knowing that, even if he shared some of her feelings, he didn't want a committed relationship. Didn't want a family. Didn't want to be tied down. Had openly stated it, and lived his life with that credo in mind.

How had this happened? How was it possible that all these years, from her teens into her thirties, she'd never experienced anything like this heady, wonderful, terrifying feeling? And because of that, had been so sure that George must have been right, that there was something fundamentally missing inside her. Whether it was her genes, her parents' lack of love for one another, who knew why, but she just wasn't capable of that kind of love.

Except she was. How she felt about Aaron proved that loud and clear.

Her hands slowly slid from her eyes, dropping into her lap. The irony was painful, yet thrilling, too.

She loved Aaron. The intense roller coaster of highs and lows these past weeks that had been knocking her all around, squeezing her chest and leaving her breathless, couldn't be mistaken for anything else.

Which meant she was fully capable of loving her baby the way she wanted to. Meant that maybe someday it was even possible she might love someone else, a man who wanted the same kind of life she did.

Aaron wasn't that man, and that knowledge painfully squeezed her heart. But he was a truly caring man—yes, he'd said some pretty awful things to her, but, as she'd guessed before, there just might be some reason for that, a reason he didn't share easily. Perhaps from his childhood, perhaps not, but everyone had issues, didn't they? She'd had plenty of her own.

Aaron's career and passion were about forming families, about bringing them together, and how wrong would it be to keep his own child a secret from him? Without giving him the chance, the opportunity, to decide if he wanted to be a part of his own child's life or not?

The calm fluttered, then settled right over her heart, and the answer was as clear as glass. He deserved to know, and their baby deserved it, too. He was a man who, even if he hadn't wanted it or planned for it, would take responsibility for his child and do everything he could to be a good father. She felt as sure of it as she was that the sun would rise tomorrow.

He probably couldn't love her the way she loved him, and that brought a heavy ache to the calm in her heart. But what was most important? That he love their child. And if somehow she was wrong, that he couldn't do that, offer that, she'd be back to where she'd expected to be all along. A single mother.

Except now she knew things would be just a little different from what she'd planned. She knew her heart would always carry an empty place that only Aaron could fill.

Last night, her plan had seemed so easy, so right. And when she'd called Aaron right after she'd made that plan, asking if he could meet her in his office at the end of the day, he'd sounded so normal, so much the caring Aaron with a warm concern in his voice, she'd convinced herself it would be okay. Difficult, yes, but okay.

Actually walking into his office at the end of the day to talk to him, though, was a different story. With her heart flying into a serious arrhythmia, creating a virtual timpani of anxiety in her chest, she thought she just might have to bail out and reschedule when she was calmer and more under control. When she might actually be able to breathe.

The office manager—Sue?—had greeted her, and something about the woman's expression upped Hope's anxiety even higher, wondering if she knew. But of course, even if she did, she couldn't know everything. Sue might know from Hope's file that she was already pregnant, but couldn't possibly know the father was Aaron.

Could she?

Lord. Hope wet her lips with her tongue and seriously

ROBIN GIANNA 181

contemplated running back out of the door. She stood, wiping her hands on her skirt, and just as she eyed her escape route Sue came over.

"Dr. Cartwright is ready to see you now."

"Oh. Okay. Thanks."

To her surprise, Sue gave her a big, warm smile and patted her on the back before leading her toward Aaron's office, nudging her inside. After a few, tentative steps, she stopped. Another smile from Sue helped her catch her breath and relax a smidge as the door clicked closed, leaving them alone.

In a very small room. That felt even smaller as she stared at Aaron's motionless back, and she nervously licked her lips. He stood looking out of the window, and his hands were clutching the back of his head, fingers entwined. Just as Hope was sucking in a calming breath and trying to rehearse what she was going to say, he turned.

And the expression on his face dried up every word on her tongue.

The man looked shaken. Pale. Staring at her as though he didn't know who or what he was looking at.

Oh, God. He knew. He already knew. And the shock and distress on his face told her loud and clear how he felt about it.

Also told her she'd been deluding herself big-time. Ridiculously hoping, even if she hadn't admitted it to herself, that he'd be as excited as she was to be having a baby. How stupid could she have been, knowing how he'd always felt about being tied down?

Embarrassment, humiliation even, slid through her veins and left her frozen.

Aaron took two unsteady steps to his desk and pressed his palms to it, still staring at her with disbelief. "I just found out… I looked at your files. I know that…you… and… I can't believe it."

The man was nearly incoherent, and, while she'd expected him to be shocked, she hadn't expected this… this horror? To think she'd believed he'd accept it, take responsibility for their baby, be there to support her. She was such a pathetic fool.

"Obviously, you already know what I came to tell you." She hated that her voice was shaking instead of cool, as she'd wanted it to be. Hated that a deep, hidden part of her had secretly hoped he'd tell her he loved her, and their child, too, that this had somehow been meant to be all along, bringing the two of them together.

"Yes. But…my God, Hope."

Every shocked word seemed to stab another sharp nail into her already battered heart. "Don't worry yourself, Aaron. I'm… I'm sorry this happened. I know this isn't what either of us wanted or expected. As far as I'm concerned, the baby is mine and only mine. Simply what I'd planned on before…this. I just felt an obligation to tell you, but since you already know, I guess we're done here. Goodbye."

She turned on shaky legs to open the door, wanting out, wanting away from him and the look on his face that spelled out painfully clear that a child binding them together was the absolute last thing he'd ever want.

"Hope. Wait."

She looked back at him, and the utter loss and confusion in his gaze sliced at her again, leaving her bleeding. "It's fine, Aaron. You can keep your life of freedom. The last thing I would ever want is for you to feel tied down and obligated." As her own father had. "You know I'd planned to be a single mother. I don't need you or any other man to support me or to make me feel whole."

She made her way out of his office and through the main door, gulping back the tears, praying she didn't make any more of a fool of herself than she already had if he showed up in front of her.

Then realized the joke was on her again, because he hadn't followed her at all.

CHAPTER THIRTEEN

AARON'S OFFICE DOOR burst open without even a knock and a Sue Calloway he'd never seen before stalked to his desk and leaned forward, giving him a look that could only be described as the evil eye.

He'd probably have been shocked by it if he weren't numb from head to toe.

"What did you do to make Hope Sanders cry?"

That shook him out of his daze. "Cry?"

"Yes, cry. She came in here looking nervous and scared, and I was sure she'd leave looking calmer, relieved, maybe even happy, but no, she had big, fat tears streaming down her face. So what did you do?"

"Nothing." Which, since his senses were finally, slowly coming back to him, had doubtless been why Hope had blown in the door then right back out.

She'd come to tell him the unbelievable news, and he'd barely been able to get a word out of his mouth, having finally gotten his hands on her chart just minutes before she showed up.

"I don't suppose you know who the father of her baby is," Sue said.

How the woman knew he couldn't imagine, but obviously that sixth sense of hers was in action. "I am. And I'm guessing that doesn't surprise you."

"Aaron." Her voice softened slightly. "From the second I saw the picture of you dancing with her, and the subtle changes in you since that day, good changes, I knew you were falling for her. I also was afraid you wouldn't let yourself."

It hadn't been a question of letting himself. He'd had no choice in the matter.

He loved her.

And he'd hurt her. Again. Let her down big-time at the exact wrong moment. But it hadn't been the shock of learning about the baby that had left him speechless. It had been the shock of realizing exactly how much he loved her, needed her, wanted her in his life. Wanted their baby. For the forever after he'd never thought he'd want with anyone. Wouldn't ever be capable of with anyone.

And because that had been a lot of change for his pitiful heart and brain to process, he'd stood there staring at her like a damn fool when she'd told him he could keep his life of freedom. A life he didn't want anymore. A life he now desperately wanted to replace with her and with their child.

He grabbed his coat, thankful his feet and mind were working again. "I need to go fix things with her, Sue."

She opened the door for him and gave him a wide smile. "You do that. Good luck."

He was damned glad he'd driven his car and not ridden his bike, and had to force himself to slow down before he got pulled over and delayed by a traffic ticket. Also needed to slow down because it was snowing, and skidding off the road wouldn't help get him to Hope so he could hold her and love her and beg her to forgive him. Again. For the third and most important time.

He ran up her snowy steps and banged on her door, his heart racing and his breath short. For the first time in his adult life, he was well and truly scared. He had no idea if Hope shared his feelings, if she wanted him in her and their baby's life, if she'd understand why he'd acted the way he had.

If she'd slam the door in his sorry face.

He banged on the door again, starting to panic that maybe she wasn't even home, that maybe she'd gone to her parents' house or something, and what would he do then? In mid-knock, it swung open, and he nearly dropped to his knees at the sight of her.

"Hope." He took in her tousled hair and her pink flannel pajamas, and she looked so sad and vulnerable it was all he could do not to sweep her up in his arms, but he knew she wouldn't welcome that after the way he'd acted. Her red-rimmed eyes and the single tear trickling down her cheek clutched at his heart, and he let himself at least reach to gently wipe it away, her cheek warm against his cold thumb. "Please let me come in. I have things I want to say to you."

"Do you?" He could see her deciding and he held his breath, praying she'd let him in and not force him to take the door off the hinges. "Funny, you didn't have much to say earlier."

"I know. And I'd like to explain why. Please."

"I know why. You don't w…want a baby to tie you down." She sniffed and swiped at another trickle of tears. "I already told you not to worry. We'll be fine without you."

"But I won't be fine without *you*. And not wanting to

be tied down isn't why I couldn't speak when you came into my office."

She didn't budge. He shook the snow from his head and tried another tack. "Even though you have every right to be upset with me, I know a caring nurse like you wouldn't want me to get hypothermia from spending the night out here, which I'll do if you don't let me in. Plus, a midwife letting her baby's father die on her front porch wouldn't be good PR for CRMU."

The tiniest curve of her lips and shake of her head had him holding his breath until she opened the door wider and stepped back. She didn't say a word, just walked toward her sofa, and he wanted to grab her up and kiss her and beg her to love him but knew there were things she had to hear from him first.

She gestured to her armchair, then sat stiffly on her sofa across from it. He pondered taking off his snowy coat, but worried she might think he was making himself a little too comfortable under the circumstances, so he sat. Their eyes met, and his nerves jangled all over again, because so much was riding on his words, and he'd done a damned poor job of expressing himself too many times the past weeks.

"When you came to my office, I'd just snooped into your file and found out you were pregnant. I'm sorry if that makes you mad, but I was worried about you."

"No need to be worried."

Her expression had cooled, and her eyes were starting to look a little hard, like blue ice, and he knew he'd better get it all said fast before she threw him out into the snow again. "I was stunned to hear about the baby, just as I'm sure you were, too. But that wasn't what shocked me. What shocked me was that, the second I read those words, I knew I loved you, Hope. More than anything or anyone in my life. And it shocked me that I felt like...like I'd come home. I've never really belonged anywhere my whole life, had been sure I never would, and in that split second all those convictions got turned on their head and I was still trying to process it all when you walked in."

Her eyes were wide on him now, and he could tell she was trying to decide if she could believe him. If he was saying it just because he felt responsible, and he moved to sit next to her, reaching to hold her hands, needing that connection. "I'm obviously a little slow to figure things out, but I finally get it. I was attracted to you the second I saw you at the party. Hell, I was attracted just seeing you in the hallway at work. And as I got to spend time with you, I loved your sense of humor and adventure. How you care for others, and how damned good you are at your job. The taste and feel of you, but I wouldn't let myself even think about loving you. Wouldn't let it happen."

"Why?" she whispered, her eyes searching his. "And why do you say you are now? I don't want our baby to force you into thinking you have to feel something, or say you feel something that you don't."

"I admit the baby was what forced me to open my eyes and my heart." He didn't want to go into the rest of it, but she deserved to know. "Forced me to look at myself and my attitudes and how I've lived. Probably I should have seen a psychologist long ago, but I'd stuffed down my past and refused to consider that it still impacted me today."

"What past? Your adoption?"

"No." He shook his head. "I told you my biological mother was unstable. But I didn't tell you all of it. She was single, older and wanted a baby. Like you. She had IVF, ending up with triplets. Apparently without much help at home. I don't know anything about her mental-health history prior to that, but she suffered from post-partum psychosis that dragged on a long time. Children's services got involved, but eventually she completely lost it and tried to kill herself. Ended up in a mental hospital. My siblings and I lived in various different foster homes, and I have vague memories of foster parents taking me to visit my mother in the hospital."

"Oh, my God, Aaron." Her hands tightened on his. "Now I understand why you were so upset with me about my IVF plans."

"I shouldn't have projected that on you, Hope, and I'm sorry."

"So what about your siblings? Do you ever see them?"

He briefly closed his eyes to that pain. "My biological mother gave us up and opted out of any contact. Not too many adoptive families want multiples, and we were separated in closed adoptions. A while back, I tried to find out who and where they are now, but had no luck. So I have a brother and sister somewhere I'll never know."

"That's…terrible." Tenderness and sympathy filled her blue eyes. "What was your biological mother's name?"

"Her name?" He stared at her, wondering why in the world she'd asked.

"Yes. You always refer to her as your biological mother, which seems so cold and distant. Maybe you do that on purpose, like she wasn't really part of your life. But for better or worse she was, Aaron. So I'd like to know her name."

"Anne. Her name was Anne." Funny how saying it did make her seem more real somehow, and not just a shadowy memory he preferred to forget.

"Anne. That's a nice name." She squeezed his hand.

"I'm so sorry you went through such difficult times. I see why you started your adoption foundation, but I have to be honest. I'm surprised you decided to become a fertility specialist, considering everything."

"I guess it was my way of helping people make informed decisions, and implant only two eggs to hopefully prevent the kind of overwhelm my mother experienced." He realized he hadn't gotten to the most important thing yet. "Hearing about our baby slammed me with a truth I'd refused to admit was a problem, Hope. A truth I finally had to overcome. That in spite of having loving parents, I ran from commitment, never let myself get close to a woman, because I didn't want to expose myself to abandonment or pain. Pathetic, but true."

"Not pathetic." She held his face between her warm palms. "Not many people have to go through what you did."

"Loving you has changed that. Changed me."

Tears sprang into her eyes, but she didn't speak, and that scared the hell out of him. But he kept going because he had to. "I love you, Hope. I love you and I love our child, and all I want is for us to be a family together forever." He touched his lips to hers, barely able to whisper the next words, afraid to hear her answer. "Will you marry me, Hope? Not because we're going to have a baby, but because I love you in a way I never knew it was possible to love someone, and I know now that I'll never be complete without you. I don't know if you feel the same way but…"

He found he couldn't finish the sentence, just stared into her beautiful eyes and willed her to love him back. Which maybe worked, or maybe she really did, because she wrapped her arms around his neck and kissed him.

"I do love you, Aaron Cartwright. So much." Her voice wobbled and her eyes filled with tears again that, this time, looked like happy ones. "We've had the same problem, you know. Until I met you, I thought something was missing inside me. Now I know what was missing was you."

Well, damn. He swallowed down the lump that formed in his throat at her words and wrapped his arms around her, holding her tight. "When I first danced with you, I thought it was fate that the music started back up just at the right time. Guess it really was."

"Is it fate that your child is going to grow up in Cambridge, so you can teach him or her how to be punt captain extraordinaire?"

"Maybe it is. But you're going to get that title first." He moved his mouth to her cheek, smiling against its softness. "You haven't answered my question, though."

"Question?"

"The 'will you marry me' question. Might not be important to you, but it's damned important to me."

She pulled back an inch, and as he looked into the blue of her eyes his chest filled with emotion all over again. If she gave him the answer he wanted, he'd get to lose himself in them every single day.

"Of course I'll marry you. I'd have to be completely crazy not to marry the world's most wonderful man."

"Can't claim that title, I know," he said against her lips. "World's luckiest man, though? With you in my life, I have that title in the bag."

EPILOGUE

"YOU'RE AT NINE CENTIMETERS, Hope, maybe even a smidge more," her midwife, Bonnie, said with a smile. "Getting close. I'll be back in just a bit to check on you."

"Doing good, sweetheart," Aaron said, dropping a kiss on her forehead. "How's it feel being on the other side of the bed?"

"Painful." She squeezed her handsome husband's hand, still a little in disbelief that he was all hers. "Being pregnant has given me a whole new appreciation for mothers everywhere. Waddling like a duck is no fun, and neither is being round as a beach ball."

"But you're the most beautiful beach-ball-shaped duck in the universe."

His eyes crinkled at the corners, until his smile was instantly wiped from his face as a contraction hit her and she moaned.

"All right. You're all right. Breathe. Breathe again."

When it was over, she let her head drop back against the pillow, and, now that the pain had faded, Aaron's anxious expression nearly made her laugh. "You'd have made a terrible midwife, and it's a good thing you became a fertility specialist instead of a practicing obstetrician. This is a normal part of the process."

"I know. But that doesn't mean I can feel blasé about you hurting." He rested his big hand on her belly and the smile came back to his face. "There's another kick. Our rugby player wants out of there."

"Or our superstar girl football player."

"And punt-boat operator. Let's hope for your sake it's not born with a pole already in hand."

She had to laugh at that horrifying visual, until she had another contraction to get through.

"These seem to be coming really close together," Aaron said, that frown dipping even deeper between his brows. "I should go find Bonnie."

"I think we can give it a few more minutes," Hope said, panting, though she had to admit he was right. They were coming fast. "Distract me with some conversation."

"Well, I was going to wait until after the baby came, but I guess I'll tell you now. Your hard work sleuthing through the newly opened California adoption records finally hit pay dirt. The Michael Krieger you thought might be my brother? Believe it or not, he is. He emailed me today."

"Oh, Aaron, that's wonderful! I'm so thrilled for—" A powerful contraction cut off her words and breath, and this one lasted so long, she thought the baby just might pop right on out. "Aaron," she gasped when she could speak again. "I think you're right. I think it's time. I—" She couldn't control the long moan, and between gasping breaths stared up at her anxious husband. "I have to push. Be ready, in case she's not back in time."

The alarm on his face would have been comical if she hadn't been hurting and pushing, and she still managed to nearly laugh as she spoke between contractions. "Why…

are you looking like that? You're an OB, not a lawyer, for heaven's sake. If…the baby comes, you can handle it."

"Right." He practically ran to the sink to wash his hands and snap on gloves before positioning himself between her legs. "All right. I'm ready. Give me another push, sweetheart."

She did, and when it was over made a mental note to be even more sympathetic to mothers giving birth, because it hurt a whole lot more than she'd expected.

"You're doing great. Wonderful. Another push."

"I take back…what I said about you not…being a good midwife," she gasped.

"Oh, my God, Hope, it's crowning! It's coming! Another big push. You're amazing. Wonderful. Our baby's almost here."

"Dear me!" Bonnie exclaimed as she ran into the room. "I'm so sorry! I never dreamed you'd go that quick…" She let Aaron continue rather than disrupting the birth, but checked Hope's vitals and hovered for when Aaron needed her.

"Oh, Aaron. Is it…?"

"Coming. Yes. One more big push, honey. I've…got it!"

To her astonishment, he really did. Their baby was actually in his hands, and he brought it wet and wriggling to lie on her chest. "It's a girl! A beautiful, gorgeous baby girl."

"Oh, Aaron. I can't believe it." She held her daughter close and stared at her tiny face and body. She thought she'd been awed every time she'd delivered a child? There was no comparison to the instant, soul-drenching love filling her chest. The baby gave a lusty cry that made both of them laugh. "Does she seem…all right?"

"She looks perfect in every way." His long fingers gently stroked her cheek. "Just like her mother."

"Here, let me take the baby and get her cleaned up, then I'll take care of you, Hope."

Bonnie carried the baby to the warming bassinet as Aaron snapped off his gloves, taking Hope's hands in his. She tore her gaze from their tiny newborn to look up at her husband, and her heart squeezed even tighter when she saw the tears streaking down his cheeks.

"Aaron." She lifted her hand to his face and gently wiped them away. "We have our miracle. I love you so much."

"I love you more than I could ever say, Hope." He leaned down to press his lips to hers. "Having you in my life is my first miracle. Thank you for that, and for giving me this second miracle, too."

She brought his head down to hers for a long kiss, and, when she pulled back, saw Bonnie standing there holding their swaddled blessing. "Who gets her first?"

"Aaron," Hope quickly said, wanting him to have that happiness. "He brought her into the world."

"And you did all the work the past nine months and today, but I'll take her anyway." His cheeks still damp, he grinned and reached for the baby, then perched on the side of the bed.

"She has your amazing blue eyes," he said softly.

"Most newborns have blue eyes."

"Not like these." He turned her a bit so Hope could see her, too, and she couldn't believe what a vivid blue they were already.

"Oh, my goodness, I guess you're right. Her hair is pretty dark, though." She ran her finger tenderly across her daughter's downy eyebrows and round cheek, still hardly believing she was really here. "So are you still good with the name we picked?"

His elated gaze stayed on their baby's tiny face. "Yes. Caroline Anne is a beautiful name. I know my mothers would have loved her every bit as much as both of us already do."

"Yes," Hope agreed, the love for her daughter practically bursting from her chest the way she'd always dreamed. "They would indeed."

* * * * *